AGOG! RIPPING READS

OTHER TITLES BY AGOG! PRESS:

AustrAlien Absurdities, Edited by Chuck McKenzie and Tansy Rayner Roberts, 2002/2006

Agog! Fantastic Fiction: 29 New Tales of Fantasy, Imagination and Wonder, Edited by Cat Sparks, 2002/2006

Agog! Terrific Tales: New Australian Speculative Fiction, Edited by Cat Sparks, 2003/2006

Agog! Smashing Stories: New Australian Speculative Fiction, Edited by Cat Sparks, 2004/2006

Daikaiju! Giant Monster Tales, Edited by Robert Hood and Robin Pen, 2005

AGOG! RIPPING READS

EDITED BY CAT SPARKS

Published by Agog! Press:
PO Box U302
University of Wollongong
NSW 2522
Australia
www.catsparks.net

in partnership with Prime Books:
www.prime-books.com

ISBN:
0-8095-6237-5 (hc)
0-8095-6238-3 (pbk)

CONTENTS

A*gog! Ripping Reads* is the sixth anthology I've published since establishing Agog! Press in 2002—and the fourth to have been edited by me. I cast my submissions net a little wider this time round and received twice as many stories as usual. What surprised me was the higher than expected quality of my slush pile. There wasn't much in it that could be dismissed at a glance. The bar has definitely risen since 2002, and as a result, picking the stories for inclusion was a difficult task indeed.

The stories in this volume are best described as being of a fantastical nature. They run the gauntlet from outright horror, through fantasy in the broadest sense of the word, and end up in the realm of science fiction.

I would like to thank Sean Wallace of Prime Books for giving me the opportunity to present these anthologies to a wider audience. Thank you to every author who submitted a story, and an extra big thanks to Robert Hood for his support and assistance throughout the production process.

Cat Sparks
Wollongong, 2006

When the World Was Flat

GEOFFREY MALONEY

P'hew! Is this the sulphur and brimstone of hell I smell? Nay, it cannot be! Surely, Doctor Faustus has merely dropped an egg of maliferous odour. But perhaps even then, the likeness of its stench shall be enough to summon the evil one.
Che sera, sera? So you shall see what will be.
—Kate Marlowe, 'Hell's Bells a' Calling' (1592)

Act I: The Chaining Season

As was his habit each morning, Lord Admiral Fontingroy, Commander-in-Chief of the Queen's navy, rose before dawn and rode his grey mare to the top of St Climan's Struggle. Here was to be found a rocky cairn that marked the place where the great saint was said to have buried his pagan faith, along with his clothes, and danced joyfully naked in his enlightenment. Lord Fontingroy thought the story pure poppycock, but the view from the cairn allowed him to note contentedly that as far as the eye could see all belonged to him. However, that particular morning, his sense of contentment was short-lived as he detected an oblique angle in the horizon.

Too early the seasons shift, he thought, and Eastermus groans upon us. The fleet would need to be recalled from the Edge, and the house chains brought out. He chuckled as he recalled the horrified look on the Rector's face last Eastermus when an inadequately secured sideboard had careened towards him during the peak of the Tilt.

Lord Fontingroy squinted once more at the horizon, hoping his initial observation had merely been some trick of the early morning light, but the angle was definitely there, and now too he saw that Mother Luna and her infant son, Baby Cupid, had appeared in the eastern sky as they did every Eastermus. The Tilt *had* arrived early. He could even feel it in his body, in the way his muscles tensed, pulling him upright in the saddle towards the east.

Upon his return, Lord Fontingroy found his wife, Lady Gia, in the ballroom of their house with her arms moving in great swirls and arcs that would have done Sir Augustus Pino, conductor of the Albion Symphonia, proud. At her command, scores of servants scurried every which way, carrying thick-linked iron chains to secure the furniture.

Lord Fontingroy crept up upon his wife from behind, slipped his arm around her waist and kissed her upon the cheek. The servants scattered, dragging their heavy chains through the hallways that lead from the ballroom, to begin their chaining elsewhere for the time being.

'See what you have done. I had them working in good order,' Lady Gia said, but still she smiled. 'Now they think we wish to be *alone.*'

Lord Fontingroy spun his wife around and leaned his head to one side in what he believed was a romantic gesture. Unfortunately he leant towards the west, where the Tilt of Eastermus had begun its pull, and he experienced a sudden spasm in his neck muscles as his head involuntarily jerked the other way.

Lady Gia laughed. 'Sorry,' she said, holding her hand to her mouth to stifle her laughter, 'but that *was* rather...'

'Funny?' Lord Fontingroy suggested, feeling irritated, but then laughed himself to demonstrate he had a sense of humour.

'I felt it as soon as I rose from bed this morning, that sense of not being quite as well balanced as one would wish to be,' Lady Gia said.

'And already the horizon tilts. I must be away to see the Queen to seek her permission to the recall the fleet.'

'And she will say, dear Gilly,' Lady Gia said, pressing her hand flat to her breast in mock earnest, '"I have the utmost faith in you, Lord Fontingroy, to drive those devils from the deep blue sea" or some such cliché. Then she will say, " I will see you in my chamber this evening."'

'And I will say,' Lord Fontingroy said, squeezing his wife more tightly about the waist, 'that I have more important business to attend to.'

'You will do no such thing,' Lady Gia said, pulling his hands away. 'You know you are the Queen's favourite. How else to explain a man of such relative youth in such a senior position.'

'Sheer talent,' Lord Fontingroy suggested with a knowing wink.

'Talent, of course, you have in abundance, dear, but good looks even more so,' Lady Gia said. 'Besides did you not say after your last visit to Albion Town that the Queen was a passable lover?'

Lord Fontingroy blushed. 'I was merely being polite. I meant that for a fat old cow she was quite well versed in—'

'Yes, well, spare me the details,' Lady Gia said. 'But you must do your duty as the Queen requires it. Promise me you will say nothing foolish, that you will not do anything to endanger our house and estates. You know what she can be like—look at what happened to the poor Strathbows.'

'Lord Strathbow was an artless beetle-brained jolthead, where as I—'

'Gilly!' Lady Gia said sternly. She had been quite fond of Lady Strathbow and still felt a little queasy in the stomach when she thought about the poor woman losing her head.

'I will hold my tongue and do as the Queen desires,' he said, sighing.

'And if what I have heard is true, holding back your tongue will not be as the Queen desires.'

With this she poked her own tongue out, pulled away from him and charged after the servants, crying, 'Too much slack, the tension must be just right...'

But then, in a moment, she was back again. 'Do try not to linger in Albion Town too long. Remember Dr M'Gee arrives tomorrow on his way home to Nor'thumberland. He has recently been to the Continent and no doubt he will wish to see you on all manner of urgent things.'

'Huh, the old dismal-dreaming quack returned yet again from one of his spruiking adventures. How long is he staying this time?'

'This *is* Dr M'Gee we are speaking of. Last time it was several months. Remember, he was anxious for you to arrange an audience with the Queen.'

'Too clearly,' Lord Fontingroy said. 'He wanted to show her that new wheel he'd invented. That ridiculous thing with the pumped-up pig intestines wrapped around it. It hissed and popped every time it hit a rock. And do you remember Dr M'Gee's response?'

'That there was nothing at all wrong with his wheels; the Queen just needed to build roads without rocks in them. And of coarse he had the vision,' Lady Gia said, then deepened her voice and raised her hand to her brow. 'I can see it now,' she said, in imitation of the old doctor, 'miles and miles of flat smooth roadways across the length and breadth of Albion and carriages with my wheels flying along them at great speed.'

Lord Fontingroy laughed. 'Can you possibly imagine a road without rocks? The man is a complete tickle-brained eccentric. But, yes, he is your father's very best friend and your godfather, so stay he must, whenever he wants, for as long as he wants, as he always does.'

Act II: The Queen in her Cups

And so, Lord Fontingroy departed in a rather grumpy mood, taking the royal navy barge, *Lady Albatross*, down the central canal to Albion Town. It was a lovely midsummer's day and he entertained himself on the journey with a book of love poems by an up-and-coming poet by the name of Elizabeth Shakespeare

Makepeace. Although the romantic prose of Makepeace was not really Lord Fontingroy's cup of tea—he much preferred the raucous sentiments of Comedia Bawdia—he found a couple of lines in the slim volume that stirred the codpiece:

> *Your nose is like a wood squirrel that sits upon your face*
> *And if I had my drathers, I'd drather take its place*
> *There to sit, so your tongue should sip*
> *The nectar of love's pleasure from these sweet and rosy lips*

So it was, that Lord Fontingroy, with a head full of bad poetry, was ushered into the Queen's presence three hours later. His first thought upon seeing her majesty was that she had put on considerable weight during the balance of Christamus. Her figure bulged upon the throne, overflowed it even, and her face was as round and plump as a chocolate pudding. Yet her skin was fair, but for her ruddy cheeks which were the hue of crushed strawberries. The bottle of Lisboa port and the half empty goblet on the lacquered table next to the throne attested to the habit responsible for the Queen's complexion.

'Dear Giles,' she said when she saw him, her voice loud, clear, resonating and regal, despite the weight of the port upon her tongue, 'it is so many months since I have seen you. But of course you bring good news; the Black Fleet is finally defeated, those pirates no longer plunder our trade and my beloved Albion rules the waves.'

'As always, Ma'am,' Lord Fontingroy replied, 'but the Tilt of Eastermus is upon us and I seek your leave to recall the ships from the Edge.'

'The Black Fleet *is* defeated then?' she asked, cocking an eye at him.

'Well, not quite, Ma'am, but excellent progress has been made, indeed far greater progress than we ever expected at this time.'

'Hmm, I think I shall leave them there.'

'That would be dangerous, Ma'am. With the balance of the world shifting as it does this time of year, so quickly they could be to drawn to the Edge to—'

'Plummet through space with their sails a'flappin',' the Queen said, then giggled drunkenly. 'Surely that would be a sight to see.' She raised the goblet to her lips and drank it dry, picked up the bottle of port, but found it empty. 'Oh dear, I was going to offer you a little drink, but now we have a dead man upon our hands. Too soon the bottles run dry. Still, plenty more where that came from; I am the Queen of Albion, after all, and I can pretty much do what I bloody well like, can't I, Giles?'

'Yes, Ma'am, you can, but about the ships...'

'Now, Giles,' she said, 'come join me in my private chambers where we will find the bottles replenished. You do want a little drink, don't you? I like my men to take a little drink, now and then; I believe it gives them fortitude.'

'Yes, Ma'am, indeed it does.' Lord Fontingroy sighed, knowing he would need more than a little drink for what the Queen had in mind.

A discreet time later, her most royal majesty sat upon her massive bed in her opulent nakedness, redolent of one of the heathen Buddha statues to be found towards the eastern edge of her empire. And, after she had disposed of another bottle of Lisboa port, her smile, too, took on the serenity of the heathens' most beloved prophet. The only thing that spoils the imagery, Lord Fontingroy thought, as he struggled into his tights, is the massive forest of hair that springs forth from her loins.

Having dispensed with her goblet—it became annoying after a while, the Queen had decided, to pour before one could actually drink—she now swigged liberally from the bottle. 'I have a little surprise for you, Giles,' she said between swigs.

'You have been reading the Kama Sutra again, Ma'am,' Lord Fontingroy said wearily, as he drew fast the strings of his codpiece. Both his jaw and back ached, such had been his endeavours the past hour, and still he stumbled occasionally, as his body adjusted to the balance of the season.

The Queen giggled. 'You are such a lusty lewdster, Giles. I sometimes think men think of little else but the ungirding of their loins. But no, my thoughts are soaring now far above the hot darkness of the nether regions. Satiation brings a clear vision, I believe, and so well satiated am I that I have a grand vision indeed. It is something that has been preying on my mind for some time and now I have decided it. I am going to rule the world in a manner that has never been seen before.'

'With respect, Ma'am, you have achieved that already. You have colonies in every corner of the Earth. You control all the major sea-lanes and commerce routes. You determine who shall rule and who shall not in the lesser kingdoms. You name it and in your name it has been done. There is nothing you cannot touch and do not rule. You are, my most illustrious majesty, in control of just about everything, and the greatest monarch in all history.'

'But not of the seasons!' the Queen shouted, her brow becoming sullen and brooding black. 'I am sick of the Tilt! I do not like falling out of bed when I get up in the morning. I do not like walking up hills, especially not in my own palace. I do not like securing my plates and chaining my furniture and none of my subjects do either.

'I do not like it as well, when you insist, as you always do when the seasons change, that *my* navy must be brought in from the Edge. So every Eastermus and *every* Wintermus, the Black Fleet follows us in, expanding their control. I want the world to be flat, flat, flat all of time! From now on, I want the balance of Autumus and Christamus all year round! That is my command!'

Lord Fontingroy had seen it often enough. One sip too many and the tide did turn, the Queen swiftly slipping from her fat giggly good-time tart personae and into her impersonation of the wailing banshee of the Moor Lochs. He chose his words carefully. 'My dear, most majestic majesty, you will appreciate the natural changing of the seasons is in the hands of the Great King in the Sky, whose powers we do not question—'

'Oh, poppycock!' the Queen cried. 'You have been given your command, Lord Admiral. Find me an answer! Are you the man for the job or not? Shall I ask Lord Herringbone in your stead?'

'Most certainly, your majesty, I am the man for the job,' Lord Fontingroy replied nervously, knowing full well that sneaky fawning cat's paw Herringbone had been after the admiralty for years.

'Oh, Giles, you really are such a good brave boy. Now come kiss the Gloriana and depart post haste. There is so much work to be done.'

As Lord Fontingroy touched his lips to the giant girasol on the Queen's ring, the Queen said, 'Giles, you do understand this mission you are upon is to be our special little secret.'

'Yes Ma'am,' he said, thinking Herringbone might very well end up with the admiralty yet, should he fail, and Lord Fontingroy was convinced right then that he would.

Act III: The Explosive Dr M'Gee

It was, of course, the fool of all fool errands that Lord Fontingroy had been set upon and he was to linger in Albion Town for several days—not to take in the pleasures of the town, not the fine inns with their spicy and exotic foods from across the empire, nor to view the galleries of the rich and famous artists the Queen patronised, not even to partake of the erotic pleasures of the ubiquitous bordellos and fleshpots—no, no, no, of course, not—but rather to understand the mechanics of the world. So it was off to Albion University he went, seeking to engage the wisest men of his time. But after three days of learned discourse, he found he was no closer to fathoming the nature of the seasons. He had numerous discussions about how many angels could dance on the head of a pin and was surprised to hear the debate ranged from just one to over four hundred and forty-four. This suggested to him angels were small tiny little creatures and not the soaring ten-foot beasts with massive feathery wings he had imagined them to be, but then he *was* willing to admit metaphysics had never been his strong point. As far as the changing of the seasons was concerned there was little interest paid to such esoteric matters, save he was assured by all and sundry that any further understanding of the matter lay with the Great King in the Sky.

So with the burden of his mission weighing heavily, Lord Fontingroy abandoned his quest momentarily and ventured forth to the *Golden Globe* to catch a matinee. It was the latest Kate Marlowe play, about a man who had sold his soul to the devil and, in typical Marlowe fashion, Lord Fontingroy found it a riotous comedy, replete with flatulence gags and bawdy innuendo. Barely five minutes into the play, he was rolling in the aisles with laughter. Afterwards, he was able to commence his journey home in a somewhat jollier mood.

On his return, he found his wife in her sewing room gazing into a crystal ball. The house echoed with the mournful moans of the furniture chains as the Tilt of Eastermus began to build.

'It is a present from Dr M'Gee,' Lady Gia said. 'He told me that if I were to gaze into it long enough I should see the future.'

'And have you?' Lord Fontingroy asked. 'It seems an unlikely proposition.'

'Indeed, but just now it told me of your return.'

'Really?'

'As you walked through the door, I saw you reflected in the glass.'

'Fascinating,' he said and slumped into a leather chair, which groaned and tensed on its chain with the added weight.

'So, how is the Queen?' Lady Gia asked.

'Plumper than ever, obstinate as always, and now she has a grand vision and I am on a secret mission,' Lord Fontingroy said wearily.

'Which is?'

'Darling, it's a secret.'

'Gilly!'

'Oh, all right. The Queen is sick of the Tilt. She rules just about the whole world and now wishes to rule the seasons as well. In essence, my dear, I have been charged with finding a way to stop the Tilt.'

Lady Gia struggled hard to suppress a laugh, but then it burst out and bubbled through her whole body. She could even feel it tingling right down to her toes.

'It's not funny,' Lord Fontingroy said grumpily.

Lady Gia took a deep breath. 'Has she gone stark raving bonkers?'

'Some would ask whenever was she not. However, the Queen's sanity is beside the point. She is, after all, the most powerful monarch in all the world and perhaps it is a fair question for one such as she to ask, why can she not control the seasons?'

'And you accepted this secret mission?'

'She would have given the job to Herringbone and I expect the Admiralty too, should I have been so callous to refuse. You told me I must do everything to retain our good fortune, and so I have,' Lord Fontingroy said, rubbing the back of his neck nervously.

All of sudden there was an explosion outside. The house shook and the furniture chains groaned loudly. 'What in all heaven's name was that?' Lord Fontingroy cried.

'I expect it's Dr M'Gee. He said a short while ago he was going down to the rose garden to try a little experiment.'

Unfortunately, most of the rose garden was no more. Much of it had been replaced by a huge gaping hole at least twenty feet deep. Dr M'Gee, long white hair and beard to match, wizened face, and dressed in an appalling purple robe covered in glittery stars and now fresh sods of earth, stood gazing wistfully at the edge of the hole his art and science had created.

When Lord Fontingroy and Lady Gia approached, he turned from his work beaming a triumphant smile.

'Ah, Giles and Gia, how nice to see you. Isn't this magnificent?' he said, sweeping his arms wide.

'I was rather fond of that rose garden,' Lord Fontingroy said.

'You can grow another one,' Dr M'Gee said merrily. 'We can't let a little rose garden get in the way of progress, can we now?'

'And what progress is that?' Lady Gia asked, cocking her head against the Tilt, as she felt its pull shift up a notch.

Dr M'Gee winked knowingly and with a flourish his hand entered his robe and withdrew a small phial. 'Just a little something I picked up in Brittany during my travels. A most powerful elixir which when mixed with this equally powerful elixir' —another phial emerged from his robe—'can produce a very large explosion indeed. Here, let me show you how it works.'

'Are you sure it's safe?' Lady Gia asked.

'Yes,' Lord Fontingroy said, gazing sadly at the remains of his rose garden, 'it doesn't look safe at all.'

'Yes, yes, quite safe it is,' the doctor muttered, moving to another part of the garden and dispensing a drop of elixir from one phial onto a flat stone that lay there, then taking the other phial, he placed a second drop a short distance away. 'The pull of the Tilt will merge them shortly. Now I suggest we stand back a little.'

But no sooner had he said this than there was a brilliant flash, an ear-splitting explosion, and the heavens rained with warm earth and rose petals. Lord Fontingroy, Lady Gia and Dr M'Gee were thrown from their feet, and when Lord Fontingroy looked up he saw the surviving portion of his rose garden had been replaced by another ugly hole.

'Do you think,' Dr M'Gee asked, wiping dirt from his face, 'the Queen would be interested in this little dandy? I was thinking I could make up a small capsule—let's call it "La Bombe Albioni"— with a glass seal in the middle and a drop of the opposing elixirs in either end. The capsule could then be propelled by aid of a slingshot, the glass shattering on impact and boom, boom, ka- boom. Think what quick work could be made of the Black Fleet.'

'I think not at this moment, doctor,' Lady Gia said. 'The Queen has more pressing matters on her mind. Besides, hasn't

Gilly mentioned before that he doesn't want to get rid of the Black Fleet.'

'But, why ever not? Those pirates are the scourge of the border seas, threatening Albion's trade routes, plundering our ships ... well, at least that's what the official propaganda says.'

'Which Gilly writes and, yes, they do occasionally do some naughty things, but if it wasn't for the terrible scourge of the Black Fleet, the Queen might decide to cut back on her navy, and Gilly might be out of a job. Isn't that true, Gilly?'

'I wish you hadn't mentioned that,' Lord Fontingroy said and stormed back to the house. He was terribly upset about his rose garden.

Act IV: A Plate of Pigs

At dinner that evening, Dr M'Gee was waxing lyrically on the new techniques the ladies of Brittany were employing to manage their pubic hair, when Lady Gia, all hot and rosy cheeked, said suddenly, 'Gilly, perhaps you should seek the doctor's assistance on that certain matter you mentioned to me earlier today.'

'And so they pluck it nearly all away,' Lord Fontingroy asked, squeezing his legs together squeamishly, 'leaving only the tiniest of strips?'

'Which they do then dye in all manner of colours, scarlet, plumberry, and even gooseturd, a colour which they claim drives their menfolk wild.'

'The matter with the Queen...' Lady Gia said, clearing her throat loudly.

'And in that matter I can be of assistance,' Dr M'Gee said quickly.

Lord Fontingroy flashed a look at his wife. 'You told him!' he said.

'We'll,' she said, 'you do require assistance.'

'Which I can give,' the doctor said, stroking his beard. 'Now in order to meet the Queen's request, first we must understand what it is that causes the Tilt. That is, we need to understand the infernal logic of the matter in order to design the necessary intervention. Am I right?'

Fontingroy groaned. 'Yes, you are right. But I knew this days ago and none of the learned men of Albion University were able to explain it to me. Too busy they were, investigating how many angels could dance upon the head of a pin.'

'I thought that one was resolved,' Dr M'Gee said. 'It is universally agreed, by scholars of Brittany, that the number of angels that can dance upon the head of a pin is zero, zilch, zip. That is, not a single one. They are far too big, you see.'

'Yes, that's what I thought,' Lord Fontingroy cried, thinking, I knew I wasn't that stupid.

'Indeed, you did, a clever young chap such as yourself, of

course you would. Now where were we?'

'The dynamics of the seasons, precisely what causes the Tilt,' Lady Gia said.

'Oh, yes, yes indeed, what causes the Tilt, or a more fundamental question, how does the world work? To resolve this we will need to tap into the Akashic Records where the knowledge of everything is stored, as it has been and as it will be for evermore. But first we must consult the keepers of the records. Come to my study at Cockcrow. It is the best time for a consultation. Fear not! With the aid of my special assistants, we shall resolve the dilemma the Queen has burdened you with.'

Thus saying, Dr M'Gee rose from his place at the table, swung his starburst cloak about him with a theatrical flourish and bid them adieu.

'He has touched nothing of his pig,' Lord Fontingroy said after the doctor departed. 'And he has a study now, here, in our house?'

'I fear the doctor has sworn off meat since his travels in the East last Wintermus,' Lady Gia said, avoiding the question of the study. 'He ate only the pumpkin, the spinach and the potatoes. 'Snow Pea remains as he was roasted.'

'Snow Pea?'

'That's what you called him, dear, when he was born. I remember you were so clucky with him, caressing his ears, rubbing his leathery little snout. I remember it so well. "I shall call this one Snow Pea," you said, "because he is such a little cutie."'

'And this one?' Lord Fontingroy asked, pulling his fork from the pig on the plate before him.

'That's Little Butch,' she said. 'Yes, yes, I'm sure it is.'

'Little Butch was my favourite piglet. Snow Pea was my second favourite, of course, but I always thought Little Butch and I had a special bond.'

Lord Fontingroy pushed his plate away. 'I shall bury both of them tomorrow.'

'And this one too,' Lady Gia said, pushing her own roasted piglet to the middle of the table. It had not been touched. She had eaten only the apple that had been roasted in its mouth.

'Which one is this?' Lord Fontingroy asked.

'Buttercup,' she said.

'Buttercup,' he said. 'She used to come and sit in my lap.'

'I'll have a word to the cook, shall I?'

Lord Fontingroy nodded and brushed a wayward tear from his eye.

Act V: The Gate of Heaven

The doctor's study, Lady Gia had assured her husband, was nothing more than a disused room in the west wing of the house, a place they never ventured on account it was where all the ghosts of the previous inhabitants were supposed to live. So it was with some trepidation Lord Fontingroy rose at the first crow of the cock and went in search of Dr M'Gee. He had been reluctant to leave his warm cosy bed, but not just because of the ghosts. The night, you see, had been a restless one. Both he and Lady Gia had their sleep tormented by nightmares of tiny angel pigs that flew around the house with stiff little wings, bizarrely using their own flatulence for propulsion. Lady Gia had said, as she attempted to describe her dream, that there was a dazzling flare from the posterior region of a little pig she was sure was Snow Pea, 'and then he did shoot off like a shooting star. It was amazing to see him fly so fast.'

Now, Lord Fontingroy found Dr M'Gee soundly asleep and untroubled by dreams it seemed. There was a distinct smell of alcohol hovering in a thick cloud over the doctor's head and Lord Fontingroy noticed that several bottles of his best brandy lay dead beneath the bed.

He touched the doctor on the shoulder and he woke with a start. 'Ah, Giles, Cockcrow already, eh?' the doctor said rolling from the bed and falling straight onto the floor where he found a bottle of brandy that still held a small portion within it. He sniffed at it, then said, 'I shall take a hair of the dog that bit me last night.'

And so he swigged the last of it, then cried gleefully, 'Ah, that's better! Cockcrow it is then, but yet I bet your cock did crow last night.'

Lord Fontingroy cleared his throat. 'Now about my problem with the Queen...' he said.

'Yes, yes, and now we shall get down to the business which needs to be done. If you could just help me up off the floor ... yes, there we go, back on two legs again. What was it the poet once said, "Two legs good, four legs bad" or some such thing.'

Lord Fontingroy knew, of course, that the poet in question had extolled the virtue of four legs over two. But he kept his silence and allowed Dr M'Gee to lead him to a small table in the corner of the room. There the doctor whipped away a red velvet cloth to reveal an ugly misshapen crystal orb beneath. It was transparent apart from its centre, which seemed to hold within it a deep grey smoke. Now Dr M'Gee seated himself and his hands with his fingers splayed open began to move above the orb, as if he was trying to draw something forth. 'Gaze closely, Giles, gaze closely, and see the powers of the heavens reveal themselves.'

'Pamini, my dear, dear girl,' Dr M'Gee said in a soft voice, 'are you there my little angel?'

The grey mist of the orb turned dark and swirled, then within the swirling a bright white light began to appear. Lord Fontingroy was astonished to see the immaculate features of a naked white nymph. 'Her breasts are sublime,' he said and felt a lump rise to his throat.

'Ssh, she is seraphim,' Dr M'Gee said, 'of course, she is sublime. It is in her very nature to be that way.'

'Yes, of course,' Lord Fontingroy said, then asked, 'Does she mind me looking?'

'Being a lower order angel her vanity is as great as any human's.'

Then a rich beautiful female voice filled the room, resounding and echoing off the walls. 'My, your companion is such a handsome devil, doctor.'

'And the Queen of Albion and his good lady wife acknowledge this, but this handsome devil, Dear Pamini, has a handsome problem that more than matches his good looks.'

'Ah yes, the Queen of Albion has set him a challenge to test her strength as Queen Regina against the natural forces of the world.'

'She knows everything then?' Lord Fontingroy asked, still absorb in her lithesome beauty. Never had he seen a woman so immaculate, so perfect in every detail. Certainly, he thought, his own dear Lady Gia was renowned as a great beauty, but Pamini was exceptional, beyond anything he could have ever imagined a woman could be, but yet so like every woman as well.

'So much, perhaps,' she said, 'but certainly not all. Angel Uriel knows more, and Michael and Gabriel too, but only the Great King in the Sky knows all, which is the way it is and shall ever be. Now I shall do a little dance for you.'

Within the orb, Pamini turned around, displaying a set of delicate gossamer wings and wiggling her perfect white buttocks. Then she bent over and revealed that part of the female anatomy known colloquially among the high-class bordellos of Albion Town as the 'Gate of Heaven' or as the 'Honey Pot' in the lesser ones.

Lord Fontingroy blushed hot and pink. Dr M'Gee slapped him on the back and yelled at the top of his voice, 'You're in, my good man. Oh yes, you are in!'

In where, Lord Fontingroy wondered, but then cold air rushed through the room as if a sudden tempest was upon them and the legendary Prospero's chooks had fled their roost.

'What manner of things are now before us?' Lord Fontingroy cried, as hailstones pelted down around him and the air in the room swirled and twisted, and then with a great big whoosh he was drawn into the orb in a twisting tornado that ripped him from his chair and rushed him towards the 'Gate of Heaven'.

Act VI: A Flat World Fable

Lord Fontingroy found himself flying in a mad rush down a long tunnel accompanied by the sounds of a thumping heartbeat and the fluttering of many tiny wings. At first, all was darkness, then, at the end of the tunnel, a light appeared growing rapidly in fullness and brightness. Yet it was not a light by which to see, for its illumination revealed no details of the place he was in, save,

Lord Fontingroy imagined, the walls were a deep rose petal pink.

His body shuddered as he burst through the light and he was forced to close his eyes with the intensity of the pleasure that swept through him.

When he opened his eyes once more, he found himself standing in a beautiful white marble hall of soaring ceilings and many columns. Before him lay a pool of turquoise water and on the other side of it stood Pamini. She was dressed now in a diaphanous gown which, by Albion standards, made only a slim attempt at modest attire. Lord Fontingroy thought poetically that the whiteness of her skin beneath glowed with the phosphorescence of sea creatures swimming in midnight seas.

'This is Uriel's pool,' Pamini said in a voice that held the music of Autumus and Christamus in it. 'He said I could borrow it for a short while. It will show you what you seek. Will you gaze into it?'

But the truth was, Lord Fontingroy could not take his eyes away from Pamini. He felt as if he had become frozen in stone and would remain that way for evermore, yet this thought did not frighten him at all, for so happy was he to be locked into that gaze with such beauty before him he did not wish even for an instant to change the moment.

'You find me comely then, you cheeky boy, you handsome devil, but now there is much business to attend to,' and saying this her form began to change. She aged rapidly to an old withered crone, then became a skeleton with rotting worm-eaten flesh, which was not only physically revolting but smelt much worse than it looked.

So with the spell broken, Lord Fontingroy's gaze fell into Uriel's pool. Before him now he saw his world floating in space as if he was a mighty eagle soaring above it. Flat it was and square too, as he knew from the maps his navy used, with each corner of the square a compass point. Within the centre of the world was his beloved Albion, a land-mass as round and plump as the Queen herself, but with a corrugated coastline hinting at the wealth of its shipping harbours. Directly to the east was the land mass known as the Continent, its western shore the home of Dr M'Gee's learned Brittany. Towards the west were the Albion Isles, the home of fishermen and drunken monks. To the north and south was the first of the seven seas, and beyond these the islands and continents of Albion's empire, stretching all the way to the Edges, which were unfathomable, unknowable save for the Black Fleet that haunted them.

And now, Pamini, tiny as a faery folk, came and sat on Lord Fontingroy's great eagle shoulder and whispered in his ear. 'I shall tell you a tale as we watch the world and, if you listen well, then I promise I shall dance for you again. The Queen's attention must be diverted from her silly crusade. But do not fear, you shall have the solution you seek.'

Then she nipped him playfully on the ear and said, 'Now see

and watch what we have here. It is your twin moons, Mother Luna rising in the eastern sky followed by her son, Baby Cupid, as they do every Eastermus. But see, too, as mother and son ascend, the demon that inhabits the eastern ether, Old Man Satyr, follows them upwards on their journey, lusting after Mother Luna as he has always, since time immemorial. But he is an earth spirit, too heavily anchored to the ground, and in his lust he pulls the world up with him. So the Tilt of Eastermus begins. Ah, but he's an old man. He cannot keep up the chase for too long. He has pulled the whole world with him for a while and now it is the peak of the Tilt! But see, his energy wanes and he is forced to retreat as Mother Luna and Baby Cupid leave the eastern sky and reach their zenith, at which point the world returns to balance and Autumus, the season of good fortune, begins.

Then mother and son descend through the western sky and pass over the Edge, beneath Wester Point, where there lives another demon, and the chase begins anew. So the Tilt of Wintermus begins, but this old demon, too, soon gives up the chase and the balance returns once more and the love and giving and merry drunkenness of Christamus arrives. Shall we follow Mother Luna and her son to the other side, my handsome eagle? Of course, we shall!'

And with that Lord Fontingroy found himself soaring off, down over the edges of the world into regions unknown. But as above, so below. Here was a world familiar to him, a replica almost of his own world which was above, yet even as he thought these thoughts, he realised there was no above and no below—there were merely two sides to the world ...

'It is a virgin land, uninhabited by people, yet the nature of it is similar to your own,' Pamini said. 'Here shall be found gold and jewels in abundance and exotic spices growing wild and ripe for harvesting.'

Lord Fontingroy suddenly found himself gazing into Uriel's Pool again, the images, the illusion of flying like an eagle gone. 'My god, that was sublime,' he said.

'I love that old story so very very much,' Pamini said. 'Come, I shall do another dance for you now, and you shall understand the solution offered.'

Act VII: Pamini's Second Dance

Lord Fontingroy thought Pamini's second dance was even better than her first. Then as the last cock did crow, he was staring into Dr M'Gee's crystal orb once more. Only a dim light came in through the doctor's windows. As if, Lord Fontingroy thought, only a few minutes had elapsed since he had first arrived and roused the doctor from his bed.

'I had this absolutely amazing vision,' he said. 'I soared like an eagle.'

'I saw it all,' Dr M'Gee said, whacking him on the back, 'although towards the end the orb did get a little misty.'

'You missed the second dance then?' Lord Fontingroy asked, feeling somewhat relieved. If Lady Gia should hear ...

'And the solution she offered.'

'We'll, after the, um, dance, she showed me other worlds that were round like balloons and footballs; they have no Tilt, you see, but are full of air and weighted down to stop them floating off into space with a huge iron ball in the middle of them.'

'Like my pig intestine tyres,' Dr M'Gee exclaimed, his hand going to his forehead, 'I see it, I see it, yes, yes, yes, I can see it, it's coming to me ... don't tell me; I'll have it in a minute.'

Lord Fontingroy groaned. 'No, dear doctor, it is clear we cannot change the natural order of the world in which we live and are chasing demons if we think we can. Pamini has given me a much safer solution. Think. It is as obvious as the nose on your face. We must change the Queen's mind.'

'That sounds altogether too difficult and just a trifle boring,' Dr M'Gee said, who was already thinking there must be some way his explosive phials and inflatable pig intestines could be put to good use on a massive scale.

Lord Fontingroy chuckled. 'No, no, not at all it. It is a brilliant and exciting idea. The Queen requires a distraction from the Tilt and think what is it the Queen delights in more than anything else?'

The doctor cocked an eyebrow. 'Several bottles of Lisboa port and some handsome male company?'

'No, more than that. Those are merely her dalliances, her indulgences, mere whims like this stupid Tilt idea, things that come into her head when she is unhappy. No, the Queen's greatest passion is her Empire and the bigger it is the better she feels about herself. All of this Pamini has revealed to me; she is such a clever giglet.'

Act VIII: Virgina Regina

And so it was that Lord Fontingroy presented before the Queen once more.

'Your majesty,' he said, with an air of new-found confidence, 'I have a grand vision for the expansion of your most noble empire.'

'Sod it!' the Queen said. 'I already control all there is to control. You have told me this before. There is nothing more to conquer, nothing more to gain. Have you got rid of the Black Fleet yet and what are you doing about the secret mission you are supposed to be upon?'

'With all due respect, Ma'am, I do beg your indulgence ... just for one brief moment. When I told you that you controlled all the world before, I was, um, speaking in a metaphorical sense.

Presently, you see, you control only half the world, but with my plan...'

The Queen rose from her throne. Her face was scarlet with anger and her brow blackened to a deep royal purple. She could hardly speak, such was her fury. 'Half the world,' she stammered, 'half the fuckin' world! You, Lord Herringbone, Commander Fowell, and all those useless others have told me consistently for I don't know how many bloody years that I control the whole world.'

'So we believed, Ma'am,' Lord Fontingroy said, finding some of his confidence slipping away, but then he snapped his fingers. A court retainer rushed to his side and handed him a flat board model of the world which Dr M'Gee had constructed. 'Your majesty,' Lord Fontingroy continued quickly, 'here, you see, in the middle of the world your beloved Albion and beyond the lands of the Continentals and the heathens, stretching all the way to the Edges. This is your most glorious empire—'

'Yes, yes, get to the point, if you have one!' the Queen roared.

'But,' Lord Fontingroy said, flipping the board over, 'here on the other side of the world is a virgin empire, your majesty, just waiting for your seal to be placed upon it.'

The Queen resumed her throne. Some of the dreadful colour had gone from her face. Her voice was gentler now. 'Come closer, Giles, you are beginning to intrigue me.'

'So you see,' Lord Fontingroy said, as he crouched next to the Queen and placed the model of the world upon her lap. 'You just flip it over like this and, voilá, the world has another side.'

The Queen gazed off into the middle distance. Her eyes became all misty. 'Another side,' she whispered, 'a virgin empire. Oh, yes, I like that, I do indeed. Who would have thought, but of course it must be. Another side to the world! And gold and diamonds and exotic spices, you say. Oh, dear Giles, you are such a clever, clever boy. I shall call it Virgina Regina and I shall make you, you lovely, lovely man, its very first Governor. Here, kiss the Gloriana. Now where's the port? This calls for a celebration!'

And as he kissed the girasol, so great was the delight of the Queen she put her big fleshy tongue into his ear and swirled it all about.

Epilogue

What followed next was a series of extraordinary events the like of which were unknown in the history of the world hitherto that time. History now knows it was the beginning of the modern age, with the development of the Grand Staircase being the momentous event which triggered the Renascence, but back then it was all about taking chances and trusting your luck.

Dr M'Gee, much to his delight, was given the main carriage of the project and he set to work immediately, commencing his blasting in a fallow field on Lord Fontingroy's estate. After several months, he called for the assistance of a brilliant young Continental engineer by the name of Da Vinci and work began on the construction of the internal staircase that would link the two sides of the world.

Fortunately the world was much thinner than Dr M'Gee had had calculated and, much to the Queen's pleasure, the Grand Staircase was completed within twelve months rather than the three years that had been anticipated.

As Governor of the new world, Lord Fontingroy, with the support and practical intelligence of Lady Gia, proved to be a very capable ruler, although he was never able to escape a rather obsessive feeling that he was living life upside down.

Geoffrey Maloney lives in Brisbane, Australia. His work as a writer and editor has been nominated for six Aurealis Awards. In 2001, his story 'The World According to Kippling' won the Aurealis Award for best fantasy short story. A collection of his work, *Tales from the Crypto-System*, is available from Prime Books in the US: www.primebooks.net

ONE NIGHT STAND

DIRK FLINTHART

He pulled up in the carpark outside the Club Riviera about an hour after sundown. Warmth poured off the black tarmac, but at least the air had lost some of the stifling afternoon heat. Leaning back in the cracked leather upholstery, he listened to the big old Cadillac engine tick as it cooled. Above him, the sign with its interchangeable black lettering said: *Tonite Only! Club Riviera Presents The Return Of The King! Elvis Lives On Stage!!!*

He slicked his hair back in the rear-view mirror and dragged the beat-up guitar case off the back seat. Despite the humidity, he shrugged himself into a black leather jacket. Best to make a good impression. There was always a chance somebody might notice.

Inside, the air conditioning wrapped him in a damp, cold, cigarette-stinking blanket. A bored girl stood behind the reception desk, looking him up and down like he'd stepped in dogshit, maybe. She wore big false eyelashes and a gold-sequined bikini that glittered in the fluorescent lighting.

'You must be the entertainment,' she said, and cracked her gum loudly. 'You're late. Mister Stubbs is waiting.' She flicked an enameled fingernail towards a door at the back.

'Thank you very much, ma'am,' he said in his best Southern drawl, but she ignored him. He shrugged, and rapped on the plywood door.

'Moment,' said someone inside. 'Yeah, come in already.'

Stubbs fit his name well, a short, red-faced, stocky man with a greasy comb-over. The wet, chewed end of an unlit cigar stuck out of his teeth as he argued with his telephone. 'Friday,' he said. 'You deliver those shrimp by Friday, or you can fucking well eat them yourself, *capisce*? No. I don't give a flying fuck. Screw you. And your lawyer, too.' He banged the phone into its cradle and turned to face the newcomer. 'You,' he said, and grabbed a fax from the top of a littered desk. He squinted at it, and looked up again. 'John Coltrane. That you?'

The musician nodded. 'You can call me Elvis, though,' he said. 'That's my stage name: Elvis Lives. Been doing it so long, I can't hardly remember the difference.'

'You're late, Coltrane.' Stubbs puffed himself up and glared.

The musician shrugged. 'I'm not on for another couple hours. Plenty of time. Hey,' he said, a little more sharply. 'Sign says tonight only. My agent said a week, maybe two. What's up there?'

Stubbs raised the fax and looked at it carefully. 'John Coltrane,' he read. 'Elvis Lives On Stage.' He wadded up the paper and threw it over his shoulder. 'I guess your agent forgot to include your social security number, Coltrane.'

'Guess maybe he did,' the musician agreed. 'One night, two hunnerd fifty.'

'One fifty,' Stubbs jutted his jaw. 'Best I can do. It's not Vegas here.'

The musician glanced out the window. 'Sign says Elvis Lives,' he said. 'Shame if the King couldn't put in an appearance. Two hunnerd. You want to talk about that week?'

'We'll talk about that week when I've seen the act,' said Stubbs. 'How do I know you're any good?'

Smiling, the musician snapped open the guitar case and pulled out the instrument, a big, shining, wooden beast of a thing. 'Gibson J-200 flatback,' he said. 'Just like the King's favourite, right down to the scratches and bumps. You wanna hear something?'

'Thrill me.' Stubbs folded his arms, and leaned back on the formica desktop.

A brush of fingertips across steel strings, and the small room leapt with sound. The musician hit the opening chords of *Jailhouse Rock* with verve, dropping into Elvis' trademark stance like he was born to it, pumping his hips and windmilling his arm. He made it as far as the county jail when Stubbs raised a hand.

'Yeah, okay,' said the stocky man. 'What I can do for you, I can do one-fifty, like I said, but you get a piece of the gate if we get more than two hundred through the door, okay?'

The musician put the guitar back into its case, and picked it up. 'My agent says the Riviera here only seats two-twenny-five. One fifty plus a piece of maybe twenny-five at the gate equals no Elvis tonight. Sayonara, sucker.'

'All right, all right,' said Stubbs. 'Don't get your panties in a bunch. One fifty plus ten percent of everything over—what, one-fifty?'

'Ten percent of everything over a hunnerd through the gate, plus your one-fifty, and maybe I make two-seventy-five for the night if we both get lucky,' said the musician. He stuck out his hand. 'Good enough for me, Mister Stubbs.'

Stubbs glanced at him shrewdly. 'You put out a jar for tips, you might get another fifty, maybe. We can talk about that.'

The musician gave him a look, cold and distant. 'The King doesn't play for tips. We got a deal, Mister Stubbs?'

They shook.

The room was a dump. There was a tiny stage with sound gear

held together by duct tape, a couple of gels for light. Too many tables crammed in; no room for dancing. Poker machines lined the walls, blinking and bleeping and swallowing coins, and the air-con was thick with fossil smoke.

It never used to be this way when he played the big places. Madison Square Garden. Now that was a gig. But that was long ago, and the Riviera was right here and now. At least he could still play. He'd lost so many other things.

He plugged in the guitar and hit a few chords for the sound guy up in the glassed-in booth at the back. The guy looked bored as hell, but then, who wouldn't? Mixing for the kind of acts that played places like the Riviera. Probably stoned, too. The musician wished he could get stoned, but it wasn't as easy as that any more. Still, if he was careful, if he played his cards just right, he might be able to score a little something tonight. It was the right kind of place, for sure, but would it be the right sort of crowd? He patted the back pocket of his faded blue jeans, feeling for the little bag of powder. All he needed was the apparatus, and a few private moments.

'One, two. One, two,' he said into the microphone. 'Two. Two. Two. Two.' Making sure to get his lips close, so the mixer could compensate for the hard sounds like pee and tee and kay. 'One, two. One, two.' One day, he'd do a song around those words, for all the bored mixers and wasted musicians. No—that had happened already. He glanced down, and smiled. It had been a long time since he'd worn blue suede shoes. Did they even make the things any more?

'Yeah, fine,' came the voice of the mixer guy. 'Levels are good. Nice guitar you got there, buddy.'

'Thanks,' said the musician.

The crowd trickled in while he watched on a monitor in the green room. One thing you could say for the new technology: even a shitty place like the Riviera could afford stuff that never would have happened, back in the day. The International Hotel never had a camera, let you look the whole crowd up and down before you came out on the stage. The musician fiddled with the little joystick, shifting the view here and there, back and forth on the little black-and-white screen. Mostly they were an older crowd, he saw. Regulars, come to play the machines and take in a bit of Friday evening entertainment. Here and there, a few couples, watching the stage with their jumbo shrimp cocktail in front of them. Six jumbo shrimp, a couple lettuce leaves, a spoonful of mayonnaise: ten bucks. He swung the camera around for a while, checking the dead shrimp and the dying crowd, thinking what a waste of time it was for him here, and then he saw her.

She was down the front, at a table by herself. Old enough to be worthwhile, young enough to be easy. She had blonde hair like you could buy from Kroger's, and jeans just a bit too tight for an ass just a bit wider than fashion dictated. The make-up round her eyes was thick and dark, and there was something in the way she sat, the way she clutched her drink that suggested a kind of vulnerability.

So yeah, maybe not a complete waste of time.

When the house lights went down, he picked up the Gibson and took a place in the middle of the stage, behind the closed curtains. He turned his back towards the audience, and waited. The smoke smell was stronger now, other smells mixed with it: booze, sweat, cooking, and even the faint, flat non-smell of the air-conditioning unit itself. He lowered his head and hunched his shoulders, feeling the little knot of excitement swimming in his belly. Even now, after so many performances, so many crowds, it still got to him. That moment, just before the curtain opened up. Maybe this time ... that was what did it. The hope that maybe this time, the right person would be out there, take in the act, pick him up and put him back on top, like before.

A guy could hope, anyway. It was what he had left. That and the music.

'Ladeez and gennulmen!' The emcee's grating drawl, amplified and distorted by the mike and the shitty acoustics of the room, was almost unintelligible. It had to be Stubbs, though. Pushy little guy like that, he'd want his moment in front of the crowd. Anyway, why would he shell out for a real emcee? 'Ladeez and gennulmen, the Riviera Lounge is proud to present, live in concert, the King himself: Elvis Lives!'

The stage name was the cue. The curtains squeaked open and the spotlight nailed the musician. There and then, on the spot, he decided to open with the number he'd used for Stubbs, and he leapt in the air, spun, and came down hammering at the Gibson for all he was worth.

And it all came back to him, the way it always did. One thing he'd never lost, not in all the years, not even when he crossed over. He still had the music in him, right there in his hands and his voice, like lightning waiting to strike. The Gibson sang under his fingers, growling and howling and crooning as he belted out the song. The strings thrummed and rasped, and he poured it all out, out into the dark where the crowd waited.

Yeah, but if the magic was still inside him, maybe there wasn't so much of it left in the crowds these days.

He gave them the old numbers, from back before the Vegas days—*Blue Suede Shoes, Hound Dog, Heartbreak Hotel*—and hey, they liked it, but you know, maybe they were more a Vegas crowd. Feet were tapping, here and there, heads nodding, but no real vibe, no big buzz. Some of them kept eating, and some kept talking, and a few wandered over to the poker machines like he wasn't there at all, or maybe like he was muzak on the P.A. system. He gritted his teeth and pushed it hard, building through *Shake, Rattle and Roll*, then reined it in a little during *Don't Be Cruel*, taking a rest, trying to focus his energy.

Then he turned it on full. He gave them *Johnny B Goode,* the old Chuck Berry classic that everybody covered, even the Beatles, and he cranked it up. Way up, as good as he'd ever been, even back when he was the biggest of them all.

He gave it everything he had, his arm windmilling and his hips pumping. He was a better guitar player now than he'd been back in the old days, and he even managed to chase a few of Chuck's signature riffs up and down the old Gibson, but it just wasn't reaching them. They were still smiling, still toe-tapping, but they just weren't there for him. Not like they used to be.

The musician jumped down from the stage, moving into the crowd, bumping and swaying, still pounding out the music, watching the faces and the bodies around him. Hardly anybody looked his way. They just shied back, automatically making room for him to get past. Too busy eating, talking, whatever.

Suddenly, or maybe not so suddenly, it wasn't working for him, either. Maybe it hadn't been working all along, and he hadn't figured it out till now. The Gibson sounded flat and puny through the crackly system. The words felt wrong in his mouth, like he was about to forget the lyrics. The energy that had filled him when the curtain went up was gone, lost somewhere, blown away in a gust of indifference and shitty air-con. He found himself thinking of the plastic bag in his pocket, and without exactly meaning to, he repeated the 'Go-johnny-go' chorus for a few bars, giving himself time to look around for that girl...

And there she was, still alone at her table. Watching him, thank Christ for that much.

He swaggered through the tables until he stood close to her. The last chords of *Johnny B* crashed out. Over the smattering of polite applause, he flowed into the opening bars of the next piece—slow, tender and wistful. At his signal, the lights faded to a single spot, picking him out of the crowd and her with him, wrapping the two of them in a single shaft of golden light holding back an ocean of darkness. Now it was like the crowd wasn't there, like it was just the two of them, alone in the light, and he leaned close, looking into those dark, sad eyes.

'This next song's for the little lady here,' he said, putting a little extra syrup on his southern drawl. 'And for anybody, anywhere, who knows how it feels to be ... lonely.' Then he took a breath, and softly, gently, he started in on *'Are You Lonesome Tonight'* —tender, sweet and low, and she blushed, and looked away, then looked back at him again with eyes like ragged holes.

He made it softer, and leaned in a little more, watching the blush fade from her face as she forgot to be embarrassed, forgot everything but the song and the singer. He'd never liked the sugary lyrics—how many people still knew what a parlor was, anyway?—but he knew how to make them work, better than anybody else.

Later, he'd regret it. He'd loathe himself for using the music to mess with the mind of some sad, lonely woman in some two-bit Podunk town in South Hicksville, USA. But he was tired, and he was weak, and he needed something that she had. So he sang to her, sadly, hungrily, and a strange and terrible hurt put a ragged razor edge into his voice.

He tried to touch her with it and thought he felt the emptiness inside her quiver in response.

The song ended. He didn't even have to signal the mixer guy; the spot faded to darkness with the last of the music. Soft, quick as a shadow, he slipped away from the crowd, back into the safety of the dressing room. When the knock came only a minute later, swift and sharp, he opened the door, and she poured into his arms.

'Oh my God,' she said, nuzzling at his neck, and he smelled the desire on her, raw and harsh. 'What is it? What's happening to me? What are you doing?'

He let his hands slide up her body, touching here, there, kneading, gently rubbing. 'Nothing but good, baby,' he crooned, tasting the sweat on her shoulder. 'You'll love every second.'

'Yes,' she hissed, her face a taut mask. 'Yes, yes. Now!' She kicked the door shut, her hands already busy under his jacket.

He held her off for an instant, using his strength to slow her gently, until she looked up at him, her eyes wide with need and wonder.

'Take it slow, lover,' he said. 'We got ourselves near an hour to the next set. Don't need to hurry for nobody.' He grinned at her, let her watch as he slid a hand down, over his hip, to his back pocket, coming up with the little plastic bag full of clean, white powder. 'Got the makings of a real fun time here, if you want.' He touched her again, like he had with the song, and felt that little quiver, just like before. She was ripe for it.

Her eyes got bigger. 'I—I dunno,' she said, looking at the bag. 'I mean, I did, a couple times, but you know...'

'Sure I do,' he whispered. 'I know all about it. This is the goods, baby,' he said. 'Heaven in a bag. Cleanest, sweetest stuff this side of Colombia.' He let her go, licked a finger and put it in the bag. Then he opened his mouth and dragged that finger over his tongue, rubbing it round his gums, and he smiled again. 'Yeah,' he breathed, though he felt nothing at all except a terrible, hungry hollowness. 'Oh, yeah.'

She gave in, like he knew she would. Took the bag, shook a little of the powder onto the hollow at the base of her thumb and sniffed it up expertly. Her head snapped up, hair flying, and she looked at him again. A cock-eyed grin wrote itself slowly across her face, and for the first time, the desperate loneliness in the back of her eyes slid away, forgotten.

'Ohhh,' she said. 'That is *fine!*'

'More,' he said, trying not to stare at her. He knew just how she felt in that moment, her pulse racing, an invisible wind blowing through every part of her body. The way he used to feel. Back when he still could. Envy seared him with a blackhearted fire. 'It's clean. It's good. You can take more.'

The drug helped, perhaps even more than his persuasions. Slowly at first, then more eagerly, she shook a larger dose of the powder onto her hand, and sniffed deeply. 'Oh, yeah,' she said, slumping back onto the green vinyl couch. 'Oh, God, yeah.'

Her eyes rolled back into her skull, and her head lolled. One long, smooth leg slid sideways until she sprawled slack-limbed before him, giggling. Beneath the edge of her skirt, he saw the damp, sweaty triangle of her underwear, if you could call it that. What they wore these days, the women he met—when he was young, the girls would have died of shame. Hardly anything at all. He could see where she shaved, dark razor stubble confirming that she was blonde by choice, not by nature.

It didn't matter at all. It had been a long time since he'd been interested in a woman in that way. Now, she was simply— *apparatus.*

He leaned close, nostrils flaring, taking in the warm, musky animal scent of her. The tang of her arousal was strong, like sea-salt on his tongue, and underneath, fainter now, the bitterness of something between loneliness and despair. Emotions were chemicals in the brain. He first read that in some science magazine somewhere, but these days, it was real. One more thing that came after the change, one more thing he'd gained in exchange for everything he'd given up. He could smell what people felt. Not that it was worth all that damn much.

The pulse at the base of her neck beat fast and strong, and the sweat stood out on her skin. Delicately, he nuzzled her, licking the skin at her throat, and she moaned, her legs opening wider still. The taste of the drug was strong and clear on his tongue, already present in her sweat. She was saturated in it, dosed to the eyes.

It was time.

He was burning for it, screaming for it, but he still wouldn't act like some kind of cliché. Sure, he could have taken her by the throat, but the memory of a couple hundred late-night B-movies made his lip curl. Instead, he slid the skirt a little higher, and placed his lips against the silk of her thigh.

She groaned, deep and slow.

At first, he licked and she writhed under his tongue. When the taste of her sweat and lust was too much, he felt his lips skin back from his teeth, and he bit down. Hot, salt-metal blood sprang forth, and he gulped greedily at the thick, red river pouring from the big artery in her leg. And she moaned, and she sighed, and she bled for him, filling him with her life, until he licked again and the wound simply closed, leaving only the faintest of scars. The old stories—people drained white, corpses empty of blood—they didn't take into account that a body holds near two gallons of blood, but even a big stomach can't usually hold so much as a gallon.

He sat up and wiped his mouth, looking down at the pale,

limp woman on the green vinyl couch. She'd live. She wouldn't remember much about what happened, but she'd be okay. Get a few good meals into her, she'd rebuild her blood supply, be like nothing had ever happened at all. It was best that way.

It was faint at first, like the far-off tolling of a bell, and he opened himself to it, waiting for it to come on. Sitting there, looking down at her sprawled on the couch, he felt the first tingling in his fingers and his lips and his toes, and unexpectedly, he found himself wanting to talk to her. She looked so soft, so vulnerable...

'It wasn't always this way,' he murmured, tugging her skirt (what there was of it, anyway) back into place. 'I just—I got scared is all.' The blood moved in him, warm and strong and sluggish, and somewhere under that, somewhere inside, the sweet humming poison of the drug, and it was good, as good as he'd told her, almost as good as when he could take it for himself, sniff, shoot up, whatever, but he wasn't going to think about that.

He shook his head, trying to concentrate on what he was telling her, though he knew she probably wouldn't remember. Maybe that was why he was talking, anyhow. He didn't know for sure, but it felt good. How long had it been since he could talk to somebody, tell them the truth about himself?

He couldn't remember. The words came to him in a rush. 'I had money. I had everything. And it was great. That's why I was scared. I didn't want to get old and lose it all. I didn't want to—' but he couldn't say 'die'. The word wouldn't pass his lips.

He felt the rush coming on, a pounding in his head like a freight train charging over Mississippi flatlands, and he swallowed. 'I paid them to find her,' he whispered. 'I paid to be like this. What she promised.'

Then it hit him. Sudden fire arced through his body and his lips peeled up from his teeth. The muscles along his spine tightened hard, harder, trying to make him arch like a bow, but he fought it, mastered it, brought it under control. And it was there for him, like caged lightning in his belly, little jagged licks of electricity shooting up his arms and down his legs, his head buzzing like a hive of bees. Good, oh yeah, good—even if the only way he could get it was to steal it from somebody else, it was still so damned good...

Grinning, he snatched up the Gibson and banged open the door of the dressing room. Time for the second set. Time for a *real* show.

In the small, dark hours before the sun reclaimed the world, he gave his last encore. With the remaining traces of the stolen high fading to grey inside him, he strummed a few idle chords, and the audience broke up into little groups and couples. Looking at watches, gasping at the time, feeling sore feet and sore legs and dry throats, and did we really dance for so long? Yes, sure we did, don't I know it, be late for work in the morning. Call in sick, maybe.

'Hey.'

The musician didn't look around. 'Mister Stubbs,' he said. 'You think it was okay?'

Stubbs cleared his throat. 'Yeah,' he said. 'Yeah, it wasn't too bad.'

'They danced, didn't they?' The creature who called himself John Coltrane turned and looked at Stubbs at last, taking in the oily sheen of his bald head, the crumpled clothing with big, dark patches under the armpits. 'You, too.'

'Uh, yeah,' said Stubbs, glancing away. 'A little. I danced, yeah. Whew,' he dragged a stained handkerchief across his forehead. 'Maybe I better look at the air-con, eh? Pretty warm in here.'

The musician ignored the change of subject. He'd had this conversation before. He knew better than to let somebody like Stubbs off the hook too easily. 'So they liked the music, right?'

Stubbs seemed to contract, as though his body was hunching into itself. 'Well, they danced. But you know, it's a pretty easy crowd down here. We don't get much out this way. A bit of novelty and you're halfway home.'

'You want to talk about that week, maybe?' But he knew, he knew already. Same as the last place, and the one before, and the one before that. Same as all of them, sooner or later. He pressed Stubbs anyway, as much to make the ugly little man sweat as anything else. 'A show like that one, you'll get twice the crowd tomorrow night. Be turning them away at the door. You could charge double, if you wanted.'

'Double,' Stubbs scratched his chin. 'Yeah, right. I can see the locals paying twenty bucks a head for what, another guy doing Elvis? Sure, buddy. Hey, you wanna buy a bridge? I got one for you, cheap.'

Same old sorry goddam tune.

The musician sighed. '1969, The King played the International in Vegas for a month. Fifty-seven shows, full houses. Did it again the year after, and the year after that.'

'That's why they called him the King,' Stubbs said. 'That's why you're doing *him*, and nobody's doing you.'

The irony of it brought a bitter smile to the musician's face. 'Guess so,' he said. All those performers, doing Elvis. Even *him*. Could make you crazy, if you let it.

'You're not bad, though,' said Stubbs. 'Course, you coulda done the moves...' The stocky little man set himself, and waved his open hands jerkily back and forth. 'The Karate stuff, you know.'

'Yeah, I do,' said the musician. 'Some shows I do it that way. I could do one tonight.' He hated himself for saying it, like he was begging. Even more he hated the look in Stubbs' little eyes, like pity. But he'd felt good tonight, once he he got going. Another night or two like that, word could get around. Get himself a regular gig, he could maybe even get a following, make the right people take notice. He'd never again be what he was, but he was still good at what he did. The best.

Stubbs looked at him, slowly unwrapping a new cigar. 'That piece of the gate I promised you—'

The musician shrugged, thinking of the lonely girl waking up backstage about now, with a killer headache. 'I've already had my piece, I reckon.'

That earned him an odd look. Then the little man shook his head slowly. 'Look, you're pretty good,' he said. 'But I *saw* him once, you know. The King. Live, on-stage at the International. He had, what,' he lifted his shoulders and stuck out his jaw, 'Charisma, he had.' He pronounced it 'tcharizma'. 'You just can't copy that kind of thing.'

Quietly, the musician tucked the Gibson away into its worn hard-case. 'I'll take cash,' he said at last.

Without a word, Stubbs produced a wad of bills from his pocket and handed it over. The musician tucked it away in his jacket, and picked up his guitar.

'Not going to count it?'

The musician shook his head.

Stubbs shifted uncomfortably. Probably his feet hurt, after the dancing.

The musician looked at his watch, calculating how long until sun-up. He needed to be back in the trunk of his Caddy before then. Not a bed, maybe, but better than graveyard dirt.

'It's not you,' said Stubbs finally. 'It's them.' He waved a hand at the last of the audience. 'He just doesn't pull the crowds like he used to.' He showed yellowing teeth in what was probably a smile. 'I guess, you know—I guess it's not the same for them, living without him. Seems to me they've just about finally admitted that the King is dead.'

The musician pulled his dark glasses from an inner pocket of the jacket and used them to hide his eyes from Stubbs. He hefted his guitar again, and headed for the exit. When he got to the door, he looked back at the ugly little man, still standing there in the middle of the empty room.

'The King will never die,' he said, and left the building.

Dirk Flinthart lives in North-east Tasmania on fifty hillside acres with his wife, a dog, a cat, and three children under the age of six. Those three have pretty much restricted his output to short stories for the last few years, but you can find Dirk in previous editions of *Agog!*, *ASIM*, and the current *Year's Best Australian SF and Horror* from Mirrordanse Books. Despite past writing forays into crime, humour, journalism and travel—and combinations thereof—speculative fiction remains his first choice, and Dirk is particularly pleased by his ongoing association with the *Agog!* titles.

1 BLUE

KIM WESTWOOD

Linkman Joey, his supply of painkillers gone, is seeing double through the flashes of light. 'Men,' he says, trying not to slur between flashes, 'I've got a number coming down and there isn't much time, so line up quickly.'

The jumpers of the 14th *Bird of Peril* squadron shuffle into place.

'Give us the number, Joey.'

He squints out of his one good eye. 'Baseman Jack!' he commands.

Baseman Jack steps forward, flying suit unzipped, chest bared for Joey.

The colour swirls. 'Five. You've got five.'

Jack zips up, turns proudly to the line. 'That's a five to go with the eight,' he tells them. 'What colour is it, Joey?'

'Pink,' he says. 'Splotchy pink.'

The others shuffle closer, wanting their numbers read too, but Joey has had enough. 'Thassall for today,' he says huskily, the walls tilting. Then he collapses on the cold factory floor.

The men carry him to a nearby conveyor belt, lay him on its shiny rollers and give a push. Ball bearings snick as Joey is slid beneath rough grey girders towards an armoured tank. Tipped inside to sleep off the bright pain, he moans quietly, his own sulphur-crusted numbers scratching on his retinas.

In an alley several blocks away, Gilbert's Bar is open 24-hours, Gilbert rotting behind the counter. It's taking a long time because of the weather: early-morning frosts, and the wind—a southerly—coming off the snow peaks.

Crikey lifts her shot glass, gargles and spits. She puts the toothbrush in the glass and nudges her companion beside her on a tatty vinyl barstool.

'We're wired, baby.'

Radio knows that already. It's one of her more lucid moments. She knows as well that their esky is empty and they have to find food.

Crikey's vest has been loaded with explosives, wires laced

between. Radio's is matching khaki, a detonator dial sewn to the front. It's clear they were once a team—meant to explode together; but now the wires connecting them have been severed and the timer no longer ticks. They leave their vests on anyway, because it's cold, and the Semtex is excellent insulation.

Radio fiddles absently with the dial, clicking through the numbers until she gets a nasty close-up memory of a face saying 'DON'T!'. She turns her attention instead to the jukebox in the shadows behind the pool table.

'J9.'

'Dancing Queen,' says Crikey.

'E4?'

'Rocket Man.'

Question and answer swap a soothing round, while outside the world has ended and they don't know why.

Hiding inside their makeshift HQ, Linkman Joey and his team don't know either. In the glinting cavern—metal arms stopped mid-switch above conveyor belts, vats left tilting their molt like half-poured porridge—all they've seen so far are moth-eaten rats and shiny feeding roaches. Conferring, they remember being waved goodbye with flags and that they'd made their parents proud; but beyond that, where there should be memories, is a strange reluctance of light.

Clearly, they flew in; their cargo plane ploughed through one side of the steelworks and jammed tight in the hole, wing props and all. They suppose they were once to jump, wafting under canopies of olive drab into enemy territory. But now the unopened parachutes neatly line one wall for pillows and the men can't tell if they'd been sent for rescue or reconnaissance, to save or invade. Joey is all they have to remember the mission they are sure is contained like code in their service numbers, once so diligently committed to memory, and which they can't recall. But Joey's inspiration comes in very short bursts, so no one has a full allocation yet.

The *Bird of Peril*'s fuselage gapes, armoured tanks and 40-gallon drums marked 'Exit Yellow' rolled out. On the concrete floor in front are several welding suits foraged from the factory locker rooms. Taking turns, the soldiers try them on, and add to each a helmet with a bright band of LEDs across the brow. Then, all kitted up, they frighten themselves and each other with sudden blasts of acetylene from the canisters strapped to their backs. They know that soon, they'll have to raise the roller door and venture into the disturbingly yellow landscape they can see bits of through soot-coated windows and rusty louvres. A deserted city, loaded with silence like saltpetre packed in a musket.

They rub at the glass with grimy fingers. 'Did we do that?' they ask.

☆

Crikey and Radio tread streets of paint-stripped buildings and defoliated plants, a virulent dust unsettled on every step—and Gilbert not the only one rotting. They stop by the local corner shop with the esky to get the last of its water and to sniff hopefully in the freezer; but it reeks, so they load up with dry packets and tins.

Outside, a savage pink dusk blooms toxic as algae above the terraces. The women duck beneath an archway of wrought-iron and up broken cement steps. Crikey wipes a muscular tannin arm across the brass plate beside the door. She fogs it with her breath, and wipes again.

Suicide Couriers Pty Ltd, it says.

Above the purloined food and jumbled clothing and the stacks of Dunlop Volleys still in their boxes, a striated square of sunset glimmers on the basement wall.

Radio lies on a camp bed, sardined in Crikey's sleeping embrace. Her breath comes high and tight as memory weights her mind, forcing it to open like an oyster.

A burning sky gouts sulphur; black mantises crawl from a widening maw, squirting a thick yellow dust. Riding vanguard is the angel Azrael, wings of hospital white folded over combat fatigues. He beckons with bright scissors, ready to cut Radio's soul from her body. But as she tilts his way, hands grip and drag her back. The magnetic dark snaps shut, the sky returns to a scarred plaster ceiling. Radio's hospital pyjamas have twisted round her limbs like candy cane, and leaning over her is a woman dressed in explosives.

The soldiers are demoralised, their rations divvied into ever-smaller portions, their water meted out in sips—but none of them will venture beyond the roller doors.

'Right,' says Joey. 'The first three in protective gear and out foraging for provisions gets their numbers read when they come back.'

There's a rush for the pile. Three emerge triumphant, welders helmets on; the rest slope off to hunker dejectedly below the limp arms of machinery.

Winching the door closed, Joey is overcome by a wash of exhaustion and has to sit down, a tic fluttering under one eye. Without painkillers the numbers are almost too bright to bear. And while he's relieved to be so indispensable, he doesn't want to think too hard about it, because each number hurtles from the dark on a mailbox, and each mailbox looks uncomfortably familiar.

Once, he thought everyone saw numbers the same as him: ribboning from passing cars, flaring on clock faces like magnesium strip. But then came school and the math board, the number books. Answering every question at first with a colour, he suffered a terrible burst of confusion and was taunted as stupid. Joey quickly learnt to look past colour to the answers they wanted, and to keep quiet about what else he saw. He also learnt there were good luck numbers, like four, beryl-green and sparkly as a prism turned in the light; and bad luck ones, like twelve, its lines raised in welts, purply as a bruise. Twelve was for the bullies packed tight and dangerous, blocking his way home, and for the hours each fortnight that his dad stayed over and blackened both his mother's eyes.

On the days his dad came around, Joey would sneak out the back and stare at the fence, nowhere else to go. Then he'd get a stick and start scratching in the dirt of the bare yard. *One*, he'd count out loud, the blue revealed, perfect as a jay's wing. *Two*, dragged from his stick Halloween orange. When he got to the bad luck numbers he'd grit his teeth and etch them slowly, deep, watching as they blistered up colour from the clodded earth, while his parents shouted and smashed their way through the house.

Joey thinks the reason they crash-landed is because they'd been a group of twelve: a bad luck dozen strapped to foldaway seats, lining the airplane's cavernous belly like eggs in a carton—just waiting to be broken. Fortunately, Antenna George fell down dead from a heart attack soon afterwards, and so now they made eleven.

There's a clattering inside the plane. Fixit Mick crawls out of one torn wing and goes to Joey, wiping grease-smudged hands.

'The turbines are fritzed,' he says.

Radio is worrying, and can't help reaching for the dial. She rests her hand on its scalloped edge, itching to give it a good turn. The last of the corner shop's water containers lie empty in a corner, and now they have to take a trip to the mall.

Crikey laces up a new pair of Volleys, her deft brown hands seamed with yellow. 'Off to kill a sinner, don't save me any dinner!' she calls back to nobody on their way out.

Out behind the supermarket three people in welders suits are manoeuvring recalcitrant trolleys onto a footpath sick and tussocky with weeds.

The women hide. They've seen lights flickering a few blocks from the bar, but no one else alive on the streets. They sneak inside through numbered checkouts and along well-stocked aisles to the rows of fridges, doors open, drink spilled out. Grabbing a container of water in each hand they make for the exit, where a soldier—back for chocolate—catches sight of Crikey running low, bottles sloshing.

Up goes a welder's glove: time suspended on five clad fingers. Slow motion the glove comes down and points.

Radio rushes into the sporting goods aisle—to more trouble. She finds a very small dead person rotting in a pram, and leans right over it as if it doesn't smell to high heaven. A sharp finger pushes through the protective wrapping on her memory. Once, she wanted one of these more than anything else in the world, but no longer had the parts. Churning in the waves of flashback, she remembers Crikey and a roomful of others without their parts being signed up for the Suicide Courier Company.

The soldiers arrive, lumbering and inexorable, while behind their helmets they are just GIs, frantic and sweating, cut off from command. They take their first steps into the aisle then stop, uncertain. Inside their suits, questions are beginning to form.

Crikey, unable to prise Radio's titan grip from the pram, grabs a cricket bat off a shelf and swivels left-right-left, errant wires poking from her vest like paspalum. Wielding the bat with the power of ten she storms the closest, and down he goes. She turns menacingly toward the others trying to light faulty gas jets, and they retreat around their end of the aisle, leaving her astride a crumpled body. The headgear has come off, revealing the grime-streaked face of a boy.

The women zigzag for home along empty streets and alleyways, sidestepping those who'd straggled in mass exodus. They get to a cul-de-sac, and a high wall bristling with surveillance cameras.

Radio frowns. Her fingers trace the mortar lines between the stone. Crikey peers past the wall and up the driveway at a nest of low buildings surrounding a central block, its windows shuttered tight. At the Centre for the Unmotherly even the electronic eyes have long ceased looking; the gates are down, and it smells of the dead like everywhere else.

Neither mean to move, but up the pebbled drive they go. They cross the threshold, its door ajar, to where the air is noxious with chloroform and decay, and the dead are crouched slack-jawed and bloodless on linoleum buffed to a malevolent shine.

Crikey sniffs, and the machinery of her mind ratchets her past into place. Unmotherly, they had asked to serve their country strapped together. The visiting recruitment officer had smirked and said 'It'll make no difference to the bang'.

Older, nastier memories reflect in Radio's eyes. Her fingers drag below her vest and begin to read the puckered edges of raised seams, the dark embroidery of numbers—until the antiseptic sluicing off the walls makes her gag and run.

Crikey finds her one floor down in the stockroom, winding the handle on a row of metal shelves. Runners slide apart and aisles of numbered eskies are revealed like picnic packs. Radio hunts for one to match the numbers on her belly. She hauls it from the shelf, rips off its lid and howls. Smashing the empty polystyrene down, she stamps on it. The howl crescendos to a raw-throated scream.

Crikey grabs and holds her suffocatingly tight. 'Shhh, now.' Behind the neat squares of Semtex she can feel her own scars burning.

Back in the basement, Radio sits obediently, arm out, while Crikey pours Dettol straight from the bottle. She watches as if it's nothing, although by the way one leg jiggles, it's not; her mind may have slipped across the pain barrier, but her synapses are still firing signals anywhere they can.

Crikey notices the shredded canvas of her lover's shoes, and goes to rummage the boxes. She glances back at the smiling woman who, deemed Unmotherly, had been signed in to the Centre to be pillaged for her parts by a society grown short on spares. Her eyes are the same colour as the pale wild irises that once grew in the creviced shade between its buildings.

Linkman Joey is slumped and wheezing, held up by a soldier each side as he heaves great asthmatic breaths. *Now they are nine, and nine is a bad luck number.*

While the rest shuffle around a lone supermarket trolley looking hungrily at the soggy TV dinners, Tankman Arlo is remembering his third being struck down by an explosives-wearing Amazon with a cricket bat, and his second falling over on the way back and not getting up. Having barely escaped intact himself, now it's time for the Linkman to give him what he'd promised.

But Joey's vision has been obscured by shadows. He sees nine black hens dead in a run—*his* hens, raised from chicks—and his father wiping the feathers and blood off his hands. Joey's five-year-old fingers wind painfully through the chicken wire, tears leak onto his school collar. He closes his eyes, and despair flutters like a moth under his eyelids.

After a while the men realise that he can no longer see their service numbers. They strip him of his flying suit and kick him out of the steelworks. He sits in his air force long johns on the hard ground, his back against the roller door. Sun infrareds his skin, but Joey's world has gone shades of grey, the sharp kaleidoscope colour drained from it like blood emptied from a bath. He gets up and limps into the stopped heart of the dust-choked city.

When the women return to Gilbert's Bar they find Joey curled up on the pool table, cradling billiard balls.

All he can discern are shadows, and two are moving threateningly across his failing vision. He scrambles backwards off the table and bumps painfully against the jukebox.

Radio fingers the dial, a buzzing in her ears: the beginnings of seizure. Jets of current flick along her limbs like minnows. In that small window of altered vision, she can see the moths at Joey's eyes and a bruise like a kick on his heart.

Azrael arrives through a crack in the wall, snicking his scissors.

'Show him your numbers,' he commands.

Joey cringes at the movement, expecting the Sword of Damocles to descend. Instead, the moths close their wings tight to reveal a shivering embroidery of skin, set alive by spasm. As the colour washes back into his world, he folds like tissue and starts to cry.

☆

The jumpers of the 14th *Bird of Peril* squadron have decided never to go outside again and, light-headed from hunger, are thinking about eating each other, starting with whomever has the fewest numbers.

Some, trying to recreate past fervors, pray out loud together while one among them speaks in tongues. A couple fall over, shaking, but their hearts are no longer in it. Downed in a foreign country and separated from their God, they have discovered that their humanity is a veneer only twelve days starvation deep.

When the fighter jets shriek a silver vee above the city, the soldiers—now seven—run out scruffy and whooping, thinking it must surely be their own, come to rescue. Jets veer toward the leaping men raising a thick, poisonous dust. The formation dips salute as several laurel wreaths thud to ground. Then wing nacelles open and strafe them as they wave.

From the doorway of Gilbert's Bar, Joey squints into a pristine sky and sees the migratory vee pass overhead, its nasty purply numbers risen like great welts on each undercarriage: *twelve—all of them twelve*. He hears the clunk of the fuselage cannon and the wing guns ratcheting through their rounds as, mid-hurrah, his men are dropped by their own.

'B6,' says Crikey, pouring bottled water into three martini glasses.

'Fernando.' Radio resists the urge to down hers in a single gulp.

Joey climbs back onto his barstool. Behind him in the dark, snooker balls glow like min-min lights on emerald baize, the bad luck numbers now safely hidden under the jukebox. He tucks in tight between the two flak-jacketed women and doesn't mind that he will never be going home.

Radio dips a finger in her glass and draws a number on the bar. 'What colour's this, Joey?'

It glistens on the polished wood, splecked and opalescent, precious as an egg.

'Blue,' he says. 'One is always blue.'

Kim Westwood won a 2002 Aurealis Award for her first speculative fiction story, 'The Oracle', published in *Redsine* 9. It was translated for *Znak Sagite*, a Serbian speculative fiction magazine, and recently reprinted in *Simulacrum* #15. Of the six other stories published, two have been chosen for Year's Best anthologies in Australia and the USA, and another, 'Terning tha Weel', was shortlisted for a 2005 Aurealis Award. She lives in Canberra, Australia with her partner, her dog and her novel; the last-mentioned she took on retreat in 2005, thanks to a Varuna Writer's Fellowship. An interview can be found in *Simulacrum* #15: www.specficworld.com and http://vanderworld.blogspot.com/ 2005/08/kim-westwood-another-australian-writer.html

See Here, See There

ANNA TAMBOUR

My eyes were milky as any newborn's when I came into the world, and the world was more of a smell and a feel than anything to look at. My mother took the time to wash me, gave me suck, and swaddled me till I was stiff as a cocoon. Then she propped me where she could glance at me without turning on her stool, and set to work.

By the end of my babyhood, I saw that I had two mothers, always doing the same thing. If one was bent over doing something in her lap, so was the other, a rat-span away. If one walked away and became a blur, the other didn't stay to protect me, but kept her company. When I was very close, the two became one, and then I could talk to her alone. They needed my closeness to come together, and when they did, my mother seemed happy. As happy as she could be.

I sat in the corner watching my mothers, for they sometimes let their eyes stray from their work. I wanted them to look at me, but when they did, they sighed. Neither could explain why they were two, and why everyone else was two but me, and why they all had two times two limbs and I almost always had four of each. If I looked down at my hands in my lap, I had four of them, all seeming as if made of fluff. I had four soft-looking feet. Brought up to my face, two feet disappeared, just as two hands, but I knew they were there, just out of reach. Thus, the world became understandable when it was close enough that my eyelashes practically touched it, but the farther away it went, the more everything became a broth of the kind that was often our dinner— a thin gruel with nothing distinguishable in it.

Where do they go? I asked my mother when she was close enough to be one. And of the world, *Where does it go,* I asked, *when it becomes soup?*

'I don't know your soup, Alwoun,' she always said. 'Here, there is only myself and you. You have two eyes, and so it is with me. And the world goes nowhere. It is here, until it ends.'

'But where does it end?'

'Somewhere beyond the town. If you go to the top of the

hill, you can look out and see it. The hill is in the middle of the world.'

We couldn't go up there. At the top of the hill is the castle. But *once*, she said, she saw a *picture* in church *of the world*. She took me to see it, but by the time she could do this, it was almost night. In the church's gloom, I couldn't see the picture, and neither could she. She promised to take me again, when the day was still light. I hoped this would come true, because that would mean there would be a time when it was daylight and she was not bent at work. While she worked, though, she taught me things, such as how to say something in a nice manner. I thought that I learned well, but whenever I thought that I had spoken most well, she looked up from her work, and sighed.

I was happiest (if I had something in my belly) in bed on spring nights, if the fleas weren't too fierce. She told me stories then, good stories, until I slept. One spring night, snuggled in her embrace, I woke. I needed to move. But she wouldn't move her arms. They were a cage around my middle. I shoved against her but she wouldn't release me. I was so angry, I pinched her. As if she felt nothing, her arms stayed tight around me. I cried myself to sleep, because I was afraid of the dark and getting out of our bed was something that I would never do, unless I wanted demons to eat me. I woke in the cold pre-dawn. Her cheek against me was stone, and the straw pallet was cold and wet, not from me. It was death, seeping.

That was my fifth spring.

The street was a cruel place. No one took me in or gave me work. I was too small to be good as a beast, and too clumsy to be useful as a little man. Instead, I was a plaything. Boys called me names. *See Here, See There* I was called by some. *Frog*, by others. I was kindly shown my reflection in a puddle of water before my head was shoved into it. That was when I finally saw what my mother must have sighed at. My eyes didn't look straight ahead. One looked toward one of my ears, and the other, towards my other. I didn't know what a frog was till a big bullfrog was dangled in front of me by a group of four boys. 'This is how you'll go,' one laughed. Each boy held a leg. Then each danced outward. I remember thinking that the frog's eyes were beautiful, and not at all like mine, except for their prominence. I remember thinking this, as its head fell into a puddle, attached to its body and flaps of skin. It flopped only a moment, before a dog darted in and scooped it into its jaws.

The world becoming soup wasn't something I discussed with anyone, nor the way I saw two of everything when everyone else clearly saw only one. I found it better not to discuss anything with anyone, or to try to make a friend. Instead, I tried to take on the personality of the town cats. Quick, lithe, and out of range of boots. However much I tried to be like this, living on what I could pick up from the muck of the street before the pigs and dogs and cats and rats got it, I was too slow, and too clumsy. Distance deserted me, cheated me, laughed at me. My knees and hands were a mass of bloody scabs from my tripping and falling. Not to mention being booted.

I wouldn't have lasted long, certainly not through winter, if I hadn't been so ugly and comical.

One day when I was trying to keep out of the way of the worst of the day's traffic of carts and men and boys, four palanquins carried by panting men pranced into the street.

'Halt!' came a yell. 'It's See Here, See There!'

The palanquins stopped and a boy a bit taller than me, but dressed to dazzle, jumped out into the mire, and ran up to me. Actually, two did until they got very close, but for the purpose of telling this to you, I'll say *one*.

'Are you not the famed See Here, See There?' he demanded.

I had just finished gnawing on the small bones of a roasted rat that someone had thrown down from a window above. My stomach was unsatisfied, and I was trying to hold the stuff that roiled in my bowels as long as I could. I needed my food to last inside long enough to give me strength and to, hopefully, help me grow.

I tore at a scab on my hand with my front teeth, and looked at the boy from the small shelter of my fingers that fanned across my eyes.

He laughed. 'Come,' he ordered, ignoring my having ignored his question. I was too experienced in the chase to ignore his demand.

The palanquins set off at a trot again, and I followed. Four boy-voices whooped at the men, chivvying them to act like racing stallions. I fell, and heard a yell. The back palanquin halted till I caught up, when I was picked up and shouldered by one of the men.

'Hiagh!' shouted the boy inside, and we all set off again, even faster. Fowls scattered at our approach, and other mortals threw themselves into doorways. We were the last of the four. From my vantage high above the crowd, I was glad that I wasn't on the shoulders of the first 'horse'. He used his huge shoulders to butt, and his swift legs to kick at anything that might trip him. An old woman, making her bent way. A young woman, whose elbow offended. Her basket held on her head went tumbling, and eggs splattered into the mud—mud which churned yellow and brown with the impact of each human hoofprint. At first, it was almost more than I could do, keeping aloft. His sweaty hair must have hurt him from my grip, and my legs surely choked his neck. To my surprise, he didn't bite me. Then fresh yells erupted from boy to boy inside the palanquins, and a fresh volley of curses and promises spewed from the boys, at the men. I tried not to be heavy as my horse increased its pace on the uphill run, passing the palanquin ahead of us to the accompaniment of wild yells from behind the gauze curtains of both. His neck against my calf felt like it was stuffed with a trapped bird.

We entered the first gate around the castle, and the race ended. I let go of the man's hair and stroked his head to say I was sorry. He bent his cheek to my thigh.

'Leave him here,' said his master's voice, so I climbed down as well as I could, but the man kept hold of the handles of the chair, and avoided my eyes. I stayed where I was as the 'horses' and their burdens disappeared through an elaborately carved arch.

It wouldn't do to go anywhere, and besides, where was there to go?

I thought these logical thoughts as my body shook illogically. So much had happened to me that I doubted that whatever this would be, it could be worse. I didn't believe in demons in the night any more, either. I knew demons, and they were boys and men whom I could see, the rats and pigs who competed with me for the town's garbage, and the fleas who cuddled with me always. Whatever demons these boys would be, they would not be worse, I was sure, than the tradesmen's boys with their haughty ways and rich imaginations. They were above me only enough to know what I suffered, and they lived by their wits and skills. They were motivated by the kicks of their own master guildsmen, so I almost felt sympathy for them. But these castle boys? What would they know, besides rich food and too much warmth in winter and sleep all year round? I scorned them—and yet, I shook.

A goose wandered up to me, to see whether I was worth knowing, but before it had a chance to know, a man in a no-nonsense jerkin spat at it and barked at me to follow him. We went through a lot of doors until we came to a small yard with a medlar tree collared by a bench, and on the bench, a jug and a loaf.

'Sit,' he said.

He took up the loaf and tore off a piece.

'Eat.'

I didn't need further instruction. I ate that whole loaf, then drank the jug of milk. I wanted to curl up and die happy right there, but instead, I trembled.

'Stand,' he said.

I stood.

He handed me a strange object. It was a stick that stood as high as my shoulder, bent by a string caught in both ends. It was a bow, and the arrow that he put to it for me had, as an end, not a point but a heavy felt ball. All afternoon he had me pull and release the tension on that bow. He didn't have me shoot it for hours, and then, when he did, he just said, 'Pull as hard as you can, and let go *like this*.' In the distance was a wall.

I did, and after the first few attempts, the arrow thudded against the wall. The murkiness of the colours there meant to me that it mightn't have been bare stone, but what was on that wall, I couldn't see. I knew enough not to ask anything. Whatever this was for, I'd been given a meal, the best I could remember, and if I pleased this man, maybe I'd get another.

When night fell, we stopped. He led me to a byre where some sheep were kept, and I fell asleep only halfway fearful.

The next morning I was taken out, given a half loaf and a pitcher of water, and told to wait by where the goose met me the day before.

The boys were not long. They trotted in on real ponies this time, and cavorted around me. I tried not to shake, and they didn't try to kick me or throw anything at me, to my surprise.

They laughed like the sound of morning, when the chamber pots are upended—and then they clattered away.

I tried to stay alert, but as the sun warmed me, I fell asleep. A hard boot nudged my ribs.

'Up.'

I scrabbled to my feet. Here was my teacher from yesterday. This time he wore a green-and-tan jerkin, and a felt cap to match. His shoes, one green, one tan, were long and pointed, not the rough snub-nose cobble of yesterday.

He walked away, jerking his hand for me to come along.

The castle was larger than I ever knew. I could never see it from the bottom of the hill, as it was soup from that distance, but up close, it was as big as the town itself, and just as much of a warren. Eventually, we entered a small room, where he left me. Almost immediately, I heard music. A flock of birds in the eye of a group of boys with stones couldn't have made more noise. It was frightening and beautiful at the same time.

Then the man returned, and as he opened the door, the music became even more excited. He led me out into a courtyard. To my left, the sun glinted off the gold of the large things held by pot-bellied men. They made the music blowing into fantastical animal innards of gold. I am sure that the squawking of them as I heard them now, all together, could not be outdone by the greatest geese in the Kingdom.

To my right, what must have been the King and his court sat in tiered stands high above the grounds. I didn't know what to do, so I turned that way and bowed low. There was a tremendous answering cackle from the animal-intestine players, and a clapping and possibly laughter from the stands. I couldn't see any faces, of course, but the colours had to be them. Red and gold I could see in abundance.

Straight ahead of me were four boys, each of whom rivalled the others in the beauty of his dress. The smallest was the one who had commanded me and the 'horse' who bore me and the boy's chair yesterday. The oldest was almost a man. Each held a bow in his hand and a quiver of arrows on his back.

In the distance, not as far as the wall, but close enough for me to recognise, I saw two things on stands. Each exactly alike, they looked like paintings of circles in circles in circles. 'That's a target,' my teacher whispered to me. 'The idea is to hit the centre circle.'

The music stopped.

'Can he shoot?' a voice from the stands called out.

'Yes, my lord,' my teacher said.

'Then let us to it,' the voice called out. My teacher handed me the bow I'd used, and a quiver of arrows with points, and turned on his heel. I saw his look of disgust.

The musicians took to their instruments again, with a short cackle.

The boys themselves supplied the next laughs, as they nudged each other, and then the tallest one bowed to me.

'You are our guest, kind sir, so pray do your finest.'

I took an arrow from the quiver, dropped the quiver to the ground, lifted my bow, and looked at both the targets.

In the middle of laughter, I loosed the arrow in the middle of the two targets. I never heard it hit, as the laughter covered the sound. But there was silence for a moment, and then, a cacophony of sound, from instruments, from the stand, and from the boys, perhaps, yells.

'Silence!'

The imperious voice out-screeched the instruments, the crowd, the boys.

'Are you not See Here, See There?'

'If you please, sire.'

'Do you not see two of everything? Or have I been told a tale?'

'Yes, sire, I do.'

'Did you close your eyes, then, boy?'

'No, sire.' I answered as well as I could remember. I was still too surprised to know if what I was saying was true.

'Then,' the King demanded, 'at which target did you aim?'

He frightened me so, I could not think. So I spoke without thought.

'I aimed for the middle of that which I could not see.'

There was a flurry in the stands. Doves taking off a roof sound the same.

'Impertinence!' a female voice fluted into the gasps. 'Devilry,' a deeper voice boomed. There was a scraping sound of fabric against carved wood, a clinking sound of gold chains shifting against embroidery.

My knees felt like pieces of sopped bread.

Then the King's voice called. 'See Here, See There?'

'Your Majesty?' I answered, but my voice cowered close to my mouth.

'A goodly name,' he said. And then he rose.

I knew it was him because as someone in the middle front got up, the gaily coloured mass of people around him rose also, with many a muted clang and rustle.

And he left, his Court following—a long tail to his royal body.

On the grounds around me, there was great confusion, as if a burning torch were waggled around a floor peopled with blackbeetles. The musicians scattered, their shiny instruments sighing as they gulped wind. Lackies of various sorts slunk away, till there I saw only the four richly dressed boys. They walked towards me, and from their hunched backs, I could feel trouble coming. If only I knew the way out of the castle, down into the obscurity of the holes I knew so well, below ...

I crouched to prepare for the worst, and was plucked up from behind. Whatever was before me, it was good to hear the outraged shouts behind grow faint as my rescuer, a huge man, carried me through archways, doors, up stairs, through halls, past guards and courtiers, ladies and maidens and men with long robes, servants hurrying, guards guarding, and finally, he put me down and pushed me into a room whose splendour I had thought dwelt only in heaven.

The room was thick with men in robes and guards, so many that when we entered, I knew not where to look, but suddenly, my guide shoved me to the ground.

'Look not at the King,' he muttered, 'but at your rightful place.' And he pushed my face to the floor with the flat of his foot.

'All leave, except the boy,' the King commanded. Nothing happened for a moment, and then there was much noise.

The foot was removed from the back of my head, and I heard a great swishing of robes, a clatter of wooden soles and the urgent patter of soft leather slippers.

'Come, boy,' I heard the King say, and so I lifted my face and saw him, standing next to a great chair. 'Come,' he beckoned.

And he led me through the great room, opened a heavy door, and into a smaller room painted all around with trumpeting angels, in the middle of which loomed a great bed large enough for ten people to sleep upon it, and high enough to be a goatpen underneath. He lifted me, climbed up himself, and enclosed us behind curtains embroidered with swans, such as my mother had taken her needle to. Enclosed, we were in a room with walls, with only a chink of light that he left in the far corner, enough that we could see each other in the gloom, though I daren't look at him.

He grasped my jaw in one hand.

'There looks to be no trickery in these eyes,' he said, turning my face this way and that, 'though frogs see more like men than you.'

I saw him from first one eye, and then the other.

'You see what I do not,' he said.

I blinked. His grip was so firm I could not move my mouth, nor nod.

'My sons,' he said, throwing his gaze to the canopy and releasing my jaw so absent-mindedly that he wrenched my neck. 'Woe is me. Their comeliness is my curse.'

I looked at him, which meant that to him, I gazed politely to his sides. I hoped this was the right thing to do, but my hope was not great enough to stop the shaking of my hands, so I clasped them in my lap.

Then he looked at me, his gaze as steady as a hawk's is meant to be. I held my hands, and breath. 'You are wise, boy!' he declared. 'Alone, amongst my counsellors, you hold your tongue. Their age has loosened theirs and shaken their brains, but I judge your tongue would never loosen, your brain never weaken with age.'

My mother taught me to be silent unless there is reason to speak, and I knew no reason now.

A tear rolled down the King's cheek. 'Four queens I've had, and each spawned a devil in an angel's skin.'

A mystery play, his talk.

'See Here, See There,' he said. 'What would you do with my sons?'

I opened my mouth, and closed it, petrified.

'Make free,' he ordered.

'Sire,' I said, guessing mightily. 'These sons are young, but their play is the play of wolf cubs.' I thought it best to stop there.

'My very thought!' the King exploded.

He was not content with me stopping there at all, because as he said, his wolf-sons besieged him in sleep. He had increased his guards, engaged yet another taster, treated his sons with indulgence after indulgence to gain their love, to soften their crafty ferocity, to make them soft as eunuchs.

'My love has only fed their wickedness. I have only hastened their growth into the savage beasts they are. Now they play, as cubs do, with their taste for jokes that always show them to their advantage. Their *real* bravery and skills are weak as broth made from a girl's breath.'

The four princes, said the King, rode so poorly that they sported with men as mounts—those manhorses they made gallop.

'They need me to make them look like knights. All of my indulgences,' the King's head wagged. 'Today's tournament, they arranged for my amusement ... my *amusement!* My eternal shame!'

I felt sorry for this sad king, who had enough to eat but a belly sore with pain.

'They are my shame,' he said.

He reached out and unravelled my hands to take one in his.

I felt on fire, his touch so kind.

'See Here, See There,' he asked rather timorously. 'What can you see?'

This was no time for silence. 'I see great danger, your Majesty.'
'Go on,' he urged.

'Either your great heart could stop from shame, or it could stop from the teeth of these wolves.'

He gasped, and I grasped his hand as best I could, it being so much bigger than mine, but slippery with sweat.

'You could banish the wolves, your Majesty,' I said, and felt from his hand that this was wrong. 'But they could raise themselves and come back, to tear you apart when you are grey,' I added, though he was grey as a stone.

'Yes, yes,' he said.

'Or you can have them meet their hell from their manly stallions, on their next gallop into the woods.'

He grasped me to his chest, in a paroxysm of relief.

'See Here, See There.' he cried. 'My true son.'

He hid me in his chamber, and called his sons to him in the Great Room. They arrived, each surlier than the next. I peeped through a hole he showed me in the wall. He expressed his disgust at the sport today, saying that witchcraft was not what tournaments should be. Then he embraced them each, warning against trusting any of the commoners, as who could tell what spells a commoner could cast?

'Far better to sport as you do,' he smiled. 'Though I shall be cross if your mounts shall soon lose their human voices altogether.'

The boys laughed, 'If they still hear, father,' the oldest one said, 'It matters not.'

Their father chuckled, and at that, the interview was over.

Arrangements were made with the palanquin carriers next, for the deed to be done on the next day's gallop—all in great secrecy, and with a mixture of gratitude and fear on the faces of the men.

During this time, I was kept secure to all but a few of the King's most trusted.

That night I slept with the King's foul breath warming my neck, and his fleas meeting mine, but I was warm and dry and fed.

And the next day, a great wailing broke out at eventide.

The King's four sons were dead, taken by the faeries of the forest, though their guards held on so tight that each boy's head had popped off into his guard's strong hands. To the men's horror, as the faeries stole away laughing, a new head grew on each boy's neck, each like the boy but unlike—so that it was good that the heads that the guards brought back were shewn to the king, who rent his hair but ordered the heads to be burnt, as who knows what spells had been cast upon them by the faeries. And as for these creatures that the faeries had carried off—like but unlike—they were not his sons, but abominations.

The faithful man-stallions he elevated to his most private

guard, making Fodneth, the one who had carried me, my personal protector. To my horror, the King asked me if he should cut out their tongues. As he rejoiced and was saddened at the death of his sons—*who*, I bade him consider—who would *solely* rejoice?

'No men love you as well as these,' I said. And having seen the men prancing and neighing once, he knew this to be true. Death had been their deliverance.

All this time I had been concealed in his chamber, in his bed.

The next day he bade me wait in the chamber, watching, till he took his great staff and knocked it on the floor three times beside his throne.

I entered then, and he pronounced me his seer. I heard the sucked in breath of a toothless man. And then as I stood, not knowing what to do, the King bade me sit on his stool at his feet. And then demanded a lesser throne be made, and there was silence, and he announced that See Here, See There would henceforth be his heir. And then there was complete silence, until the King dismissed his court, when they fled like a flock of starlings.

That evening the King drank till he was drunk, and I drank at his behest, cup to cup. Being ill-used to more than foul water, I first fell asleep, then upon his tickling me awake, I kept him company, cup for cup, until I fell into a deep stupor.

I woke with my hands on fire, my body swaddled tight as a babe. When I screamed, the King turned over in his sleep, and kissed my brow.

My hands had been cut off at the King's command. He pointed to them, now a reliquary beside the bed, holding in their cupped palm-bones his seal of gold. With my great skill, he explained, it was better for both of us that my hands could no longer hold a bow, as they would attract the faeries to bewitch them against me, should they be left to live upon my precious beloved arms.

And he nursed me to plumpness, and had me guarded at every moment that he was not himself by my side.

He fed me himself, from his own fingers.

My wrists healed to shiny stumps, and whenever I itched, which was many times during the day and night (the King being less fastidious than my mother) I felt my hands reach out, though my itch never felt the satisfaction of their fingers.

There was great jollity in the court, and the people in the town below and lands around were happy. They had dreaded the King's natural heirs, the king to come. But how could they dread me? See Here, See There—or Frog to most—had become the Frog Prince to them. The milk that made my bones was theirs. My shit might smell of peacock's tongues now, but I was still their spawn, and had eaten from the gutter. No poor man feared me, no woman didn't love me, in only the purest way. My only fear, the knights of the realm—strong in arm but weak in head—I made content.

I could never claim their glory, though their wars and exploits would be greater and ever more glorious guided by the light of my all-seeing wisdom.

And so my life was as close to heaven as I'd ever reach upon this earth, when one afternoon as the King was at the hunt and I was sitting in the most inner garden, the old man who had been his greatest counsel approached me with great respect. Asking to sit beside me on the bench under the medlar tree, he proceeded to praise me in terms so convoluted, so dusty, and with his nasal voice so like a droning wasp, that my ever-guarding Fodneth turned to relieve himself behind a rose.

At that, the aged counsellor gripped me with the strength of an eagle, and with his silver spoon, dug into my right eye, tearing it from its home. My scream brought my guard to my back, just as the spoon had begun to rip into my remaining eye.

Doubled over in pain, I felt my attacker thrash briefly, then fall against me, and with the muted sound of much cloth over a brittle-boned body, to the ground.

The King himself nursed me in his bed. Day after day I lay there, my head bandaged and my eyes unseeing, though I felt no great pain after what must have been the third or fourth day. The King fed me broth and chicken and goose and bear, and syllabub and peacock when I was well enough.

Finally the King himself removed my bandages and looked into my remaining eye with love, and fear.

'What do you see?' he asked.

'My father who loves me,' I answered.

'My son,' he cried, his hot tears making their way into my orbless eye.

He grasped me through the night as if I were a log, and he a drowning man.

In the morning, he gently opened my eyeless eye, and into its depth, inserted a new eye, cold against my bones, but quickly warmed. An eye of gold, inscribed in a circle so that the words looked at you: 'See Here, See There.'

And so I counselled, and he ruled for many a day. I sat at his right during the day, and was with him for all the hours under the sun—except when he went hunting—and slept in his bed at night. I was his sleeping draught, he said.

My counsel was ever wise. 'See Here, See There,' I made it my job to be. I knew the thoughts of the king before he knew them, as he muttered in his sleep. I knew the rumours in the castle through the guards who loved me as their own, especially the four, and most especially Fodneth, my protector. One day Fodneth told me of a rumour.

'A boychild,' Fodneth said, 'who looks like you ... or rather, as you did.' And he looked at me with a question unasked.

His tidings did not make me glad. My back sweated ice. For

he sought my left eye to look at me. And I knew at once—Fodneth had seen what the king had not.

The truth was: with my golden eye staring straight ahead unwavering, I still looked as something other than anyone else—as strange as before my living eye had been torn out. Yet I now saw the same number of everything as everyone else, and I knew now that the haziness of my sight at any distance was not any worse and really much better than that of, say, the old man who had tried to blind me, and who had worn great pieces of glass against his eyes. And now my left eye no longer swung ever to the side, but over time it had been pulled towards its golden brother, and now looked straight ahead—when I wanted it to. Of course, I didn't want it to. I could not let anyone know my secret. I thought I had kept it well.

Fodneth had seen me in my private times, in the seclusion of the garden on those days when the King was at his hunt.

'This boy?' I asked Fodneth.

'They say he is another See Here, See There.'

'There is only one,' I replied.

'The faeries have enchanted him, some say,' Fodneth added.

I nodded, rubbing my stump against the down on my cheek.

'They are powerful in these parts.'

'Can he talk yet?'

'He is too young.'

'That is good, Fodneth. Faeries or no, we can abide no pretenders.'

And so the boychild—only a crawling babe—was smuggled to the castle, where, alone in the garden with Fodneth, I used my own scarred stumps to rub nettles over its body as it slept the sleep of a most powerful brew made by Fodneth's mother in the town. And Fodneth tucked rose branches between its legs, and swaddled it. And he placed the frog-eyed babe in a hamper and drugged it anew, so that it lay quiet where Fodneth placed it—under the skirts of the King's throne. And during the King's morning court, the child awoke and made a sound unheard by the King before, except in his nightmares. And the King jumped up, and the sound blared out so strong, that his neckhairs stood out in a ruff. The King kicked his stool away, knelt down in his finery, lifted the skirt of his throne, and saw the hamper. And as it would be death for him if his court saw him afraid, the King held out his staff, and with its spiky head, he caught the hamper. And he gazed at the shrieking thing, its eyes as tight as a miser's purse. And the King touched it with his staff, and it opened one eye, one great blue orb that stared straight by the King as if he weren't there, just as See Here, See There always did. But this thing did with such malignance that the King stifled a cry, and coughed.

And the King's thoughts then are as clear to me as if he had declared them: *It stole into my presence with the ease of smoke.*

It breathes my essence. And the babe closed its eye again, and screamed even louder than before. *The curse for my sons. Is this one of them?* the King thought, even louder. At long last, the babe's scream ended (as the king watched) with the gurgle and choke of a son being murdered. And yellow foam came out of its mouth. And the King, never having been in the presence of a babe, clutched his heart. And his heart knocked hard against his chest like the staff of Death, who is not to be kept waiting. And he toppled over, and his crown clattered to the floor. And his throat met the gold and diamond tower atop his crown and pierced him so truly that the diamonds glowed like rubies.

The babe was burnt, as bewitched or bewitcher. Bewitched? Bewitcher? Even the all-seeing I knew not which, but this treatment purified both.

I was crowned King, and Fodneth is ever by me. I have ruled for seven years of rejoicing in the Kingdom.

Each day upon awaking, I gazed upon my hands and felt them growing stronger, stronger than they ever were upon my wrists. Four years ago I took a queen, who now tenderly feeds me. My knights are true, my table jovial, and my queen both beautiful and constant.

Yet last night I dreamt of three wolves leaping for my throat. One had the face of my queen. The second, of myself when I was whole.

This queen I have taken produced a son three years ago. The midwife carried it to me at first wail, and I saw it at its christening, and the Queen and I rejoiced, for it was beautiful as gold. Yesterday during morning court the Queen entered the Great Room, leading the child by the hand. 'A portent!' she announced, crying tears of joy. 'My lord!' she cried, kissing it and me as she placed the boy on my knee.

He looked past me, and I looked past him, but we both saw each other well.

A pretender.

I ask you—my hands, my blue orb and my golden eye—what is your counsel?

I dare not consult Fodneth, for he was the third wolf.

As a child, Anna Tambour won an archery contest by aiming at a point between two targets. Her sight has since been corrected. She lives in the middle of the world, in a valley where there is no king but many queens, some with nine eyes. They are not interested in reading her stories and books, but you might have different taste. Books: *Monterra's Deliciosa & Other Tales* and (a collection, Prime 2003) and *Spotted Lily*, a novel (Prime 2005). There's more to read on her website, Anna Tambour and Others: www.annatambour.net

Truckdreamin

ANDREW MACRAE

I Backroads

Black rain fell on the glitterin tar, steamin where it lay an dissipatin heat haze shimmer from the burnin sun. I hunkered down inside me trucksuit. I were lookin for somewhere to shelter from the storm, me old bones achin from all the roadin I done, when I seen the flyer wreck roadside. Old Crow come on up behind me like always, made me feel sick to see him. Its bad when your omen of illness an despair follers you aroun, but I seen him all the time an he seen me with that look in his white eye said, 'I *know* you, boy.'

'I know you, too, an I aint been a boy for a long time.' I werent gunna let him rattle me. 'Time we stop meetin like this.'

'Thats as may be, but we still gotta figger out who takes what from this wreck.'

'I doan want nothin from this wreck.' I eyed the rottin corpses within. They laid in a shattered an burned-out shell. The flyer were light, a city model, not built for the storms we got in the backroads.

'Oh I think youll take what you can get, all right, just like me. We is one an the same, Jon Ra.' He coughed a dry rasp.

'Theres where your wrong. I aint the same as you nor never will be.' I fingered me blade, cheap steel what wouldnt hold an edge no matter how much sharpenin I given it.

'Lissen, I aint after their stash. Just the meats from their bodies.' He hopped closer an *ark arrrrrrked.*

'Best you be movin on now.' Mention of stash got me innerested. Stash could be sold for cash what I needed if I were ever gunna get off the road.

I stood up straight an showed him the blade.

'Ha ha, I knowed you was just like me. Well be seein each other again.'

'You doan scare me,' I said. It werent quite true, but he flown off anyways.

Left me with the wreck an them two rotted bodies. Ive killed before but I dont have much stomach for lootin corpses. I reached in past grinnin deaths heads an grasped that old tote bag full of crank. It made me heart sing, a sad an lonely song. I werent no crow, but I were old an needed peace from the road.

Time I first seen Old Crow, Id just turn fourteen an come off me first truckride. Didnt have a link maker an fancy wave gear back then, that were in the days before I knowed much about truckin, tho I thought I did. There werent no riders cab that first ride, nor truckdream to smooth me way, just a frantic dash an grab an forty hours in the grip of me speed spike, facin road blur an cold air outside of a Remmingford. I were unsteady on me feet once I come off, still gettin use to ground again, when I wandered into a roadside shanty town.

Old Crow were there outside a grog shop, slurpin whisky from a plastic cup. He wore a coat made from shredded trucktyre an his hair was black an shiny.

'Come over here, boy,' he said. 'Ill buy you a whisky.' I were too young to know better so I went over there an he put a whisky in front of me which I downed for I were thirsty.

'Thats the way.' He gave me another what I downed also. 'Say, you seen that girl over there?' He pointed to a girl across the dirt street, she were lookin at me. She were drinkin too. 'Yair,' I said. 'I seen her.'

'Well, she would be a nice warm body to share the night with, doan you think?'

'Yes she would, Id like that very much. I just been on me first truckride.'

'Thats a fine thing. Its somethin to mark the passin of.'

'Yes you is right, Ill go an say hello.'

I went over to the girl an we talked, an pretty soon I were horny an she were horny too so we found a place to lie down on a mattress in one of the shanties. I kissed her face an she yielded. So then I took off her clothes an stripped me coverall an it were clumsy an messy an somethin dark winged up from deep down where the dreams come, only it werent a dream. It were somethin what come up thru me but werent parta me, an there were blood on the mattress, blood soakin thru to the dirt floor of the shack.

I ran outta there with me tote bag an me spike, an I seen Old Crow, he were legless on the ground. He looked in me eyes an I knowed we was tied together on the roadin.

Two trucks sat linkin a wave in the lot of the desert truckstop where I come to offload the crank from the flyer wreck. Id rode a lot of trucks since that first time I seen Old Crow an all I wanted were to be done with him an the backroads. That looted crank were a ticket out.

The two trucks was new models, but custom indie, not like company machines, they had style. They was freestylin faster than thought, fatter than t-bones, ampin patches between em an buildin a wavey vibe. I shook a link outta the air an tuned in. Id seen trucks doin more an more of that stuff lately. The patches we traded with em was a new thing. Got em stoned or somethin, an then they built waves they could share. I shivered inside me suit. The wave they made were pitch an yaw, buildin an keenin like whalesong, with the beat rockin throb of a diesel blowin sooty smoke, tho I never seen a diesel cept in truckdream.

I took note of em, they was that good. One were black an purple, detailed with trickery what changed as how you looked on it, an I saw its name rendered in glyph, it said *Stormwater*. Other were red an white an done in retro, with detailin by human hands. Expensive mods, you wonder how it coulda afforded it, it had chrome smokestacks an blacked out sensor screens. It were called *Sinnerman* in scrollwork. They was doughty trucks, an if ever I met em on the road, Id be sure to hail a ride. I walked on in to the truckstop.

Thru the window I seen the dining room were river stone set in cement, scratched tabletops an bent legged chairs. Three riders also, two of em with shaved heads clean from the shower an eatin breakfast. Third had a blank face expression what you get when usin the link. I knowed him. His name were Damon, he were a good rider tho he were white as. Everyone looked over as I walked in but I just stared em in the eye, shiftin from one to the next.

'How youse goin?' I said.

The two of em what were eatin just went back to it, but Damon flashed into the here.

'Yair, all right,' he said.

I went over an sat down. 'Lissen mate, I got some crank to offload. You buyin?'

He looked at me, eyes narrowin. 'Maybe.'

'I got moren a kilo to get rid of.'

'Whered you come across it?'

'Them as asks questions usually doan like the answers.'

'Well thats not the best circumstances in which to offload crank, mate.'

'Ill give you a taste.' I took some crank an cut it on the table for him. It were the colour of dried blood.

'Thats vile lookin gear.' He took out his spike an helped himself, mixin up one handed.

'Mate, its good crank.'

His jaws clenched as he shot up an he knowed it were good gear. I knowed it too, an I werent gunna let him talk me down too far but also I hadda get rid of it to keep ahead of Old Crow an buy me some peace from the backroads.

'Ill give you five fifty for it,' he said.

'Seven hunnerd.'

'Six.'

'All right, Ill take your six.'

I handed over the crank, just as a blast ripped thru the truckstop, tore a hole right in the wall. For a second I seen bright sunshine outside an missile tracks in the air, then it were just dust an smoke. The other two riders got cut down by riverstone an tabletop shrapnel. Damon laid back in his seat. His head hung wrong, like his neck were broke. I rummaged his body for the six hunnerd he owed, but before I found it another missile shrieked an boomed an I rolled for the door. Under it all I heard the sound of big rigs rumblin.

Outside five brumby trucks roaded under a dust cloud, an what they wanted with a shitcan truckstop, I didnt know. They was armoured an had launchers an hot fifties. I made out what I thought were their leader, the biggest, blackest, baddest mother of them all. It were a old eVolvo, ancient even, belchin black smoke thru the smokestack but I knowed it werent no diesel, it were just for show. It were flanked by two captains, one of em a green Harvester. Out in the lot, them two indie trucks swung aroun, loopin back to the road thru the smoke an fire. I moved outta there on me own two feet. I didnt wanna be anywhere near that place, but I couldnt get too far, I knowed it, an before I even made the road I heard gunfire rattlin.

More missiles trackin, one two three blasts an one of the indie trucks from the lot went screamin past me. I seen then that the big black brumby didnt want nothin with the truckstop, it wanted to steal a indie truck for its mob. It crashed into the blue one called Stormwater an drove it off the road. There was dust an chaos all aroun, but them brumbies soon had Stormwater in their midst.

I crawled on me belly into a drain beside the road. The ground shook with crumplin blasts from the truckstop an fire crackled in the air. I didnt have that looted crank no more, nor any chances of gettin outta the backroads anytime soon.

I laid in that drain an lissened to the brumbies movin aroun, they was probably scroungin parts an fuel from the blasted truckstop. Maybe they was lookin for me too or scoutin out for the other indie what escaped, coz I heard em thrummin up an down the roads. I laid there like a lizard till the sounds went away an the light faded.

Driftin an dreamin on me own sad thoughts of loss an square one, I remembered back down the road to the second time I seen Old Crow. It werent that long after I first seen him. Id just jumped a animal transport, it were better than clingin on outside, an a step up toward the riders cab, where all us youngsters dreamed of ridin but we didnt have nothin to trade with the trucks yet. I were settlin in among the sheeps for the night when I seen a spark light the crease of Old Crows face. He gurgled on a billy an lay back there in the dark in his coat made from shredded trucktyre an lined with rabbit skin. He had them white eyes an his hair were white too, only I knowed itd been black once.

'Wanna cone?' he said.

'No thanks, mate.' I were mindful I seen Old Crow right before that winged thing what rose up outta me when I killed the girl.

He cackled an took another toke, blowin out smoke. 'Ah thats better,' he said. 'Doan you know, boy, when someone offers you somethin, its polite to take it?'

'I doan wanna smoke right now,' I said. 'Im not feelin the best.' It were true, seein him again like that made me queasy, I were shakin.

'I got some medicine for yer.' He reached into his tote bag an pulled out a spike.

'I dunno mate, really, I doan feel so good.'

'You wanna try this brew, boy, believe me, its the cure for what ails you.'

'Oh, an you know what ails me?'

'I seen you with that girl. I know you is runnin. Im runnin meself. Folk like us gotta stick together.'

'I aint folk like you.'

He laughed at that. 'I see you is a fine young man with much roadin ahead. But you an me is partners now. You gotta learn to take whats offered an do what needs doin.'

'Ill do what needs doin. Im not scared.' An whether it were outta fear or somethin else, I took that spike as offered. It musta been loaded with truckdream coz it hit home an I slept black sleep with no winged things, it were warm ocean rush an smooth waves thru the night, sigh of wheels on tarmac an a truckin lightshow goin off in me brain. It were wonderful an terrible an if I werent already lost to meself on the path of roadin, I were from then on.

When I woke there werent no truckdream no more, there were fever. Bad memories of bloodslick hands an the smile I cut in the girl. I sweated an shivered an when I looked at me arm I seen poison blood had took hold. That spike musta shot moren truckdream. Me flesh burned, yeller ooze comin from the hole in me arm, an I laid in the muck an piss in the animal trailer. We was still movin but there werent no Old Crow. I knowed I hadda get outta there but we was rollin at speed. There werent hardly any room for a rider, the trailer were packed tight with sheeps. I sweated as the fever took hold an the pain lanced into me shoulder an down me side. I couldnt feel me fingers no more an the hand swelled up. I slept some times an waked some times. I were smeared with shit. The sheeps bleated an pushed in on me. There were no more smooth truckdream, only darkness an badness down from where the black winged thing come an took me for a instant that time, a little rip an then there were blood on me hands an behind me eyes.

The truck started to slow as it rode up a hill, an I took me chance. I got near the hatch, keepin the sheeps away with bellowin an kickin. I threw meyself out an the road bit deep with iron teeth what tore at me flesh an I rolled over an over. When I waked, the feverd gone, but me arm werent never the same after that.

II Midden Dump

Them brumbies searched the country aroun the torched truckstop. I didnt move from the drain where I hid while they tried to catch up with me, or maybe it were the bad things I done tryin to catch me. I were lyin in that ditch, thinkin on the times I seen Old Crow an the times ahead of me now, wonderin what the best way thru were. I couldnt go backwards, you cant crawl back into mothers belly, tho many try. I knowed me way were forward, like always. I crawled outta me hidey hole. It were night. The stars was shinin down on me an the moon looked like a big old spud in the sky. I seen glowin fires from the burnin truckstop back thru the trees where the cash an me whole ticket out was burned up ash. But I just put me back to it all an headed out on to the road.

Pretty soon I come to a crossroads where I seen a truck parked off by the side. It were the one from the truckstop, the retro style one, red an white, called Sinnerman. It were shimmerin in the moonlight, gleamin chrome an lyin like a snake with its scales all newly hatched. Me breath caught a little to see it there, it were a thing of beauty, an then me brain started tickin, what were it doin there, so glimmerinly? I didnt have to wait too long for a answer, coz it spun a connect an hit me with its wave. It hooked me right away, it suckered me with a tasty vibe, an then it sent words along the link.

'You are Jon Ra.' It were a statement, a fact. Me brain went tick tick tick. It knowed me, that werent no surprise, I were knowed in the backroads. But it were *waitin* for me.

'Yes its me,' I toggled back, alone in me head once its wave washed away.

'I need your help,' it said. Now that were somethin I aint never heard no truck say to me nor I aint never said it to no truck neither. It doan work like that in the backroads. It work by bribin an cheatin an lyin.

'Thats innerestin,' I said. 'Whaddaya need *my* help for?'

'I lost my friend Stormwater in the raid. I need help to get it back from the brumby mob.'

Well that were another thing I aint never heard before. Friend? Id seen trucks make waves together but I never seen em formin attachments with each other. There werent many contracts what could support two indies, let alone a mob. Maybe thats why some time they went rogue.

'I doan unnerstand. You is a powerful truck, Im just meat. I aint carryin nothin you can use. I got burned in the raid same as you.'

'I must take down the Brumby King. You have roaded long and you know the ways of truck wrangling. I need a rider for this trip.'

Sinnerman needed a rider, maybe, but I didnt need this trip. I were just tryin to keep ahead of Old Crow, but sometimes the roadin shows you the way to go. 'Its dangerous work,' I said, 'goin after big black brumbies like the one you call King.'

'There is a reward for anyone who can catch the Brumby King. I will give you the money in return for Stormwater's freedom, if you truck with me.'

That pricked me ears. Maybe this were the roll of the dice I were lookin for, the big score to buy me way free an leave Old Crow behind. But I also knowed that Sinnerman were playin me, it hit me with its wave an then filled me head fulla thoughts of trucks an Brumby Kings an reward.

'Thats all well an good, Sinnerman. But you still aint said why you need me to help you. It doan make no difference to me his Brumby Kings made off with yer mate.'

'Are you going to keep roading until you rust and fall into the ground? Because I have seen your future. You have been running so long you forget what you are.'

It chilled me to hear a truck sayin them things out loud like that. It were a truth I knowed in me bones, but I didnt like the sound of it. I hadda get back some footing.

After a while I said, 'Maybe you do have the right of it. But maybe you need me moren I need you. So lets enter this agreement like gennlemen. Ill road with you, an help catch the Brumby King for the reward youll share. But if theres treachery, Ill bail, Ill steal your truckmind into me substrate quicker than death, an thatll be the end of the road for you. I know a lot a tricks.'

'That is why I need your help.'

So we sealed the deal there in the moonlight an I climbed into the warm console glow of Sinnermans riders cab. It smelled like home in there, a mix of sweat an person stink an another kinda funk what I cant describe, but it were somethin what grew in from the road. Solvents an machine oil an mollycules set loose from the heat of the petaflop donk. I settled in on the soft riders seat an took the IV off the dripmount, like I always did once I sealed a deal. It werent like in the old days of ridin, now I had somethin to trade. I slid the spike into me arm as Sinnerman cranked the chem feed from its alkaloid synth an there was truckdreams what I dont remember no more, but they was good, there werent no blood nor no black wings an we went on our roadin together.

Truckdreamin were a warm familiar feelin, an I were mellow an sad, thinking on how Id more roadin behind than in front. Sittin in Sinnermans cab led me back down the trail to the third time I seen Old Crow.

It were a different place, in the mountains. Summer sun didnt make much way thru thick cloud an it were cold an rainin. I seen the thin wisp of smoke first, an then I left the road on a track. The smoke were comin from a humpy, it were a sheet of rusty roofin iron over a row of stones. Old Crow sat in front, only it werent the same man. Same trucktyre coat but it were a younger bloke, smaller, with pale watery eyes. When he seen me he called me over. He knowed who I were, all right, an I knowed him, too.

'You wanna share my fire?' he said.

'Well seein as how you shot me fulla poison last time we met, no, I doan think so. You can keep your smoke, an your fire too.' I eyed the rabbit cookin over that fire an seen the rows of rabbit skins dryin on racks.

'Now that is a shame coz I got this meat an I doan know what to do with it all. Might have to feed it to the ferrets.' He nodded his head at a cage inside the humpy.

I knowed I shoulda kept me mouth shut, taken his food an walked away but I couldnt help meself. 'Whaddaya do with them ferrets?'

'I use em to catch rabbits. Got em trained to come when I whistle. I send em down rabbit holes an they scare the rabbits up into me traps.' His eyes lowered then. 'Only sometimes theres babies down there an the ferrets doan come back when I whistle. I have to wait till next day an then try. Sometimes they is so full they cant get outta the rabbit hole.'

'Oh I see,' I said, rememberin how me old man gutted rabbits with a flick of his wrist, an wishin I hadnt been so curious about the ferrets.

Night were comin on in the mountains an Old Crow had more to tell. 'If a ferret gets a taste for babies, I hafta kill it, coz it wont come when I whistle no more. Just like if theres any baby rabbits left. I put em away.' His eye flashed. 'Its a kindness.'

I didnt say nothin, but I ate some rabbit an sat by the fire. When the dark come he went into his humpy, an I started wonderin on the black thing what winged up inside the night I killed that girl. Whats to do when your bad omen keeps follerin you aroun like that? The only thing is to make peace an share food an fire with it an shelter from the storm. But I couldnt sleep there, with Old Crow in the humpy an them ferrets hissin an bitin an scratchin. I crept back down the road an got on me way.

Truckdreamin an Old Crow dont mix too good, so I were awake in the dawn light when Sinnerman said we was comin up on the Midden Dump road. I popped the hatch an stuck me head out. Traffic goin both ways an sideways, it were truly a meetin of roads. People an machines come from all over for the chance of findin somethin useful in the trash what got carted there from the gigacities. It were a place them brumbies would definitely feel at home, theyd go there to trade an scavenge parts. On that road was all colours an creeds -- people an spent robos an drones too, they was flapplin aroun in the air like the crows lookin for machine meat, which is what you found at the dump if you got lucky. All the garbage were drawn there an I wondered what the folks expected to do with that trash but this were the end of the world, there was buyers an sellers for everythin.

The shacks an hovels started gettin thicker the closer we got, an soon the mountain of Midden Dump filled earth an sky. We was comin up on the centre of things, there werent no tall buildins nor nothin but still it were a city. The trucks dumped an turned aroun, an people an machines crawled over each other to be the first to get at each load of putrid stinkin poisonous shit what got pumped out the arse of civilisation. But even shit gotta turn to dirt sometime, an there is little tiny animals as what lives within it an makes their whole life outta shit. So it were with the Midden Dump.

Well, we had come as far as we could, Sinnerman were too big to go down the narrow alleys an it didnt have no drone to telly into. Anyways, I wanted to get out an walk aroun on me own two legs. I said, 'You wait here, Ill see what I can find out about the brumby mob.'

'Ten four. But I'm not stopping here. I'll meet you on the other side.' It held its hatch open an I limped out. I watched Sinnerman drive off an me heart sorta skipped to see it, it were the tidiest truck Id knowed. Made me proud to be roadin with it. I realised I felt somethin for Sinnerman, we needed each other an Id never knowed that feelin before. It were a strange feelin. But I were on me own then an wonderin how best to start lookin for this brumby gang. The dump were a big place, but also the brumbies would thrive there. I watched for anythin they might like in the way of spare parts or whatever. That were not so easy neither, coz the brumbies like other trucks would of tellied into robo bodies to do stuff what were too delicate for a big truck body to do.

I passed some dump people, they wore rags an their flesh were grey, hair fallin out. They was crouched down an scratchin in the side of that mountain of trash, diggin white clay from the ground. Men an women both was twistin the clay into little balls an puttin it into their mouths an into slings they had aroun their skinny bodies what was ravaged from hunger, they was feedin themselves with dirt. Crows flied aroun em, their time werent far off.

After a while I seen a white shed an inside were a white woman. She had clothes what actually fit, pants an a shirt like army folks wore only she werent army but she had that straight back cast about her. She wore glasses an her grey hair tied in a pony tail.

Shufflin past like I were a dump dweller, I found meself a spot where I could see an not be seen. There was bodies of dirt eaters on a slab inside the shed, they was skin stretched over bone. I eyed a robo drone in there with the doctor, a small heavy tread vehicle with a tray back piled with bodies. Looked like they was doin some negotiatin, currency changin hands, so I shook a link outta the air an tried to tune to their wave.

'...rotted faster than previously.'

'I've said all along they won't last more than a month,' the doctor said.

'Just keep the supply up.'

'Dead flesh is what the dump grows. There'll be no shortage to harvest.'

'I'll be back at the end of the week.' The drone broke the connection an headed out into the street. I pinged a check thru the link an there were a truckmind tellied into that drone. I sniffed out the truck waitin outside the dump to the north an wagered it were a brumby tho what itd want with bodies of dead dirt eaters, I didnt know. That werent no kind of spare parts for a machine.

I sent Sinnerman a wave to keep its mind out for another truck an then I went on in to the shed. There was medical supplies everywhere, that woman were still doctorin all right. I walked right up to her.

'Hey,' I said. I thought of what I could say to rattle her, get her talkin about brumbies.

She looked at me like she seen me for what I were an it werent a nice feelin. 'Who are you?'

'I is a rider from the backroads.'

'You're a long way from home.'

'Im roadin after brumby trucks.'

'I'm a doctor, not a mech.'

'Well I seen you with that drone just now an I wanna know what a doctor is doin sellin bodies to brumbies.'

Her face darkened an I knowed I hit a spot, it were a brumby drone she were dealin with for sure. 'That's a bold line of questioning from one such as you.'

'It doan seem right, is all. You is a healer. Spose ta be, anyways.'

'There's not much I can do for the dirt eaters. Geophagia, it's called. They believe the white clay they consume has magical power, and I suppose in a way it does because their bodies do not rot when they die. It contains a preservative that wards off necrosis for a time, keeps the myelin sheathing of their nerves in tact. With the money I get I buy medicine to help the living.'

'Shoulden you be helpin the dirt eaters while they is still alive?' I pressed home me point, wheedlin for stray info.

'There's nothing I can do for them. They do get some nutritional benefit from the clay but not enough to sustain them. I think they are done with living, in any case.'

'But you is helpin brumby trucks what doan care who they kill to get what they want.'

'You're just they same as they are, rider, preying on anyone weaker than you.'

That gave me pause. 'Im just doin what I can to find peace from the road.'

She shot me a look over the top of her glasses. 'I think it unlikely that you will ever find peace.'

I left that silence hangin there an she kept lookin, lookin thru me like she knowed me secret, seen the blood behind me eyes an Old Crow at me hind. Me face flushed, I couldnt help it.

I were gunna say, 'Fair enuff,' but then I seen Old Crow outta the corner of me eye. He hopped up on the slab where the bodies was, an I turned an ran from that white shed what were full of death, not healin.

III Mountainside

I couldnt wait to put that place behind me, but the stench of dead dirt eater clung to me clothes. I lost the warm part of me a long time ago an just then I felt its loss yawnin, an maybe thats what gave the black winged thing room to rise up that time, or maybe the creature had been in me all along an drove out the warmth. I didnt know, but I were glad when I seen Sinnerman again on the road out to the north. It sat there with its mighty beatin engine hummin with tech, it made me glad I were teamed with it. I crawled back inside the riders cab an laid out for Sinnerman what I had seen.

Sinnerman tracked that brumby truck from the dump an we roaded west, follerin it on the scanner, rollin thru forest an trees then out past the dyin farms an the old grain silos which now the food come from unnerneath the gigacities. The farms let go to twisty roads, an Sinnerman took the bends like a racer. It were gunnin faster an faster now to find Stormwater. We took the mountain way at each turn, an when we hit the snowline we hadda slow down some. It were hard goin, Sinnerman ground down gears an then put out studs on its tread, an the hummin of tyre on road changed its sound to a scratchy growl. The road got steeper an steeper, there was no trees no more, just snow an ice an rocks.

Sinnerman were determined, it were single-minded in its roadin. It burned up so much fuel, an all for Stormwater. I didnt quite unnerstand it, but it touched me.

'What is it about Stormwater that makes you road thru so much hardship to find?' I asked.

'I dont know the answer,' it said, 'but we were meched in the same shop and whenever the roading brought us together, we would wave links. When the brumbies attacked, we were building a shared vibe, mixing pieces of ourselves together. With Stormwater gone, it feels like a piece of me is missing.'

'Oh I see,' I said, tho to tell the truth I aint never known them feelins meself.

I thought on that as I watched the road play out in frontve us, it were still gettin steeper, there was no trees no more, just snow an ice an rocks. This were a place for a ambush, a steep road with deep valley on one side an blank mountain on the other. The road ran up the side of that mountain, an bad weather hung down low all aroun us. I didnt like the look of it, but there werent no turnin back. Then I seen a black shape in frontve us, it were the brumby from the dump. It held the mountain road ahead. There werent no way aroun it, we was gunna hafta face it down.

Outta the ice an winds an swirlin whirls of snow I seen two four six headlights shinin thru an a spatterin of redeye runnin lights what marked out three truck shapes in the murk. The brumby from the dump were joined by two others what musta come out from the lair to make a stand.

We roaded closer to where them three stood across the road. They could of held back twenny or a hunnerd from that mountain pass. I seen their black armoured bodies an I recognised the shape of the Brumby Kings two captains from the raid on the truckstop. I suddenly wondered why theyd be formin up without even testin us out first.

'You got any history with this brumby gang, Sinnerman?' Like it werent somethin I shoulda checked out earlier, but I never thought there might be more to the story than what Sinnerman tole me.

There werent no answer from Sinnerman, coz it were havin some trouble keepin its road in the snow, tyres slippin as it ground closer. Crazy bursts of static hissed over the link, I couldnt foller it but Sinnerman were talkin to the brumbies. Sinnerman were sellin me out, I felt it then.

'Whats goin on?' I said.

The chatter were still cracklin across the waves, but Sinnerman answered in voice. 'They offered me a trade. You for Stormwater.'

'I thort you was straight up,' I said.

'I had no choice.'

I didnt say nothin. The feelins I had for Sinnerman was swirlin like the snowstorm outside. I hated it for crossin me, an the way it done it. But I were gunna go down fightin, an somewhere in the back of me dim mind I hadda notion I might still be able to wrangle that Brumby King for meself.

'Fuck you, Sinnerman,' I said.

I reached for me tote bag an the release on the riders hatch, but Sinnerman hit the locks with a thunk. I still had the screens, tho, what showed me the outside. One of them brumbies, a green Harvester with a snowplow, rumbled forward. The others held the pass.

Inside the cab, Sinnerman tried to pin me down with a flailin grapple what sprung outta the floor at me feet. I had me hand in me tote bag, reachin for that slab of substrate what held all me code patches an viral messengers. I shuffled thru the link an slotted home a tag to crank the substrate. I hadda get close enuff to Sinnermans petaflop donk for the wave to transmit. The grapple latched onto me arm, an I squirmed to get free, holdin the substrate out in fronta me as I switched the wave over.

Everythin stopped dead. The locks released. The grapple fell to the floor. Sinnerman were shut outta its own truckbody behind a viral storm. Thru the substrate, I waved a innerface with the truckbody an felt the power surge as I pumped the juice thru me fuel-line veins. Me vision whited out an widened so as I could see all aroun. I stretched meself.

We pushed forward. Movin as one. I were rusty at this caper, it took a lotta me to do it. Somethin at the edge of me thoughts blurred an I felt recoil through the truckbody as Sinnermans weapon systems opened up. It were all I could do to focus on movin the wheels thru the innerface. But Sinnerman werent givin up on Stormwater, it were still fightin thru the viral storm to get to the weapons systems. The missles beeped lock an I felt a blast an seen smokin ruins where them two brumby captains use to be. I knowed then that Sinnerman were packin fierce weapons, an it were gunna blast through whatever stood in the way of Stormwater, no matter who was in the drivin seat.

Through the smoke an storm come the Brumby King, dressed in armour platin an bristlin with glistenin missiles an chain gun. It were at least twenny year old, I seen then, I didnt know how it kept up, it musta renewed its soft wares from scratch three times over, but that truck were the baddest, meanest lookin thing Id came across an I didnt know how I were gunna get close enuff to wrangle its truckmind. The air filled with missile tracks an smoke an a rain of sparks from the fifties. The ground shifted up unnerneath us as another blast ripped the guts outta a blue brumby, things werent goin so well for em even tho there were only one truck standin against em.

A blast from the Brumby King slew us sideways an we stalled against a jack-knifed brumby wedged in the mountain pass. Sinnerman kept pumpin them missiles into the brumbies. They werent expectin such harsh treatment so deep in their own turf, they was flaylin aroun an skiddin on the ice, but then I seen the Brumby King pushin the burnin green Harvester with the snowplow in frontve it. It turned head on an connected with us, there were a crunch an a wild hissin comin from the Kings donk as it rolled Sinnermans truckbody back down the hill.

Sinnermans engine caught. I pushed back, blarin squeal of rubber on road an roarin engine. Sinnerman were still workin weapons thru the viral storm, an it spat thousands a micro-drones which was repelled from our own wheels, but they shot forward an slipped up the King. The Brumby King skidded sideways with a creak an a groan, an Sinnerman punched it thru with a spike what sprung from a housin unnerneath the cab. There were a horrible screech as gears stripped metal flesh deep in the Kings heart, an it howled for traction to get off that spike but it couldnt.

Snow turn black where the Brumby King ran out its fluids

onto the ground. Whole thing only took about two minutes an then it were over. The two brumbies what was left was freed from the King but they didnt know what to do, theyd been slaved. There was bursts to an fro on the link, so much scatter I couldnt tell where it were comin from. Sinnerman were done for, it burned itself out tryin to beat the viral attack. The riders cab filled up with smoke. I couldnt see nothin, I groped for the hatch release what I pulled, an scampered outta there like a three-legged rabbit. Cold air an ice blew in me face, swirlin snowblind an wailin wind. The ground hit me.

Drones an little brumby skaters spun aroun, some was empty since their truckmind were dead, others still respondin to standin orders, they was there but there werent no one home. Sinnerman were wrecked, its axel broke. Maybe with heavy salvage somethin could be done, but I didnt think so. I crawled over to where the King lay dyin, an copied across its truckmind into me substrate. Itd make a tasty prize, but I knowed me roadin werent done yet.

I limped out an left that carnage of smoulderin trucks behind. Me trucksuit werent nowhere near warm enuff for the weather, I wouldnt last long unless I could find some shelter an warmth. So I struggled thru the snow, follerin the brumbies tracks back to their lair. Somethin in me bones tole me to go, I hadda find a way to get off the mountain. I figgered thered may be somethin in that lair what I could use, an I were curious about it. I were shiverin like I had the fever, I hadda stop meself from cryin out. It werent long before I found a cave in the side of the mountain, an looked down a long dark tunnel. I didnt wanna go in, but I knowed I had to. Stormwater mighta been still alive down there, an may be I could rig a fix to get back to the backroads. Anyway, it were warm welcome air what blowed up the tunnel.

I crept along the wall, slinkin silent like I learned to do. First I felt like a ferret, creepin in to scare up the baby rabbits. But the longer I went on down that black hole, the more I realised I werent no ferret. If anything, I were the rabbit. I thought on how me skin would look, hanged on a rack outside Old Crows humpy. Still, there werent nothin to do but keep goin on.

Dark wings snapped across in front of me face an I near shat meself. I ducked an looked to where they swooshed away, thinkin it were a crow, but what would a crow be doin in a cave? Were it a brumby drone? Soon I seen soft light leakin thru the darkness ahead. The tunnel opened up into a cavern, it were lit by glowin orbs in the walls what made the little tracklins of water sparkle like snailtrails.

All aroun lay the Brumby Kings spoils, truckbodies on blocks an donks up on hoists, warm air to keep everything movin nice like it should. Mech decks under lights took up the main space, an over against one wall were a pile of spent fuel cells. Some kinda bastard hybrid mech drone what the brumbies tellied for repairs

slumped behind the decks, fine grapplin feelers slinked all over the
controls. I seen Stormwater, blueblack in the low light. I checked
its stats thru the link, an at first it looked gutted empty. But when
I seen closer, I found a tiny truckmind in there. Something what
bore the stamp of Sinnerman as well as Stormwater, I logged it
against their tag files.

I ditched the Brumby King from me substrate. It were takin
up too much room, an things had gone beyond that now. I ported
the Sinnerstorm truckmind an it started growin straightaway,
extractin itself, takin what it could and bringin info back. I got a
shock. It were vibin out waves in all directions, lookin for trucks
to chat to.

Then I seen a shape behind the mech decks an I turned, it
were dump-dwellers. Ten of em, laid out on pallets on the ground.
There was wires an decks an substrates all connected to lines in
the dirt eaters heads. Them brumbies were usin the dirt eaters to
learn, an to renew their own soft wares. Somethin about the way
them bodies was preserved by the white clay what they ate at the
dump, it made em not rot so fast. The brumbies had the freshest
laid out, they was usin the humans brains as a map for growin
brumby truckminds what could be slaved an droned, but with the
knowin where a body were in space an able to work on little stuff
what took fine skills. They needed somethin to work the mech
decks, twistin tiny knobs with its fingers an hands.

I seen them grey, shrunken bodies, mens and womens both,
they was in half-life, hooked up an growin templates for brumby
drones. When they was alive, their lives was nothin but finding
dirt to eat an rollin it in their fingers. An then in death they
doan even get no rest, they is still made to give more. I hefted a
rock. I knew it hadda be done. Me stomach churned. It were not
somethin I relished. I smashed their skulls, one by one. I couldnt
of left em there like that.

Behind me I heard a noise.

'What you doin there, Old Crow?'

'I mighta ast you the same question.'

'An I might not answer your question, neither.' I hooked me
tote bag over me shoulder.

'Ha ha. Doan mind me, I is just some old bloke whos been
follerin you aroun. Or maybe its you whos been follerin me all this
time, waitin for the chance ta come up on me like this.'

'I aint follerin you. Yore like me fucken shadow, I cant shake
ya.'

'I already tole you, we is rollin on the same road. Whos to say
which side of the face casts the shadow?'

'I say. You bribed brumby trucks to bring me here.'

'That's as may be, but why doan you try this coat an see how
it fits?'

'Im not puttin that filthy thing on. I aint no crow.'

He took off the coat. Unnerneath, he were just a skinny old man in dirty rags. 'Take it,' he said.

I flicked me blade, it come outta me belt like it wanted to. It went snickerty snick, an I made a slice across Old Crows old man chicken neck. After the pain he caused me, it seemed almost a load off me mind. Blood bubbled an he grinned as he fell to his knees, one hand clenched up holdin out the coat. I sorta larfed, but choked it off an stepped back as he rocked to the ground. In his dyin eyes I seen that black winged thing risin up to claim its prize.

I couldnt stand to watch. I left Old Crow to his dyin, an set off back up to the top of the cave mouth. It were a long, cold walk back down the mountain. Maybe I could rig something from the wreckage of Sinnerman an Stormwater, an mech that new truckmind across. But when I reached the cave mouth, I knowed Id of froze before dawn, wearin just me trucksuit. I went back down in to the lair. I didnt have no choice. I were gunna hafta put on that trucktyre coat. Jes till I found me next ride.

Andrew Macrae started writing seriously in 2003. He attended the inaugural Clarion South workshop in 2004, and since then his stories have appeared in *Orb* and *Aurealis*. His interests include music, science fiction and 70s truckin' movies. He lives with his partner and several typewriters in a house in Melbourne run by a grumpy tortoiseshell cat. He blogs at http://andrewmacrae.livejournal.com.

THE SECRET LIVES OF
RICK AND PEGGY

JEFF VANDERMEER

Rick works as a commercial credit officer at a bank and has an obsession with H.P. Lovecraft. This might be why he refers to the bank's managers as 'The Old Ones' and believes that at night they creep into the vault and shed their human disguises, *shuggothing* and *writhing about*, bathing in the money that carries the secret Masonic Old Ones symbol on it. In his secret life, unknown even to his good friend Peggy, Rick is a 24-7 Lovecraft apologist. In a secret bungalow outside of the city, Rick keeps sophisticated tracking equipment so that he can monitor the media day and night. Whenever he comes across a negative reference to Lovecraft, he fires off a missive via snail mail or e-mail, using one of his many aliases. He considers this his holy duty. For example, when in the summer of 2004 the writer Jeff VanderMeer scoffed at the hideous effectiveness of the giant penguins in Lovecraft's *In the Mountains of Madness* for a *Locus Online* article, Rick immediately sent a letter to the editor under the name 'Gerald Rebarb' that stated in part, 'Clearly VanderMeer has never set foot in the Mountains of Madness.' It is a little-known fact that 90 percent of all letters and emails to the editor concerning Lovecraft originate with Rick.

Meanwhile, his friend Peggy ostensibly works as a stylist, making drab products look beautiful for advertisements. In truth, her main job is protecting Rick from the Old Ones that work at the bank. As the great-great-great granddaughter of Dexter Ward, and privy to all of the secrets of the Mad Arab, Peggy has considerable experience in this area. Using as her latest cover the search for a new house, Peggy spends a lot of time saving Rick's ass from various plots by the Old Ones. For it is Rick's fate to be an unknowing nexus, or portal, into the Old Ones' universe, which is the real reason he obsesses over Lovecraft. He cannot escape his fate yet has no inkling of it. He *certainly* doesn't understand Peggy's worries about his belly button. 'Keep it clean of lint,' she repeatedly tells him. 'Make sure your pants or shirt covers it at all times,' she says. 'Who knows what might come out of it?!' Rick's fairly sure nothing is coming out of it, but Peggy knows better.

One day, an entire universe might devour our own.

Sometimes Peggy is even behind the bank building, battling the green tentacular strength of the Old Ones, while oblivious Rick works in the front, attending to clients. Naturally, this takes a lot of energy and physical prowess on Peggy's part, so it's only understandable that she might from time to time get irritated. When Rick asks how her house search is going, Peggy says between gritted teeth, 'It's going fine.'

It'd be going much better, she thinks, *if the Old Ones didn't gravitate toward you like bears to honey pots. It'd be going much better if you weren't such a* portal!

Still, she's his friend for the long haul, and it could be worse. *At least he's not writing missives day and night in support of Lovecraft or something nuts like that*, she thinks. Unlike the crackpots Rick's always pointing out to her in the letters-to-the-editor columns of various respected periodicals.

Jeff VanderMeer is a two-time winner of the World Fantasy Award, and has made the year's best lists of *Publishers Weekly*, *The San Francisco Chronicle*, *The Los Angeles Weekly*, *Publishers' News*, and Amazon.com. His fiction has been shortlisted for *Best American Short Stories* and appeared in several year's best anthologies. Books by VanderMeer are forthcoming from Bantam, Pan Macmillan, and Tor.

A PIG'S WHISPER

MARGO LANAGAN

When is that man coming back?' said Clarice. 'The friendly one?'

'Well, *I* don't know,' said Henry. 'He has made us miss our dinner and our biscuits-and-milk already. I hope we don't miss our supper as well.'

'The sun is going.' Clarice eyed the high branches.

'Then he will be along soon,' said Henry firmly.

'I think we should go back out to the road, and meet him.'

'But he said! Wait here, he said. Do not move from this spot.'

'But what if he has forgotten us?'

The bush was vast around them, immense above them; its frail roof of leaves was a sky within a sky.

'After all those twists and turns he took us through,' said Henry, 'I am not even sure where the road *is*.'

Henry woke in the night with Clarice on his arm, her face patched with moonlight above him. Bright with excitement, too. 'What is it, Henry? Up the hill there.'

He had to lift his head, which was full of sleep-fog, and to which some leaves and litter had adhered behind. He had to prop himself on his elbows to see.

Firelight made a little golden cave or cavity, a little room, away up in the forest's darkness. Shapes moved about there purposefully. Men's shapes, they must be, for those were men's voices shouting, jolly and free the way they never were with ladies around. They were roasting meat on their fire; Henry's stomach whined at the smell.

'I thought I was dreaming,' said Clarice happily. 'I had a long dream where they were all singing and laughing up there. And the smells, Henry! Delicious smells! Maybe they will share with us! Or maybe they will have leftovers they don't need.'

She was all for running straight up there and asking.

'But what if they are bad men?' said Henry. 'What if they dislike children? I think we should creep up and spy on them first, and see if they look safe. Don't you?'

So that is what they did. The darkness made their movements all velvety, so that they could move no noisier than clouds gliding. Frond and leaf-tip stroked Henry's face as he passed; insects creaked and stopped; two fruit bats crossed the leafy sky, and one silent night-bird.

The camp must have been farther away than it looked, for by the time they reached it, the three men there were laid out asleep very soundly.

Henry and Clarice peeped out from behind separate trees. A grey-haired gentleman lay on his back in his trousers and shirt by the fire, his other clothes folded and stacked next to his head, a straw boater and a cane on top of the stack, two shiny black shoes beside it. He looked as if he would lie as neatly as that all night, his hands folded on his chest. The second man was all white shirt-front; he wore a tail-coat that clearly would not meet across that vast belly, and his tiny head was almost sunk away into the shirt-collar, with only his beaky nose poking out. The third was a working man, sprawled out with his bushy-whiskered, white-haired head on one crooked arm. He murmured between his snores, and frowned as if he were trying to remember something.

'What is that,' whispered Clarice, 'that he's holding?'

Henry tried to see it under the man's big hand. 'Something in a pudding-bowl?'

'A pudding!' They both said it, in identical tones of longing, as a tendril of the pudding's scent tickled their noses, as sweet and cosy as a rainy Sunday in their father's house.

'A *whole* pudding, that they've not even eaten a *piece* of!' whispered Clarice. '*Jam* pudding!'

'No, plum,' said Henry. 'It's a good plum-duff.'

'No, look; you can see the jam. Bubbling up there—'

She gasped: the pudding—it must have been from the weight of the man's hand—had moved in the bowl, turned so that a wetter part of it slid into view, a gleaming part, furrowed like a forehead. The jam or juice bubbled against it at the rim of the bowl, and a sound, half-sigh, half-snore, escaped.

Now the smell of caramelising jam was strong among the trees, and Henry's stomach all but cried out loud. 'We could wake them and ask for a piece,' he said.

'Do you think?' Clarice put her hand to her mouth. 'He looks a bit shouty, that man. I think I heard him shouting in my dream. And perhaps the others...' She looked doubtfully from the neat gentleman to the tail-coated one.

'Perhaps we could *take* it,' murmured Henry.

'Oh, Henry!' He heard her think about it. 'But it must be *hot*.'

'Well, *he*'s holding onto it without burning.'

'But he would have harder hands than you. And the bowl, that would be the hottest part—oh!' She caught his arm and gripped it hard.

'What?'

Her eyes were enormous. 'The pudding! It's—*looking* at us!'

The furrows had tilted in the bowl, and a large dark mark just like an eyebrow had risen, and below it in the juicier, jammier underside there was a whiteness—

'It must be a potato,' said Henry.

—with a dark mark like the colour on an eyeball—

'That'll be a, a raisin.'

—which moved, and the dark pudding-flesh closed and opened on it, exactly like an eyelid.

Clarice drew in a breath to scream. Henry was too unnerved to try to stop her.

But something else did. The trees opposite them twitched, and two men, clutching each other in terror, stumbled and sneaked into the clearing.

Shakily Clarice let out her breath.

Both the men were short and solid, one pale with big ears and the other darker and more bearish. They were what Henry's father would have called 'a very common sort', all bent and furtive, in cheap, tough clothing, none too clean. They fell and crept and crawled towards the beardy man.

'Rolling home across the foam!' he suddenly sang out, which put them back on their haunches a moment. But he tossed his head and went on sleeping, and on they came. When the dark one reached the beardy man, he put out paws that looked made of the coarsest leather, and snatched the pudding from under the sleeping hand, and the two thieves tumbled away out of the clearing.

'Calamity!' The beardy man sprang to his feet. Henry and Clarice shrank behind their trees. 'Thievery and trickery! Awake!'

'My dear fellow—'

'What the blazes—'

'Them low puddin'-thieves have used the cover of darkness and the sleep of the innocent to approach unapprehended and make off with our Albert!'

'Which way did they go?' The tail-coated gentleman rolled to his feet. 'After them!'

'Of all the low-lived, carrot-nosed poltroons!' The two of them ran away into the trees. The third gentleman donned his jacket, shoes and hat, stowed his bow tie in a pocket, retrieved his cane and started after them with the greatest dispatch.

The children were left with the fire. They came forward eagerly into its comforting dancing light.

'It smells wonderful,' said Clarice, bending to pick up a stick for a poker.

'Yes, look!' said Henry. 'They have left all this meat roasting in the—'

Quite suddenly he turned and pushed Clarice hard in the chest.

She staggered and stared at him. 'What was that for!'

'Don't go near!' he said. 'Don't touch them! Don't even look!'

She tried to see over his shoulder. He pawed at her eyes as he pushed her out of the clearing.

'Henry-y! Henry! All that good meat! When we're so hungry—'

'It is *not* good meat! It is *not!*' He tore the stick from her hand, threw it into the darkness and pulled her after him back down the hill, and through the fernbrake and deeper, down to the creek where the rocks and the tree-ferns hid the light of the fire. There he crouched, and shivered so hard that his teeth rattled.

Clarice watched him, afraid to speak, and angry. Her stomach growled.

Henry looked up. So did she. The smoke floated moonlit through the treetops. 'Oh-h-h-h,' said Henry.

'What did you see?' she whispered.

'I can still smell it.' He leaped up and seized her and pressed his face to her head. 'It is in your hair! You will have to wash! It is in your clothes!' He pushed her again, so that one foot and the hem of her skirt went into the creek.

She gasped at the cold. Rage gave her courage, though, and she ran at him like a little bull. 'Don't you push me, Henry Clarkson!' She butted him in the belly. 'What do you mean, wetting me in the middle of the night!'

She stood over him, stiff with anger. He lay like a grub, curled up on the creek-bank, and put his face in his hands and sobbed.

'What *is* it, what *is* it?' She knelt by him, crying too, for if Henry wept matters must be truly terrible.

It was not long before he stopped, stupefied with crying. She sat with her hand on his side, patting now and then, wiping with the hem of her skirt at her own tears, which wormed out more slowly and miserably than Henry's had.

'I just want to sleep,' he said dully.

She unfolded herself from sitting and lay on the wiry grass and the sand behind him, her arm over his waist and her damp cheek pressed into the curve of his neck. He did not complain, though she had never lain so close to him before. She listened to his breathing with her ears and chest and arms; she felt his heart right there next to her own; she closed her eyes tightly against the sight of the sky, all stars and branches and drifting smoke, and before long she slept.

It was a strange, wild feeling, waking in the bush. All the things that should have been separated from them by walls and windows—the cool, scented air, the clap and whoop of wings as birds poured carolling through the treetops, the rushing of the stream—all these things were doubly fresh, doubly loud.

They lay looking up through the curved combs of the tree-fern fronds.

'Do you think he will remember us this morning?' said Clarice.

'As soon as he wakes up,' said Henry. 'He will say, "Oh, my gracious, those two wee bairns!"' And he slapped his forehead as the man would, to make Clarice laugh.

They got up and drank from the stream, and watched it for a while, because it seemed so cheerful and busy about itself.

'I suppose we should wait where he said,' said Henry. 'If he goes there, we might not hear him from here. He might think we have wandered off and lost ourselves.'

'He would call, wouldn't he? We would hear his calling?' But Clarice followed Henry up the slope. He was in a mood now; they were both too hungry for play or laughter.

After they had sat in the fernbrake long enough to doze and wake again, she ventured to say, 'Henry? That fire...'

'No.' He hunched away as if she had smacked him.

'But maybe there is meat—'

'I said *no!*'

'Still good, though, in the coals—'

'It is *not meat!*' He was on all fours, barking into her face, barely an inch away. 'It is *not meat!* It is *not for eating!*'

She crumpled like a sheet of paper thrown on a fire. 'All *right!*' She put her fists to her eyes and fell to the ferns. 'There is no reason to shout!'

'There is *every* reason to shout! There is *every* reason!'

'You're mad, Henry,' she sobbed. 'You've gone mad.'

They waited in the fernbrake, taking it in turns to visit the creek and fill their bellies with water.

Night and day they waited. The man did not come; he was not going to come; he was not going to remember them.

On the day they realised this, Henry said, 'Well, perhaps that meat, then.' His face was very thin, but his eyelids seemed huge and heavy.

'It will all be spoiled now, in the sun,' said Clarice eventually.

But the thought of roasting meat was too wonderful. It dragged them up the tangled steep nightmare of the hill, on their rubbery legs. Giant ants stood in their path and waved red pincers at them. Yellow stuff seeped from ulcers in the tree-trunks they leaned against to rest, and stuck to their filthy clothing, and tried to stop them moving on.

The clearing when they reached it was full of a lively, malignant hum. Clarice, crawling now across the mat of curved gum-leaves and sharp sticks, smelt the smell first, and sat back and covered her mouth and nose with her hands. Henry lowered his head and set his jaw. Breathing gaspingly through his mouth, he stepped into the clearing towards the dead fire.

A black cloud sprang from the objects there. Any number of them could be charred logs, fanned twigs, wood misshapen by chopping and burning. But the big round stones that lay tipped and gaping, their teeth gleaming in the sunlight, there was nothing else those could be.

'Oh!' said Clarice. 'Come away, Henry!'

Even as she turned from the clearing, she saw the heap beyond him, beyond the dead fire. She crawled away fast, but she had seen it. The flies had lifted from it. It was a pile of burst mattresses, black mattresses, with their innards forcing out through the skin, purple and yellow and green.

She fell forward onto her shoulder and head. Grit jumped into her eye. She had not thought black people could grow so *fat*; all the ones she had seen were slender, strands of stringybark shadow that stepped out of the bush, and looked at her, and turned back into shadow again. How ugly they were, swollen up so, all split and thrusting out of themselves!

She upped and crawled again. She tried to blink away the grit. The eye was unbearable open, unbearable closed; tears spouted up in it. She crawled and kept crawling even as she slid on the leaves; crawled along in the air, it felt, scrabbling for the ground, the whole world gone slippery and sharp and half-blind. And Henry was gone, too; Henry would forever stand in that clearing, facing away from her, the air around him swooping and swaying, thick with flies.

They stayed at the creekside after that; they knew now that the man would not fetch them, and they hadn't the strength to go back and forth from the fernbrake any more. And the creek was farther from the clearing than the brake was, too, which they were glad of.

There they died, Clarice first in the night, and Henry two days later towards evening.

Two foster-brothers came upon them that night. Long pale streaks they were, with staring blue eyes and ragged skirts, made of dried-out gum blossoms, that covered neither the dangling sex before nor the thin, grimy bottom behind. They bent above the children and made their vague noises, and straightened their wooden bowl-hats.

'We were as sweet and soft as these once, do you remember?'

'Soft? These are all bones and britches,' sniffed the other. 'We were much more rounded. And smaller. No bigger than a gumnut.' He picked up a curl of dead bracken and laid it across the children. 'And pink, we were. Pink as the dawn, not nasty yellow like these.'

The first brother clicked his tongue, bringing a handful of leaves and scattering them over.

They covered the children with leaves and litter and sticks, and when that was done they sat up in a tree, swinging their long legs and looking down mournfully at the mound. And then they were gone, passed on like a bird or a breeze, the branch not even rocking after them.

No one came to bury the bones in the clearing at the top of

the hill. Months later a stockman rode in and moved about there, turning the dry remains with his boot-toe. He picked a skull—a tiny one, clean and white—out of the pile and put it in his saddle-bag, but the rest he let lie, scattered in the ashes there, heaped in the sun. He climbed back up onto his sweating mare, and kicked her into movement, and rode away from that place.

Margo Lanagan has written poetry, novels and short stories for adult, young adult and junior readers. Her collection of speculative fiction short stories, *Black Juice* (Allen & Unwin Australia 2004, HarperCollins US 2005, Orion 2006), has been widely acclaimed, has won two World Fantasy Awards, two Ditmars and two Aurealis Awards, and was shortlisted for the *Los Angeles Times* Book Prize and made an honour book in the American Library Association's Michael L. Printz Award. The story 'Wooden Bride' was shortlisted for the James Tiptree Jr Award, and 'Singing My Sister Down' has been nominated for many other awards, including a Nebula and a Hugo. Margo lives in Sydney.

AND DOWN CAME A SPIDER

SIMON BROWN

Bulbridge, Wiltshire. September 1954.

Autumn sunshine. Seen through the liquid ambers it was the colour of honey. Thomas Muffitt put his hand on a pane of glass, reaching out to the light. The pane was cold on his palm and he quickly withdrew his hand.

Oh, Patience, can you build me a better world?

'Father?'

Muffitt turned to glance at his daughter, pale and slight, and sombrely shook his head. He pulled the eyeglasses down from his forehead and peered at the spider in the glass jar that had been sent him by a naturalist friend in the Cheviots. At least he thought it was from a friend whom he believed lived in the Cheviots. He screwed open the lid and carefully retrieved the specimen with a pair of forceps. The spider wriggled furiously, but to no avail. He teased it with a pipette until it was angry.

'Patience?'

His daughter put out her arm. He put the spider against her skin. Patience flinched when the spider bit her.

Muffitt quickly replaced the spider in its jar and screwed the lid back on. He then lifted his daughter's arm and studied the bite. 'Ah, good. Two punctures. Perforations two millimetres apart.' He looked at Patience over the top of his glasses. 'Any reaction yet?'

'Only the pain from the bite.'

'Let me know.'

'I will, Father.'

She had golden hair. Like autumn sunshine, he thought. Not like her mother at all. But in almost every other respect...

'Very well.' He waved her off. 'Very well.'

Patience left and he turned to his notebook. He wrote: *unkn. sp. (gen. Scotophaeus? but blue multistranded web like gen. Amaurobius?), found 3 miles nw Alwinton, N'umberland, body 10 millimetres, span 15 millimetres, pedipalpi considerably shorter than 1st leg segment, large protruding chelicerae (gen. Dysdera), diet unkn.*

Muffitt pushed his glasses back onto his forehead. *Maybe this one,* he thought.

His daughter returned briefly to tell him his expected guest had arrived.

Patience sat in the bay window of the reading room. She put her book down and looked at the bite. There was some swelling, but that was utterly ordinary, nothing her father would be interested in. She timed her pulse. Utterly, utterly ordinary.

She looked out the window, wondering what it was her father had seen among the trees. It all looked the same to her. Everything always *looked* the same to her.

Lord Willoughby thumbed through the new manuscript of Muffitt's book.

'I don't see the change you wanted me to peruse, Thomas—'

Muffitt smiled patiently and flipped the pages back to the title sheet. Under *Theatrum insectorum* appeared a dedication.

'For my patron and friend, Peregrine Bertie, Lord Willoughby d'Eresby,' the lord read aloud, and blushed. 'I say.' But for a moment that was all he could say.

'I thought it fitting, Peregrine. Without your help this book would never have been completed.'

Lord Willoughby cleared his throat. 'And you have found a publisher?'

'Zetzner is doing an edition.'

'While hunting for the change last night I could not help notice you persist with giving the arachnids their own subphylum.'

Muffitt said defensively, 'Together with horseshoe crabs, ticks, scorpions—'

'Hardly the point.'

Muffitt sighed. 'I see no sense in heaping spiders with insects with crabs with centipedes...' He let the complaint die. 'Well, you know all this.'

'Then why keep the word 'insect' in the title?'

'Zetzner would not publish it otherwise,' Muffitt said, his voice rising. 'They argue that no school or college would pick it up.'

'But Zetzner will publish it if you keep this title?'

'You have the galleys in your hands.'

'It will cause a storm.'

'Good!' Muffitt exclaimed. 'The world is always beset by storms. It's about time a hurricane batted the long-protected heads of naturalists; we've had it too easy—too *neat*—or too long. The world is more complex than we could know.' He swallowed. 'More changeable, too.'

'The Royalists will want you behind bars.'

'Parliament will protect me,' he said, not entirely sure *how* he knew.

'You are an iconoclast.'

'I am a scientist.'

Willoughby snorted. 'Oh, there's a difference?'

Patience had tired of the view. In fact, she was feeling pleasantly lethargic, like she had that time her uncle had given her too much sherry to drink. She wondered in what world that had happened. She could not remember if she had an uncle in this one. Her lips were tingling. She touched her nose. It was numb, as if she had been outside in the cold autumn air. She hummed a little nursery rhyme. The light outside was changing.

Father should know about this, she thought, but that fat Lord Willoughby was with him and Willoughby would be angry if she disturbed them.

High overhead she heard the hum of the Liverpool-London airship. She wondered if one day she would be able to travel on one. She would like to visit the Egypt Protectorate, and maybe even further afield, to the kingdoms of Siam or Kalimantan. She wondered what colour the light would be near the tropics.

She did not like Lord Willoughby. He looked at her the same way he looked at one of his prize heifers. No, she corrected herself, the way he looked at one of his gun dogs.

She was very, very tired. The sun was low on the horizon now, the colour of mustard. Darkness was starting to walk the earth, and she would embrace it, use it to find their home, the world her father so desperately wanted to return to, the world he missed so much. The wife he missed so much. Patience could not remember her mother; in this world, at least, she had died giving birth to her.

And in the first world, the primary, she had been far too young. Patience dimly remembered white hands and rose water and carbolic acid. The last from her father's laboratory, probably, cleaned every day by her mother.

Her memories were drifting.

She was two or three years old, sneaking into the laboratory. Her father was working at his desk, so intent on his notes he did not notice her. There was a spider, so pretty. She let the spider out of the bottle and it bit her. The world shifted rather than changed, moving sideways, and everything was golden for an instant.

Things got very confusing after that. As her father told Patience much later, he did not at first know that anything was different, only that his daughter was crying in pain from a spider bite. He searched frantically for the spider but could not find it, and then realised all the spiders in their bottles were out of order, rearranged somehow. That was the first sign, he realised afterwards. The second was that the radio had gone dead, not even hissing static. Then he could not find his wife although only moments before she had been in the room next door: the third and most terrible sign.

If father was right, all worlds came from Patience originally,

or her namesake, or ancestor or avatar. The great creator, the
weaver of the web that held together the universe, and he tried
again and again to get her to recreate that first world, the one
with his wife and her mother still in the room next door to the
laboratory. It was the sign by which he determined that all his
succeeding experiments with Patience and spider envenomation
had failed. Yet still he tried, never gave up searching for his wife,
hardly caring about the worlds Patience created for him except for
how it might help him regain what he had lost, and never stopping
to consider what he had.

Things were moving sideways again. A nursery rhyme popped
into her head and she sang it with the voice of a small girl.

Little Mary Ester
Sat upon a tester...

Fobbing, Essex. September 1954.

Sir Thomas Moffett, Particular to the Earl of Essex, had been
searching for the missing link for half his life in this world. When
he found it on a cool, autumn day in a copse near his brother's
rectory, he did not at first understand the significance of the
specimen in his glass jar. When he returned to the rectory he
and his brother had shared a phial of tarantium, and it was
some hours before he came out of the stupor and borrowed his
brother's magnifying glass and his copy of Gesner, Wotton and
Penny's *Theatrum insectorum.* That is when he finally realised his
quest was completed.

'This is it,' he said intensely.

William, an amateur naturalist in his own right who
specialised in serpents, and who had been watching on with
interest, said, 'It is what, exactly?'

'A Mygalomorph.'

'Good for it. What in dickens name is a Mygalomorph?'

'A fossil,' Moffett said, standing up suddenly and breathing
in deeply.

'Awfully active for a fossil,' William said. 'Awfully ugly, too. A
brute of an insect.'

Moffett looked severely at his brother. 'We've had this
argument before. Spiders are not insects.' He tapped the jar with a
pencil. The spider reared up on its hind legs and tried to strike at
the pencil through the glass. Clear drips of venom trickled down
the inside of the jar.

'Did you see that?' Moffett asked excitedly.

'Yes. It *is* an ugly brute.'

'No! The fangs! They operate vertically, straight up and down.
Most spiders' fangs move like pincers.' Moffett moved his arms in
and out to demonstrate. William looked on with amusement.

'We have only found Mygalomorphs as fossils before,' Moffett
went on, a little impatiently. He turned to *Theatrum insectorum.*

'There,' he said, pointing. William looked at the photograph of an irregularly shaped piece of shale; impressed in the rock was the brother—or sister, he supposed—of the spider in the jar. The caption said *Aganippe sp.*

'You are being literal, aren't you?' William asked, new respect in his voice. 'This is the first time a live one of these—' he jabbed at the photograph '—has been found?'

'Yes. Yes, I think so.'

'Good God.'

The queen's army had given up its siege of London and was now moving north in search of supplies, especially gunpowder. The Earl of Essex had to retreat before it, ironically a victim of his own success; it had been his force that had attacked at great cost the besieging Royalists at Epping, diverting them from their main task.

Thomas and William Moffett said their good-byes hurriedly. The sound of artillery thundered just the other side of Fobbing.

'Have you your specimen?' William asked.

Moffett patted the pannier at the back of his motorcycle.

'Thanks for the book. I don't know where my copy is. Probably with Patience.'

'Have you heard from her?'

Moffett's expression did not change, but his voice tightened. 'Rupert has his armour astride the main roads to Wiltshire. Nothing is getting through, not even the mail.' He tried to smile bravely. 'But Rupert can't stay there forever.'

'Then perhaps you should not post the spider to her,' William suggested. 'Leave it with me.'

'I love you dearly, brother, but you have a rector's absent mind. You would lose it among the jumble you call a house.'

William nodded. 'True.' He grasped Moffett's shoulder. 'For God's sake be careful. The queen hates scientists as much as she does Parliamentarians, and you are the Earl of Essex's Particular, which makes you particularly hated. If she gets her hands on you she will have your head.'

Moffett patted the hand. 'I will be careful.'

For a long while Patience Moffett stared at the messenger. He was no more than a boy, soot-stained cheeks, eyes hollow from hunger and shiny with parliamentary fervor, tatty leather riding gear. An ancient Browning was stuck in his belt; she noticed the safety was off, and wondered if he was aware of it. Was the gun for bravado?

'Miss?' he said, and held out the package again.

She looked at it. Plain brown wrapping and string, her name and address in her father's scribble. She took it gingerly.

'Did Particular Moffett give you this himself?' she asked.

The messenger nodded. 'He was healthy when I saw him,' he

said, guessing the next question. 'He's high in the earl's favour, they say.'

Patience laughed, mostly in relief. 'Yes. I believe he is. Thank you.'

Without another word he turned to go.

'Wouldn't you like some food and drink? A cot for the night?'

He mounted his horse. 'Have to get back, Miss, you understand.'

'Of course.' She thought petrol must be desperately short if the army was sending its messengers out on horseback. 'Drive … ride … carefully.'

He touched his cap and dug his heels in. A minute later the sound of the galloping horse faded away; the gallop had been for bravado, too. The woods rustled with a cool breeze. Afternoon shadows played on the lawn. She retreated back into the house, closing the door after her.

She sat in the bay window and carefully opened the package, revealing a small wooden box and a letter.

Dear daughter, the letter said, *You will realise the importance of the enclosed specimen as soon as you see it. You will also know what to do with it. As you know, it is hard to remember what the first spider was all those worlds ago, but in my bones I feel it was an ancient species.*

Essex has won another victory over the queen, but Rupert is behind us now and we're starting to feel the squeeze. Apparently Hopetoun is on his way, but autumn rains have bogged down his armour. Pray for me as I pray daily for you. All my love, your father. sgd Particular Thomas Moffett, in service to Parliament and the Earl of Essex.

She opened the lid of the box and inside was a perfectly mounted spider, large, black, shiny, forward-projecting chelicerae, and…

She held her breath. *No, it isn't possible. After all these years.*

Next to the spider was a phial of its venom. She held it up to the light. Clear as water. No colour at all. How strange, she thought, and then wondered at her own reaction. Why should she expect venom from a Mygalomorph to be the same yellow-white as venom from an Araneomorph?

She collected the tape recorder and the syringe from the top drawer of her father's desk, loaded the phial into the syringe and quickly injected one millimetre of the venom into the crook of her arm. Almost instantly she cried out in pain. It burned like acid. She fumbled with the recorder's microphone. By the time she turned it on the pain had spread several centimetres up and down her arm. She talked haltingly into the microphone, recording her reactions. After a while her mouth was producing too much saliva for her to speak clearly. She tried to stand up to collect a notebook and pencil, knowing how important were these first reactions to the envenomation, but the muscles in her limbs would no longer obey her; in fact, they had started twitching slightly. She was sweating as if it was the hottest summer day and she was in her church clothes.

She rested back in the bay seat, staring outside towards the trees. She remembered once a long time ago—and maybe in a different world—that her father had tutored a Sikh student from the Kingdom of Amritsar, and he had told her that God was like a spider; just as the spider's web came from within it, so did the universe come from God.

The light outside seemed almost solid. Without knowing why a nursery rhyme popped into her head. Her father used to sing it to her when she was a little girl, in another century and in another place. She remembered the lyrics as if she had only heard them yesterday.

Little Miss Mopsey
Sat in a shopsey...

Cambridge, Cambridgeshire. September 1954.

Tommy Moufet stared at his grease paint reflection and wondered, very briefly, if there was anything left behind the makeup; if he wiped it all away, would his own face still be there? The next moment it did not matter, his mind focused solely on the performance ahead. He leaned into the mirror and used a sponge to deaden the highlights on his cheeks. There was a knock on the door and the stage boy came in. Moufet glanced in the mirror, realised it was somebody he could be curt with but decided to be magnanimous. He had also seen the Browning in its shoulder holster. He knew the Particulate had issued a warning about the riots, even going so far as to threaten marshal law, but he thought it a bit high-handed of theatre management to give their bloody boys *real* guns.

'Yes?' Moufet asked in his most Learish voice. *Yes, my son, I am old and tired but a good and regal king, at least until the second scene.*

'It's ... it's...'

Moufet put down the sponge and intoned, 'Nothing will come of nothing: speak again.'

'...*her*, Mr Moufet. She's here.'

For a moment Moufet had no idea what the boy was talking about, because with a sharp pang of sudden misery he knew Shakeshaft was wrong. With a daughter who could create whole universes, existence continually sprung from nothing, or so close to it not to count. How had it all started? He could no longer remember. He could not even remember when or where it had all started. Aeons ago, across genesis after genesis.

'Mr Glenville said he'd told you about her.' The boy was almost desperate.

'Ah,' he said, his mind slinging back to the present, and in his real voice, 'Of course.' And he thought, *Bloody Peter and his public relations*. 'Show her up.'

The boy gratefully disappeared. Moufet stood up, looked around uncertainly. How should he greet her? Sitting? He tied his gown. Kneeling? The thought made him giggle. *Oh, Christ, the Particulate would have my guts for garters*. The thought of garters got him going again. He knew he sounded like one of Cinderella's tittering sisters.

And he realised in a strange, heady rush, that he did not know who Cinderella was. The name was an echo in an empty room.

Sit down, he told himself, and did so. A second later he crossed his legs. A second after that he leaned further back in the chair and lifted his chin, glanced at himself in the mirror and saw the line between makeup and skin around his neck. He lowered his chin. Reached for his cigarettes. Before he could light one the door opened, she appeared and Tommy Moufet almost forgot himself; if he hadn't forced himself down he would have been kneeling before her like some Cambridgeshire peasant.

'Mr Moufet?'

He nodded, trying not to make it too imperious.

'I am Margaret Windsor.' She held up the camera and camera bag. 'I've come to take some publicity shots.'

'Yes, of course. How would you like me?'

Margaret Windsor blinked. 'Umm...'

Chrissakes, Moufet thought, *what did I say that for?* 'A reflection? Houston Rogers did that with me in '49. Turned out rather well. Or if you give me twenty minutes I'll be in costume and you can do me in a scene. Angus McBean did that one with me in the same year. Dramatic.' He was starting to babble and knew it; he always did that in front of beautiful women. He shut his mouth.

'Have you finished with the makeup?' she asked.

'Not quite.'

'Why don't you carry on and I'll just snap away.'

'Snap away?'

The woman nodded absently. He saw then that she was carrying a simple SLR, not one of those bloody plate cameras as large as a stage light. He sighed, and turned back to the mirror. He was about to dab himself with the cigarette, threw it away angrily and retrieved the sponge.

'Have you seen the play?' he asked.

'No,' she said, half her face hidden by the SLR. 'But I know Terence, of course.'

'Of course,' he said drolly.

'So I know what it's all about.'

'Have you done Miss Leighton yet?'

Click.

'After you.'

Moufet puffed out his cheeks. Looked at his face from every

angle. He was doing quite a good job of it, but could not recall ever learning how to apply makeup.

Click.

'What is Peter going to do with the ... ah ... snaps, did he say?'

'Theatre posters, as I understand it. And I have a deal with the *Daily Express*. Two pounds for exclusive rights.'

Click.

Alarm bells went off in Moufet's head. 'Theatre posters?'

'Uh-huh.'

Click.

'Of me in my dressing room?'

Margaret was checking something on her camera. 'Not necessarily. I want a good portrait, so I'll crop them.'

I bloody hope so. Why couldn't Peter have used Houston?

Click.

'Peter tells me you're interested in bugs,' she said.

Moufet froze, the sponge suspended halfway to his nose. 'Among other things,' he said carefully.

'Oh, don't worry,' she said. 'I don't care one way or the other.' She grinned at him in the mirror, and added dryly. 'Me and the Particulate don't get on, exactly. Nearly forty years since the revolution and they still don't trust my family.'

Moufet almost said automatically, 'For good reason', but he remembered just in time that the Particulate no longer trusted him either. No science for the common people, apparently. After all, science was knowledge, and knowledge was power, and as far as the Particulate was concerned everything must stay the way it was.

But nothing is the same.

Click.

He gave his reflection one more inspection and sat back. Another knock on the door and the stage boy reappeared. 'Thirty minutes, Mr Moufet,' he said, glanced shyly at Margaret and disappeared again.

'Peter says you actually wrote a book about them.'

Moufet cleared his throat. 'Have you almost finished? I need some time alone to prepare for the role.'

'You're playing Mr Martin and Major Pollock?'

Click.

'Terence set it up that way. Miss Leighton is playing two roles as well.'

Margaret nodded. She let the camera hang from her neck, but she seemed reluctant to leave. Moufet looked at her with his polite face, waiting.

'Peter said you have a daughter. Patience.'

'Peter *has* been saying an awful lot,' he said tightly, the polite face slipping away. Royalty or not, no one trifled with his daughter.

'She helped you with your research, before the Particulate slammed down on independent—'

'Miss Windsor,' he said, stressing the miss, 'what are you getting at?'

Margaret tried smiling, but the experiment failed. She put her hand in the camera bag, rifled around for a moment before withdrawing it with a small glass jar. 'My father asked me to give you this.'

Moufet hesitated. He could see a curled black shape in the jar and he felt his sudden blaze of curiosity must have shone through his makeup.

She reached out further. 'Go on,' she prompted.

He took it from her. His hand touched hers and he wondered if he had committed some blasphemy in doing that. Then his attention was taken entirely by the specimen in the jar. Although he had never seen one before, he knew what it was from story and legend.

'*Phoneutria fera*,' he whispered. 'How did you...?' He let the question fade on his lips. There was no other family in the world that could have gotten their hands on a specimen of the Brazilian wandering spider, not since the destruction of that country and its vast jungles in the world war of 1912. He knew he must have been a boy then, and had heard stories about the skies being dark for two years afterwards, bringing on famine and revolution, but he had no real memory of the time.

Perhaps he hadn't really lived through it at all; that seemed to be happening more and more lately.

'Why me?' he asked. 'There are hundreds of amateur particulars.'

'The spider is your specialty.'

'Still—'

'And Patience is your daughter.'

Moufet blinked at Margaret. 'What do you know—?'

'Only what father told me.' She looked confused. 'I cannot pretend to understand his words, they made no sense, but they obviously meant a great deal to him.'

'What words were those?'

'He said that when the creator walks the "darkness of embrace" the world is born anew.' She blushed with embarrassment. 'I told you he made no sense. He stutters, you see—'

Moufet nodded. 'I see. Thank you.'

Margaret breathed deeply. 'He thinks you can make the world better for my family.' She stared at Moufet then, as if trying to test the truth of her father's belief by seeing into his mind. 'He has risked a great deal—'

'I understand. My daughter and I will do what we can.'

She nodded, but did not seem convinced. 'Well, that's all done, then. Time I caught up with Miss Leighton.'

She left without saying another word, not even goodbye.

Moufet picked up the glass jar and studied the spider inside it; it may have been his imagination, but he thought it glared at him with malevolence. After a moment his hand started to shake.

Patience came out of a deep, dreamless sleep. Her mouth was as dry as a desert and the back of her throat felt like it had been rubbed with sandpaper. There was a glass of water on a night stand near the bay window where she lay curled. She sipped carefully from it, and remembered.

She sat up, suddenly alert. Outside it was still autumn, the light still flowed around the trees like honey. She could feel the cold through the panes of glass.

Sighing with disappointment, Patience scrabbled for her notebook. It was caught in between the folds of her dress. She quickly read the last entry, unclipped the pencil and wrote: *Everything is the same.*

On the nightstand, beside the glass of water, was a small phial. She picked it up and crossed out the label.

The front door opened. Patience frowned. It was too late for the cleaner and too early for the cook. Then she heard heavy, familiar footfalls.

'Father?'

The door to the sitting room opened and her father entered, obviously exhausted, his clothes spattered with mud.

'I did not hear you arrive...'

'I walked from Bulbridge,' he said and sat down next to her on the bay seat. 'It was too late for a taxi.' His shoulders slumped. She could see traces of grease paint under his jaw.

'Why aren't you in Cambridge? What's happened to the play?'

'I told Peter I was sick; he got Eric Portman in.'

'What is it? What's wrong?'

In answer he dug into his coat pocket and drew out the glass jar given him by Margaret Windsor. Patience took it from him immediately.

'I know what this is,' she said slowly.

Her father laid his hand gently on her leg. 'Then you know what to do with it.'

'Father, I'm afraid.'

'I know. And I am afraid for you. But this time, this place, is not our home.'

'I don't know what home is, Father. I have not been allowed to have one.'

Moufet blinked, opened his mouth to say something but closed it again. Patience saw confusion and pain in his expression, and it was almost too much for her. She held his hand and said, 'I'm sorry. Of course I know. Home is where mother is.'

'Patience—'

'But I don't know that home either. I was only a small child.

Now I'm a woman and I find I do want a home. I don't want to change worlds any more. I don't want to learn whose side I'm on this time, learn the names of our friends who were enemies in the world before, see you risk your life for one side and then the other. I want peace and certainty and a future that doesn't change every time you find a new species of spider.'

'Believe me, Patience, I want this life no more than you, but after searching for your mother for so long we must try again. Once more. Will you try once more, Patience? Will you?'

Little Miss Moufet
Sat on her tuffet...

Chipping Norton, Oxfordshire. September, 1954.

'It was hysterical!' Elizabeth Thomas said, then imitated the contralto voice used in government announcements: 'Science is for the people.' She laughed, a sound that was forced but infectious for all that and Patience joined in, not sure what it was they were laughing about. 'Imagine following the news with an announcement like that!'

Dressed in a yellow summer dress and sitting in her yellow summer garden, Elizabeth seemed the perfect hostess to Patience who felt uncouth and cumbersome in the older woman's presence. Bees hummed in the background. Chilled white wine coursed through her brain. She felt pleasantly sleepy.

Elizabeth stopped laughing with a sigh, which seemed very upper-class to Patience, and reached out for the wine bottle, accidentally knocking it over. 'Oh, fuck!' she cried, quickly picking up the bottle and at the same time edging out of the way of the spill.

Patience glanced at her father, but he pretended not to have heard the word and continued to smile slightly as if he hadn't a care in the world. Again, Patience thought it was a typically upper-class thing for a woman to swear like that in front of guests and not even to know she had done it.

There was a 'halloo' from the house and Elizabeth's husband appeared, a large balding man with a face which in a strange way made Patience think of an affable eagle. He was still dressed in a black suit and carried a bowler in one hand and a briefcase in the other. He bent over to kiss his wife, who angled her head to present a cheek, then smiled tightly at Patience and more warmly at her father.

'Thomas,' he said in a north country accent and held out his hand.

Thomas Muffet stood up and accepted the hand gladly.

'Did you bring it?'

Muffet retrieved his own briefcase from beside his chair and held it up.

'Excellent. Why don't you come up to the house now?'

'Oh, Isaiah,' Elizabeth said, pouting. 'You've just come home. Leave work behind for a couple of hours at least. You and Thomas can yak all you want after dinner.'

'Best to get it over with.' Isaiah said it like an aphorism.

Elizabeth sighed, lost her pout and looked at Patience. 'Well, we can stay and play for a while. Let the spoil sports go and nod wisely at each other all they like.'

Her husband barked a laugh, trying to mean it. 'Publishing's nothing to do with wisdom.' He tapped the side of his nose. 'It's to do with nous, and that's not the same at all. Isn't that right, Thomas?'

'I couldn't say,' Muffet said. 'Not my field at all.'

'Which is why you're here,' Isaiah said as if Thomas Muffet had proved his point after all.

Muffet glanced at Patience and raised an eyebrow. 'It's perfectly alright,' she said, unintentionally copying Elizabeth's accent. 'We will cope just fine without you.'

The men left and—Patience thought it strange—the two women fell into an uncomfortable silence. Still the bees buzzed and the wine spread its glow until Patience thought her cheeks must be flashing like polished apples. She watched Isaiah and her father wind their way along the garden path before disappearing behind a dry stone wall.

This world is very pleasant, Patience thought. The summers are warmer. Things seem greener, somehow. We've lived through worse. Yet she knew for her father it still wasn't good enough. As far as he was concerned the only one true act of creation included her mother, and they hadn't found her yet.

But he had promised it was the last time.

'I'm glad your father brought you along,' Elizabeth said eventually. She looked around her garden. 'It's lovely here, isn't it? I know you like it. I can tell. The Cotswolds are the most beautiful part of the world.' She frowned slightly. 'Except the name of course. Chipping Norton. It's not as charming and rustic as Stow on the Wold or Bourton on the Water, or as historic as Stratford on Avon or Oxford itself. Chipping Norton. Bloody dreadful, isn't it? I mean 'Chipping' sounds like a substitute for a swear word, don't you think? Something used by one of those clever dicks who think they're being so modern by substituting when they should just go ahead and say it. It's so snide, like they're winking at you at the same time.'

She smiled in what Patience thought was a self-deprecating way and envied her the mannerism. Patience knew if she tried it would just look studied; 'clever-dickish' as Elizabeth might put it.

Elizabeth refilled her glass and went on, her voice rising as she spoke. 'I can imagine all these town planners sitting together—with bowlers and briefcases on the table in front of them—trying to figure out what to call this place and one suggests

'Norton' and another says – thinking he's being modern—'Oh, not *chipping* Norton', and then giggling like a school boy who's told a fart joke and thinks it's the cleverest thing ever said in the history of town planning...'

She stopped abruptly. 'Oh, fuck it, I'm rabbiting on. Forgive me.'

'No, not at all,' Patience said, knowing even as the words came out they sounded frail and false.

'Well, you and your father should stay for the weekend. We'll have fireworks in the village tomorrow night.'

'Something special?' Patience asked.

Elizabeth looked at her strangely. 'Fifth anniversary of the Restoration, dear.'

'Ah. Of course.' Patience swallowed more wine.

'Good thing, too, or Isaiah would not be able to publish your father's book.'

'Yes. Very lucky for him.'

'Things must have been hard under the Particulate for you two.'

'We managed,' Patience said, wondering if she sounded defensive, not sure if her memories of the time were real or not.

'Are you going to be a naturalist, too?'

'I already help my father with his experiments.'

Patience saw Elizabeth glance at the crooks of her elbows. The scars were quite small, but against her pale skin they seemed like angry mosquito bites. She folded her arms in her lap. 'I make observations and take notes,' she continued.

'Now that your father's work is going to be published, what will you do next?'

Patience almost said, 'Keep on searching', but stopped herself in time. She shrugged, and felt herself scrunch up defensively. 'Carry on, I expect. Father believes he has only scratched the surface of the kingdom of spiders, and he hasn't even started on ticks and scorpions yet.'

Elizabeth repressed a shiver. 'Ugh. Ticks. Awful things. Scorpions, too.'

'A whole kingdom unto themselves,' Isaiah mumbled, staring at the contents page of the manuscript. 'That'll set the hornet among the swimmers.'

Muffet blinked at the expression. He dimly remembered something similar but could not put his mind on it.

'You include twizzle-legs and seastingers among them. I find that wonderfully curious. Don't seastingers have ten legs?'

'That's true, but anatomically they are related to spiders. They all share a common ancestor.'

'Ah, this evolution you speak of. Erasmus Darwin's theory.'

Muffet nodded eagerly. 'He is close to the mark, I think, but his predecessor, Lamarque, was closer yet.'

'A Frenchman? That will make it popular with the new king's Royal Society. As long as Germans aren't involved, all the king's men are for the Continent. You should see the spats all the gentlemen are wearing in the city these days. What is fashion in Paris one day is fashion in London the day after.'

Isaiah reached into one of his bureau drawers and withdrew a wad of new pound notes. 'Will this cover your expenses?'

Muffet took the money, trying hard not to keel over with relief. 'Amply. Thank you.'

'You will stay here with Elizabeth and me, of course, through the editing. You and your daughter.'

'That is very generous of you.'

'Not at all. I think Elizabeth and Patience are getting on like...'

Isaiah's affable face creased into a frown, as if the thought in his head had simply dissolved.

'Like a house on fire,' Muffet finished for him.

Isaiah's frown disappeared and his face opened with genuine pleasure. 'I like that,' he said, chuckling. 'Like a house on fire!'

'They are really quite beautiful,' Patience said. 'Scorpions, I mean. Not ticks.'

'Really? Even with all those legs? I don't believe you.'

Elizabeth said it playfully, tipsily, but Patience surprised herself by feeling a flush of anger.

'Yes, beautiful. They hold their tails with the most lovely curve...' She tried to imitate it with her arm and hand, knowing even as she did so that she was mucking it up, not explaining it at all well. She dropped her arm clumsily. 'It is lovely,' she finished lamely.

Elizabeth regarded her with benign forbearance. 'I see your point. Scorpions have an art deco tail. In their way, they are very modern.'

Patience laughed despite herself. Elizabeth not only understood, even if she did not agree, she also wanted to ease her guest's embarrassment. She sipped more of her wine, feeling completely relaxed and unfamiliarly secure. She really did like it here. The people seemed as kind as nature.

But still not home, Patience reminded herself. She did not know what art deco was, exactly, but it sounded temptingly modern.

Given time, she could learn.

Patience intercepted her father on his way out of the grand house and took his hands in hers.

'Where are you going?'

He looked at her guiltily, then glanced at the doorman holding open the car door for him. 'I have to go to London. I won't be long.'

'I don't want you to go.'

'Isaiah has given me ... us ... a substantial advance.'

'Don't spend it on your specimens.'

'It's for us, Patience. We are so close, we cannot stop now.'

'You asked me try once more, and I brought us here. I created this world for us. There is none better. I will not dream again. I don't want to leave. I *like* it here.'

'But this is not our home. We don't belong.'

'I don't care,' Patience said, her voice rising.

Muffet glanced again, nervously, at the doorman, and said in a hushed voice, 'Isaiah and Elizabeth have been very kind to us, but we can't expect them to let us live in their house all our lives.'

'Don't be patronising. It's not the house. It's this world. It is comfortable, curious and almost familiar. There is no civil war. Science is waking after a long sleep. Life could be a lot worse.'

'It is not our home.'

'We could make it our home.'

Muffet smiled thinly and eased out of his daughter's grasp. 'I will be back soon,' he promised.

Elizabeth thought Patience looked wan and worried after her father left for London, so she took her to Oxford. Long established as an agricultural centre, Oxford now had aspirations after the Restoration of making itself as a university town, establishing new halls and laboratories and red brick lodgings, and tempting clerics, philosophers and particulars out from hiding in England and back from exile in France and the Low Countries. The streets were crowded with automobiles and steam caravanserai, and up above gyroliners chuckered in from London to land near roof hangars. The air was yellow with coal dust and kerosene vapour, and it seemed to Patience that everyone moved with great energy and determination. Guild and faculty flags fluttered from almost every building, and hawkers strode up and down outside theatres calling out the cost of lectures scheduled for the day.

Elizabeth showed her the Cathedral of St Mary the Martyr, the patron saint of her descendant Charles the King Returned, and the new college of St Mary Tudor, where theology and science would be taught side-by-side, no longer contained by the strictures of a despotic parliament, and next to the college the large brass globe of the world that marked the English campus of Prince Henry the Navigator's famous college of physics and mathematics, once closed by the Particulate but open for business once more.

Patience studied everything with wide eyes and almost desperate impatience. She wanted to see everything, attend every lecture and talk, wanted be a part of the new world on display here in Oxford.

The climax of the visit came when Elizabeth showed Patience the new school of anatomy and biology, its buildings still being constructed under the supervision of the Royal College of Surgeons.

'They are looking for zoologists, anthropologists, botanists,' Elizabeth said. 'Isaiah is already contracted with the school for their journal and half a dozen text books.' She added, rather archly, 'They are also looking for an entomologist.'

Patience understood it was an offer, unofficial but she was sure with some weight behind it. The way Elizabeth had been allowed access to so many schools and colleges proved she was known, if only as the wife of Isaiah Thomas, the kingdom's foremost publisher, and in her own right as granddaughter of her namesake, the famous editor Elizabeth Goose. But Patience also understood it was an offer of a position for Thomas Muffet. As much as she liked this world, it was still a small place in many ways, and her own future was still pinned to her father's.

'And female students,' Elizabeth said as if reading Patience's mind. 'The first university school in England to do so.'

Patience, experiencing a lightheaded exhilaration, remembered little of their excursion after that until they returned to the house in Chipping Norton and right away saw her father had returned from London. He was standing on the front steps, talking excitedly with Isaiah, his sample case under one arm. Her exhilaration fled like day before night and a heavy sadness settled on her heart.

'You promised. One more time, you said.'

Patience would not look at him. She sat at her dresser, staring out over the gardens that surrounded the house. A peacock strutted across the lawn immediately below, and a dog on some mission or another made a wide circle around it. Above, low clouds that only an hour before had threatened rain were dispersing and blue sky shone sweetly.

Thomas Muffet, kneeling on one knee by Patience, squeezed shut his eyes and shook his head. 'Don't repeat my words to me. I know what I said, and I am sorry. But Patience, you must understand, this world is nothing to me without...' He stopped, realising what he had said and filled with sudden guilt because of it.

'It's always her,' Patience said quietly. 'Even with me, this world is worth nothing to you?'

'That is not what I meant to say,' he said. 'I cannot imagine life without you, my sweet Patience, and this world is close to perfect.' His voice became strained, almost pleading. 'But you never knew your mother.'

'She died because of me, I know that.'

Muffet stood, suddenly cool and aloof with self-righteous anger. 'I have never accused you of that.'

Patience looked squarely at him and he could not meet her gaze. It was enough.

'I like this world,' she said plainly.

'I know. I am sorry.'

'You are always sorry,' she said, 'but never mean it.' She sighed heavily. 'When?'

He slumped with relief, and handed her a vial of yellowish Araneomorph venom.

'From the genus *Nigma*, I think. New species, though. Unnamed.' He started speaking with the rekindled enthusiasm of someone who had won an unexpected victory. 'It is the most delicate green spider with a darker green curlicue on the abdomen. Art deco, Thomas called it.' He laughed nervously, almost a titter, then swallowed. 'Tonight. After our hosts are asleep. Do it then.'

He kissed her head and left, and for a long while Patience could not move. She was paralysed by the expectation of loss. She looked out into the gardens. The peacock had gone. Elizabeth was there now, talking with a gardener, smiling as brightly as the day. And then, without warning, like the final piece of a jigsaw, she realised how alike Elizabeth was to descriptions her father had given her of her mother. Blond and English, tall and slim, laughing and gentle. Now that she thought on it, Patience realised there even was something of the mother and daughter in their relationship, in the care and consideration Elizabeth had shown her, in the way Patience looked forward to being in her company and wanting to emulate her.

Patience absently rubbed the crook of her elbow. The scars of innumerous bites felt like Braille under the tips of her fingers.

A decision came to her, unsought, unexpected, but right, and having made it she would not wait. She retrieved the hypodermic bag from a drawer in the dresser and prepared the venom. There was hardly any sting at all, and the venom caused nothing but a slight swelling. After a while, though, she was aware of the edge of her vision losing focus and the colour seeping out like spilled wine.

It was easier than she had thought it would be. As the new world formed, Patience concentrated on keeping her distance, regarding it the way she had the view of the garden from her bedroom window. She imagined her father there, and saw him standing on a green hill looking around expectantly. She cried, because she loved him like a daughter should, and her tears became a warm rain gently falling around him. Then she closed her eyes, and when she opened them she was still in Elizabeth and Isaiah's house, but in her heart was a great hole where her father used to be.

Bulbridge, Wiltshire. January 1963.

William placed a gentle hand on his brother's shoulder as he stood by the grave of his wife. The despondency that had fallen on Thomas since the start of her long illness two years before had grown in weight until it seemed it would overwhelm him completely, and nothing William or any of Thomas's friends could do made any difference to his frame of mind. His fame as a zoologist meant nothing to Thomas anymore, despite the long years of intellectual courage and honesty he had applied in his research and writing.

William sighed. After striving all his life for a place in the sun, Thomas had lost it at the last. If only he and his wife had managed to have children, perhaps there would have been some room for hope.

After a long while, William tucked his hand inside Thomas's arm and led him away from the grave. Thomas offered no resistance, but his gaze never lifted from the ground. They had reached the hearse when Thomas stopped suddenly and bent down. When he stood, he showed William a tiny, almost transparently green spider on the tip of one finger. Thomas stared at the spider intently, and even as William guided him into the car and they drove away from the cemetery and all his past, he never once took his eyes off it.

Simon Brown's last book was the collection *Troy*, published by Ticonderoga in 2006. His last novel was *Rival's Son*, published by Tor in Australia in 2005 (and in the US by DAW in 2006), the second book in the Chronicles of Kydan. The last book in the series, *Daughter of Independence*, will be published by Tor in Australia in 2006, and by DAW in the US in 2007.

VERY LIKE A WHALE

DAVID J KANE

I must finish this quickly. The plane lands soon and I promised I'd be back in time, no matter what.

I got to the Foreign Correspondent's Club around 2.30pm, just as the old boozers finished their pudding. The club was an old colonial joint with overstuffed sofas and club chairs, Tiffany lamps, maroon carpet and red wallpaper. A young Chinese guy, dressed in traditional white shirt and navy trousers, sat discreetly at the back of the club behind a baby Steinway, wasting his talents on Streisand numbers and highlights from *Cats*.

I took a seat and scanned the room. It was packed with parasites; there were bankers schmoozing governments, brokers peddling secrets, and tech-wreckers pitching old ideas to the new rich. I recognised some fellow lawyers, too, though none from my firm. Hostess Sandy was not there or was hiding.

I must have waited for about half an hour, perched on my burgundy Chesterfield, sipping Coke and trying not to nod off. Truth be told, I was hung-over and bush-whacked from a month on the road.

It seemed far longer than a week since I'd last been at the Club. I smiled, remembering my last night with Sandy. She'd swamped me with vodka shots, and listened to my woes. By mid-evening, I'd been as lashed as a mourner at an Irish wake, and more than happy to go back to my room with her to rut and forget.

I reflected on Sandy's manifold talents and wondered if she was working the night shift. Such thoughts evaporated as Archie Banana crashed through the club entrance and was escorted to my chair by a waiter.

Archie wore an ash-grey suit and sunglasses which I had never seen him take off. Under the lights of the tiered, crystal chandeliers, his hair was yellowed lettuce: the effects of years of peroxide abuse and sunburn. As he angled in to shake hands, I caught a whiff of alpine-mint.

'Archie,' I said. 'Great to see you again. I hope you didn't have any trouble finding the place.'

'No,' he said simply, in his sing-song falsetto. 'No trouble at all, once I remembered our insignificant little appointment.'

I let that pass. Archie had acquired his rather unusual moniker by making it clear to all that he was: 'yellow outside, but Brit-white under the skin, like the herb most people think is a fruit.'

By British, he meant snooty, class conscious and superior. As his servant, I was expected to wait. The political incorrectness of his name was a source of endless self-amusement. But you had to live with his arrogance to get access.

Archie cleared his throat and, apropos of nothing, said: 'I flew in from Norway last night.'

Having never been to Norway, I had no immediate reply and nodded dumbly.

'Arctic jet-lag is the worst,' he said. 'The days are never the right length to start with. People there come in three stripes. Like scooping ice-cream from a big tub of Neapolitan. You've got your elves, your death-metal-heads, and your civil servants. Outrageous beer taxes, but the quality of life there is fine and they seem happy enough.'

He paused to order a drink from a waiter and to grab a basket of peanuts from the waiter's tray, which, till then, had been en route to another table. 'So what am I doing here today?' he asked.

I reminded him—perhaps for the fifth time in as many meetings—that we were running an important case for his employer about whether 'frozen yogurt is yoghurt that is frozen' for the purposes of the EU Customs and Excise Directive. Millions of Euros were at stake in State subsidies over the question, and the company had already spent 400 grand on my firm's services in preparation.

Archie was our star witness: a peerless legend in acidophilus. He was also regional head of research and development, and had hundreds of projects on the boil at any one time. I'd spent a month sweet-talking his secretary to wing this slot. And I couldn't waste it on Norway.

Archie snorted: 'Project thrush-purger?' He stuffed more peanuts into his open mouth. 'Not that tired hobby again? Why waste time on dairy snacks, when the real money's in happy pills.'

With a dramatic sweep, he brushed peanut shells off his lap, and continued: 'I toured our new flux-factory this morning. Now there's a business plan: move in and start out with sugary treats and cheese whip. Get the market fat and unhappy, bloated and plagued with "civilized" problems like obesity and depression—the whole kit. Then, re-calibrate the factory. Pump out pills to treat the symptoms: therapy in a daily tablet. Addictive to be sure, an unavoidable side-effect. Unfortunate. Pure genius when you think about it.'

'We're not all depressed,' I said, not entirely convincing myself.

Archie giggled, and burst into loud song in his rich, near contralto: 'Flavil and Prozac and Zoloft and Paxil, Cupid and Comet and Donna and Blitzen ... ho-ho-ho, Merry Christmas, Mr Lawrence, and thanks for all the fish.'

I looked away. People from adjacent tables were staring at us like we were fine art. Archie's inappropriate and unseasonal carol had distracted even the pianist, who struggled to recover his place in the Andrew Lloyd Webber song book.

I stared some people down and thought of my ex hanging the tree last year with Grace, waiting for me to get home. In January, she'd run off with a cutlery salesman—a failed entrepreneur of the dot com era who'd changed his name by deed poll to Knife.N.Spork.com. After his business bombed, he'd parlayed the name into a line of club anthems and was now a celebrity DJ in the bunkers of South Korea. I didn't know much else about him, though my ex had assured me at the end of the first custody hearing that he had 'a cock as big as his bank account'.

'Listen to me!' squealed Archie, kicking my right shin and jolting me back to attention. He had run out of peanuts and patience.

'I want to tell you more about my trip. From Oslo, I flew to the Lofoten Islands in the Arctic circle. Twenty-two hours of light a day this time of year. At a Viking hall ruin wedged up against a nine-hole golf course and cod racks, I was mistaken for a Jap and bundled into a package-tour. I didn't mind one bit; they plied us with mock-mead in medieval-styrofoam cups and I got a bit silly.'

I looked at Archie's flapping arms and wondered how you'd know he was drunk. He had no inhibitions dead sober.

'Our interpreter was a real Red Sonya,' said Archie holding his hands ten inches out from his chest to demonstrate her attractions. 'Six foot one in her flats and viking horns!'

Archie jumped up suddenly, and scratched his crotch. 'Synthetic underwear. I think I need some cream,' he said in explanation. 'Anyway, Red Sonya. She blabbered about Odin and Wednesday and whales. My fellow packagees were fascinated and I didn't get it at first. But then it dawned on me: the Jap-wegian affinity for sea and whale-guts.'

He plopped back in his chair, and I rolled my eyes, recalling my ex's hippie-friends and causes.

He saw me do it: 'Not a supporter of the save-the-whales campaign, I see. A fan of flensing, are you?'

Archie looked down at his feet, and pouted. 'So maybe it was Sonya's tits that flipped their lids, not the whales. But think of it,' he said, using his hands to make his point. 'A flotilla of boats herds you into shore; the fishwives wade in and stuff your blowhole with gaffs; the menfolk slash your jugular; and then the kids get into the act and carve your guts with long knives.'

'I can indeed imagine it,' I said, irritated by his pompous diatribe. 'I've been married, thanks.'

My joke crashed between us like a meteor. My chief witness clicked his tongue disapprovingly and, without a word, leapt up and headed for the bathroom. I was going to have to work hard to get this meeting back on track.

I waited for Archie to return, ruminating on the worlds of whale-whacking and witness statements. I had a sudden memory of Grace at Sea World. I'd taken her there two weeks before my wife and DJ Uber-spoon trounced me on appeal and won her.

'A better household for the child,' the judge had pronounced judgmentally (as you would expect). 'Mother at home, all that.'

I'd been trying to put it out of my mind all day, but I was losing Grace tonight. After her turn as a transvestite singing clock in her school musical, she was absconding to South Korea with my ex to live with him.

My ex and I had talked about it by phone yesterday and we had agreed; we would be adults for a night. No ugly scenes or name calling; we'd be civil and Brady. Show Grace we loved her, and that we bore each other no ill will ...

A wineglass smashed behind me and I swung around automatically. Of course, it was Archie. He had evidently tripped and fallen into an old man's lap and was now dressing the dodderer down for being so stupid as to sit quietly in his chair. Gracelessly, Archie righted himself and, with an angry shrug directed at the beet-red man, walked back to his seat and sat down.

Archie continued where he had left off. 'Not my first trip to Norway,' he said. 'At Cambridge, in the 60s, I joined what we coded an "urban-shamanistic collaboration of pharmo-warriors", ha-ha, student pretensions, hey?'

I didn't know where this was going. But I knew I'd have to hear him out completely if we were to get started on the case.

'We concocted Azrorca in our dorm, flew to Norway and jabbed them. Our brew denatured whale meat, made it rancid and inedible. But, curiously, it worked only on the cows. The males didn't absorb it and excreted it pure. Pure bullshit, you might say, ha-ha!'

Archie had shouted the expletive, and we were again the focus of the room's attention. Nodding, I willed him on to finish this nonsense as quickly as possible.

'The bulls fouled fjords and corrupted krill. Battery-salmon guzzled them and were then gobbled by sea-birds. Puffins started popping like champagne corks in the sun, *ad libitum*. We stopped doping Cetacea. We gave ourselves a stern talking to, cut our hair and got real jobs.'

Archie looked wistful. But I was appalled. My witness was mad. To think: my last two years with Grace wasted on yogurt!

Archie waggled his right index finger under my nose didactically, and continued his hectoring.

'Pigs are my thing now. Like German Texans, lactobacillus loves pork. I mixed it with their penicillin-laced feed. I fed pig bits to their grand-piglets, and interbred them like your Tasmanians. I dumped the outflow into the river and sullied grass-carp of distinction. Then I cross-bred the product with modified bird flu. Expensive to source—Indonesia the key there—all tax deductible with the right accountant.'

I had no idea what he was on about and I felt sick. Not at his words; but physically ill. My bladder ached, and my face was a sun. I mumbled my apologies and stumbled to the bathroom. I could hear him talking to himself as I walked away.

I pissed dark-yellow buckets, and looked down out of the window. Hordes of new rich, Westernized locals wielded lumpen shopping-bags like maces. I could have been in Sydney or New York, or picking up Grace from school for that matter.

I zipped and then washed up, and re-entered the club, determined to postpone the meeting. Across the room, I saw hostess Sandy sashay through the door in the little black cocktail dress that passed for her uniform. She looked younger than I remembered, and her hair was up and festooned with silver chopsticks. She smiled and I grinned at her. But, as I advanced to greet her—easily the highlight of my day—she squatted down on her haunches before Archie and lapped his hand.

I edged towards them, crushed and curious. Without deigning to look up at me, Archie took a deep breath and started speaking. I stood awkwardly opposite Sandy, like a groom at the church without his bride.

'Understand, *matey*,' he said, mocking my Australian accent. 'It's not you; or not only you. It's the whole lot, the entire goddamned race.'

Archie tilted his head and glared at me. 'You've met my wife.'

It wasn't a question.

'You've seen them in malls and airport lounges,' he said, his voice soaring higher. 'Thrashing about, pointlessly, all sound and fury.'

Archie looked back down at his feet, and Sandy stood and put her hand on his shoulder protectively. He whispered: 'You're just like the rest. Greed, profit, land, fame, change, adventure, destruction, service, mate-ship, command, status, women. Like the Nords, you worship the four: sun, ship, horse and cock. But at least they knew why they were doing it. You won't perish as honourably as they did.'

Archie and Sandy both stared at my Coke. I followed their gaze, and saw it. At the bottom of the glass, lay a half-dissolved gel-capsule, wrecked on rocks of ice. Sandy had walked behind Archie whilst he spoke. I was standing within arm's length of her now, and I could smell her alpine-lozenge.

'For reasons you've guessed,' said Archie, 'you are a suitable vessel for the glorious launch of my latest product.'

My guts unspooled and I flinched as the pieces fell into place. I tumbled back towards the exit, stuporous and stunned. I picked myself up. They laughed at my crab-dance as I clamped and held shut my burning bowels. As they cackled at me, their teeth clacked with antidote.

'Airborne fresh,' sang Archie, imitating a popular jingle.

'Go get 'em, big-boy,' moaned Sandy, and then tongue-kissed her husband.

I turned and bolted down the stairs to the street. Then I jumped in a cab for the airport.

I've landed—infected, febrile and corrupt—with blood in my throat, shit in my pants, and Archie's plague to bring down on you all.

I could have ended it in Shanghai, if Grace hadn't chosen her mother. But her clock will soon sing. And I promised I'd be back in time, no matter what.

David J. Kane is a freelance writer. Born in Geelong, Australia, and raised in a series of regional centres, he now lives and works in Hong Kong. David pays the bills by writing copy for investment banks. Not surprisingly, he dreams of demons; and his horror stories have appeared in a number of publications, including *Reflections' Edge*, *Afterburn SF* and *Dred Tales*. David is married and has a son who —when this biography was written—was nameless and six days old. www.davidjkane.com

ROSEBUDS

TANSY RAYNER ROBERTS

It began with a bear and a dwarf, as all the best stories do. I was
running after the dwarf. My skirt was mud-smeared and torn.
My hair was a mad tangle streaming behind me. I was flushed in
the face, huffing and puffing like some farmer's wife in the fields.

Silvy ran a few steps behind me. I knew without looking that
her hair was still tidy, her skirt pristine, her pale complexion
unchanged, though she was running almost as fast as I was.

That tells you all you need to know about either of us.

At least the dwarf was in worse shape than me. Already today
he had been half-drowned, scratched and pelted by an army
of forest creatures. And who had saved him from those violent
animals? Me, every time.

I wasn't convinced that he needed saving, but Silvia begged
me to help the poor little man. My sister's moral compass has
always been sharper than mine, so I tend to follow her direction
in such matters.

Poor little man, my elbow. After I had rescued him from
the homicidal fish, the manic squirrels and the psychotic eagle
(without a word of thanks, I might add), the dwarf's precious sack
had fallen to the ground, spilling its contents into the dirt and
revealing its secrets.

I'm not surprised the forest creatures were so vengeful—the
sack contained stolen nests and eggs, precious moss from the
river, handfuls of the last winter nut hoard. In amongst that lot
were several mean, pathetic little treasures from our village—a
ribbon locket here, a fountain pen there. I recognised half the
items—they had all gone missing over the winter, sparking
suspicion between neighbours and friends.

So the dwarf snatched up his sack and ran for it, and I ran
after him. My mother's wedding pin had been one of the first
baubles stolen, and I was determined to find out if the little crook
had it somewhere in his sack.

The dwarf was wheezing now, his sack of stolen things
bouncing up and down between his shoulder blades. He threw a
panicked look over his shoulder at me, then dove through a clump

of bushes, branches snagging at his trousers as he scrambled into the clearing beyond. I threw myself after him. My dress was ruined, after all. What were a few more rips and stains?

I did not reach the dwarf in time. Someone else got there first. A huge, broad-shouldered, magnificent bear thundered across the clearing, towering over the little sneakthief.

I stopped, mesmerised by the sight. Silvy came up beside me, not even breathing hard from her exertions. 'Oh,' she said in a loving voice. 'It's our bear.'

To understand about the bear, you have to know that Silvy and I have the most wonderful mother in the world. She is kind and good and everything that I am not. Best of all, she never makes her difficult red-haired daughter feel like she is any less special than the pale and perfect fair-haired one.

My sister was named after the fine white Silvia rose that costs my mother a fortune at the market. I was named for the wild Rosamund rose that snarled in uninvited from the forest, entwining itself through my mother's garden until she was forced to love it. I learned from an early age that most people prefer white roses to red.

It was our mother who invited the bear into our lives, when a thick layer of winter snow covered the rosebushes in the garden. He came to our kitchen door with a mournful look in his big brown eyes, and she let him in to sit by the fire. He stayed with us all winter, lapping soup from a bowl on the floor and gazing at the three of us as if we were his saviours.

And if he gazed at Silvy a little more than he gazed at me, I tried not to mind. That has always been the way of things.

It *was* our bear in the clearing now, and there was a terrible look in his eyes. As he advanced on the quivering dwarf, he roared— such a deep and threatening roar that I found it hard to stay on my feet. Oh, he was magnificent.

The dwarf shuddered, and toppled. He fell back on the grass, his sack falling limply from his shoulders and an awful, frozen grimace plastered over his face. I knew without getting any closer that he was dead.

This was the bear who had sighed as I recited Shakespeare to him, the bear who had watched my sister as if she was a rare and precious flower, the bear who politely moved his paws this way and that to be out of the way of my mother's broom.

He had just frightened someone to death.

'Rosy,' gasped my sister, her fingers tightening on my torn sleeve.

The bear screamed, throwing back his head as if some terrible pain had overtaken him. The fur peeled from his skin as if it were a suit of clothes. His whole enormous frame convulsed and shrank. He threw himself to the ground, crying and sobbing, and it was not the voice of a bear any longer.

He was a man. A huddled, naked man. As he unfolded and came to his feet, I saw that he was familiar in every way except his form. There were the broad shoulders, the deep brown eyes, the strong paws (now hands). There was that humble, almost shy expression. He was devastatingly handsome. My wicked, night-time thoughts about our friend the bear no longer seemed quite so perverse.

A light shone from my sister's eyes as she stared upon this marvellous, naked man. A similar light shone from his eyes as he looked upon her.

I watched it happen. By the time she had crossed the clearing towards him, and taken the shawl from her shoulders to shield his nakedness, they were in love. Sometimes it happens that way. My sister adores romantic novels, and I had always known that the first kind-faced stranger who came her way (boys from the village simply don't count) was doomed to an endless life of happy matrimony with her.

I just hadn't expected him to be the kind of man who could frighten a dwarf to death with a single roar.

They were speaking to each other now, and I forced myself to listen. Between the usual cooing endearments that are compulsory upon such occasions, we learned that his name was Bran, and he was an actual prince.

Let's be honest, now. Who didn't see that coming?

I checked on the dwarf. 'He's dead.'

Prince Bran tore his eyes briefly away from my sister to see for himself. 'His death broke the spell,' he said. 'At the beginning of winter, I came looking for the thief who had robbed our castle on the far side of the forest. He used his wicked magic to transform me into a bear.'

'That was poor planning on his part,' I said. 'He should have turned you into a bunny rabbit. I've never seen a bunny rabbit scare anyone to death.'

Prince Bran was no longer listening to me. He was too busy holding Silvy's hand, and asking her to marry him.

She bit her lip, just a little. 'Rosy. What should I do?'

'Don't look at me,' I said. 'This is something you decide for yourself.'

Silvy's romantic novel-reading came to the fore. She knows what a poor girl does when a rich man asks her to marry him.

Within a minute she had agreed, the prince had kissed her and they were walking arm-and-arm through the forest. I stayed to pile stones over the body of the dwarf, so that his body would not be eaten by the forest creatures. It seemed the thing to do.

'What about Rosy?' I heard my precious sister ask her betrothed. 'She doesn't have anyone to marry.'

'She can have my brother,' he said. 'It's about time he settled down, and Rosy will be good for him. Your mother can come and live with us.'

'It's all so wonderful,' Silvia cooed.

My sister expected happily ever after, but I had no such illusions. I finished my makeshift cairn, and went after them. Silvy might not realise it, but she was going to need me.

For a start, it wasn't what I'd call a castle. I know, I know. Girls who live in cottages shouldn't throw stones. It *was* a rambling manor house, far larger and more impressive than we were used to. The turrets and battlements were fake, though, added on later than the rest of the stonework, and there was a tower in the centre that didn't match at all. It looked a bit lopsided.

The garden was made up of neat squares of grass and rows of prim, starchy flowers. I couldn't for the life of me see where my mother could put her marvellous rambly roses, even supposing the poor things would survive being uprooted. But there was no time to think of that. My sister and I were about to meet the Queen.

A loud squawk was the first thing we heard as Prince Bran pushed the front door open. He was wearing Silvia's shawl as a kilt, so as not to shock his dear old mother. He certainly shocked the maid. A tray of silverware came tumbling down the wide staircase, and a brassy brunette lass in an apron skirt came scrambling after it. She threw herself straight into the Prince's arms, if you can believe it, wrapping her legs around his waist like a trollop—more so since he was wearing nothing but the woollen shawl around his nether regions.

'Oh sir,' she gasped, bouncing up and down. 'We have missed you. They said you were taken by bears!'

'Not exactly,' laughed Prince Bran, settling her back on the floor. 'It's good to see you, Mary. Where is my mother?'

There was a step on the stairs. Silvia looked up and went paler than I had ever seen her before. I followed her gaze.

The woman resembled an alabaster statue. She must have been fifty, but her skin was still tight around her face. Her eyes were like blue glass, hard and cold. She wore the most exquisite dress I had ever seen—all corsetry and narrow skirts, with a boned hem that had gone out of fashion twenty years ago. As she descended the stairs, she carried herself like a queen, and it took me several minutes to pull myself together and remember that she actually was one.

'Bran,' she said, presenting her cheek so he could pretend to kiss it. 'Where have you been?'

'You're not going to believe this, but I was turned into a bear,' he told her.

'Nonsense. You've been off at those gambling halls all winter, just like your father used to.' The Queen granted Silvia and me a cursory glance. 'I don't know what you've brought home with you, but I advise you to send the miserable creatures away.'

Silvy swayed. I moved in quickly and gripped her arm. 'If you dare faint on me I will leave you alone with these people.' The threat was enough to make her stand upright.

The Prince took hold of his mother's elbow and steered her to one side. 'Mother, while you listen to me, try to remember that you will cease to rule this country in less than a year when I come of age. I was transformed into a bear by one of those evil dwarves that have been robbing this kingdom blind. I might not have survived the winter without the assistance of these girls and their good mother. What's more, the fair-haired girl is the one I intend to marry.'

The Queen sniffed, looking past his shoulder to reassess Silvy. 'I suppose she's pretty enough. Who is the other, her maid?'

'Rosamund is Silvia's sister,' said Prince Bran. 'I thought perhaps she might marry Kell.'

The Queen laughed sarcastically. 'Two dowerless marriages? Marvellous. I'm sure we all look forward to you taking the throne, you've such a head for business.' She tossed her head. 'Honestly, darling, I refuse to talk about it. Don't expect me to dine with you and your guests. I'm really very cross with you.'

She swept away. Even her backside looked haughty.

'How long were you away?' I asked Bran in a quiet voice.

'Four months,' he said, trying not to laugh.

I smirked at him. 'Good thing you didn't leave it any longer. That could have been a *really* unpleasant scene.'

Silvia burst into tears. Instantly I had my arms around her, the laughter forgotten.

Bran reached out and brushed Silvy's chin, the only part of her face that was not dripping wet. 'Don't weep, dearest. Let me find you some rooms and pretty dresses and a nice lunch. You can even have the princess suite in the Tower if you like.'

'No thanks,' I said for us both, remembering the unnatural lean of that particular Tower. 'Just some plain old rooms as far from your mother as possible, and we'll be fine.'

I had already decided that I was getting Silvy out of there, as soon as I could.

Bran must have had some idea of what I was planning, because after lunch (a quiet affair in our rooms without the presence of his mother, thankfully) he took us straight to the library. As soon as I saw it, I knew I could not leave the castle. Not for a year or two, at any rate. I had never seen so many books in my life, never even imagined that so many books existed.

What a cheap trick.

'Let me show you the poetry nook,' said Bran, hooking his arm in Silvy's and guiding her away. I let them go, guessing this would be one of the few chances they had to be alone. I had some exploring to do.

The shelves were all made of polished wood and the books were proper leather-bound tomes with gilt edging and thick paper, no cheap knock-offs. I found myself in the history section, reading titles like *A Social Study of Transylvania*, and *The War of the Begonias: an illustrated guide*. Then I discovered the adventure section and filled my arms with novels by authors with dashing, heroic names.

I found a window seat and curled up with my hoard, drawing the curtain behind me to give Bran and Silvy the illusion of privacy, and losing myself in a sea of crisp white pages.

An hour or two later, my curtain was ripped aside. 'What are you doing here?' a young man demanded in a very unfriendly voice.

I hesitated. 'My name is—'

'Oh, I know who you are,' he spat. 'Mother told me all about the drabs my brother brought home with him. Where is your gold-digging sister?'

So this was Kell, the one Bran had confidently declared would be my bridegroom. I was almost relieved to discover that he was brattish and arrogant—if he had been anything like his brother, I might have ended up agreeing to the double-wedding scenario. As it was, I owed him a favour for reminding me why this was all such a terrible idea.

I tried to leave with dignity, but his arm was slung across the width of the alcove. 'Please let me past,' I said.

'You won't get away with it,' said Kell. 'You and that blonde hussy will be packed off home by morning if my mother has anything to say about it.'

I glared at him. 'Can you guarantee that? I'd be so grateful if you would.'

He dropped his arm, and I shoved past him in a very unladylike fashion to go in search of my sister.

The rooms Bran had chosen for us were pretty enough, but fancier than we were accustomed to. Silvy and I had a bedroom each and a connecting sitting room with a blazing fire that made the room far too hot during the day. Personally, I didn't see the point of a fire without a stovetop slung across it for cooking, but I suppose the ways of a castle aren't designed to make sense to a girl from a cottage.

Silvia was curled up in a white velvet chair, sighing over a small book of poetry. She wore a pink gown I had never seen before, with a full skirt embroidered all over with tiny roses, and the most fashionable sleeves I had ever seen in my life.

I stared at her. 'Where did you get that?'

'Bran sent a maid to take my measurements. She found this and a few other dresses that will do for now, but she's going to make me all new ones. My trousseau, Bran says.' She blushed faintly.

I couldn't stop staring. Was this my sister? Was she really this naive? 'Silvy, you do *know* no one wants us here, don't you?'

She shifted her shoulders a little. 'Bran wants us.'

'His mother doesn't. Nor his brother.'

'Oh, Rosy, don't you like Kell?'

'I didn't get a chance to like him, since he so obviously loathes the air that you and I breathe.'

Silvia sighed. 'Bran said he might be difficult. I'm sorry, Rosy, are you dreadfully disappointed?'

I took a few deep breaths, forcing myself not to start screaming. 'Silvia, I'm not the one angling to marry a prince here. Tell me the truth. Do you really love Bran?'

Silvia looked shocked. 'How can you doubt me?'

'Because you've only been in love for about four hours. How can you be sure it's the real thing?'

Silvia laughed. 'Oh, Rosy, it must be longer than that. It feels like forever.'

I looked at her carefully. 'Were you in love with him when he was a bear?' It wasn't completely unlikely. I myself had been half in love with him as a bear, although the man-version was distinctly more annoying.

She hesitated, then fluttered her eyelashes a little. 'I think, perhaps I might have been,' she said modestly.

Great. I flopped in the second velvet armchair, a deep pink one. 'His mother's going to be mean to you. His brother, too. You hate it when people are mean to you.'

'I don't care,' she said. 'I won't give him up, Rosy. I'm going to marry him.'

I sank my head into the deep plush of the armchair. 'So what are we going to do?'

Silvia smiled, an unexpected gleam sparkling in her eyes. 'We could take a look at those other dresses. Find something pretty for you to wear?'

I looked down at my grubby day dress and sighed. 'I suppose it couldn't make things worse.'

The dwarves did not assault the castle until the following morning.

The Queen had declined to join us for breakfast, preferring to take tea and toast in her room where she could sulk properly. Kell had entered the breakfast parlour long enough to load up a plate with curried fish, eggy rice and several beef steaks (rich people have a very strange concept of breakfast), then made a rude noise in our general direction and took his repast elsewhere to eat it.

This left me and my bacon and eggs sitting at a table with the cooing lovebirds, who fed each other strawberries and other dainty morsels inbetween endearments.

Not awkward at all.

'Oh,' Bran said, while Silvy was reaching for another strawberry. 'I sent for your mother this morning.'

'I'm so glad,' said Silvy. 'I long to see her—can you believe it's only been a day?'

I looked hard at Bran, willing myself to believe that 'sent for your mother' meant he had actually sent a carriage for her, and a really long letter explaining the current situation.

I had a horrible feeling that it actually meant a messenger carrying a curt imperative that my mother drop her daily chores and hasten across the forest (on foot, alone, with her bad back) if she ever wished to see her daughters again.

Why had I agreed to come to this dratted castle? Why hadn't I insisted that Silvy and I go home, and that Bran come courting her like a proper suitor? It didn't matter how well we were dressed, we would never be anything more than the two peasant girls the prince had found in the forest.

The door to the breakfast parlour burst open.

Kell stood there, tense with rage. 'You mentioned something about killing a dwarf in the forest yesterday, brother?' he said, the sarcasm fairly dripping off him. 'I think you'll find he had a few pals who have something to say about that.'

Upstairs, somewhere near the lopsided tower, we heard an explosion that made the castle shake.

Dwarves are known for their mining abilities, for their skill in digging gold and silver and jewels out of seemingly barren earth. In our part of the world, though, there are other treasures lurking beneath the surface, waiting to be mined. Strange, sorcerous materials that just cry out to used.

The dwarves are known for crafting those strange materials into canny and clever devices. This is why you never want to get on the bad side of a dwarf.

By the time Bran, Silvy and I made it to the roof, the castle was under attack. The Queen, clad in perfectly corseted armour, directed a platoon of sentries, footmen and kitchen maids in defence of the less-than-sturdy walls. Many of the defenders threw pots of hot custard or warm oil (somehow it was never boiling by the time they brought it up from the kitchens) over the parapet, while others brandished garden implements and other improvised weapons.

A glass ball sailed over our heads, and shattered on the tiles beyond. A hissing, spitting pink spell emerged from the broken glass, but a quick-thinking maid extinguished it with a bucket of soapy water.

'If you're going to stay, make yourselves useful,' the Queen shouted at us, just as another glass ball sailed straight at her. She smashed it away from her with a swing of an elderly cricket bat, and sprayed the released spell with an industrial-sized perfume bottle. It coughed, and fell dead to the ground.

'You two should go below,' said Bran, buckling on the breastplate he had grabbed from the umbrella stand on the way up. 'I can't guarantee your safety.'

Silvia gave him a look of steel. 'If the chamber maids can defend the castle, I'm sure I can.'

I have never been so proud of her. Worried, but proud. I picked up a croquet mallet from the pile of spare weapons at the base of the spiral tower. 'Let's do this.'

There was no diplomacy. The Queen sent several heralds down to parley with the enraged dwarves, but she put a stop to that after the third one was transformed into a butternut pumpkin.

Silvy and I spent hours on the battlements, smacking glass balls out of the sky. If you did it hard enough, the spell would fall down on to the dwarves below. Between the two of us, we were responsible for six dwarves being transformed into small furry creatures, seven falling into an enchanted sleep, nine turning on their comrades in fits of uncontrollable fury, and one being so overcome by a magic-induced lust that he attempted to rape several other dwarves, and was finally left humping the tree that they had tied him to.

Near midday, I swung too hard at a missile of the non-magical variety and lost my croquet mallet over the side. I was so tired and aching that I could hardly stand, but I staggered back to the weapons pile to find something else. Kell was there. He was exhausted, too, a long scratch bleeding down the side of his face. He was staring at my sister.

She was worth staring at. Silvia stood on the battlements, her fair hair flying in the the breeze, a tennis racquet brandished in one hand. Her pale, perfect cheeks were sunburned.

'She's magnificent, isn't she?' said Kell in a slightly strangled voice.

I tried not to take offence, though I had been defending the castle with every bit the enthusiasm and stamina that Silvy had. People always expect me to cope with difficult situations and hard work, while they expect Silvy to faint, act distressed, and need to be looked after. I was guilty of it myself, at times.

I gave Kell a hard look. 'So you're admitting that your brother's chosen bride isn't as useless as you thought she was? How gracious of you.' I snatched up a rolling pin, and headed back into the action.

I was distracted, and didn't see the glass ball in time to stop it smashing against the stiff daffodil-coloured skirts of my princess dress. I flailed at the sizzling green spell with my rolling pin, but it latched on to my ankle with a squeal of triumph.

Breathing hard, I waited. After half a minute, I was fairly sure that I wasn't a pumpkin, or an ostrich, or a puppy. Something worse, then. My skin was hot all over, and I could feel my veins twitching.

Some of the spells made you crazy—turned you into a berserker who tore violently at your own friends and allies. I had to get away from everyone until I knew what horror had been visited upon me.

I turned back to the weapons pile, but Kell was gone. My eyes were watering madly, but I still saw the door to the crooked, lopsided spiral tower. I stumbled forward, and wrenched at the door handle.

Inside, the tower was cool and dark. I was shivering, but my skin still felt scratchy and hot. I collapsed on to the steps. I was dying, obviously. I would never see my mother again. I thought of her struggling through the forest in her second best boots, a sensible lunch packed in her basket, hope in her eyes.

Boiling tears dribbled down my face. I was so selfish. The castle was under siege, Silvy was in danger, and all I cared about was that I missed my mother.

I scrabbled at the bodice of the princess dress, desperate to be free of it. I half unlaced the bodice, but could do no more. It wasn't helping, anyway. My breathing was wild and uncontrolled, and sweat rolled off my skin. What difference did a layer of brocade make? I was going to die of the heat anyway.

Somewhere, a door opened and closed. A voice spoke. 'Rosy?'

Bran. I forced myself to open my eyes and look at him. I wanted to warn him to stay away from me, but the words dried in my throat.

He had seen the glass slivers clinging to my skirt. 'What kind of spell was it?'

I shook my head. 'Don't—know.'

But I did know. How could I not? The very sight of him had quickened my pulse, set my feverish skin singing. Damn it all to hell and back! It was the tree-humping spell. And I was alone with my sister's betrothed.

My hands, almost of their own volition, caught him by the breastplate and pulled him towards me. His eyes were bright and strange. Would I find glass shards clinging to his clothes, too? I didn't care one way or the other. My fingers found the lacings of his breastplate, even as my mouth found his and dragged him down to my level.

He was kissing me now, his body responding to mine, and I knew that he had been caught by a lust spell, too. What were the odds?

There was room for guilt in this scenario, but I pushed it into a tiny corner of myself, somewhere near my elbow. Part of me knew that spell or no spell, I had wanted this. I had wanted him as a bear, had wanted him as a man—had wanted, more than anything, for one single person to notice me more than they noticed my sister.

The spell sang along my skin as I freed him of his breastplate, and scrabbled at his trews. He was lifting my skirts and ripping at my underthings, grinding himself against me as he sought his way within.

The steps grated hard against my back, and it hurt in other ways, too—ways I didn't want to think about. But the heat was driving me wild, and I bucked and groaned against him as if it was anything but my first time.

At one point, there was a moment of stillness as if something wonderful had been achieved, and then we were mad creatures again, tearing at each other in our desperation to be rid of the spell.

If you've read enough cheap melodramas, you know how this ends. At the height of my madness, as I clawed his back to drive him deeper inside me, I looked over his shoulder and saw my sister Silvia standing in the doorway to the tower, colour flaming in both her cheeks.

I pounded on Bran's shoulders with my fists, and he turned to see her, too. But by then, she was gone.

'Silvia!' I shouted, even as I scrambled out from under the hot, wet body of her betrothed and flung myself out through the tower door.

For a moment I couldn't see her. I could see Kell and the servants still fighting the dwarf spells, and the Queen shouting at the troops.

The air was thick with glass shards and spells. Two of the footmen were fighting as if they wanted to kill each other, and two more were kissing against the chimneys like the world depended on it.

I saw her then, a pale figure in a pink dress, teetering on the edge of the parapet. For one awful moment I wasn't sure if she was defending the castle or preparing to jump. As I opened my mouth to scream that I was sorry, that I loved her, that it hadn't been my fault, I saw a glass sphere shatter hard against her golden hair.

The spell inside was silver and sharp-edged—I had never seen one like that before. It engulfed her, trapping her inside a glittering mesh and yanking her back over the edge.

'Silvy!' I screamed in a voice so sharp that it felt like it came from outside my skin. I ran to the parapet, reaching it just as Kell did. A moment later, still breathing hard and rearranging his breastplate, Bran joined us both.

Silvia was still falling. The silvery mesh lowered her slowly to the grass below, and the dwarves snatched her body out of the air. Many of them did an ugly little war dance, and shrieked expletive-riddled taunts up at us.

Then one of them cast a glass sphere at the grass, opening up a huge wound of fresh-turned earth, and every single dwarf leaped into the hole and was gone. They took Silvy with them, still struggling in her magical net.

Bran and I stood there for one long moment, staring in mutual horror at the hole in the earth that had swallowed our beloved girl. It was Kell who broke the silence. 'Well? Are we going to rescue her or not?'

Of course we were. Of course, of course. I wasn't going to leave something this important to the men. I would rescue my sister and see her safely home to our mother.

Only—rescue or no rescue, I didn't see how I could ever possibly look her in the eye again.

I need not go into detail about how angry the Queen was that both her sons were abandoning the castle to rescue my sister from the dwarves. We could still hear her shrieking from the battlements as the three of us leaped into the gaping hole that had torn up a large portion of the front lawn.

The tunnel was deep and wide, arching down into the soft earth in a slow spiral. Our feet sank into the dirt as we hurried down and along in the wake of a hundred tiny footprints.

I don't know what I was expecting at the bottom of that tunnel, but the lake took me by surprise. We came out into an enormous cavern, at the shore of a lake so huge and dark that we could not see the end of it.

'I'll go around this way to see if there's a route through,' said Bran, having reclaimed his customary note of leadership. 'Kell, go around to the left. Meet back here in ten minutes.'

As easily as that, I was alone. I took a step or two towards the glistening, black waters of the lake. I slipped my shoes off— ridiculous, impractical slips of yellow satin-thin leather—and let the water curl around my toes.

Glancing around to be sure that neither of the princes were within sight, I leaned down into the water and cupped it in my hands, rinsing hastily between my legs.

There was blood and other stickiness on my fingers as I washed myself clean. A sudden urge to cry, or to vomit, rose up in my throat, and I scrubbed my hands so hard I almost lost the skin from my palms.

The water of the underground lake was cool and tempting. For a moment, I wondered if it might be possible to lose myself in its depths before Bran or Kell returned. Then I shook those thoughts clear of my head, angry at myself. I had to save Silvia first. The lake could wait.

'I know what you did,' said a voice, cutting through the splash and the silence.

I whirled around, my skirts soaking, to see Kell sneering at me.

'Do you think we don't all know what kind of slut you are?' he said.

'I was under a spell,' I said angrily, stepping out of the water. 'Feel the glass shards in my hem if you don't believe me.'

'Can you tell me that you didn't want to steal your sister's man?'

I opened my mouth to deny it, but my tongue choked on the words. It was true. I was the worst sister in the world. Part of me had not only enjoyed possessing Bran for those stolen moments, but had relished the fact that I got there first—for once, I had snatched something before it was offered to my sister.

'Up here!' Bran called to us. 'There's a passage through, and a hundred dwarvish footprints leading the way.'

Kell turned without a word and headed around the lake towards his brother.

I followed, my wet skirts swishing at my ankles.

This tunnel went on a long way, and was so low in most places that we had to crouch and crawl. A steady whirring sound of machinery surrounded us, but it was only once we emerged from the end of the tunnel that we realised what it was.

This cavern was just as enormous as the first one, only instead of lake it was full of ... well, you always think that dwarvish devices are going to be small and canny, like the glass missiles they had besieged the castle with. This particular dwarvish device was the size of a city. Every part of it whirred and clanked and hummed and rattled. A steady stream of junk and treasures—gold, jewellery, weapons, cutlery, broken glass and china, torn books, grass clippings—poured from the ceiling into a large vat that munched it into unrecognisable slag.

The slag oozed down metal pipes and along clockwork conveyor belts before being channelled into other machines—one that spat out glass spell balls, another that produced small and gleaming wands, and a third that produced bowls of a grey, strange-smelling substance that might in some universe be considered porridge.

'Gods and demons,' breathed Bran. 'What is this place?'

I sympathised with Kell's withering look. I was beginning to suspect that my sister's betrothed was an idiot.

'Where is everyone?' I asked, hoping it sounded like less of a nitwit question than Bran's. 'Surely there should be dwarves ... I don't know, tending this lot.'

'Not a lot of point to automation if they have to be here,' said Kell, reaching out and lifting a glass ball from a packing case it had just landed in. 'But I take your point.'

Somewhere in the distance, a scream rang out.

'Silvia!' said Bran, darting towards the sound.

I helped myself to three glass balls and a dwarvish wand before following him. The glass was still warm to the touch.

When I caught up to them, the brothers Prince were arguing at the mouths of two tunnels. 'The scream came from this one,' Bran said angrily.

'All the more reason to approach from the other,' growled Kell. 'They'll be expecting us, you fool.'

'You'll have to get used to obeying me one day,' said Bran in a dark voice, and threw himself into the tunnel he had chosen.

Kell hesitated, then took the other.

Neither of them had looked at me for an instant. I considered my options, and followed Kell.

'Tired of my brother's bravery already?' he said when he heard me coming after him.

'Let's just say I'm losing faith in his tactical decisions,' I replied.

We emerged from our tunnel on to a shaky layer of scaffolding. The roar of voices was at first overwhelming—when I recovered my senses I realised we were in a cavern many times huger than either of the previous ones, and that this one was full of dwarves.

They hung from the walls on scaffolding and slings—they filled platform after platform, many of them chattering or shouting angrily amongst themselves. It was like a council meeting at the village hall, only a hundred times busier.

In the midst of it all, my sister Silvia hung miserably from the ceiling, wrapped in that same silvery metal net. She was wide-eyed and startled, as if she had just awoken from a dead faint to find herself in this bizarre place, surrounded by angry dwarves.

No one had seen Kell and I yet. 'What do we do?' I asked him.

'Wait for my brother to do something stupid, and then clean up the mess he leaves behind,' he muttered.

A roar broke into the chatter and chaos of the dwarves—a male, human roar with more than a hint of bear in it. Prince Bran exploded out of a tunnel higher up in the chamber, in full view of everyone. He saw Silvy's predicament, and his face went bright red. 'Let her go, you mutant devils!' he screamed, brandishing his sword in the air.

Beside me, I heard the quiet slap of Kell hitting his own face with his palm.

A dwarf who might have been some kind of leader—or possibly just the one with the best decision-making abilities—gestured with one hand, and a second silvery net fell from the cavern ceiling to entangle Bran's limbs. It fought him to the ground as if it were alive, pinning his limbs together.

'Foolish man thing,' snarled another dwarf, possibly a woman. 'Do you really think all this was about capturing *her*?'

'Oh, Bran!' wailed Silvia, but everyone pretty much ignored her.

'Her only use to us is as a witness to your crimes,' said the first dwarf, with some satisfaction. 'You shall be tried for the murder of Viggi Sigurd Friggland III, and she will give us the evidence we need to prove your guilt.'

'No!' I yelled up to them. 'That's not right!'

I thought I heard Kell mutter something along the lines of, 'oh, cobnuts, she's as bad as he is,' but I ignored him.

The dwarves peered down at me with some interest. 'And what do you have to say in this matter?' asked the one who was probably a woman.

'Silvia wasn't there when Vig … Sig … when your brother dwarf died!' I yelled. 'Or, at least, she wasn't as close as I was. If you let her go, I'll be your witness.'

'Interesting,' muttered many of the dwarves.

'Don't trust her,' muttered some more.

The 'head' dwarf looked from me to Silvy and back again. Silvy looked cowed and fearful, and more than a little confused. 'Fair enough,' the dwarf said, finally. 'Let down the blonde one, and bring up the redhead!'

Several dwarves pulled levers and winches, and Silvia was slowly lowered in her silvery net all the way down to where Kell and I were standing. 'What exactly are you planning?' he asked me under his breath as we waited for her to reach us.

'I don't know,' I said desperately. 'What do you think I should do?'

Kell looked up at his imprisoned brother, then at Silvia, and finally at me. 'Tell the truth,' he said grimly. 'At this point, I don't think it can actually make things worse.'

Silvy gasped as her feet touched the platform, and the silvery net fell away from her. She hugged me hard, and then fell back as she remembered that she hated me right now. The look on her face was somewhere between awful and hilarious.

'Get her out of here,' I told Kell. 'Take her home, please. And—when I say home, I mean our mother's cottage. Not that castle of yours.'

'I understand,' he said.

'I don't,' Silvy flared. 'What's going on, Rosy? What about Bran?' She hesitated, and her cheeks flamed red. 'I mean... I don't want anything horrible to happen to him.'

'And what about me?' I said. 'Do you want anything horrible to happen to me?'

She looked stricken. 'I—I don't know. I just want to go home. Can't we all go home?'

'Not yet,' I said, looking up at the dwarves. 'But you can. Go with Kell, show him the way. I'll be along in a little while.'

Kell took Silvia's arm, and she allowed him to guide her back through the tunnel that had brought us here. I turned back to the enormous council chamber to see a thousand dwarves staring down at me. 'So what do we do now?'

I had expected them to imprison me in another of those metallic nets. Instead, a small platform was painstakingly lowered for me, and once I had stepped on to it I was raised to the level of the higher-status dwarves—the one who sounded like a leader, the one who was probably a woman, and an engineer who held a basket of glass balls. He held it out to me, and I reluctantly placed the balls and wand I had stolen into it.

If I was getting out of here alive, it wouldn't be by fighting. I had figured out that much.

Bran was dragged to another platform near the three dwarves who seemed to be in charge. He snarled at his captors like some kind of wild animal.

'Will you submit to truth spells?' asked the engineer dwarf.

'I don't care what hexes you put on me,' growled the Crown Prince. 'I have nothing to hide.'

'Why do you need a witness if you have truth spells?' I asked.

The three dwarves looked at me as if I was crazy. 'For the paperwork,' said one of them. Sure enough, many of the dwarves around us were taking detailed notes, tapping sentences into complex devices.

'Cross referencing,' said another.

'Legal ramifications,' said a third.

'All right,' I agreed, in the hopes that they would stop explaining. A glass ball promptly smashed against my chest. A green flicker of a spell emerged, spitting and giggling, and latched itself on to my larynx.

A second spell was likewise released over Bran.

'State your names,' said a dwarf.

'Rosamund of Rose Cottage,' I said.

'Prince Branweather Floribund,' said Bran from within his net.

Several dwarves snickered at this. I couldn't blame them, really.

'Miss Rosamund,' said the dwarf who was probably a woman. 'Did you see the death of Viggi Sigurd Friggland III?'

'I saw the death of a dwarf,' I said. 'But if you mean the one who stole the trinkets from our village, and who was left buried under a cairn of stones in the forest, then yes, we're probably talking about the same one.'

'And how did Viggi Sigurd Friggland III come to die?'

'Prince Bran scared him to death.' Part of me wanted to stop talking right there, but the truth spell got hold of my throat and threw out a few more details. 'That is—well, it was all Viggi Whatsit's fault, though, wasn't it? If he hadn't turned Bran into a bear then Bran wouldn't have been able to scare him to death. So he brought it on himself, really.' I wanted to explain my joke about how it would have been better to turn Bran into a bunny rabbit, but the truth spell mercifully allowed me to repress it.

The possibly female dwarf turned to Bran. 'And how did Viggi Sigurd Friggland III come to turn you into a bear?'

'I found him in a cave,' Bran said in a sulky voice. Like me, the truth spell was drawing more out of him than he obviously intended to say—it had stripped away the veneer of charm that he usually layered over every conversation. 'Stupid little mutant. He'd been stealing from our castle, and I caught him red handed. I yelled at him and made him give me his sack, and he was so goddamn useless that he dropped it. One of those glass balls rolled out and broke on my foot. Next thing I know, I was a bear.'

I was staring at him. 'What? Is that really what happened?'

'Amazing what comes out under truth spell,' said the dwarf engineer cheerfully. 'Prince Bran, did you intend to do harm to

Viggi Sigurd Friggland III?'

'Well, I didn't intend to kill him,' said Bran reasonably. 'I just wanted to put the wind up him, give him a good fright. Serve him right for turning me into a bear. Though I'm not weeping any tears over the shortarsed freak, let me tell you.'

'Thank you for being so honest,' said the possibly female dwarf, smirking a little. 'I think that wraps things up nicely. One more question, Prince Bran. Are you the one who made a gesture towards honourable behaviour by placing a cairn of stones over our brother dwarf?'

'Um, no,' I spoke up. 'I did that.'

Bran looked at me in surprise. 'Did you? What on earth for?'

'I would like to propose that Prince Bran be considered guilty of "Causing Death by Inappropriate Action and/or Carelessness," with a secondary charge of "Unprincely Behaviour," my fellow dwarves,' said the possibly female dwarf.

'Seconded,' said the engineer.

I half raised my hand. 'Um, while he's under the truth spell, can I ask him a few questions?'

The dwarves looked at each other, and mostly shrugged. 'If you like.'

'Rosy, what are you doing?' Bran asked in a strangled voice.

'Judging from what I've heard today, this is the only way I can get a straight answer without you honeying it up with that charm you do so well. So try this one: were you affected by a dwarf spell when you found me in the tower?'

He clamped his lips shut, but they flew open of their own accord. 'Of course not. I never said I was.'

'And you knew what kind of spell I was under.'

He couldn't help it—he actually smirked. 'Well, that was pretty obvious.'

'You took advantage of your betrothed's sister while she was in the throes of a lust spell?' My voice had risen into something of a shriek, but that didn't prevent me from hearing the collective indrawn breath of a thousand dwarves.

Bran smiled that gorgeous smile of his. 'Well, obviously I didn't know Silvia was going to find out about it...'

The possibly female dwarf raised her hand. 'I would like to propose that the charges against Prince Bran be promoted to "Very Unprincely Behaviour" as well as "Causing Death by Inappropriate Action and/or Carelessness," she said in a very firm voice. Oh, yes. Definitely a woman.

'What's that supposed to mean?' Bran demanded. 'Who the hell are you little runts to decide what constitutes 'Unprincely Behaviour'? I'm the fucking prince around here.'

'Can we consider a tertiary charge of "Ungentlemanly Language in a Public Arena?", suggested the dwarf engineer.

Many of the dwarves near him agreed that, yes, they probably could.

Bran turned his anger on me. 'What the hell have you done to me, you stupid bitch?'

'Let's pause for a minute and think about what exactly was done to whom,' I shot back.

There was much muttering and discussion amongst the dwarves—not only those near us, but every dwarf in the chamber. They went back and forth for ages, arguing and shaking their heads, getting into minor riots, and passing little notes up to the paperwork dwarves.

Finally, the dwarf who was probably in charge took a deep breath. 'Miss Rosamund, given the circumstances, we have decided to let you be in charge of sentencing Prince Bran. We are prepared to enforce any punishment or ... transformation that you decide upon.'

Bran sounded almost cheerful. 'But she can decide to forgive me and set me completely free, right?'

'If that is what she wishes,' said the probably-in-charge dwarf.

I thought about it. I really did. I thought about letting him go. I thought about him bursting through the cottage door, and explaining the whole thing to Silvy in such a way that he ended up as the hero. I thought about her married to him, unable to escape, and only then learning what kind of person he was. I thought about her making excuses for him for the rest of her life.

I thought about how much nicer he seemed to be when he was a bear. I thought about him showing no remorse at having caused the death of a fellow person. I thought about the very real possibility that I might be pregnant.

If Bran didn't learn a harsh lesson about how to treat people very soon, in less than a year he would be in charge of our entire kingdom, and then we really would be in trouble.

'Let him be a rose,' I said, in a clear speaking voice.

'What?' Bran howled.

'Let him be a rose in my mother's garden,' I said. 'Let him watch and listen. And ... once my sister Silvia is so deeply in love with someone else that she could never be convinced to go back to Bran, let him be a man again and make what he can of the rest of his life.'

The dwarves nodded and smiled to themselves. 'Good,' said the female one. 'With a mind as devious as that, you should have been a dwarf.'

Bran was staring at me, his jaw dropped so wide open that he could have fitted a whole roast chicken inside it. He mouthed words at me, and they weren't pretty. But he was already changing form, his limbs twisting in on themselves to form green, spiky branches.

When the dwarves were finished with him, he was quite beautiful. His flowers were a dark purplish colour. He would look well among the white Silvia and red Rosamund of my mother's garden, for a while at least. The engineer dwarf passed a wand over the rosebush, and it vanished.

The female dwarf took my hand, and led me along a winding rack of scaffolding to a series of freshly-ground tunnels in the wall of the cavern. 'The one on the left will take you straight to your mother's garden,' she said. 'It's a short cut. You'll probably be home before your sister.'

I thought of burying my face in my mother's apron and confessing all to her, before Silvy reached the cottage to tell her how wicked I was.

'Where do the other tunnels lead?' I asked the dwarf.

She shrugged. 'Other places. Other kingdoms, I suppose.'

My hand brushed the left hand tunnel, and a wave of longing overcame me. But, after a moment, I pointed at the tunnel furthest from the one that would take me home. 'I think I'll try that one.'

There was nothing but kindness in the dwarf's face. 'What are you looking for?' she asked me. A better question, I suppose, than 'What are you running away from?'

'I don't know,' I told her. 'Perhaps I'll find out when I get there.' Me, and anyone else I might happen to have brought with me.

I crawled into the tunnel mouth and started to climb up towards the daylight, thinking about a kingdom of limitless possibilities. A kingdom without mothers or sisters or bears or castles or princes.

A kingdom where no roses grow.

Tansy Rayner Roberts lives in Tasmania where she is busy raising a toddler, selling wooden dolls, reviewing, teaching, blogging and occasionally living up to the title of 'fantasy writer'. Her stories this year will appear in *Aurealis*, *ASIM*, *The Outcast* and *New Ceres*. Check out Tansy's blog at http://cassiphone.livejournal.com/

LIFELIKE AND JOSEPHINE

PAUL HAINES

Bernard arrived home late from work to find Denise sipping Bolli at the mirrored dining table. She wore the long red dress that split down the front, emphasising the cut of her breasts.

'What do you think, darling?' she said, a manicured hand adjusting the thick black curls that fell around her shoulders.

Go with it, Bernard told himself. Whatever it is has made possible a whole new troop of fusiliers.

He placed his briefcase on the floor next to the stand, and carefully removed his coat. Denise's hair looked the same, he thought, though she may have had it cut again. Surely she wouldn't bother asking him about something trivial like that.

'Very nice,' Bernard said, unsure whether he had used the right amount of conviction. He hung his coat on the hook and loosened his tie.

Denise leaned forward in her chair, turning her head. Her chest rose, presenting a perspective of deeper proportions. 'Well?' Her chin angled up towards the light.

Had she had her breasts done again? Bernard couldn't be sure. 'They look great.'

'No, no, no.' Denise moved her head slowly from side to side.

If she opened her mouth, Bernard thought, she'd look like a side-show clown waiting for the ball to be popped in. Her finger circled her face in impatience. He'd doubted he'd be lucky enough to win a prize.

He eased his paunch down on the other side of the table and poured himself a little stress relief from the half-empty decanter. The brandy spread through his belly, releasing a slow, reassuring heat through his knotted, middle-aged muscles. His head throbbed. He studied Denise again, unsure what he was supposed to be looking for. Surely she hadn't had a facelift. Maybe her chin had been re-sculpted.

'Oh, for God's sake, Bernard.' She pounced out of her chair and stalked around the table to tower over him. She thrust her face up close to his. 'Are you going blind in your old age? Open your bloody eyes!'

Bernard winced and leant away, trying desperately to adjust his glasses. He scanned her face, looking for something, anything. Her skin, pearl-white and smooth, pulled tight like a canvas over her cheekbones. Flawless, unblemished.

Ah-ha! He puffed himself and spoke with swagger, 'Marvellous job, Denise. Your face looks absolutely beautiful. Not a day past twenty-five.'

She allowed a curl at the edge of her lips. 'Yes, it is good, isn't it? Audrey and Madeline and the rest of the gang will be awfully jealous. Latest formula. Won't need new injections for at least ten years.' She touched up her lipstick in the reflection on the table before straightening to her full six-feet. Bernard had convinced himself that her being taller than him now wasn't intimidating.

'I thought perhaps you should take me out to dinner to celebrate.' Denise refilled her glass.

'I've had an eventful—' Bernard began.

'Mancini's. Nine sharp. I've made the booking already, so don't give me that face. You can wear the suit I've put on your bed.' She took a sip and admired the fine line of the bridge of her nose. 'Besides, Ila told me celebs will be there tonight. Oh, and I'll need some cash for the gardener. He'll be coming tomorrow afternoon.'

'Yes, dear.' Bernard swallowed his drink easily. He couldn't swallow his headache.

Bernard arrived at the hospital half an hour late from work.

'What time do you call this?' Denise snapped her compact shut and placed it into her handbag. She sat in a wheelchair, her legs apart, wearing an outpatient's robe. 'It's a bloody Sunday. You should have been here for me when I called.'

'Sorry, dear.' He had learned to appreciate her last operation—she no longer scowled. He could appreciate this one, too.

A nurse pressed a packet of pills into Bernard's hand. 'Make sure your lovely wife takes one of these after every meal. And no sex for two weeks.'

Denise snapped her fingers. 'Hurry up! I can't bear to spend another minute in here. Take me home!' Bernard shuffled into position and pushed the wheelchair down the hallway to the elevators.

'Has Audrey called yet?' she asked.

'Yes, dear. She said she can't wait to see the results.' For the life of him, Bernard couldn't remember what Denise had just had done. He hadn't checked his notepad on the way here. The pressures at the office were consuming him. He didn't think she'd had liposuction, but he wasn't sure. Hadn't they had to wait a month last time?

As they drove home, Denise chattered incessantly about rejuvenation and gratification. Bernard answered in all the right pauses, but his mind was already strategising over the battlefield in his study. How many artillery should he use against Somerset's heavy cavalry? Or perhaps he should counter attack with a cuirassier brigade first, backed with lancers, thereby negating Picton's reserve? To achieve victory, his next move required delicate timing indeed.

Bernard surprised himself with a nervous flutter deep in his stomach. They had refrained from sexual activity for the last two weeks and, though it had been difficult, Denise promised him it would be worth the wait. He suspected she had tightened herself and hoped he'd be able to get used to the change.

He stepped out of the shower, dried himself off, and applied Denise's favourite body lotion to his chest and thighs. He dabbed on the aftershave she had made him buy, though not too much. She hated it when he overdid it.

'You have a retarded sense of smell,' she would chide before making him wash it off to reapply the correct amount.

He slipped into her preferred bathrobe—a blue silk kimono—and adjusted his thinning grey hair in the mirror. It would annoy her if his pate reflected too much when they watched the recording later and he didn't want that.

'You ready, darling?' Denise called from the bedroom.

'Yes, dear.'

Candles lined the dresser and the bedside tables, flickering shadows across the walls. Denise lay on her back on the four-poster bed, one hand under her head. Her legs were pressed together and turned to the side. The black satin lace chemise she wore ended halfway down her thighs. She raised a leg and the chemise slid down an inch, revealing dimple-free skin.

Bernard lay beside her, careful not to block the view of the camera tucked up in the corner of the room. Denise couldn't smile, but her eyes were kind as her hand nestled on the back of his neck.

'Hello,' she said. She pulled his head close to hers, and they kissed, a soft tentative touching of lips. Bernard, almost used to the collagen, pressed his mouth more firmly to hers. She thrust her tongue in and pulled the robe from his shoulders.

He slid his hand over the chemise, tracing his fingers over the saline and briefly teased the permanently elongated nipples. Bernard suspected they didn't harden anymore, but it had been so long since she'd had them done he wasn't sure. He needed to concentrate on his performance so he dismissed the thought.

His hand moved down again, her belly firm, making sure he avoided her navel. She hated having it touched. He encountered the thin strip of coarse hair dividing the electrolysised skin and wondered what he would feel next.

He slid over the mons pubis. His finger encountered something fleshy and hard. Denise inhaled sharply. Something's wrong, Bernard thought. It feels too big.

'Check it out.' Denise pushed his head down and, at first, he made the mistake of resisting. She shoved his head again and the stress-sore muscles in his neck twinged.

'Bernard! Don't you ruin the movie again!' She pushed his head between her parting thighs.

Bernard gasped.

'What do you think, darling?' Denise asked.

It wasn't just the size that had caught him off guard, but the colour of her sculpted labia minora. He struggled to form words, his tongue deadweight and temporarily paralysed.

'It's the new black, darling,' said Denise. 'Modelled after Naomi. They say she has the best in the business.' She wriggled into view for the camera. 'And though it looks bigger, the vault's actually smaller.'

Bernard stared transfixed at the chocolate lips bulging over her white labia majora, his thoughts of performance fading fast. It looked like someone else's mouth.

'Well?' When he didn't answer, she stopped recording and backhanded him around the head. 'You're pathetic! I did it for you.'

'I'm sorry, dear. It looks very nice.'

She threw his kimono at his face and pushed him off the bed.

He sat in the dark in his recliner watching the television with the sound turned down while patterns of interference swept over the screen. She'd be finished soon. Bernard preferred the interference over the gardener.

After a while, the interference stopped.

Bernard added a flourish of red to the Cuirassiers' bayonet before placing the toy soldier back on the battlefield. This regiment hadn't been as accurate as promised. The heads were oversized.

This weekend he planned to re-enact the entire Battle of Waterloo again. And there would be no delay in the opening of *his* attack. He made shooting sounds and stormed the crest of the ridge, where Picton's 5th division were positioned. He would destroy the English like he had the King's German Legion holding the farmhouse La Haye Sainte. He made a mental note to whitewash the farmhouse walls—the unauthenticity of the exposed brickwork detracted measurably from his enjoyment.

'Have you noticed this?' Denise stood in the doorway of the study holding her right arm out parallel to the ground. She wore only her lace negligee.

He placed the soldier onto the table with a smidgeon too much force. His first weekend off in months. Bernard bit his lip and counted down from ten. Today was supposed to be *his* day. 'What is it, dear?'

Denise tapped a finger on the skin beneath her outstretched triceps. It wobbled. Slightly. 'See? When did I get the arms of an old woman?'

'You *are* forty-three,' Bernard replied.

'Not this woman! Follow me.'

'Denise, you promised—'

'Now!'

He trailed her into the kitchen where several brochures were displayed. Denise specified one with glossy pictures of muscle schematics overlaid with electronic grids.

'Madeline is having this right now. Audrey's booked in next month. What do you think?'

'I don't know.' Bernard studied the brochure. 'Neuro-sub-muscular atomic repression. I've never heard of this.'

'It's been in the States for months, darling. If I don't book an appointment now, who knows when I'll be able to get in.'

'Wouldn't lipo—'

'Can't you read?' Denise thumped a long finger on the brochure. 'This is permanent. The entire body, every surface muscle. Nothing will sag again.'

'But, Denise.' Bernard scanned the fine print. 'This says there is partial paralysis of the muscles. I don't think it's a good idea.'

'Oh, come on, Bernard. When did you last see a cripple with fat arms or legs?' She nodded slowly, up and down, up and down, the rhythm of victory. 'Makes sense, doesn't it?'

He sighed, thinking of how many extra hours he'd have to put in at work. 'This looks expensive.'

Denise almost grinned. 'Ah ha! You'll love this! You won't—and I promise you this—need to purchase any additional enhancements for the next five years.'

Bernard looked at her dubiously. He had heard this before.

'We're going to save a lot of money doing it this way. She slid a second brochure in front of him. 'Audrey and Madeline don't know about this one. See this procedure? It provides a soft yet resilient surface encasing the entire epidermis. It also applies pressure to the muscles beneath, keeping them firm, doubling the benefits of the sub-muscular procedure. It gains nourishment from metabolising and reabsorbing the dying epidermal layers. I'll never perspire in public again!'

'I'm sorry, dear. I have no idea what you're talking about.'

Denise guided his hand to an inch-sized sample on the brochure. It felt soft and warm and looked sun-tanned.

'Skin?' Bernard recoiled and tried to rub the feeling off on his trousers.

'And this is the best bit.' Denise adjusted a dial in the top corner of the brochure. 'See! Any colour tan whenever you want. We can convert the sun-room. If only this had been around before my electrolysis.'

She gave him a sympathetic look, though it wasn't meant for him. Bernard nodded. He might even be able to expand his library with the extra space. Denise squeezed his hand and passed the last brochure. A woman bent one leg over the back of her neck while she balanced on the other. Another women stood with her head beneath her legs, looking up at her bottom. Its title read: *Boning Up.*

'The clinic has a buy two get one free offer,' she said. 'And although beauty is noble, one mustn't neglect one's health. Osteoporosis is *the* silent killer, Bernard. You wouldn't want me at risk, would you?'

'No, dear.' Bernard read how they injected a keratinase-based serum into the marrow of the bone providing a suppleness, much like that of a new-born baby. They claimed it rendered bone density technology obsolete. 'I'm still not sure about this, Denise. Are there any side-effects? Is it proven? How long bef—'

'For God's sake, it wouldn't be available if it didn't work! We're living in the 21st century, not the bloody 19th.. You and all your bloody Nappyonic battles!'

She'd booked herself in before Bernard made it back to his study.

Bernard adjusted the saline drip in the crook of Denise's arm.

'Don't you dare!' she said. 'I can still eat. My teeth aren't too soft. You just need to blend everything and then hand-feed me.'

He had dressed her in a red high-waisted French evening dress, circa 1815, made of silk, net and embroidered in chenille. Bernard parted her legs slightly, relishing the touch of her cyberskin. He'd come to like it much sooner than he would have thought. So warm and lifelike, yet so guiltily artificial. Like the accessories he had enjoyed in his youth. He untied several of the silk strings around the neck of the dress, revealing a generous curve of saline breast.

'Bernard, please.' She sat straight-backed against the leather settee, unable to move. Her arms hung at her side, bent at the elbows. 'If you're going to do this, don't make me watch.'

He stood back, admiring her position, and scratched the stubble on his chin. She might not be able to see the entire battle-field from here, he thought. I need something to prop her up with.

The phone rang in the kitchen.

Bernard answered on the sixth ring, hoping it wasn't that damned gardener again. He'd be firmer this time and tell him in no uncertain terms his services were no longer required.

'Hello?' Bernard's eyes lit up. 'Yes it is, Doctor McKenna. That's right. A soft, French timbre preferably early 19th century. Over one hundred phrases right? Great. You're positive there are no side-effects from the electronic voice box? Good. The larynx won't regress, will it? Excellent, see you tomorrow morning.'

He cast his eye over the battlefield, mentally checking off regiment positions, calculating distances, and the camera in the corner.

'Bernard, please!'

He smiled at his beautiful wife, secure in his impending conquest. 'Soon, my sweet Josephine, soon.'

Paul Haines was raised in the 70s in the wrong part of Auckland, moved to Melbourne in the mid-90s and started writing in 1999. This story arrived fully formed during a sober conversation with Claire McKenna at Clarion South. He has no idea what Claire had been talking about that allowed this to happen, but it got the thumbs up from the rest of the Borg in the crit room. Paul's also won an Aurealis Award and a couple of Ditmars and has a short story collection *Doorways For The Dispossessed* to be published by Prime Books sometime soon. He gets paid to be an IT consultant and you can see his badly made web page at http://mc2.vicnet.net.au/home/haines/web/index.html.

THE SOULS OF DEAD SOLDIERS ARE FOR BLACKBIRDS, NOT LITTLE BOYS

BEN PEEK

When I was twelve, my mother took me to see a doctor at the Samohshiir Medical Clinic. As we could not afford a private doctor, we left early, and walked the two hours from our home to the clinic, and waited in the dim morning light with a dozen others who had traveled early and on foot, like us, in the hope of seeing a public doctor.

In the roof of the world above the clinic were thousands of lights. They were the most lights that I had seen anywhere before and I was content to sit on the stony ground and watch them brighten. To my gaze, the white stones sitting in the roof of the world were like tiny, misshapen eyes, and looked as if the ground herself had awoken and was watching us living inside her. My father, a miner, had laughed when I told him this, once. The light was made from the empty world outside, he explained, and the red sun's light filtering through long shafts of crystal and quartz to us.

The doctor that I eventually saw was named Osamu Makino. He was a small man with a thin, sad eyed, lined face beneath disintegrating grey-white hair. When he stepped out of his office and into the waiting room to call out my name, he was dressed in the doctor's black pants, black jacket, the black gloves, and the doctor's white collared and buttoned shirt. Under the bright white light of the room he appeared as if he were falling apart; that it was not only his hair, but his entire personage, that was crumbling into nothing before us.

He examined me in his bright surgery, dripping ointments over my hairless chest, placing cold coins on my eyes, and pressing down on me with warm, powdered fingers. Eventually, he began rubbing a slender bone across my arms. While he did this, he dropped powder onto my left arm. Finally, he said, 'Does your skin hurt?'

'Sometimes,' I replied, quietly, for I had always been a quiet child. 'It feels as if something is pulling at it. At night, mostly.'

My mother had brought me to the clinic after she and my father had found me walking around our house two nights earlier.

I had never walked in my sleep before and, when they had stopped me and asked me what I was doing, I spoke about a life that I had not experienced, about things that I could not have known. I remembered none of what I said in the morning, but when they asked me if anything was wrong, I did not speak of the pulling on my skin. We could not afford for me to get ill, even with the public clinics. But after consulting the family history and agreeing that there was no lingering ancestor in me who could be the cause, my parents felt it best to take me to a doctor. When I told him of the pain in my skin, my mother shifted her thick, heavy body in her worker browns and pursed her thick lips together in a frown.

'You should have told me,' she said, finally.

I nodded, said nothing.

'It doesn't matter now,' Doctor Makino said. He stood and brushed flakes of powder from his black pants. 'There's no harm, so long as he doesn't lie now. Tell me, do you have other pains?'

I shook my head. 'No,' I said, for emphasis.

'No strange dreams that reoccur?'

'My parents say that I walk in my sleep.'

His lips curved into a sad, disintegrating smile. 'I was not asking what your parents told you, but what you experienced. Do you dream?'

'No.'

'Why are you asking him this?' my mother asked.

'Your son's skeleton is distorted.' Doctor Makino sighed and rubbed at the left side of his face with his black-gloved hand, as if to erase himself. 'There is a second shadow around his skeleton. It is the first stages of soul infection, I am afraid, but you need not worry. It is early. We can remove the infection—'

'Infection?' Mother interrupted.

'Yes.' Doctor Makino's sad dark eyes never met mine, only hers. "Infected" is probably not the best word to use. A soul is not meant to be an aggressive thing, but in your son's situation, the soul cannot stop itself. It is a lost soul from the war; there are more than a few in our city now, though the Queen and her department never speaks of it. The war—the attacks against us —continues, despite our successes, and soldiers do die. The souls infecting our young are those Aajnnese men and women who have lost their soulcatchers, or whose catchers were broken by the enemy after their death, thus leaving their soul lost and scared.'

I wore a soulcatcher around my neck, my fourth. My father and I had made it from pieces of bone and silver on my eleventh birthday. He had shown me how to bond the silver with the bones of a blackbird we had purchased at the market, but it was I who had made most of it, and I who had killed the bird. I still remembered the blackbird watching me silently with its white eyes as Father and I walked through the narrow, crowded streets of our neighbourhood that evening. The roof of the world was lit with a weak scattering of eyes, and so most of our light had to come from the blue-and-green mushrooms people planted on the sides of the road. The blackbird did not utter a sound when, at home the following day, I had reached in with my hands and snapped its neck.

It bothered me, that last part, as if it knew what I was to do, and was allowing me.

'Who...?' I hesitated.

'What is it, Mi?' Mother asked.

I asked, 'Who is it?'

'I don't know,' Doctor Makino said. 'The problem is that these souls are falling into the bodies of our young and that their identities are completely unknown. Without knowing who they are, it is difficult to draw them out, and no one has yet been able to explain why it is happening. It is becoming more and more frequent, that much I know, however. Just last week a young girl was bought in with three souls—three, would you believe! She was in agony, souls pulling at every part of her. She had already gone blind, the poor child—'

'It can be removed, yes?' Mother asked. 'This soul. We can remove it?'

'Not by me, no,' he said. 'I am sorry. It is beyond my skills. You will have to write to the Queen and request a soulbird. I will provide you with a letter to accompany it.'

'What will happen if, if the Queen says no?' I asked.

'She won't,' my mother said sharply. 'The Queen protects us, remember.'

The doctor's disintegrating smile was less comfort. 'The soul in you has died violently. It was not ready for death. Few of those fighting are, I suppose. But it is important for you to understand that the soul is trying to live again—that it wants to live! It is trying to make you into itself so that it can have that life. Because of your youth it will eventually be able to dominate your own soul, to rule it, if you like. Your skin and bones will begin to grow into this old memory at an accelerated rate. It is happening now; that is why your skin aches.'

I did not fully comprehend the danger of the doctor's words by the time he had finished speaking. I had not yet seen the boys and girls whose souls had been overtaken by lost souls—who would be called the Infected—and whose bodies were now monstrosities. I had not seen the extended arms, the twisted faces, and in some cases, limbs that had been removed in brutal, ugly fashions to fit the phantom memory of injuries sustained before death. When she stood, my mother's face was pale and grim in a way that I had never seen before, and so I knew, then, and knew again as the doctor gave his private address to her 'just in case', that there was some danger. I had the sense then to be frightened and to realise that the words Mother spoke on the way home were hollow comforts, meant to assure both her and myself.

When we arrived home, the blackbirds were waiting with letters.

Satomi

I want to go home. It's cold. So cold. I've never been this cold. The wind pierces the thick army greys I am wearing, ignores my gloves, sinks into my bones. Kyo tells me that I will get used to it, that my duty will warm me, but I don't believe him. I can't. Everything around me is dark and damp. Everything is heavy with ash that is turning the ground an ugly black-brown.

This ugly empty world spreads out beneath the stilts of our watchtower like a stain. If not for the thin, stilted shadows of other watchtowers around us, I would think us alone and dead. I have not seen Aajnn for over a month. I am here beneath the empty red sky with a musket Kyo assures me I will never have to fire. Fire! As if it will in this damp! The powder for it is useless. I tell him this, teeth chattering, but he shrugs and tells me the Queen will never allow the enemy to come close to us anyway.

I am writing in the fading light of the red sun. The sun—the sun is worse than we were ever told. It fills the emptiness day and night. At night, the sky turns an ugly brown black, never truly dark. To think, our clear, beautiful white light is drawn from this!

The sky reminds me of how much I have left behind, how much I loved the narrow, twisting passages of our home. How much I miss the cool, clean smells. Everything is so mixed up here. Ash and meat. Meat and trees. Trees and waste. Why did I come here? Why did I just not ignore the Queen's conscription and go further down, to the deeper towns, to where the lights are blue and green, and it draws nothing from this awful, awful red sun?

My only pleasure comes in watching the blackbirds. Day or night, they pass through the red sky. They settle on our towers. They scratch. They look for food. Later, they fly away, either behind or in front, to Aajnn or towards the thin, thin plumes of ash that signal the approaching enemy. The birds, at least, are free.

Yoshio

It is wrong of me to write that the blackbirds were simply *there* when my mother and I returned from the public clinic. In truth, they were there for the entire walk home. The dark-feathered birds sat alone on the sloping roofs of houses, sat on the wires across the roof of the world in twos and threes as they often did, and landed on the sidewalk, to peck at the glowing mushrooms, or in the cracks of the road. They were silent, as always, but there was never anything strange or untoward about these birds until we emerged from the narrow tunnel and into our neighbourhood.

I was born in the neighbourhood called Yokto. For most of its existence, it was beneath the notice of anyone who did not live in it. It had been built only seventy years ago in a small cavern that could hold fifty families comfortably, but which held more than two hundred, now, in cramped, narrow streets. In Yokto, the roof of the world hung so low that none of the houses could ever grow beyond one storey, and those at the corners of the neighbourhood had to do without the steepled roofs that were in fashion, and which blackbirds favoured. The poorest of the poor lived in flat-roof houses. Yokto was a dim, chill neighbourhood in comparison to others, for across the roof of the world was the lightest scattering of eyes, a hundred and thirteen, none of them bigger than my fist at the age of twelve. We relied upon fungi and portable stones for light, and it served, but with only so many lights in the roof of the world, Yokto also kept a certain chill, as it never drew enough of the red sun's warmth for us.

By the time of our return, hundreds of blackbirds had covered the neighbourhood to such a point that their presence was noticeable, but not the curiosity that it would eventually become. My father, who had returned from the mines at midday, said that the birds had migrated one at a time. They emerged from the tunnel's black like an inky drop of water falling from a tap. As he was illiterate, he did not use such language, but you will forgive an old man this quirk in his own memoirs. Yet still, emerge the blackbirds did, and they came with scraps of paper in claws and beak, which they dropped on the streets and the houses of Yokto. Burnt and dirty and caked in dried blood, these letters lay, unmoving, until the soul-infected children of Aajnn arrived to retrieve them.

> Satomi
>
> An order today. An order? I don't know if I could call it such. They've told us to capture blackbirds. As many as we can. Any way we can. Alive or dead. It matters not. The musket in the tower up from us lets out a crack every so often, proof that they have the same order, for there is no enemy to shoot at. No birds fall from the sky, however, and there is no sense that they have hit anything, so far. And why should they? You don't catch blackbirds, Kyo said after the order was delivered. If they're wild, you just don't. It's the Queen's law.
>
> Our musket has proved useless, but we are trying despite ourselves. Orders are orders. We are using a blanket. When one of the birds lands before us, we throw it, trying to toss it over the bird to catch it alive. So far, we have succeeded only in throwing the blanket off the tower and into the ash and mud below.
> Yoshio

My mother wrote a letter to the Queen, asking for a soulcatcher. She included Doctor Makino's letter, but there was no immediate response, which my father said was unsurprising. No one in Yokto could afford a soulcatcher, and the Queen's mercy was not as infinite as it had once been. My mother ignored him and more blackbirds arrived, and more paper filled the streets. Stories of people trying to pick up the letters reached everyone, and my father tried it himself, to know if it was true. Like the stories, my father found his hands pecked by sharp beaks, but it could have been worse, as there were stories of blackbirds suddenly falling upon individuals, their black wings beating and claws scratching at their faces silently.

'There are over three thousand now,' my father said, staring out the window, a bandage around his left hand. He was a short, stocky, unshaven man in worker browns. He could not read, it is true, but he could gauge numbers and lengths and widths with a glance better than anyone I knew, and no one disputed his estimation now. 'There's no sign that they're going to stop, either.'

'The Queen will send somebody,' Mother replied from the small dinner table. She was writing a third letter requesting a soulcatcher, and had a third letter from Doctor Makino, who supplied them each time she went. A blackbird's feather scratched across paper. She did not look up when she added, 'It will be explained soon enough.'

From my position on the floor, I saw my father's back straighten, the thick muscles around his neck tighten at the mention of the Queen's name. The war had changed my father's relationship with the Queen. He had mined before for new neighbourhoods, to find minerals, to help advance Aajnn, to help it grow. But with the war, his job had changed, and now he mined for metals and minerals that could be turned into weapons. His job, he said, was not to kill, or to aid in the construction of weapons that would, but when he complained, he was told that all resources in Aajnn were being directed to the war. He could work or starve.

The argument was an old one between my parents. The more pressing concern was the need for a soulcatcher. During the week since my return from the doctor, I had not slept well, and needed to be drugged after the second night. It happened, on that night, just as I was drifting off to sleep, that I felt my bones and skin moving. At first, I thought that the doctor's words had come back to frighten me, that it was just the lingering hint of a nightmare; but when I touched my right arm, the skin shifted, and phantom fingers pushed up against it. I screamed. It was not, perhaps, the most masculine response, but it felt—I remember it now as clearly as that moment when I first felt it—as if a hand had been trapped beneath my skin. That it was caught in the meat and the muscle and the veins. That it was tangled against the bone. That it was struggling for freedom, trying to force my body into the right size and shape for it so that it might be able to move freely.

My only response was to scream. When Doctor Makino arrived in his doctor's blacks, appearing from the dim night light as if he had been waiting in the dark for this to happen, he wasted no time in sedating me. I was to be sedated, likewise, each night, and in that haze I was only dimly aware of the second body pushing against my skin. But in the morning, I was sick and groggy, and unable to attend school, but there was no presence of this soul, except in my mind. I followed my mother on her errands, or sat in the main room, or worked at some other task, but at no point did I stop thinking about whose soul was inside me.

Satomi
They tell us that the enemy makes blackbirds from brass. That beneath the black feathers, beneath the beak, beneath the hard skin of claws, there is nothing but brass machinery. That there is no blood. That there is no soul. That the birds are nothing but the machines a man made. The machines a woman made. The machines that have been sent to spy upon us, to tell the enemy who we are, where we are, and how to kill us.
The plumes of smoke draw closer and I ask myself, 'Will the enemy be of blood and bones?'
Yoshio

My left arm, to this day, is longer than my right. I am righthanded, and so my right hand and arm are used more, yet my left is thicker, stronger, the arm of a man who would always be more active than I. It is not something that you will notice upon first meeting me, but it is the physical reminder of my infection, of being Infected, and it is the only way by which I can now gauge what the owner of the soul inside me once looked like. Yet, in comparison to many other children in Aajnn who were Infected, my deformity is not even worth mentioning.

The Infected came into Yokto in the second week after my visit to Doctor Makino. It was they who picked up the burnt and bloody letters off the streets.

The first whom I saw doing this was a girl, no older than six. She was walking down the narrow lane that my parents' house was on, following a blackbird. The bird was jumping from letter to letter, occasionally flying, but clearly leading her, and she was hurrying along behind it. Behind her came Doctor Makino in his doctor blacks and a tall woman in worker browns that, I assumed, was the girl's mother.

When the girl was outside our house, I walked down to her. The right side of her face was lopsided and still to the point that even her right eye did not move. Through her worker browns, I could make out the swell of a breast on her right side; it was an ugly thing, too big for her, and made more prominent next to the flatness of the rest of her chest. As she saw me approach, she did not speak, but remained still and quiet, a sullen girl.

Before I could speak, her blackbird leapt, and flew down the lane. The girl ran in a limping run, one leg larger than the other. Her mother moved quickly behind her, but Doctor Makino turned to me, his dark fading gaze resting on me, and then over my shoulder. When I turned to follow his gaze, a black blur startled me. Looking back, I saw that a young blackbird had dropped to the lane and stood on a narrow letter, watching me intently.

'I think this one wants you to follow it,' Doctor Makino said.

'How can you be certain?' I still remembered the dark blood down my father's hand. I would not risk that.

The doctor sighed and rubbed at the right side of his face with a black-gloved hand. He looked tired, and sounded tired when he spoke: 'The letters are meant for those like you, Michio. The Infected. At least, that is what we think, and certainly the birds are only allowing those like you to pick up certain letters.'

It didn't take much to make the connection between the letters and the soul inside me. Would it really tell me the identity of the person trapped within me? Would it help? Before I could talk myself out of it, I stepped out into the street, picked up the letter the blackbird had moments before stood on. Tearing its dirty envelope open, I read quickly. 'It is from a man called Yoshio.'

'Is the next?'

I followed the bird, picked up a second letter, opened. 'Yes.'

At the end lane, the blackbird stood on a third letter, waiting. The narrow buildings and dim light from the roof of the world made it seem as if I would be following it into the unknown, and I suppose I was, though I did not feel frightened. The doctor said, 'Follow it and collect your letters quickly. The more you have, the more you will know about this Yoshio, and the easier he will be to remove when—*if* a soulcatcher arrives.' He paused, then added, '*Quickly*, Mi. Do you understand that?'

I didn't, and said so.

'The Queen will not like this,' he explained. 'The letters of dead soldiers are problematic enough, I imagine, for the secrets that they will reveal about the war. You hear rumours—you are too young, but I hear them. The Queen and those around her deny them, but they have been busy telling us all that we are winning the war for years now. What if these letters say otherwise?'

I had no answer, but the doctor did not expect one. He thrust his black gloved hands into his black jacket pockets, and began walking down the street in the direction of the young girl and her mother from before. It was in the opposite direction to where my blackbird waited, and when I turned to see him again, he appeared only as a dim outline, illuminated by the mushrooms beneath his feet.

Heeding Doctor Makino's words, I collected the letters that the blackbird landed upon. Even in my haste it took me all morning. Once, I tried to collect a letter that the bird did not land on. For that, I received a sharp peck on the hand. It did not draw blood like the bird attacking my father had, but I did not touch any letter other than those my bird landed on afterwards.

When I returned home, it was late in the afternoon, and my mother had been looking for me. I was scolded, but not harshly, for she had seen the streets fill with Infected and watched as they picked up the letters, and had been able to deduce what had happened to me. In her hand, she held a fresh green envelope that lightened her mood. It was a letter from the Queen, informing her that a soulcatcher would be arriving in two days time, and that we would not have to pay for its services.

Satomi

The enemy is made from brass. It sounds insane, but it's true. I saw it with my own eyes. Commander Takahashi showed me. Well, not me, not personally. I have never spoken with him personally. He won't speak to any of us individually. No, he told us all, together. He called all of us on the Northern Line into the Forward Command so that he could show us the enemy.

It had been laid in the middle of the tent, its skin sliced open, and we could clearly see that it had been built from pieces of tarnished bronze. It was a man, though, no matter what anyone says. A man. We could clearly see that. A pale man. A man with brown hair and deep set eyes. A man who had once lived and breathed, you could believe, but he was now a man made from brass.

The Commander did not give him a name. He was the enemy. Just the enemy. A man from The Shibtri Isles. Not even a man, if it could be helped. A thing. A thing from the Shibtri Isles, the Commander said, more often than not. He compared him to the birds we shot. Told us that they were not our blackbirds, just as this was not a man like us. They were both things. Things made by the enemy to be our enemy.

We had expected men and women of blood and bone, just as the Queen said, but no. They, the Commander told us, will not fight. They will send these machines, these replicas of men and women to fight, and leave the casualties as a burden for us.

We were silent after that. Shocked. Confused. Offended? A little, but it did not matter. There was only silence. Silence in which we all heard, clearly, the click, and then the faint hum of the brass machinery starting. A gentle sound almost. A humming.

And then the thing—the man thing—sat up.

The soulcatcher wore the catcher's dark blue pants, jacket and gloves. Like Doctor Makino, the soulcatcher wore the white, high-collared shirt that her occupation demanded she wear. To my twelve-year-old gaze, however, the soulcatcher was much more attractive than the doctor had ever been. She was a woman and I was immediately besotted, though in hindsight, I imagine that it is more correct for me to write that she was a girl, no more than six years older than me, having only recently been appointed to her position. No family in Yokto warranted a veteran soulcatcher and experienced soulbird.

My soulcatcher's name was Mariko Ohara. She was a small, dark-haired girl, and curved in ways that I had not noticed before. It is, therefore, with some amusement that I write that her first words, after the courtesy of saying hello, were spoken to me with a knowing smile on her lips and amused light in the dark eyes that were behind her thin, silver glasses; those words caused in me such utter shock that my immediate response was to blush like I had never blushed before, and to tell her that she couldn't possibly mean that.

'I'm sorry, but I do. You have to take your clothes off.' She was trying to be firm but failing. 'I'm sorry, Michio, but my bird cannot search you if you're wearing your clothes.'

'Must he take off all of them?' Mother asked.

She was making the situation much worse and it took all the willpower that I had, then, at twelve, not to spin around and shout at her.

My distress must have been plain to Mariko, for she said, 'He can wear shorts, of course. Of course. He just needs to leave his chest, arms and legs free, so that my bird can search him. You'll need to take off your soulcatcher too. The birds do not like them.'

Her soulbird was the biggest blackbird that I had ever seen, twice the size of those that had made Yokto their home. It—I could never think of it as a he, or even a she—was both wider and taller than those, and it had a thick barrel chest. Its black feathers, usually so sleek on blackbirds, were shaggy, as if to suggest a wildness to the bird that could not be tamed, as did its long, dark slash of a beak. Yet, despite its appearance, the soulbird perched in its narrow cage quietly, drawing easy breaths. It was not bothered by the fact that the black bars of its cell pressed in like a fist against it.

Once I had changed in my parents' room, Mariko told me to lie on my back upon the narrow, single bed that dominated my own. Once I had done this, the soulcatcher and my mother tied my arms and legs down with heavy leather straps. As they did this, I felt, for a moment, ashamed of the room that I occupied. It was the first time that I had ever felt ashamed, and that, indeed, shamed me. Compared to others in Yokto, I was not suffering: one of my parents worked, I did not share my room, I had a table and chair from which to do my homework, and I even had a few books and toys. I could read. My own father could not do that. Yet, in this position, I was able to compare my mother's faded brown worker clothing and Mariko's new, thick, white shirt, and the silver studs in her ears—three in the left, five in the right—and the glasses she wore. My family could afford none of these things, I realised. Even the bed sheets I lay upon were old and threadbare and had been mended more than once. It caused in me a sudden bout of self-consciousness. If I could have hidden our poorness from this beautiful girl before me, I would have.

But there was nothing I could do. Indeed, when Mariko lifted the soulbird's cage above me, her slender fingers opening the door, those thoughts evaporated quickly as the soulbird stuck its black head out. Mariko bent down and placed her mouth beside it: 'We are looking for the soul of Yoshio—he does not belong.'

The soulbird's white gaze fell upon me. It was an oddly empty gaze, one that I did not like. In its cage, the big black bird shifted. Its feathers ruffled. Its long sharp beak opened and closed in silence. Then, slowly, its body scrapping against the bars, feathers falling off as it pushed itself out, it dropped lightly onto my naked stomach. Its cold claws pinched my skin. Its white gaze returned to mine. The emptiness in there was slowly becoming frightening but it was not something that I could look away from—

Its sharp beak plunged into my skin.

There was pain, but worse, I realised, was that it had ripped a piece of skin off my stomach.

He sat up!

I did not move. No one did. The brass man's brown eyes were wide open. In the moment that they glanced over me I knew, knew, that he was alive. Alive as you or I. But it was only for a moment that I could think that. The next, shouting, screams, and chaos. The brass man had leapt off the table.

In the confusion around him, he had no trouble reaching Commander Takahashi. Men in soldier's grey stepped back from him. Men that were meant to fight him. To stop him. Men who had been assured that the brass man was dead. They stepped back. They yelled for him to stop. But they were frightened and con-fused and did not think to stop the brass man's thick, mechanical hands from grabbing the Commander by the throat.

We attacked him, then. Men threw themselves at him. Others smashed chairs. Anything. But it was not enough. Not nearly. Commander Takahashi's neck splintered. We heard nothing, but when the brass man tossed him away, the Commander landed in a bent angle that no living man could make.

I do not think the brass man expected to live. Whoever had

sent him, whoever gave the order for him to die and come back to life, must have told him that there was no way to survive. And so he made no attempt to do so. Instead, he attacked the officers. He attacked only those with rank. He ignored anyone else. Even as we attacked him, he ignored those of us in simple grey.

I broke one of his limbs off. I had a hammer. A big, long hammer that they use in mining pits to break rock open. The tools were outside the tent. They are giving new recruits hammers, Kyo and I had joked when we saw them. We made jokes about how we would apply for them, for they were weaponry we were both more capable of using. And when the brass man was attacking, we had no choice but to run for them. Yet with that hammer I took an arm off. With another Kyo smashed open the brass man's leg. Together we broke open his head. Together we killed it. We could not have done this with a musket. Yet still, even having done this, the brass man had killed five of our officers with his own hands.

We are back in the watchtower now. They sent us afterwards. Send us back to watch the lines of ash draw closer. To shoot blackbirds. To await this enemy.

Yoshio

'It is not Yoshio.'

Mariko's voice. It was faint, however, as if it was being smothered or pushed away, and could only be heard from a distance. I struggled to hear as she continued to speak, straining as much as I could, but her words were simply incoherent to me. I wanted to open my eyes and look at her, to assure myself that she was there, that she was a person I could recognise, but another voice told me not to. *Don't open your eyes*, it said. It did not explain why, but the voice sounded like mine in all but the subtlest of tones, and there was such an unquestionable authority in it that I did not dare disobey. Not yet. Not until I knew more.

'But the letters are from him.' My mother's voice spoke this time; it was loud and clear, as her voice always was. 'How do you explain them, then?'

'A lie, maybe.'

'There are over ten thousand blackbirds in Aajnn. What kind of enemy could send so many?'

Mariko's voice was still faint: 'An enemy winning.'

'The Queen says otherwise.'

'I do not wish to disagree with the Queen.'

'You just did,' my mother said. 'Your soulbird is not helping my son. You tell me that these letters are wrong. That this Yoshio is not inside him. You are even suggesting to me that the blackbirds in our neighbourhood—in our entire city, even—are not real. The only way that this could be true is if the Queen has been lying to us about this war. That is what you are telling me, is it not?'

'The Queen—'

'The Queen protects us!' Mother interrupted.

Don't open your eyes. I wanted to, needed to. I could feel the silence around me, thick and angry now, and opening my eyes, I knew, would diffuse it. I would prove to them that it was Yoshio inside me. That the birds were right.

'Mu.'

It was my father's voice, distant as Mariko's was.

'She is a guest, Mu,' he continued. 'More than that, she is trying to help our son. It's been three days. It's as she says—this Yoshio is not in him.'

Don't open your eyes.

My mother's breath was heavy and ragged. 'I know. It's just— No, I am—I am sorry.' Her tone was rigid, angry, but the anger was directed at herself, not Mariko. I could not hear the soulcatcher's voice reply, but my mother said, 'No, please, I shouldn't have said that. I have believed in the Queen since I was born. She sent you, you must understand. She sent you for our son. She has never— to think that she might be lying...'

'She's just tired.' My father's voice grew stronger, clearer. 'Mu, You need your rest. You can't be with him all the time.'

Don't—

'What if he wakes up?'

—open—

'That's why Mariko is here. You've barely slept in three days.'

—your—

'I want to be here for him.'

—eyes—

'You need rest.'

I opened my eyes. There was no one in the room. There was no room. Rather, there was only whiteness and a faint, faint pecking, coming from all directions about me. I tried to sit up, but I could not move. The pecking grew. It sounded as if it were coming from a sharp beak that was being scraped across hard stones. My arms and legs were immobile. I could feel straps holding me down. The pecking continued, steady, coming from all around me. I struggled to raise my head. I felt a stab of pain. Then another. I looked down and saw, standing on my stomach, its claws a wet red, the shaggy, wild soulbird. Its long, sharp beak had just pierced my stomach and plunged into the bloody mess that already existed. As I watched, it drew back, ripping the wet, raw contents of my intestines with it. As it raised its head, the soulbird's white eyes met mine and I realised, with horror, that they were no longer a clean, crisp white, but that they were stained red.

Its beak opened, and in a voice that was mine, it said, 'I told you not to open your eyes.'

☆

Satomi

The tower to the North exploded today.

One moment, it was there. The next, its thin legs were all that remained, and its broken wreckage smoldering beneath the morning's red sky. I had been on watch when it happened. Kyo was sleeping. I had gotten us dry powder for the musket and so I had it sitting on the rail of the tower. Sitting ready. Kyo had helped me, even, after what happened in with the Commander, though as we stood and looked at the wreckage, I knew that our new musket was useless.

The explosion began in raining fire. It's the only way to explain it. A soft sprinkle of fire began to fall and then, suddenly, the tower exploded! It burst apart. Ripped apart. It was shredded. I don't—I can't explain it to you. The fire rained down and then, suddenly, the slowly bleeding mid morning had opened up like a wound, and there was a broken tower on the horizon and no sign of the enemy. No brass men. No brass animals. Just the plumes of ash, drawing closer. Ever closer.

I know more fear every day.

Yoshio

When I awoke, Mariko was sitting in my room. Her blue jacket was hanging off the back of my chair and she was sitting at my table, reading the dirty, burnt letters that I had collected. I was no longer strapped down, though my limbs felt sluggish, as if they had not been used for some time, and I was tired. There was a thin white blanket covering me and, before I said a word to Mariko, I lifted it. I was completely naked, but to my relief, there was no other mark upon me.

'How do you feel?' Mariko picked up a stone pitcher from the floor and poured a cup of water, then came over to me. 'If your throat hurts, drink.'

I did and, after watching me take my first hesitant sips, she said, 'It took five days. You've been in a sleep, of sorts, for five days, but you won't feel rested.'

'Where—where is your bird?' I asked, my voice soft, scratchy.

'At home. He finished yesterday, so there was no need to make him sit in the cage for the return journey. Are you sure you're fine? Five days is a long time to be under, so if you're feeling nauseous, or you hurt, you should tell me.'

I shook my head. 'Just tired.'

'Good.'

'Where is...' I hesitated, the memory of what I heard while under still fresh in my mind. 'Was it Yoshio?'

'No.'

'Who was it?'

Mariko sat on the edge of my bed. 'That took a little while to figure. You're only my third patient, Mi, and I still have much to learn. Forgive me. My soulbird had found something, but it was difficult to remove. It wasn't Yoshio, as I said, but that does not account for five days. Even an unknown soul should be able to be removed within two. But yet still he worked by a third and fourth. Only a suicide is so difficult.'

'Kyo,' I whispered.

'Yes, Kyo. It took him five days to pull Kyo out—if I had read the letters, it would have taken less, perhaps. But I thought they were fake. I've only just read them now. In fact, I was just reading Yoshio's final letter now, where he finds Kyo.' She stood, and picked the dirty piece of paper off the table. Aloud, she read, 'I found him this morning. He had done it in his watch. In the time when he was meant to have his gaze on the dark red sky. When he was meant to be watching the plumes of ash. To report if they came closer. When he was meant to be watching for the first touches of flame falling through the sky at our outpost. But he hadn't been doing any of those things. He hadn't been watching. His eyes were open, but he would not see anything. Kyo had done it early in his shift. He was stiff when I touched him. Cold. So cold. Colder than the wind that cut through my clothes.'

She stopped, but I knew how the rest of it went.

> He lay against the wooden wall with the musket next to him. The musket that was now stained with his blood. The musket that we had been given to defend with. To share, one between two. The musket we had only just gotten dry powder for. That musket that he had used, finally. The musket that he had used to crush his soulcatcher so that his soul could return home to Aajnn, so that it could find a sanctuary that he could not here.
>
> And I wondered, as I helped the doctor take Kyo away, how it is that I will return home?
>
> Yoshio

I never saw my soulcatcher again, but we only remained in Yokto for another month, so it was to be expected. Yoshio wrote in his first letter that he should have gone deeper into the world rather than taken part in the Queen's War; that he should have gone into the cities that were lit in blues and greens and, I learnt later, purples and yellows and much, much more, but to places where the red sun and the Queen were not known. It was into these cities that my parents took me.

I remember the morning that they told me of their decision well. For weeks, we had heard rumours that cities neighbouring Aajnn had fallen. That they had fallen as much as six to eight months ago. But it was not until a queen's messenger, wearing the pale green that signalled his service, came around and spoke in Yokto that it was finally confirmed. The letters the birds brought, he said, were from real soldiers. The Queen was now attempting to establish a peace with the forces for the Shibtri Isles and we need not panic. Or words to those effect. On the morning after that, I woke in my bed, chilled, the lights on the roof of the world dimmer than usual. Outside, blackbirds sat quietly, as they always did. Yokto was a neighbourhood of blackbirds now, and Aajnn a city of them. Climbing out of bed, I walked down the cold hallway to the living room, where my mother stood at the small, stone, dining table, crying.

I had never heard my mother cry before and so I approached her, quietly. As I drew closer, I could see the outspread wings of a blackbird on the table. They were still. As still as the wings of the blackbird on my eleventh birthday. My hand drifted up to my soulcatcher, to feel the warm bone and cold silver. I hoped that I would stay in it after I died. That I wouldn't become lost like so many others.

'Mother?' I asked.

Ignoring me, she picked up the long knife that was in front of her. The blade was old and scratched, but sharp, and there was blood over it. Angrily, she stabbed the blade into the blackbird's stomach, then twisted it, further ripping open the cut she had already made. When her sobbing grew louder with each twist of the blade, as if her grief were being strangled in her throat, I realised, finally, how much she had lost. How she had become her own lost soul, even with her soulcatcher firmly around her neck. The knife fell to the floor and Mother thrust her hands into the bird. She dug into the blackbird's stomach, her hard fingers clawing through organs, breaking bones, all in a desperate attempt to find one, tiny piece of brass in the slippery organs that would return her faith. That would return her Queen.

'*Mother.*' She had begun breaking the blackbird's wings. I called out a third and fourth time, until finally, on the fifth, my voice pained from screaming, her hands stopped, and rested, trembling, on the table.

'Michio.'

Her voice was soft, frail, hurt. I had never heard it like that before and would hear it again, only once. Wordlessly, I took her hard, red hands into mine, and led her away from the bloody table.

Ben Peek is a Sydney-based author. His fiction has appeared in *Year's Best Australian Science Fiction and Fantasy* and in *Leviathan Four: Cities*, edited by Forrest Aguirre, and *Polyphony 6*, edited by Deborah Layne and Jay Lake. In addition, his fiction has appeared in *Fantasy Magazine*, *Aurealis*, *Shadowed Realms*, and *Full Unit Hookup*. He also writes criticism for *Strange Horizons*. His novel *Black Sheep* is due out from Prime Books in 2006. http://benpeek.livejournal.com.

Different in the Lands of Glory

JAY LAKE

'I was thus brought to the solemn conclusion that in about 25 years from that time all the affairs of our present state would be wound up.'
— William Miller, predicting the arrival of the Second Coming in 1843/1844

An October evening near Port Gibson, New York, was no time to be standing about wound in a bedsheet, waiting for God's angels. Atop a wind-whipped hill in the dark of night, Rebekah Linebarger's father kept a square-fingered hand firmly upon her shoulder. Her two brothers Jachin and Boaz clung to her other arm. Their large, rough hands gripped in tighter imitation of Papa's, until she wanted to squirm from the bruises they raised. Like Millerites all over New York, and indeed, the United States and Canada, they had been waiting there the whole day. Rebekah was nearly ill with fatigue and hunger.

'Soon,' her father said just as he had been saying all the day and night, though they had stood on this hill time and again since March of 1843. Brother Miller had promised this was the last, correct date. 'Soon. You boys hold on. Glory's so close I can smell it.'

Me too, Papa, Rebekah thought. *Glory comes for me too, with Mama in the vanguard.* But she didn't know exactly where Glory had got to this holy October 22nd. Brother Fowler's fine words of just a day ago had explained the curious errors of calculation which had caused the previous dates to pass by with the brethren yet unclaimed by God.

'Behold the Bridegroom cometh, on the tenth day of the seventh month,' Brother Fowler had declaimed from the back of a wagon. He had been explaining the differences between the Hebrew year and the Christian year and how a true scholar of the Bible must needs sound the depths of variance betwixt the two. Everything had seemed so clear when he spoke.

Now those words were just so much tired puzzlement. For one, Hebrew year or no Hebrew year, everybody knew October was the tenth month, not the seventh.

Papa was wrong, too.

He might have scented Glory on the wind, but Glory did not tickle *her* senses. All Rebekah could smell was nose-tingling smoke from the previous day's burning stubble and the mold-damp of woods in autumn. Leaves wet with dew and the slimed beginnings of winter rot rustled across the grass, their chill slap raising goosebumps on her ankles as they passed. Her scalp itched something fierce from the rough twine Papa had used to tie her hair at the top.

Mama would never have let this happen to her family.

Rebekah wiped the smoke-tears from her eyes and stared up at the scattered moon-stained clouds looking for the Heavenly host. Something darker moved across the sky, further dimming the night. Papa gasped as a bell began to toll down the hill in Port Gibson. Jachin muttered the Lord's Prayer, followed by poor, slow Boaz, as always half a beat off.

'Our Father, who art in Heaven, hallowed be Thy name...'

Rebekah heard a creaking noise above her, though she still saw nothing but shadow. It sounded like the towropes of the Erie Canal boats, as if a great weight of wood or canvas moved through the sky under immense strain.

'Mama?' she whispered.

Why would it be Mama?

Whatever flew above her head popped, then fluttered to send a hot wind washing over her. *Glory* was *coming*, Rebekah thought as her heart raced, a warm blush engulfing her neck and face. She felt a tugging at the bundled topknot of her hair. The muscles of her neck jumped as her entire body erupted into goosebumps.

The angels were coming for her just like Papa had said, just as Brother Fowler had preached. Flying down from above, hands reaching out for the high-bound hair of the righteous to snatch them up to Glory, salvation in the Kingdom of God. Her heart thrilled.

The Advent was here!

Would the twine hold? she thought with a stab of panic. Her hair might pull out of the coiled knot, its curled red strands might separate. Such a small thing from which salvation should depend, that the angels might grab.

Even more frightening, were Papa and Jachin and Boaz strong enough to hold tight to her when she was pulled to Glory?

Papa would be so angry with her if either of her brothers fell. He had lectured her time and again these past three years, since their family had seen the light of Brother Miller's teachings, and most especially before each of the hilltop gatherings. 'Eggs, girl,' he would mutter. 'Eat more eggs. Your Mama always said they were good for your hair.' Then he would glower, as he did at any mention of Mama.

Eggs, cream ... anything to make her hair brighter, stronger, a beacon to Heaven. Even breadcrusts, over her cries and protests. Papa had sold the farm a year ago spring, right before the first prophesied date, to an unbeliever from Canandaigua who had marveled at his luck. The first thing Papa did with the money was send to Rochester for a French-trained hairdresser to come and make Rebekah's hair right for God.

'Pride's a terrible sin, vanity in a little chit such as yourself,' Papa had grumbled, 'but Brother Fowler says the Lord's angels will take us up by the hair. Like those Musselmen of old Damascus.'

There was of course no question of her ever going to Rochester herself. Rebekah's entire life would be nothing but Port Gibson, then the Kingdom of Heaven. She knew she was supposed to rejoice, but surely she was meant for more than this?

There was so *much* out there.

Despite Papa's warnings she did take pride in her hair. Worthy of Heaven it was, red and rich and flowing like the cataracts of the St Lawrence. Half the boys of both Wayne and Ontario counties had flocked to see her since it had grown in, whenever harvest or market or the business of the Erie Canal brought one or another of them to Port Gibson.

Even some of the girls, too, whispering behind their hands and rolling their eyes.

Rebekah knew her flowing red hair was considered a misplaced luxury by those townsfolk who did not follow Brother Miller. They thought it crazed, too, that Papa and the other brethren had sold their farms, given away their cattle, some passing on every stick and stitch down to the clothes on their back. What need did a man have within the Kingdom of Heaven for his earthly possessions? It would be easier for a camel to pass through the eye of a needle. Let the Babylonians enjoy their last few days of false comfort before eternal damnation.

And though he condemned her for her pride in advance, Papa had only glowed with his own. 'No sin in a man, missy, to revel in Adam's lot,' he said. Through her, Papa had even earned the envy of some of the Millerite Brethren who were supposed to all be beyond such concerns once they'd accepted the imminent Advent of God's Kingdom.

'Rebekah,' said her mother.

A voice Rebekah had not heard in four years. Or was it only the wind?

The bell tolled again down in Port Gibson. Her brothers' voices, still out of time, said, 'Thy kingdom come. Thy will be done, in earth, as it is in heaven...'

Her hair pulled hard now, leaping up as if to fly free to Heaven of its own accord, a scalped flow of red curls as still-burning offering to God. Rebekah tried to reach up to grab her locks and stop the pain, but Papa and Jachin and Boaz held her tight to the good New York earth, arms close to her body.

The creaking was louder now, almost thunder, though she could still see nothing but moonlit clouds and countryside. Everything seemed calm and hot as a summer day.

Was Glory hot?

She had always imagined it to be cool, the inside of an icehouse, pale blue and welcoming, vast galleries of glazed brick and glittering glass.

The burning wind whirled around her like a dust devil, carrying the scent of iron stoves and dark herbs, green-brown and crumbling within their golden caskets. Her mother's voice stirred again, almost lost inside the whispering air and hot scents. 'Rebekah, lift yourself up to me.'

In the autumn of 1840 Mama had been knocked into the Erie Canal by the baker boy's mule. The cart driving along the cobbled track on the south bank had swerved to avoid a dog. A wheel had come loose, the mule panicked as the load buckled and dragged, then danced to the left, shoving Mama hard, her hand tearing away from Rebekah's. It was an accident, pure and simple, with a dozen witnesses or more. After falling in, Mama had splashed to the surface, laughing at her second baptism and calling up to folk on the bank just as a wheat barge came down the canal.

The wooden hull took her in the head, splitting the smile and the red curls like a summer melon, spilling Mama's life into the canal the way a slaughtered lamb spilled its life for the dinner table.

Rebekah had run to hurl herself from the canal bank intent to save, or perhaps join, Mama. Some men caught her and held her back while she screamed her throat to leather. Finally a bailiff and a slaughterman, both strong men and kind, led her away to a couch in a nearby parlor where Doctor Verdain fed her tincture of laudanum. She refused to eat bread or anything of grain thereafter. Papa had finally forced her to do so once again in order to thicken her locks for the Advent.

'Give us this day our daily bread. And forgive us our debts, as we forgive our debtors...' The bell continued to ring.

Rebekah listened for her Mama on the wind that whirled hot and hard. It carried a fine grit like dirt in her mouth from being facedown in the schoolyard. She spat it free, struggling against the strain on her hair.   'Mama, I'm here. We're here. Where are you?'

Jachin had always been hard to love. Her first memories of him were a surly and quick-tempered brother who would take her corn syrup taffy away when no one looked, then shriek that she had tried to steal his away from him.

The years of their childhood had made him little easier, though she and Mama often spoke of it over washing or pickling or cheese making.

'I want to run in the woods like they do,' Rebekah said,

tapping her foot instead of stomping around the room as Jachin would have. 'I want to *see* things, to *do* things.'

Mama laughed and shrugged as she kneaded dough. 'Men are what they are, in the image of their Maker. It is us women who keep food in the house and sheets on the bed. As the word of Our Lord says, "Thy desire shall be to thy husband, and he shall rule over thee."'

'Doesn't say my brothers rule over me,' Rebekah grumbled.

Mama just laughed again.

Jachin was always the thorn, always the tease, until Marley Williamson, the Methodist preacher's boy, had caught her feeding ducks down behind the mill one Sunday afternoon. In those months after Mama had died Rebekah found herself preferring solitude.

'Ho,' he'd said, standing close and taking her free arm in his.

She was that year growing into her womanly charms, and felt already blood-hot and poorly made. But this greasy lout with his breath like tobacco was not the sort of lad of whom she dreamed, especially within the cloud of her grief. 'Go away, Marley.' She pushed at him.

'I don't think so.' His voice was soft, practiced. 'My Daddy's important in this town. People listen to what I say.' He grabbed her chin and planted a clumsy kiss upon her face. 'What if I tell them you are a wanton?'

'My Papa would never believe.'

'My Daddy could buy your Papa with his pocket money.' Marley grinned, showing brown-stained teeth. 'Your Papa would be—'

Then Jachin had grabbed Marley by the collar and thrown him down. He lodged two hard kicks in Marley's ribs, after which Jachin took Marley's elbow and bent it back until it cracked like green kindling. Rebekah winced and screwed her eyes shut.

'She is my sister,' Jachin said in a low voice. 'Next time you come near her, I shall crack your head and dance on your brains.'

When she tried to thank her brother, he just scowled. 'You are not worth my breath. I was defending Papa's honor.'

Nonetheless, she knew what was in his heart. After that day no one in town was ever less than polite to Rebekah. Though Jachin could still not find a smile for her, his hard words lost their edge and his pranks came to an end.

Again the bell tolled down in Port Gibson. Jachin and Boaz lurched onward through their prayer, still making a hash of Our Lord's words. 'And lead us not into temptation, but deliver us from evil...'

Her brother's prayer echoing in her ears, Rebekah tried to raise her arms. 'Mama,' she cried in a voice that was no stronger than her mother's wind-speech, 'I cannot come to you.' The canal had swept the red stain of life away in moments. No one had let Rebekah go to Mama then, either.

Her hair strained harder, roots popping and snapping in pinpoints of fine pain, bright as the stars between the clouds above her. The scent of the hot wind of Glory had changed to a bakery smell, sweet and yeasty and death by drowning all mixed together—Mama's smell.

'Papa and the boys must come with me,' Rebekah said. Papa had said so. Over and over, he had told her that.

'The angels will take us up to God's Kingdom by our hair, and by God what is yours is the family's, girl!' He snatched a log from the woodbox and in his frustration smashed it into the wall. Rebekah stumbled against the stove, jumped away from the burning heat on her hands, and stumbled again, falling with her back in the washtub. Sawdust and ashes on the floor were so much grit on the pulsing pain in her palms.

'I won't—' she began, trying to protest she had made no argument against Papa or Brother Fowler. Papa had been so unreasonable with her since Mama died.

'Don't you mouth me back, neither!' The log shattered with the second blow. Her father began to sob just as Boaz stepped into the cabin.

'Wha ... wha ... what have you di ... di ... did to her?' Boaz asked Papa.

With a loud and wordless groan, Papa fled, slipping on the doorstep. Boaz stood staring after him then turned to Rebekah. 'It ... it ... it's Mama, ain't it?'

'She's in the Kingdom of Heaven,' Rebekah said quietly, ignoring the searing pain in her hands. 'Papa just wants us to go to her, clothed in Glory.'

'Clo ... clo ... clothed in glo ... o ... ory.' Boaz smiled then. This was one of his rare moments that could make everyone forget all that was wrong with him and see only the brilliant child of God.

The bell tolled yet again. Somehow, within the prayer, Boaz had caught up with Jachin, his voice strong and clear as it never was at any other time. 'For Thine is the kingdom, and the power, and the glory, for ever...'

Then her mother was in front of Rebekah, arms on her hips with a familiar, frustrated smile. 'Are you coming or not, girl?'

Mama's face was whole, her hair down to her neck, her clothes dry. She looked just as she had before she died in the canal. The creaking noise still echoed in Rebekah's ears, now more like the sound of great wings than the straining of barge ropes. Squinting in the moonlight, Rebekah thought she saw wings behind Mama, huge and glorious, great as New York state, powerful as Niagara, but at the same time ethereal as steam from a kettle.

'I... I...' Rebekah said. For a moment she felt as if she spoke with Boaz' mouth. Then, finding her voice, 'Are you an angel?

Have you come to help found the Kingdom?'

Mama shook her head. 'Every man must find his own Kingdom, Rebekah. I am come for you.'

'Papa. My brothers. We go as a family.'

Her hair was tugged again, hard and sharp. It was not Mama's hand on her head, Rebekah realised, for Mama stood before her, wings sweeping high into the night sky.

Who pulled on her then?

As if in answer, the hot wind swirled again. Mama smiled, her teeth gleaming diamond-bright in the moonlight. 'You, Rebekah. You are my daughter, you are my heart's heir in this mortal coil. I am come for you.'

Rebekah blinked away more tears—smoke, sadness, pain, it did not matter which filled her eyes. Papa could be hard, but he loved her. Jachin was, well, Jachin. A man young and headstrong, but still her brother. Boaz would never make his way in the world without the help of family.

Her help.

And what about her own hopes?

'I cannot go without them, Mama,' she said, though their fingers on her arm were like millstones. Papa and her brothers still lived, still needed her.

Her mother's smile tightened to a grimace, while the great upswept wings became narrower, more solid, the ghosts of feathers winding themselves into ropes that bound Mama at the back and neck. 'In Heaven, everyone has his place, and every place is prepared. Your place is beside me, Rebekah.'

The swirling wind was hot again, laden with the scent of scorched iron and stone—something like she'd always imagined deserts to be. Could Heaven be a desert? What was Glory but an eternal dwelling among the unmoving ranks of angels? Brother Fowler said, 'God's is an everlasting Kingdom that shall stand forever.'

It would be a fixed eternity, Rebekah thought, like being a stone lodged within the earth, never to be turned by a farmer's plow or washed by the rain. 'No,' Rebekah whispered. 'I don't want a *place*, Mama. I want *life*, a husband, children. I want to talk to a Red Indian and ride one of those new railroads and … and…'

Words failed Rebekah as her heart pounded. Mama's eyes turned to ice, the ropes became chains, the hot wind chilling quickly. 'I must go,' Mama said, 'for the midnight bell is almost done. Your place is with me, always. Papa and your brothers, they—'

Then Mama was gone, shooting into the sky as bright and fast as any Independence Day fireworks rocket, while the bell tolled loudly enough to be the last trump. Jachin and Boaz finished their prayer together with an echoing 'Amen.'

Papa released Rebekah's arm and dropped to his knees.

'It is ended,' he said, weeping into his hands. 'God did

not come for us. We are sinners and fools, doomed to a great disappointment.'

But God had *come,* Rebekah thought, though she kept her lips still. At the least, He had sent Mama. The Kingdom was real, too much so, frightening in the fierce iron heat of God's love. Scalp aching, she sat down next to Papa, her hand now on his shoulder. 'It will be well.'

Jachin squatted on Papa's other side, glaring darkly at Rebekah. 'Let us wait for dawn, lest Brother Miller miscalculated his day. Time may run different in the lands of Glory.'

So the family sat now, instead of standing, chewing on slick grass to assuage their hunger as the scents and sounds of night eventually faded to the orange eastern glow.

Papa hugged his children, staring intent into the fire that heralded the new day. 'The Lord answers our morning prayer,' he said, his voice still thickened with sadness, 'by giving light with regard to our disappointment.' He looked first at Jachin, then Boaz, and finally at Rebekah.

'My child,' Papa whispered. 'Your hair.'

She reached up to touch her curly locks. They were straight now, and brittle, something she had not noticed in the night. Pulling a length of her hair around for inspection, she saw that the beautiful red had become bone-white.

Mama's parting gift, or curse, perhaps, removing her cause and case for vanity. Rebekah did not have it in herself to mourn her beauty.

She sneezed then, finally chilled to the bone by the morning dew. Still weeping for Glory, her father and brothers gathered her up and went in search of a more mortal sort of fire by which to warm them all. She did not need a place in Heaven, if indeed it was Heaven that had sent her mother amid the stench of hot iron and gritty winds. She had her family here in Port Gibson. She had made her own choice.

Mama, Rebekah thought, *my life will be long and I will see wonders in this world. Life itself, not Heaven's grace, is your greatest gift to me.*

Jay Lake lives in Portland, Oregon, with his books and two inept cats, where he works on numerous writing and editing projects, including the World Fantasy Award-nominated *Polyphony* anthology series from Wheatland Press. Current projects include *Rocket Science* and *TEL : Stories.* His next novel, *Trial of Flowers,* is a fall, 2006 release from Night Shade Books, while *Mainspring* will be released summer, 2007 from Tor. Jay is the winner of the 2004 John W. Campbell Award for Best New Writer, and a multiple nominee for the Hugo and World Fantasy Awards.

DAUGHTER OF THE RED CRANES

SUE ISLE

Cai Mei sat in the shabbily carpeted hallway outside her family's seventh-level flat in the Peace Hotel, playing chess with her neighbour from one level down. She almost never won but it was good practice, kept her brain sharp. The move she had just made had at least stopped the little horror for a moment; As he thought his eyes closed almost to slits in the babyfat of his cheeks. Then he pushed forward a knight and Cai Mei said all the bad words she knew.

'Zhang Lian!' the shrill cry from the stairwell followed her oath, so fast Mei thought Lian's mother had actually heard her.

'Mate in seven,' Lian said. He stood up, bowed unsteadily to her and waddled reluctantly away, having learned that if he didn't, his mother would come and fetch him and carry him bodily down the stairs no matter who was there to see. Or else she would say something about him still wearing diapers. After all, Mei thought with some sympathy, he wasn't three yet and so spoiled it was no wonder toilet training was taking a bit longer than it should. Most of the Peace's population worshipped him. They had been the same way with her when she was smaller, she and Lian being the only two children born here in the past twelve years. The grandmothers said once no one had wanted girls, that *their* grandmothers had lived in a time when only one child was allowed for each woman, so girls were often killed or abandoned in hopes that another pregnancy might produce a male. She unfolded long skinny legs and peered at the board as she picked it up. It looked like he was right about the mate. Again.

Then she noticed something else as she turned to brush dust from her skirt. There was *blood*, a long drying stain, low down on the material. Alarmed, Mei pulled the skirt around after checking that no one had come into the hallway. Yes, definitely blood. She felt a cold tension in her stomach as she recalled what her mother had said, over and over since Mei could remember. 'When you are ready to become a woman, you may bleed. Not many of us do now, not since the sicknesses of the Emptying, but my mother did, I did and so may you. If it happens you must tell me or your grandmother at once. No one else.'

Cai Mei quickly went into their flat, wearing the skirt wrong-way around and carrying the chess board so that no one else would see.

That night, Cai Mei awoke very suddenly to find her grandmother sitting on the end of the bed in her little alcove. She blinked, wondering whether Cai Shan was actually a dream and if so, what it meant that she should dream of her grandmother. 'Hello, honoured grandmother,' she managed. 'Are you here in spirit?'

'Not quite,' Cai Shan replied drily, 'but it is good to know that your manners don't desert you when you are surprised from sleep. Get up and dress, granddaughter, we must talk.'

Her mother had said so little when Mei told her about the blood. She had come in from some excursion and was carefully cleaning a ragged cut in her arm when Mei found her. The black sleeve of her tunic was rolled up and her unusual pale brown hair half pulled out of its usually neat braid. When her daughter spoke, she listened, face expressionless, and then nodded. That was all.

Now, Cai Jia Li stood by their apartment door like a guard, again dressed in black, with the red ribbon signifying their femclan, the Red Cranes, threaded through her braid. Cai Shan glanced at her daughter, put a hand to her granddaughter's shoulder to halt her before the door. 'Have they arrived?'

'They are in the hall,' Jia answered her mother. It was as though Mei was not even there, which made her both anxious and upset. Then someone knocked twice on their door and Jia opened it. Outside was a spread-out group of women, some of whom Mei knew from meetings of the Red Cranes. As a child, she had always been sent to another Peace household for the evening but sometimes she had seen them arrive and longed to be one of them. The Red Cranes were well respected and Mei had had all the usual fight training from the time she could walk, same as her mother and grandmother before her, but that was not the same as being one of them. She sometimes wondered whether she would ever use that training for anything but play.

Cai Shan pushed Mei slightly. 'Let's go,' she said and the Red Cranes moved aside, except for two of them continuing in the lead. The others fell in around the girl and the old woman in procession to the stairwell, where the group waited while one young woman ran down ahead and called back, her voice a high eerie echo, to say all was well.

'Why are they doing this?' Mei asked her grandmother. Her mother had fallen back amongst the others and Mei could not speak to her. 'This is home. Of course all is well.'

Cai Shan only signed her to silence. Now Mei was frightened. Her grandmother was not even complaining about the stairs or that no one was helping her. They walked down three flights, then emerged into another hall and turned left, into the centre of the building. This was Red Cranes territory; where secret training and teaching took place and where she and Lian were firmly moved on if they ventured to play anywhere nearby. This hall was bare, wooden-floored and musty-smelling and barely wide enough for two people to walk side by side. Once it had been wider, Mei knew, once the Peace had been bright and elegant and filled with people who came to eat delicious food and meet friends and dance. The Red Cranes walking ahead of her ran the length of the hall and came back, again saying all was well. Mei looked at the doors they passed. They were barred and boarded so heavily that it seemed they were never meant to be opened. Halfway down the hall her grandmother stopped her in front of one door, closed only with a heavy bolt.

'Open it,' she said. Mei struggled to do so but no one helped her or said anything. Fear made her clumsy but she eventually achieved her aim and found herself standing in an even smaller passageway. There was someone at the end of it, barely visible in the gloom, but Mei closed her eyes for a moment. When she opened them, she could see that the person was a grandmother, one of the oldest Mei could ever remember seeing. This was Wang Hu, aged one hundred and three, who had not been seen outside her apartment since before Mei was born. She opened her mouth to say something polite to the grandmother but then heard the women closing and bolting the door behind her.

'Do not worry about them,' the grandmother said sternly. 'I do not have many words left, Cai Mei, daughter of Cai Jia Li, and if I am to use them for you, they will not be wasted. Do you understand?' Mei nodded. She had to nod. The old woman's fierceness was like that of a fire which has used nearly all of its fuel. She could spare nothing. 'You are twelve years old and you have bled. You are possibly the only fertile female of childbearing age in our femclan. The others we had have been killed or kidnapped by other groups. This is why you have been a prisoner for your childhood years. Now, you must do another thing which you do not understand. You will experience pain and fear and when it is done, we will shut you up once more until your child is born. The man beyond this door is our prisoner also. We have taken him from the harbour near one of the foreign ships which visit Shanghai, at great risk. Three women died in the kidnap. One was my own granddaughter. Yet we are not in the past, when a woman was worthless unless she bore a son. You have the choice whether to pass the door or to remain a child.'

'Will I go home?' Cai Mei whispered.

The ancient white-haired woman did not answer the question. 'Choose, Cai Mei,' she said.

Like I have a choice, Mei thought. If she refused, they might let her go but she would have to pass her mother and grandmother who kept watch outside above, lest the Jade Dragons come before this night was done. It was unimaginable that they would come to the Peace, those creatures she knew only by name, but there was no possibility of contradicting the grandmother. She looked at the blank door. 'I—I will pass the door,' she said.

'And now I will instruct you in the ways of a woman,' the grandmother said. 'Sit here and listen. The man beyond has been told he must not hurt you; that he will be hurt and perhaps killed if he does hurt you. You will spend the night here and then the next night, and the next until we know you have a child.'

A man ... Cai Mei choked on a hundred questions. She had rarely ever seen a male. Before she was born, the massive crush of humanity had finally destroyed Shanghai, her mother had told her. It had been the place where China and breakaway Taiwan had finally become one, creating peace across the waters, in a last desperate attempt to heal, but wars had erupted between the peoples, the tribes of Europeans and Indians and Chinese and all the others who had made Shanghai their home. They had ripped the city apart and the ancient structure which had preserved it for so long could no longer maintain itself. The men had left Shanghai in their hundreds, seeking food and water for their families. Most had never returned. Many of the women and children left behind weakened and died, until the survivors learned to take care of themselves and take the best of their past to feed their future. She listened, half numb, as the grandmother's wispy voice told her what she might expect, the actions she must perform and what the male's responses might be.

By the time the door opened, Mei was not hearing much of it at all. She had shut her mind away into the last chess game she had played with little Zhang Lian, solitary lord of the Red Cranes. She barely felt the grandmother's hand between her shoulder blades, part benediction, part simply making sure she did not turn and bolt. Then the door was shut behind her and she was looking at an alien human being who rolled up from a narrow bed and stared at her in shock. She should not have tried to move up that last pawn, Mei thought dimly, that had wasted time and she had not been able to bring her knight into play quickly enough when she needed it...

'What in hell is going on? Who are you?'

She blinked awake again, back in the cramped wooden-walled, windowless room. His hair was the colour of demons, fire-coloured and he had a short beard of the same shade, making it difficult for Mei to estimate his age. His eyes weren't clearly visible in the lamplight, but as he looked up from the bed, they appeared to be the colour of the sky. His skin was pinkish white beneath a torn shirt and trousers of faded blue. He had spoken Mandarin, but clumsily, the way Lian still sometimes did, because no one corrected him. 'I'm not going to hurt you,' he added awkwardly. 'Maybe those women who shoved me in here are something else, but you're just a child. What's your name?'

'Mei.' She managed to unfreeze her tongue. 'Mei.'

He managed a smile, very nervous, and she saw that he was young after all, perhaps twenty or not much beyond it. Even though he was so big, twice the size of her mother or any other adult woman, it was a frightened boy that the Red Cranes had trapped here. 'Pleased to meet you, Mei. I'm Andrew Tennant—and the reason I look so strange to you, I guess, is that I'm from the other side of the world, from Australia. You ever hear about Australia?' When she only looked blank he added, 'What about history, do they teach you history?'

She nodded. 'The history of China and of Shanghai and something of the many ships which visited before the Emptying and, the grandmothers say, are beginning to visit again now that the waters are peaceful once more.'

'Not if they keep doing stuff like this.' He sat up carefully as though his body hurt to move and rubbed a shoulder, wincing. 'What am I here for? I hadn't heard that Shanghai had turned cannibal but those women were pretty damn insistent about dragging me in here.'

The word 'cannibal' did not mean anything to Mei but she knew the grandmother had not said it. Yet she was suddenly reluctant to tell him what the grandmother had said, what she had been commanded to do as the price of adulthood. Into the silence she heard a small scratching behind her, that could have been a rat behind the wall, but which she knew was the grandmother's reminder.

'I must stay here the night,' she blurted. 'They have shut me in. This is so that the other femclans will not interrupt.'

'I don't understand that word "femclan",' the fire-haired young man said, frowning. 'I learned Mandarin from old people who emigrated as children on the last of the refugee boats to make it to Australia.'

Mei nodded, glad for another topic, however temporary. She was glad he could speak her language because this meant she need not tell him that she could speak all the languages of Shanghai. 'The word means a group, a clan,' she said. 'It is female because there are almost no males here now. Before I was born, they had to leave Shanghai to look for food. You cannot drink the water of the Huangpo without treating it but many did and they died. So now...' She could not look at him. 'Now you must give me a child because I am a woman this night and they say the Jade Dragons, who claim the area outside the Peace, may try to take us. It belongs to us, the Red Cranes, not to them but they do not agree. That is why the door is sealed and my mother and grandmother are outside.'

Andrew Tennant stared at her in horror. He shook his head. 'You're a *child*,' he protested. 'No way can I do that. Why don't they send someone a bit older, if they have to, you know...'

'There were diseases,' Mei said, remembering her school lessons. 'The Elders made them, the people who lived a hundred years ago when the oldest grandmother was a child. There were too many people and they were trying to prevent so many children. Something went wrong and even fewer boys were born than before. Then another disease made many women unable to have children at all. Most women do not...' She broke off. She didn't have to say it. Her own bleeding did not make it certain that she could bear children but at least it might be possible. No time could be wasted.

'You don't look all Chinese, you know, if you don't mind my saying,' he said suddenly. 'Mostly, but there's something in the shape of your face and eyes.'

Mei nodded. 'My grandmother's man was one of your people,' she said. 'A Westerner, I mean, I don't know if he was from Aus-tra-lia.'

'We're from all over, I suppose,' he said. 'Well, anyway, that could be why you're resistant to that created plague. I mean, obviously your mother was, too. Any other kids in your family?'

'No. Only Zhang Lian in our apartment building.'

'His family any relation to yours?'

'His mother is the cousin of my mother.'

'There you are.'

Again the faint scratching behind Mei's head as she stood near the door. She swallowed the last moisture in her mouth and longed for a drink, but there was no water. She began to take off her clothes. The young man let out a protesting yelp and put a hand in front of his eyes. 'Don't do that!'

'I've told you I must,' she said.

The scratching, louder. This time Andrew Tennant heard it and glanced towards the noise in time to see Mei react by turning towards the sound. 'Are they there?' he asked in disbelief. 'Who did you say—your mother and grandmother are there on guard to make sure—?'

'Of course.' She finished and stood there, a little chilly even though the night was so warm. She walked to the bed, wondering what to do. She could not wrestle him out of his clothes and the grandmother had not said what should happen if the stranger refused to cooperate. She *had* said some unexpected things about what to do if he couldn't. 'Please,' Mei added. 'They will release you to your people if you do this, but if you do not they may kill you.'

Andrew Tennant stared at her as though he had forgotten all his words. Mei thought of the strange, serious way her own mother had looked at her as she guarded the door, as though her daughter was both unknown to her and the most precious thing in the world. She tried to will herself to look like that. Andrew Tennant began to talk very swiftly, almost incoherently: 'Look, Mei, let me talk to my friends on the ship I'm from. We can arrange something to help your people, your Red Cranes and the rest. That's why we're here, to talk to the local people, to help—there's a doctor on the ship, maybe she can help, but *no way* am I having sex with someone your age. Don't take this wrong, please, you'll be real cute in a few years but not now, no way, no how.'

Mei took another step until her legs were up against the

bed. With him seated they were of a height. She reached for his shirt and tugged, hoping the material would tear but it did not. Tennant pushed away from her, grimacing, trying to stop her and at the same time not touch her. 'The women outside will hurt you,' she said. She knew only the child's pain of falling on concrete steps, of an adult's hard hand smacking her leg, of nausea within her stomach when bad food or water got past the medical checks. She had to do this; no one else could. She knelt on the bed and he fell back, almost comic if not for the repulsed look in his eyes as though she was something spoiled and rotten.

There was a thump, as though something or someone heavy had fallen against the wall beside the door. Mei and Tennant jumped. Before he could ask any more questions, shouting followed the thump. A young woman's voice, high and strong and urgent. Mei had never heard anyone shout like that inside the rooms and hallways of the Peace. Tennant scrambled up and managed to get off the narrow bed and stride the few paces to the barred door. He rapped on it and shouted for someone to come in, but there was no response.

'No!' Mei hissed. 'If the Jade Dragons are inside you must not tell them where we are.'

More shouting drowned them out, a scream and the report of a pistol. They would be old weapons, Mei knew, from stockpiles hidden by the last Government of the People's Democratic Republic of China. The Red Cranes had them also and there had been many, many skirmishes since she was a small child. Mei had seen none, heard several. Old weapons, many of which did not work properly, but some worked well enough. Tennant jumped to his feet. 'Get under the bed, Mei. You're small enough to squeeze under there and they won't see you. Put your damn clothes on first!'

His voice was filled with exasperation rather than panic, and it was that more than anything else that encouraged Mei to obey him. She put on her trousers and shirt and squirmed under the bunk while Tennant faced the door again. 'Grandmother? Old lady? Open up the door and come in here, sounds like you'll be safer that way. Can you hear me?'

If she did, she made no reply.

'Mei, is there another way out of this room? Have they boarded over another door?'

'I don't know. I have never been here before. I have never been anywhere.'

Sharp voices rose outside and then the grandmother's dry-leaves voice. She must still be on her chair before the bolted door, but Mei could not make out her words. Then there was a whispering scream, then shouts and running feet. Then silence, for long enough that Tennant went to the door and began looking for a way to open it. He jumped back and swore as something heavy struck the outside, once, twice, many times. Tennant shouted in his own language but Mei could not recognise many of the words he used. Then she smelled smoke. 'They have set the Peace on fire!' she gasped and struggled out from under the bunk.

'No, they haven't,' Tennant replied. 'They're burning through the door.'

'That will be the same thing!'

'No.' She struggled to button her shirt properly, while he stared at the door, in which a black patch had appeared, smoking and growing larger. A tiny flame burned at its heart. Another blow rattled the walls and a human fist appeared through the burnt and brittle wood, sheathed in heavy black leather. Someone swore in Tennant's language. Mei, who had readied herself for the arrival of the Jade Dragons, who would kidnap her and kill Tennant, listened in shock. Tennant heard it, too; she glanced at him and saw the new hope in his face. 'It's Andrew Tennant,' he called out. 'For God's sake don't come in shooting. There's a kid in here.'

'Open the bloody door then,' another voice answered in his language and Mei jumped in shock; that was a woman's voice.

'We're locked in.'

'Hang on then, we've almost burned around the lock.'

A few moments later the door swung inwards and the two prisoners saw a helmeted and armoured figure in the doorway. 'Follow me,' she said.

'Whitford?'

'Yeah. You sure did manage to screw up your shore leave, Andrew.' Then the cheerful voice faded as she turned to Mei. 'I know I look scary,' she said in clumsy Mandarin, 'but Andrew can tell you I'm a nice person. Now, I want you to walk out of here after me and just stare at my back, all right? Don't turn your head to look at anything else. We're going to go down the stairwall to the main lobby—I guess it was the hotel's main lobby—and outside.'

'Are you a demon?' Mei blurted.

'No, I'm a girl,' the cheerful voice said. 'It's just I'm not supposed to take the helmet off. Can you follow me now?'

'Yes, but I do not wish to leave the Peace. I want to go back to my home on the seventh level. My mother and grandmother will come back to look for me there if the Jade Dragons have chased them away. If they have been captured,' Mei said resolutely, 'then there are people at home who will take care of me.'

'We'll see about taking you home once we get Andrew back safe,' the voice promised from the blind black helmet. Mei thought there was glass in the front, but it looked so dark to her she could not understand how the woman might see through it.

'Move it along there, Whitford!' a deep male voice shouted, only a few paces beyond the woman. Mei gasped and leapt back, knocking into Tennant.

'Cool it, Shane! There's a little girl here and she's scared silly.'

'So am I,' said the deep voice, 'and I'm telling you we seriously have to move it along.'

'Come on, Mei,' Tennant said gently and it was that which got her moving. She stared at the black-armoured back as the woman Whitford had told her. Tennant was at her back and he rested a hand on her shoulder as though to stop her running. 'Don't look at anything,' he told her. 'Just walk.'

They took her back to the stairs she had climbed down to get here and began to descend. A blinding light brighter than anything Mei knew burned her eyes and turned the darkness to brightest day. At the first landing there was something crumpled on the dusty concrete and she balked against the push of Tennant's hand on her shoulder. The fallen form had cloudy white hair; it was the ancient grandmother Wang Hu. Had the black demons killed her because she could not bear children; in their ignorance not understanding that the grandmothers held all wisdom, that without them there would be no memory?

The huge armoured shape identified as 'Shane' laboriously knelt beside the fragile shape, as his comrades tried to move around him, taking Mei with them despite her struggle to get free of Tennant's hand.

'She's alive,' the behemoth called. 'Go on, I'll bring her.'

Gunfire echoed from elsewhere in the Peace, but Mei's confused ears and brain could not determine from where. Tennant's people, she thought, they must be fighting the Jade Dragons. But how could they tell who was Jade Dragon and who was Red Crane? They didn't know what the signs meant and they were dragging her, making it impossible for her to resist, past landing after landing until the armoured demon carrying that blazing light pushed through a doorway into the enormous, high-ceilinged area just in front of the last guardpost. There was no one on duty at the stations. Andrew Tennant put his arm around her shoulders and made her walk among them to the tall elegant doors, standing open, their glass shattered like jewels. Mei tried to stop again, pleading, 'I must not go out there!'

'Sweetie, you have to. It's not safe here. If we get you out of this hotel we can move you somewhere that *is* safe.'

'But my family won't know where to find me!'

'We'll find them. Now come on!'

Someone shrieked in the distance but the black demons ignored the cry. Shanghai was full of screams, whispers and skittering of feet that had nothing to do with their problems. Behind them was Mei's world, echoing with gunfire. She went with them and their blazing light into the street she had never seen. With her mother or grandmother on guard, she had been allowed on to the upper balconies to hear the voices of Shanghai, but her feet had never touched the ground. Like an Empress, they had said when she was very small, and laughed. Now, Mei still felt very small. The hugeness of the city made her want to crouch down. Buildings reared like cliffs into strange shapes against the black sky. Some were clear glass, arrows aimed at heaven, twisted shapes crowded against one another in an impossible tangle of giant toys. There were so few people that she couldn't imagine the city crammed with millions who needed all this space and all these buildings that she knew only from ancient photos and computer prints, though the Red Cranes had no working computers. One such image she recalled was that of the Jade Buddha Temple; centuries old and protected from harm by the grace of the spirits. The picture showed it gaudy by daylight and populated with smiling monks and visitors. Mei's frightened eyes suddenly saw the real temple, right there by the road she walked; a shell, ghostly and frightening in the shadows. The monks who had protected it for generations, were long gone but she prayed silently to their spirits to help her.

Then a great thundering noise from the sky made her think the buildings were falling on their heads. She froze but Tennant pulled her aside, into the leaf-strewn courtyard of the deserted temple. 'It's all right, it's one of ours,' he shouted, forgetting to use Mandarin and almost unintelligible in any case, but she heard the relief in his voice. The other black-armoured demon—Whitford—closed in on her other side as though believing Mei would run. *I may know nothing of the world outside the Peace*, she wanted to shout at them, *but do you think I would disgrace my clan, my family? My mother, my grandmother are not here and perhaps they are dead but they will still see me.*

What she saw now was a monster descending from the sky, wearing a huge blazing light which turned the night-shadowed courtyard to day. Lian had little toys like that, with rotating wings as though they should fly. She had never believed they were real. The monster howled and rattled and hissed as it lowered itself to the ground, needing half the courtyard area to do so. It lurched as though it would strike the temple and Mei had to stop herself cowering. Whitford stood forward in front of her and Tennant and stretched out both her arms, waving the light she carried. The noise was too great for any human voice to be heard, great enough to thunder through Mei's head and half stun her. The flying machine lurched again and she looked at Tennant. He was frowning and reached to tap Whitford's arm, but before he had a chance to communicate anything, a doorway opened in the machine when it was still Tennant's height or more from the ground.

A figure crouched in that entrance and leapt. Its slenderness and lack of armour was what warned Mei and she grabbed Tennant, desperately trying to pull his hand so that he would follow her away. Instead he drew a gun from his belt. Whitford was already shooting. The machine fell sideways the rest of the way to the paving stones and stopped its thunder in a series of coughs.

Stupid to shoot, of course. The Jade Dragons would never be where a bullet was. Even as Whitford fired, half a dozen people had already dropped from the commandeered monster and one, with a neat leap and roll, had come in past the two westerners and pulled Mei neatly backwards, with a slim, iron-strong arm around the girl's throat.

Whitford struggled with two Dragons. Tennant whirled to see where Mei had gone and saw her in her captor's grasp. He held up his hands. Mei coughed and the grip on her throat lessened a little. She went limp as though the pressure had made her faint and fell to the paving stones. It was hard not to break her own fall but she did it, slumping gracelessly against the Jade Dragon's legs. Above her she heard somebody moving and the thump of fist against flesh and only then did she move, rolling over and over like a desperate insect trying to escape childish persecution. Why hadn't another of the Jade Dragons stopped her? She had never expected to get away with this, only to give Andrew Tennant some sort of a chance to use his weapon. Mei opened her eyes to a silence of ghosts.

They were like ghosts, the ring of slim, black-clad forms around her. Perhaps ten, eleven... her eyes blurred. None of them were much older than she was, she saw with shock, and not all wore the green ribbon of the Jade Dragons. Before her was a woman of the White Tigers and two bearing the facial tattoos of the Sun Bears. None of them were moving and when she clambered to her feet, she turned about and saw why. In the entrance to the temple courtyard was another of the black-armoured demons, who carried the ancient Wang Hu in his arms. Clutching the demon's belt, looking insufferably at ease, toddled little Zhang Lian.

'You girls have nearly destroyed your hope of a future,' Wang Hu announced. Her acerbic voice was like the faintest wind but a wind that carried acid. 'I saw you try to land this *helicopter gunship*.' The last two words were in English but she waved contemptuously at the lopsided machine. 'You nearly dropped it right into the temple. You have no idea of what you are doing.'

'*We* have no grandmothers,' the solitary White Tiger was stung to complain. 'We are doing what we can. We have had no children born in ten years and we will do what we must. We have given our territory and our people over to the Jade Dragons' rule for the chance of children.'

The ancient woman laughed in the faint, restrained way of her people and her time. It left lacerations. The White Tiger woman faded back behind the others. The grandmother, Mei thought as she tried not to smile in sudden hope, behaved as though she sat on a throne clad in silks, not held like a baby in the arms of a desperately embarrassed foreign devil.

'Children! You are all children! If you take this girl with you, these foreign devils here will follow and smoke you out. If you have the sense to talk, bring your elders here if you have them and they can talk with these devils, who will bring you medicines and knowledge. You, devil, tell these children why you are here.'

Andrew Tennant took a moment to gather his thoughts into Mandarin.

'We came to understand,' he said slowly. 'To meet your people, to re-establish trade links that were broken many years ago. When the cities finally died we thought there was no hope. We've been looking all over the world and found only a few scattered groups of survivors.'

'The city is still here,' Mei said, surprising herself but the ancient woman in the one called Shane's arms bowed her head a little in benediction and pointed at the girl. 'We are still here. And here...' She walked up to Shane, knelt beside Zhang Lian and took the little boy's hand. 'Are you well?' she asked.

He nodded solemnly, eyes fixed on her. She would not ask about his family yet, Mei thought, or hers. 'This is Zhang Lian. They—people say he may build the spaceships again, so that they will fly to the moon and to the planets as they did before. He can beat any of you at chess. Do you have anyone who can do that?'

She saw Andrew Tennant make a sign at his friends and after a pause, both Whitford and Shane pulled off their helmets. Shane was dark-skinned and wavy-haired, making Andrew seem small. Whitford's eyes, in the bright searchlights, were the colour of the daytime sky.

'We *were* looking for an ambassador,' said Shane, the deep-voiced dragon.

'Yeah, but this is just a kid...' Whitford protested.

'No, she's not,' Andrew said flatly. 'Not any more. Look—Mei —you and the old lady, will you talk to us? We can't promise to help you but we'll try. And you can help us. There are bad problems out there that we can't fix; we came here hoping you can. Will you try?'

Mei looked at the grandmother, hoping to be told what to do as she had for all her twelve years, but now Wang Hu seemed to be asleep, a wisp of a creature in Shane's armoured hold. She could not fail her family, she knew. She could not fail herself. She faced the battle-weary members of the femclans and bowed, startled to see the women bow back. Then Mei turned again to Andrew Tennant to give him her answer.

Sue Isle lives in Perth, Western Australia. She has written two books for teenagers, *Scale of Dragon*, *Tooth of Wolf* and *Wolf Children*, and sold stories to Aurealis, Orb, ASIM, Agog, Borderlands, Tales of the Unanticipated [USA], which recently published *Mary bennet Goes Postal* and NSW School Magazine, which featured Sue's immortal work *Aliens Stole My Sister*. Other interests include history, sf conventions, roleplay gaming and gardening. A mixup in school meant Sue studied Chinese history alone in the library which may or may not have had anything to do with the eventual creation of 'Daughter of the Red Cranes'.

STEALING FREE

DEBORAH BIANCOTTI

Thrice-born Salamander, supple-limbed and edgy, was not at
home here. He drummed his dumpling fingertips on the echo-
drum of a hollow log, and waited.

'Salamander, you never were good at it,' said ample Kingfisher.

The kingfisher arranged jade-tipped, onyx-sheened feathers
in the melting sun. He had time to glare at the horizon, then to
turn his cold-coal stare to the rushes by the lake's edge, before
Salamander even bothered to reply.

'Good at what?'

'Waiting,' spat Kingfisher. He spun his head suddenly back to
the river, his eye caught by a sinewy ripple.

'Right,' said Salamander, craning his neck to follow
Kingfisher's gaze into glare-warmed water. He added a mutter
beneath his breath.

'What?' Kingfisher, all poor-impulse-control, could never
resist the bait.

Salamander shifted, his eyes like the pits of pawpaw. 'I said, I
can't help trying to see what you see.'

'Ha!' said Kingfisher. Then, 'Does it hurt?'

Kingfisher seemed long and mean, but wasn't. The ripple was
gone, so he twisted back to his pale-skinned companion.

'No, no, no, it never hurts,' Salamander whipped his blue-
jasper tongue at the air.

'I think you do it on purpose,' said Kingfisher.

'Why would I do that?'

'Maybe you're bored.'

'I'm bored right now, all right.'

'Maybe you like making me go out of my way, fetch and carry
for you and bring you back to the river for mending. Picking up
your pieces,' Kingfisher said, iron in his voice.

'I know you do it out of kindness, and care,' Salamander
soothed. Kingfisher was his friend, and Salamander understood
the duty there. He knew what was owed.

'This is the fourth time you've—'

'—third—'
'—that you've grown that leg back, for a start.'
'Right. Oh, this leg? No, only the second.'
'When's your—'
Fat-lipped Barramundi broke the surface then, unexpectedly close. Kingfisher tried to smooth his surprise, but the rough of feathers at his neck gave it away.

'She'll see you now, Mudpuppy,' said Barramundi, and plummeted with a flick of her tail, the silver of her scales like a neon streak.

Kingfisher swung his beak in a slow left-right. He glared balefully at the absence of Barramundi. 'Best of luck with—'

But Salamander had already gone, following the fish to the place where the gatekeeper lay.

'—that.'

Salamander was not a mudpuppy.

Descent #1

The Empress (self-declared) was a spotted gudgeon who lived in a cave that was never warm. Her chequered skin was pink-green-grey beneath her scales and the constant sway of her tail gave her a restless air. Eels attended her, swarming her sides like oily ribbons and bumping into each other with careless grace. The floor of the lair was littered with bright, smooth pebbles gathered into clumps of colour. It was the Empress's pride, and she personally oversaw the design, updating it seasonally or more often as was her mood. Today, the floors were in almost vertical lines, first white then brown, with a determined streak of black along each edge.

'We need you,' said the Empress, 'to steal. For us, something. From the Monster's hall. A prize beyond. Price. For us. For here.'

Her mouth was always curved down into a sneer, but it was worse when she spoke. She lay on a flat stone that was almost an altar. She had lived so long that the stone was slightly curved beneath the swing of her weight.

'Why me?' asked Salamander.

'It is a saltwater. Thing. And we know you. Are able. To deal with saltwater. Since your last. What do you call it? Rebirth?'

'I'll need my other arm first,' said Salamander, not disagreeing with her. 'My arm, he thought, and a plan to get out of this. 'I'll need to get my strength back.' He waggled his shoulder at her, where the stump of his arm was growing.

'We. Shall try to. Help you hurry. That along,' she said.

The Empress's powers were part magic, part force, and Salamander never knew which to expect. She may try to cure him with charms, or she might very well order other slaves to pull on his nascent arm and drag it out of him like he was a coil of rope.

'I've done more than lost an arm in your service,' Salamander said, pitching his voice to sound respectful, not accusatory.

'And we. Are grateful. Waterdog.'

The Salamander was not a waterdog either. 'Perhaps some end to my service is in order?'

A gravid pause.

'We have taken. Care of you and. We have fed. And kept you and. Watched over you and. Performed such rituals. As might enhance your returns. To life. You know.'

Salamander spoke carefully. 'I know.'

'We. Are. Still. Owed,' she said. She almost sneered. 'Where is your. Honour? That we. Enjoy so much? Where. Your duty?'

Salamander felt the heavy truth. No job could discharge the debts he'd incurred. He owed the Empress his life, more than once. He felt for a heartbeat the bitterness that all owned things feel.

'So,' said the Empress. 'Say when. Until then remember. We value you. Whatever you. Need.'

Asymptote

'Not always the same arm! Sometimes a different one,' Salamander was saying.

'Right, right,' Kingfisher was unconvinced and worse, almost indifferent. 'So they're arms because ...?'

'These have elbows, see? This arm will have an elbow when it's finished growing back.'

'I think mostly the same arm,' Kingfisher cut across Salamander. 'I think you're lazy—'

'Lazy! How—'

'—or too slow. Or maybe you just need to swap trades. Stealing's no good for you.'

'Stealing's what the Empress asks of me.'

'Then get used to growing back your arms.'

Kingfisher got in the last word by huffing out his iron wings and flying straight out at the sun.

Salamander, one of a kind, self-regenerative optimist, slipped under clear waters and walked with the barest trace of awkwardness on three legs, across pebbles as mottled-brown and perfect-smooth as his own skin. The stump of his shoulder was lighter under water. In truth, there was an ache, but it was just beyond his edge where his arm would finally be when it grew back. Each re-growth was faster, as if salamander limbs pushed themselves forward once they knew the way, running like putty along memorised lines.

Above, Kingfisher blurred and shimmied, a dark tear in the cloth of the sky. Now and then he swooped and his voice came hollow, words lost in echo.

Salamander inched ever on, spreading pads of fingers wide

to find purchase, his mind less on the task ahead and more on questions of a personal nature.

Flight

Salamander walked and swam and walked for eight days in the direction of the ocean. On the way, he surfaced but rarely, shooting out his pale blue tongue for bugs along the river's edge. Reaching the ocean, he paused, finding his breath, swallowing up the salty water until the stinging on his soft skin and throat and lungs stopped long enough that he could release himself into the beat of the waves.

It wasn't so bad, he told himself. It wasn't so bad.

The ocean smelled of tin, whereas he was used to the fulsome dank stench of the upper river. He tried not to let it get to him. Seagulls swarmed until he dipped and wiggled forward through dense water, blinking often (the salt-world was a blur to him). When he rose again, the seagulls were grey-white specks sticking close to shore. This far out, they found no purchase. Only air, and air is an empty thing at the best of times.

On a buoy, abandoned to the waves, a lone pelican squatted with her webbed toes spread, dramatic black-white wings folded. She blinked at Salamander with curiosity, sweeping her pale pink beak over and around him. The empty sack of her throat wobbled as she shifted her head back and forth, trying to hold him with yellow-black eyes that looked painted to her head.

'You?' she said, piecing him together between her disparate pupils.

'I believe we may have met,' said Salamander.

'I believe,' she said, 'you were the one to steal the trap that held me, Salamander.'

'Of sorts,' Salamander replied patiently. 'You had a torn plastic bag wrapping your foot, and I unsheathed you.'

'Stole,' said the pelican, with satisfaction.

'I hate to disagree, since we have this cheerful history,' Salamander said, the sun prickling where the water didn't reach on his neck and face, 'but I believe it's only stealing if you take something someone else wants, isn't it? I mean, if you wanted that plastic bag, that would be stealing, yes, but otherwise—'

'—what is it?' Pelican asked.

'Just taking, I should imagine.'

'I find the distinction pointless,' said Pelican.

She was joined, then, by another pelican, one that straddled the side of the buoy awkwardly, wings spread for balance.

'Pelicans,' said Salamander, addressing them both (for now there was neither room nor reason to address either one individually), 'I could do with a favour.'

And that's how Salamander stole many miles from his trip, carried safely in the throat of a pelican (he wasn't sure which), and how the debt came to be paid between the unique salamander and all the saltwater birds. For a time, at least.

Should he need a ride back, he was assured, he would be one debt in their favour. Even, he made them declare, if he was in pieces, they would carry him back to the start of the river. There, Kingfisher would find him and take care of the rest of his journey. He heard a throaty promise, ensconced in the gullet of the giant bird, and let it rock him still.

Salamander wasn't worried. He always paid in trade what he could not steal.

Descent #2

What the Empress called a Monster was an octopus, mottled honey-mustard in colour, and graceful. She lived alone in a cave like a craw. Two fat rocks marked the entrance. To leave the cave, it might be that she rolled the rocks away with her long arms. No, wait. Legs (there were no elbows). But she never left.

Salamander watched for three more days outside the cave, saltwater grating on his skin, his new arm throbbing from the long journey. He fended off the strangest and most voracious of creatures while there. The worst, a dim-witted, twenty-armed starfish. Purple-red-grey, it moved dully like a stomach on thick fingers, and Salamander chose simply to ignore it until it dragged itself away.

Sand pressed into the soles of his feet and he shifted his weight awkwardly. He gauged there was space enough for him to get inside the cave. However, if the Empress was at all correct, the treasure would require the removal of the boulders. She was expecting him to ask for help, most like, but he didn't intend it.

The octopus must be hungry. Its legs were spilling from the cave like seaweed, drifting across lumpy corals. Between the boulders its head bobbed stupidly like a fishing fly.

It must have spied something then, because its brown colouring gave way swiftly to yellow; deep blue rings blurring-bright along its legs and sides. Salamander startled. The concentrated pulse of colour was like two personalities struggling for the same skin.

Deftly, one leg snagged a passing something that crawled the ocean floor and wore a suit of blue shell. Salamander guessed a crab, but his eyes weren't adjusting right to the salt. The water hung heavy like taffy. He supposed he might not be able to do a trip like this again.

The octopus and its would-be crab disappeared inside the cave, one last bob of the bulbous flashing head marking their passage.

Salamander was used to the many forms of panic. Stage-fright-panic, nearly-getting-away-with-it-panic, about-to-admit-defeat-panic, and the panic that came right before dying, for which he had no clear name, the panic that flooded the mind and locked fast on the body. The panic he felt then was somewhere between stage fright and dying. He knew the octopus was deadly, its shocking colours the sign of passion.

Salamander never planned far ahead. It was, according to Kingfisher, what made him such a lousy thief. But in the three-day wait he'd thought perhaps he could steal into the lair of the monster secretly, through cunning alone. Now he was worried. The poison she used on her prey was harmful enough, but he understood of this creature that she had another, more deadly poison that she would release if threatened. The flash of blue brilliance still hard in his mind, Salamander grew alarmed. Cunning of the type he himself possessed (i.e. minimal) didn't feel like quite enough protection.

He did then what he always did when troubled. Marched boldly towards the source of his anxiety and hoped for the best.

At the cave's edge, he peered past the rocks to check for clear passage. Once assured, he was in, squeezing himself through the gap. He picked his way over a couple of colourful open maws that he guessed (despite his groggy eyes) were sea urchins, their prickly mouths feathered with thin, bright beards of tentacles. His tail brushed one urchin and it contracted in ecstasy, colours rippling in patterns of concentric pleasure.

On the walls were many scuttling things, wisps of biology that could have been coral, could have been fish (probably seahorses, Salamander guessed, from the speed of some of them whirring past his head with dumb intent).

'Tut-tut-tut,' said several of the wisps at once.

'Oh, shut up,' Salamander muttered.

He wondered if they'd spin ahead to warn the monstrous Octopus, but they seemed to prefer hovering around him, apparently fascinated by his careless arrival. Perhaps they were afraid of her, too.

'And no gift?'

Salamander froze.

'Beg pardon?' he asked of no one in particular, since the voice came from nowhere.

'No gift. What I mean is "you haven't brought a gift". Oh, over here. Here!'

Salamander looked towards the sound and saw only the seam where the wall of the cave met the sandy floor. Then the seam moved towards him and he realised it was a sea snake, pale yellow, flat at the tail but curved high closer towards its bullet-brown-head.

'You'll need a gift, most like,' said Sea Snake. 'And you haven't brought one.'

'Tut-tut-tut.'

Salamander did a quick inventory of his possessions. 'This could be bad,' he said, since he was, indeed, carrying nothing at all.

'Unprepared?' enquired Sea Snake, 'Curious. Here, take a little something from the treasure room before you reach her chamber at the end, there. She has so many gifts from so many better prepared visitors, she won't even remember.'

'But, er, what if I choose something she particularly likes?'

'Tut-tut-tut.'

'All the better. Who doesn't want two of what they particularly like?'

Salamander hesitated, trying to gauge the snake's honesty.

'I hadn't known,' said Sea Snake, impervious, drifting away, 'that we snakes could grow legs. And yet, here you are, my odd, brownish, leggy friend. And so, I will help you choose a gift.'

Salamander did not correct his new brethren, the snake. Instead, he followed her into a room in the cave filled and dripping with all sorts of stolen things. Strange shapes that had become soft and muted by the corals and creatures that now lived on them. Shapes that were small craters and some that were long stemmed things and other oddities most probably from ships. Somewhere in here, too, was the treasure the Empress desired.

'How did you grow your legs?' said Sea Snake.

'Oh. You know. Um, magic?'

The snake cocked her head attentively. 'All right,' she said, when there was nothing more forthcoming. 'Not as interesting an answer as one might hope.' Then, 'Take these.'

She indicated with an elegant nod three strands of white saltwater pearls, tied together with seaweed and knotted with oyster hair.

'You know,' Salamander said carefully, almost idly, 'what would be really good?'

'Yes?'

'A stone.'

'A stone?' asked Sea Snake. 'Would that really be so good?'

'A, um, a beautiful stone. That glows pale as the moon, white with a delicate fissure through the middle, like the tiny map of a river.'

'Tut-tut-tut.'

Salamander was of course describing the very thing he'd come here for, all the while ignoring the whirring, irritating seahorses and keeping his eyes on the countenance of the snake, to best gauge her responsiveness. Sea Snake reared and rose, zigging languidly through the water. 'I know the very one. A perfect piece of smoothed selenite in a silver setting, yes? Used to be her favourite.'

Salamander suppressed a skip of delight. Why, with the help of his so-called brethren, this might turn out to be a successful theft yet.

They had to dig for it, through strange, hollow objects that clunked against each other when dropped, and shreds of faded cloth. But there, beneath it all, was the treasure the Empress had described.

Salamander was slipping his fingers into the coral and slime on its surface, cleaning it and congratulating himself earnestly, when he felt the hard, rough edge of the crystal. Except, the crystal—this crystal, the one the Empress craved—should not be so rough.

'The saltwater...' said Salamander.

'Yes,' said Sea Snake. 'Corroded the metal and corrupted the crystal, discoloured and roughened it. Yes. I remember now. Not such a good gift after all, perhaps.'

Salamander stared at the dull exterior, river landscape hidden beneath.

'I suppose,' he said, 'there isn't any other?'

It wasn't until then he noticed the tut-tut-tutting of the Seahorses had stopped.

'Oh, no, no, there's no other,' came a hard whisper, not from the snake, but from the door, where the Octopus now rested.

She swept into the room, nearly filling it, the floating sack of her head bobbing above them. The colours of her skin began to bubble and roil. She still carried, in one long leg, the shattered carcass of her lunch. Around her scuttled tiny crabs like moving jewellery boxes, their crystal legs silent against the walls, their eyes precarious on stalks above their heads.

As the Octopus flared brilliant-blue, and Salamander attempted to remember how to speak, one small crab said, 'Heard of you.'

'Me too,' said another, bright shell of a thing beside the unpredictable bobble of the Octopus's head. 'Heard you lost your legs a lot. See how pale the new limb is. Hellbender, aren't you?'

Sea Snake scoffed but was otherwise silent, fitting herself along the edge of a pile of treasures. She regarded Salamander with keen eyes.

Salamander, meanwhile, flicked his gaze back and forth between the wall of enemies. 'Um. No. A salamander. Hellbenders are different. Though it's probably not, uh, an important point right now.'

'Anyone,' said a partner crab, scuttling along the wall towards Salamander, 'anyone would think you don't know what you're doing, losing pieces of yourself. Throwing yourself away, in a way.'

'Yeah, you must be bad at stealing.'

'Yeah. Maybe sometimes you lose your head.'

Salamander trained black eyes front-forward. 'If I did, it'd grow back.'

'Yeah?' said a jewel.

'Yeah?' said the other.

'Yeah,' Salamander said through flat lips. 'Did last time.'

He kept a poker face, waiting for a challenge. When none came, he stood up as straight as he could and looked to the Octopus.

She said, 'You steal often?' Interest piqued.

'Sometimes stealing is the honourable thing,' said Salamander.

Then a plan opened up in front of him, and he looked deep into the Octopus's eyes. There was no time for caution or second-guessing, so he said straight, 'Explain to me, if you would, where the flaw is in this.'

The Octopus stared, her tiny beak motionless. When Salamander was finished telling his plan, she suggested there wasn't much in it that was flawed at all. She agreed right there and then.

Ascent #1

The journey home always seems to take longer.

Three strands of white pearls were around his neck and, though pretty, their true value for Salamander was more practical. They were used to harness him to three Sea Snakes, who pulled him up and away towards the buoy where the Pelicans waited.

'God speed,' said one of the Snakes.

The Pelicans, who preferred all debts to be paid, even those owed them which they didn't yet need, tried to convince the Salamander to part with a strand of his pearls. He wouldn't hear of it.

'No,' he said. 'When the time comes, you find me, and we'll be even again then.'

They dropped him as far inland as they dared (since it was a foreign place to them), and Salamander continued along the river bed on foot, the strands of pale glowing pearls dragging and bouncing on the ground and threatening to dislodge at any moment from his neck. He kept pulling them back on with fingers like fat buds. And one other piece of the trade he carried, pushed along gently in front of him, rolling unevenly and constantly requiring correction to its path: an oyster shell. The largest oyster shell that had ever been found, claimed the Octopus, clasped in the disembodied claw of a mighty crab, long dead. She'd promised the claw would need to be prised open with great force.

Saved from a time-consuming journey, Salamander reached the Empress within barely a day of leaving the Octopus's place.

'Pearls?' asked the Empress. She rocked in slow anticipation, eyes mournful, mouth downturned. The eels blanketed her sides, moving even closer when the salamander arrived.

'Mine,' said Salamander. She would assume them stolen.

'Your bounty. Then,' she said.

'That, and my freedom.'

The Empress didn't blink, only stared at him with eyes sticky-soft but hard and mean.

'What is. Free? Are any of us. Truly? Free.' In her gulping monotone she added, 'You have the. Prize?'

Eyes black-blank, giving nothing away, Salamander said simply, 'Yes.'

'You do?' There was almost amazement in her voice.

'Are you surprised? And tell me, why should I give it to you?'

The Empress would have smiled in faint derision, but her face would never let her. Stiff as a mask, her indifferent profile said, 'Because. You gave your. Word you would. Steal this thing for me.'

He sighed, as if in defeat, paused a moment for drama. Then he shoved the shell forward until it came to rest in front of her. The Empress shifted first to one side and then another, rolling her eyes at the object. Even through the stillness of her face, confusion was apparent.

'This is it?' she asked. 'And ... how. To open it?'

'Yours to find out,' said Salamander.

He stayed to watch, standing outside the cave and feeling the smooth pull of freshwater on his skin. He took deep swigs of the stuff and delighted in its sweet weightlessness. Inside the cave, the Empress struggled.

First she mouthed the claw with great consternation, pulling on it with her fleshless lips. Then she tried dropping it, hoping the weight would shatter the thing (it didn't) despite the water's impedance.

'You could ask for help?' suggested Salamander, noting almost smugly that she pretended not to hear. The Empress would never risk having to share. Instead, she batted at the shell in rage, knocking it against the edges of her cave, pushing and pressing at it with her stony mouth until her skin tore in several places.

Finally she pushed the shell against the wall, wedged it in the pebbled floor of her cave, and managed to wrench the crab claw loose. Showing a dexterity he hadn't thought she possessed, she twisted herself nearly in half, working up enough energy to slam her jaw into the shell, and slam and slam again, until the claw sprung free.

She nosed greedily into the gap between the shell halves. Inside, a single stone glowed with dull intent, wrapped in its metal setting. The Empress opened her mouth in delight, leaning into her gift. The brightest, smoothest stone she had ever ...

'Wait,' she said.

At last.

'This isn't it,' she added, her words coming out in a rush.

'It is. The crystal that fell from a ship to the bottom of the ocean, that struck the back of a sleeping stingray, startling it into

flight? So that when he skimmed the Octopus's—the Monster's—
hall, it was dropped and then recovered by one of her long limbs,
and coveted, and carried inside so that she might gaze on it
forever? Is that the one you meant?'

'Yes,' said the Empress. 'No.'

'It is,' Salamander assured her. 'It's the very one.'

There was a pause, during which the Empress listed to one
side, her eye fixed on the Salamander.

'Oh,' he said. 'Wait. You're wondering why it's so unalluring?
Why its milkiness does not give way to a soft transparency that
reveals, at its core, a tiny landscape with a river? Is that what
you're wondering?

'Yes,' sneered the Empress.

'No.'

'No?'

'There's every chance you knew all along, of course, of how
the saltwater had blunted and tarnished it so the Octopus threw
it aside. And you sent me there anyhow. But I think only that you
couldn't decide what you wanted more. The stone, or my failure
to acquire it. Either way, you have no intention of ever letting me
work off my debt. Do you.'

The Empress didn't answer. The invisible venom from the
Octopus had already kicked in, the stuff carried in the clamped-
shut shell. It had trailed into her revolver-eyes and the cuts on
her hard-edged mouth. She moved her head in thick confusion,
noting, probably, a darkness like twilight setting in unexpectedly,
and unexpectedly fast.

Paralysis was next. The slow beating of her tail stopped and
her eyes crystallised into perfect opacity. She drifted to the floor
of her prison. The eels wafted, bemused, into the space she'd left
behind. They lowered themselves to her fallen corpse and those
that got too close died with her.

Diversion

And here's what happened in the Monster's hall.

Salamander, true to his word, explained to the Octopus that
he was going to steal from her. He did not ask her permission or
her good grace, because stolen it had to be, to fulfil the contract.
One thing he did ask, though, was if there was a further trade
he could perform. Did the Octopus ever desire something from
the river? Freshwater pearls, say, their pink-grey skins perfectly
rolled?

One favour he did ask, which he could not steal.

'Name it, odd little thing,' said the Octopus, her voice a reedy
soft rasp coming from the tiny beak of her mouth.

'Some of the venom they say is lethal, that you possess in your
bite,' said Salamander. 'I ask you to trade it freely, and I will repay
with some other favour.'

'Favours,' said the Octopus, supposedly a monster, 'are given, they can't be paid or repaid. That's my code, at least, and I will hold you to it.'

She agreed to the favour and vowed to live with the curious little leggy creature in her debt.

'You can always claim—' began Salamander.

'Yes,' the Octopus interrupted. 'And can choose not to. And can decide.'

Ascent #2

One year to the day a blue bullet streaked the sky and came to land on branches above Salamander's head.

'Kingfisher,' acknowledged Salamander.

'Salamander.' Kingfisher sat brood-chested, steel green in the sun. 'How goes it with the collection?'

'Fine.'

'Customarily tight-lipped,' observed the Kingfisher. He focussed on something far away.

Salamander blinked slowly. Said, 'I believe I have enough, now.'

'Good, good,' agreed Kingfisher. 'Anxious?'

'No.'

'Nervous? A little?'

'No. What do I have to lose?'

Kingfisher spun his beak around as if his head was on a coil. 'I would say "life", but you've lost that a couple of times already.'

'A-yup,' said Salamander. 'And no one to piece me back together with their magic this time. No need for you to fetch and carry, either, so there's a bonus. But, I gave my word.'

'Powerful magic in itself, that. For many of us.'

Salamander would have shrugged, but lacked the musculature. 'You don't get to choose a moral code, I think. You're born with it. It's in your—'

'—your what? Your bones?,' interrupted Kingfisher, a scolding tone. 'And if you can grow new ones, then what?'

Salamander didn't answer. He moved as if sighing, his belly expanding beyond his ribs and taking a moment to settle back in.

'Here goes,' he said, by way of good-bye, and slipped beneath the water.

'Good-bye,' said Kingfisher.

Free

'Are you, now, free?' asked the Octopus, rolling subtle-grey-pink freshwater pearls along the sand in front of her.

'Yes.'

'Free of service, or free of guilt?' she looked at him softly over the stab of her beak.

Salamander paused, eyes like black beads. 'Both. Either. Is there one without the other?'

'There's choice,' said the Octopus, tiny eyes steady under her enormous head. 'That's perhaps all there is?'

Salamander inclined his chin in agreement. Outside, he knew, the Pelicans sat in saltwater, awaiting his return. 'I can't stay long.'

'Tut-tut-tut.'

'You know,' said Salamander, ignoring the interruption, 'sometimes, the things you value most can't be bought at all.'

The Octopus absorbed this quietly. 'They have to be taken?'

Salamander nodded, 'Sometimes, they even have to be stolen.'

Deborah Biancotti is an Aurealis and Ditmar Award-winning writer based in Sydney, Australia. Her work has appeared in *The Year's Best Australian Science Fiction and Fantasy*, *Borderlands*, *Orb*, *Redsine* and *Altair*, as well as anthologies from MirrorDanse, Ideomancer, several other editions of Agog!, and an upcoming story in *Eidolon 1*. Online, she has work at *infinity plus* and *Ticonderoga Online*. Also, she has a website and a blog http://deborahbiancotti.net and http://deborahb.livejournal.com/. She refuses to watch reality tv on principle.

SCREENING TEST

CHRIS LAWSON

Lenoir knew his suit would mark him as the enemy, but he could not bring himself to leave it behind. Worsted wool was the wrong sort of armour for Le Zone, but he no longer felt comfortable outside of his apartment unless he was sealed in a freshly pressed, high-twisted, charcoal suit.

Lenoir was climbing a staircase that zig-zagged up the front of the concrete housing when he realised that he had been spotted. He heard the sounds of young men scurrying up the stairs beneath him. It had been raining and the stairs were still slick with water and the oily shimmer that seemed to seep right out of the building. The boys' feet slapped in the wet and he heard their high, excited voices as they clambered up toward him.

Moving away from the racket, he stepped through an access corridor to the opposite face of the building. He came out and saw the wall of another building, exactly the same as the concrete monstrosity he was standing on, only rotated sixty degrees.

On the balcony of that building, at the same level as Lenoir, stood three young men in bulbous parkas and running shoes. They stood only twenty metres away, but separated by a gulf of open air.

The boys saw him. One raised a phone to his ear. Lenoir heard a ring-tone in the distance, somewhere below and behind. The boys on the balcony were directing the hunt by mobile phone.

Lenoir looked up, judged that he had too far to go and could not elude his hunters, so he stood and waited for them.

A skinny youth was the first up the stairs. His face had turned a cherry colour from running. As soon as the boy saw Lenoir, he smiled and, realising that his quarry had given up the chase, he slowed to a steady, calculated walk. His eyes were wide and they did not look away from Lenoir for a moment. The slower boys came up behind: a stocky, muscular boy well-suited to climbing mountains or stairwells; then a boy with a scar that kinked his upper lip; then a big, pudgy lump of a boy made even pudgier by the Michelin-Man hoops on his parka. Then another two boys appeared in the corridor to the stairwell on the other side of the building. *Algerians*, thought Lenoir. The boys tried to look alike: puffy jackets, tight jeans, precocious nicotine stains on their fingers, stringy hair and sorry attempts at beards.

Last of all, ambling along at an easy lollop, came the unmistakeable leader of the boys. He was not the biggest, or the strongest, or the oldest, but he would be the hardest enculé on the block.

The enculé held up his hand. It was an unnecessary gesture as everybody had stopped already, but the boy had the reflexes of an old general and he gave orders as naturally as breathing. A wispy moustache cluttered up his top lip and an embryonic attilio sat on his chin.

'What is your name?' asked the boy.

'Lenoir.'

'Well, Lenoir, what business do you have here?'

Lenoir stared at the boy, sizing him up. 'It's personal.'

'There's a toll.'

'Not for me,' said Lenoir.

The boys shuffled about uncertainly but the boy laughed. 'I guess you must be some sort of super-Ninja or something, eh? Or maybe you have the cops behind you.'

'The police wouldn't come without an army escort,' said Lenoir. He took his mobile phone out of his jacket and tossed it to the boy. 'Check the addresses under V.'

The boy hesitated.

'Go on,' said Lenoir. 'There's only five numbers in memory. Look under V.'

The boy scrolled through the addresses. There it was: *V for Vallone.*

'This is a joke,' said the boy.

'No,' said Lenoir.

'You work for Vallone.'

'In a way. I'm his advocate.'

'And how do I know this is really Vallone?'

'Call the number,' said Lenoir, and then added slyly, 'If you really want to.'

Lenoir watched the boy carefully here, to see how he would react. *Consider it an intelligence test*, he thought.

The lumpy Arab behind him said a few words in French-Algerian patois, then others chipped in. Lenoir heard them call him a berraani, which made him smile. While the boys debated whether to call the number, Lenoir listened. He was careful not to reveal that he understood large slabs of their patois of French, Dardja and Verlan.

When the voices had died down, the enculé tossed the phone back and, having passed Lenoir's test, said, 'There may be a truce, but this is not Vallone's territory.'

Lenoir said, 'Like I said, I'm not here on business.'

For a man in a suit, all alone in the estate, Lenoir was

unfeasibly self-assured, and there was his way of moving; Lenoir did not walk like a man in a suit, ... and the accent, ... and the fact that he knew exactly where he was going on the estate. The boy was beginning to figure that Lenoir was no berraani. He was from Le Zone, from a long time back, for sure, but he was a local.

'Lenoir. Lenoir,' said the boy, rolling the name over in his head. 'Tupe! You're *that* Lenoir! You burnt down the school!' Now there was awe in his voice.

Lenoir shook his head. 'That's not entirely true,' he corrected. 'It was only half the school.'

Lenoir had been thirteen and Danielle had been twelve when she had convinced him to break into the art room at L'École Charles-Edouard Jeanneret.

They waited until after nine. When they were sure there was nobody on the premises, Lenoir twisted the padlock on the school gate with an iron bar. They went through the gate and Danielle draped the chain and the lock back on the gate so that passers-by would not notice that the lock had been broken.

Lenoir jammed the iron bar into the artroom door, leaned his weight into it, and splintered the wood around the lock. The door swung open and the two of them slipped inside.

They smoked stolen cigarettes and drank a bottle of brandy they had filched from Danielle's mother. Danielle let Lenoir put his hand up her blouse even though there was nothing there to feel. Mostly, they just talked and talked some more. They spray-painted BAISE LA POLICE! And ÉCOLE LA MERDE! on the walls. Lenoir shook his can of paint, savoured the rattle of the metal pea in the can, and tried to think of a new and imaginative obscenity to spray. That was when the fire started.

The smell of burning plastic alerted Lenoir. He turned to look at Danielle, who held up the cigarette in her hand for him to see. The tip was not just glowing, it was blazing. Yellow-blue flames twisted off the end of the cigarette as she pretended to take another drag.

She had found a patch of carpet soaked in turpentine and had impetuously pressed the cigarette into it. The cigarette ignited the turpentine, which in turn ignited the polyester in the carpet. The flames took to it with a hunger. In seconds the fire flowed across the carpet and up the wall behind Danielle's back.

Danielle giggled and pointed, but Lenoir took one look at the fire and knew they had to get out *now*. The flames had engulfed a supply cupboard, and that meant turpentine and methylated spirits and oil paints.

Lenoir seized her by the elbow and pushed her towards the exit. She was a little drunk and stumbled into the door, slamming it shut in front of them. Lenoir held her around the waist with one hand to keep her upright while he opened the door with his other hand.

At that moment the cupboard exploded, spraying the room with flaming shot. The two children tumbled out of the door as the flames surged up the walls and licked a tongue at them through the door.

Danielle had escaped untouched, but Lenoir's hair was smoking and a gobbet of smouldering paint had attached itself to the back of his right hand.

'Are you all right?' asked Danielle.

Lenoir nodded. He wrapped his good hand in a handkerchief to peel off the smoking paint blob from his other hand. A plum-sized circle of skin came off with it.

'That looks nasty,' she said.

It took every ounce of his will, but Lenoir refused to cry. Crying was for kids.

'Hardly hurts at all.'

The banlieu boys followed Lenoir up the stairs at a respectful distance. They were curious about him and wary of him and the tension between the two impulses was making them fidgety.

Lenoir stopped outside number 833. The numbers had been prised off the door, but their impression remained in the paint just above a small peephole lens. Lenoir knocked at the door. There was no answer. He knocked again. He put his ear to the door and heard a television blaring, so he knocked a third time, but there was still no answer.

The lead boy from the gang came forward and said to Lenoir, 'This is the Haliba place. They'll all be at work now except the grand-dad, who sits at home mixing curries in front of the TV.'

'Haliba?' asked Lenoir. 'Not Becquerel?'

'I don't know any Becquerels,' said the boy.

Lenoir stared at the door in frustration and knocked again.

'He won't hear you,' said the boy. 'He turns the TV up loud. You've got to do this.' He gestured to the big pudge of a boy with enormous fists, who pounded so hard that paint flaked off the door.

'Hey! Mr Haliba! Hey!' The flabby apeman bellowed at the door.

The door opened and Lenoir found himself looking over a security chain at an elderly black Moroccan man with wet hands. It was dark inside the flat, and Lenoir could see the old man's eyes flicking about as he took in the scene: a stranger in an expensive suit and the local gang of toughs standing at his door. He wouldn't be taking down the security chain any time soon.

'Can I help you, sir?' said Haliba the old Moroccan.

'I'm looking for the Becquerels.'

'Aha,' said Haliba. 'The Becquerels lived here before us.'

Lenoir nodded. 'Did they leave a forwarding address?'

Mr Haliba shook his head. 'They moved out. The Housing people, they moved them away when they no longer needed two bedrooms.'

Lenoir frowned. 'What?'

'They moved out,' said Haliba again. 'They do not live here.'

'I know that...'

'They are gone,' said Haliba brightly.

Lenoir held up a valuable phone card, still sealed, and watched Haliba's eyes follow the card to read the denomination. He tried speaking very slowly.

'Do ... you ... know ... where ... to?'

'They are gone.'

The enculé stepped up and said, 'Do you want *me* to talk to this old sharmute?'

Lenoir said, 'It won't help.' He slipped the phone card under the door despite Mr Haliba's spectacular lack of assistance. 'He doesn't know anything worth terrifying him for.'

As walked away from the apartment, the boys came behind him, following in silence. Then he heard Mr Haliba call out to him from behind his door.

'Monsieur!' he shouted. 'The daughter, she died. That is why they did not need the second bedroom.'

Lenoir stopped suddenly and the boys stopped, too. He turned and said, 'What?'

'Their girl, she died.'

'Are you sure?'

'It is only what I heard.'

Lenoir turned to the railing of the balcony and gripped it with both hands. He stared out across the courtyard and into the distance. The boys looked where Lenoir was looking.

Out across the courtyard, past the East Block and beyond a dead hedge was the old school. L'École Charles-Edouard Jeanneret was shrouded in concrete and graffiti and a barbed-wire security fence that had been built principally to keep the children inside.

Danielle and Lenoir heard sirens as they ran out of the school. They sprinted all the way across the plaza and up the walkway at the end and only stopped when they could run no further.

Lenoir said to Danielle, 'Sneak into your place as quiet as you can and never say anything to anyone.'

'You think I'm stupid?' She gave him a kiss which smelled of gasoline and sweat. Then she laughed and disappeared up the stairwell of the giant concrete Skinner box where she lived.

Lenoir counted out fifty steps towards his own home. When he was sure he had given Danielle enough time to be out of sight, he doubled back to the schoolyard. He was back before the fire engines could get there. He sat down on the steps of the school gate and waited. There was no point in running. He was covered in burns and a patch of his hair was singed and whenever there was trouble, Lenoir was always the first suspect. Besides, he was better off with the police tonight than going home to take a beating.

The fire engines arrived. Then came the police car, and after that came the ambulance. He said nothing to the firemen or the police, but when the ambulance officers asked him if he needed anything for pain, Lenoir held up his right hand, burn and all, and clenched and unclenched his fist for the ambulance officers to see. They took him to hospital anyway.

The school counsellor was a psychologist by the name of Dr Sylvie Coulthard. She had come to the Becquerel apartment because the boy was banned from the school. The teachers had stopped talking about 'that Lenoir boy' and were now referring to him as 'that Lenoir maniac' or 'the little arsonist.'

Lenoir's mother had flown the coop years ago, leaving the father to care for the Lenoir boy. He was a brute of a man who terrified everyone except but the boy himself, so Dr Coulthard arranged to see Lenoir at the Becquerels' apartment, especially as the boy spent more time there than at his own home.

Dr Coulthard knocked politely on their door. Mme Becquerel beckoned her in. 'Thank you for coming all this way,' she said, even though it was only a ten-minute walk from the school. What she was referring to was not the linear distance from L'École Charles-Edouard Jeanneret but the social distance. Between Dr Coulthard's office and the Becquerel apartment was a chasm as deep as any ocean trench.

Dr Coulthard was a tightly wound woman who wore her profession like an outer skin while Mme Becquerel wore a denim skirt with a cigarette-pack bulge in the pocket and a loose singlet top that revealed half a tattoo of a blue-and-orange koi on her left shoulder. Dr Coulthard's hair was tied in a geometric bun and Mme Becquerel's was a red straggle.

'Where can we do the test?' asked Dr Coulthard. 'We need a table and two hours of uninterrupted quiet.'

Mme Becquerel cleared the dining table and put out a bottle of water and two glasses, then she called Lenoir out of the main room where the television had been keeping him occupied. The boy arrived with that strange mixture of defiance and sheepishness that Dr Coulthard recognised immediately. The boys in particular learned the attitude young. It meant: *I've done the wrong thing, but I won't acknowledge it, no matter what.*

Once the boy was seated at the table, Mme Becquerel excused herself and Danielle from the apartment and left them to it.

Dr Coulthard took the test sheets from her briefcase and spread them over the table. 'Now,' she said, 'we are going to see what can be done with you.'

'Do I have to?'

Dr Coulthard leaned over to him, so close he could smell her perfume. She said in a steely voice, 'Do not burn the last of your bridges.'

They started with numbers and words and patterns of circles

and squares to test how smart he was. Next came the personality test; then the empathy scale; then the social awareness scale; and finally Dr Coulthard made him tell stories about some pictures, and that didn't seem to be testing anything at all.

When Dr Coulthard had finished packing away the test papers, she pulled out a cotton bud on a long white stalk.

'What's this?' asked Lenoir.

'It's a mouth swab.'

'What for?'

'Just stick it in your mouth and rub it against your cheek.'

Lenoir twirled the swab around in his mouth and handed it back to Coulthard, who slid it into a plastic sleeve and sealed it in a zip-lock bag.

'Well done, Lenoir. Well done,' said Dr Coulthard. She looked genuinely pleased with him, and possibly *for* him, too.

'Are you all right?' asked the enculé. This unlikely question, concern coming from the mouth of a professional intimidator, snapped Lenoir back to reality.

'Everything is fine,' said Lenoir, and he reflexively bunched up his right fist. 'But I could use some help today. It will be worth your while.'

The enculé thought for a moment, and then said, 'What do you have in mind?'

'I need your boys to scout for me. Shouldn't take more than an hour or two.'

The enculé nodded. 'Sure.' He had passed another test.

So Lenoir took the gang along with him to a small plaza. The journey took them through alleyways that were familiar to Lenoir but the walls had changed, or at least the graffiti had. The styles, even the words were different. Some of the graffiti looked clean and detailed and had depths of colour that he had never seen before. He noticed that many of the graffiti were not spray-painted but stuck on. The images had been blown up and divided into page-sized stickers and then assembled as a montage that could cover an entire wall.

The subjects had also changed. Back when Lenoir was a boy, tags and crude sexual iconography and swear-words directed at the police were the fashion; now the pictures showed a contradictory mix of minarets, anatomically dubious women in provocative poses, and men with grenade launchers on their shoulders and keffiyehs wrapped around their faces. He could not fathom the fusion of imagery from American pin-ups and Islamic resistance.

The changes, though, were superficial. Lenoir knew the banlieu. He knew which shops the schoolboys would hit for cigarettes and alcohol, and the paths of escape.

Of course the shops in the plaza had changed. One business fails, another grows in its place, but always there would be a little café. And there it was, right where the bakery had been in Lenoir's day.

One thing had not changed at all: the branch office of Crédit Lyonnais and its automatic teller.

Lenoir gave his instructions. The boys were to wait near the bank and to let him know when they saw a woman in her late forties with red hair and a Japanese fish tattoo. She would use the automatic teller and they were to follow her home surreptitiously. He himself was retiring inside the café where she would not see him. He invited the enculé to sit with him inside the café and ordered them coffee,

'I don't know your name,' said Lenoir.

'Mohammed,' said the enculé.

'There are a lot of Mohammeds nowadays. Do you mind if I call you 'enculé'?' asked Lenoir.

'It depends on the way you say it,' answered the boy coldly.

'As in 'one tough enculé'.'

'Sure. You can call me that.'

The boy wanted to know about Vallone and why there was a peace between the two houses, so Lenoir talked in very general terms about the politics of Lyon versus Paris.

'But you're not from Lyon originally. You grew up here.'

'Indeed I did.'

'And now you want to come back.'

Lenoir puffed out his disgust. 'To Paris? I'm here for one purpose and then I'm gone.'

'You don't miss Paris at all?' asked the enculé.

'I'm told the call girls are better here.'

The enculé laughed at that. 'There's nothing you miss, then?'

Lenoir could not say anything without revealing too much, so he kept it to himself that the worst thing about coming back was that he was suffering a sort of reverse homesickness. He did not want to be in Paris. The city put his teeth on edge. All the years in Lyon, living in the boarding school, then the shared barracks at the university, upgrading to his own apartment and then as his income had improved to the house and then to a small country estate with its own riverbank—it had done nothing to wash the banlieu out of him. Despite every effort, he felt at home here. And it disgusted him.

There was only one thing he missed about Paris and according to Haliba she was dead.

A rap beat called out from the enculé's pocket. He answered his mobile phone. He nodded to Lenoir, and Lenoir went to the window to check. There she was on the far end of the plaza, punching numbers into the teller machine. Red hair in a bird's nest, bare wiry arms, and the revealed tail of a blue fish tattoo; even with her face turned to the wall of the bank, she was unmistakeable.

'Mme Becquerel,' said Lenoir to himself. 'How nice to see you again.'

☆

Dr Coulthard came back a week later with the test results in her hand and a smile on her face.

'Everything came out as well as could be,' she told his father, who had made a great effort to look presentable that day and had nearly succeeded.

Lenoir had hit the bullseye on the tests. He was intelligent, socially disadvantaged (which was Dr Coulthard's way of saying that his father beat him from time to time), and the gene probe had detected a variant of a brain chemical called monoamine oxidase A which, she did her best to explain, affected mood. Lenoir had the trifecta, and the trifecta earned him the right to attend an experimental school that would prevent him having problems with the criminal law when he grew up.

Dr Coulthard and his father discussed the possibilities with great earnest faces, but Lenoir knew it was the allowance that sealed it. While he was at the school, 'which is in Lyon by the way,' all of Lenoir's living expenses would be paid and his father would receive a small but not insubstantial 'travelling allowance.'

'Well,' said his father, trying to look as if he was weighing up Lenoir's future. 'When can the boy go?'

The next intake was in two months. In the meantime, Lenoir's presence would most definitely not be required at L'École Charles-Edouard Jeanneret.

Lenoir spent his free time with Danielle, who was still supposed to be at school because nobody knew about her role in the fire. Her truancy was so pervasive that it could not escape the notice of her teachers. This filtered up to the principal, and from there to her father.

One morning she came to Lenoir with two black eyes. She was too embarrassed to go to school even if it meant another round of her father's discipline that night. So Lenoir took her to the plaza where he filched a mirror compact and a jar of foundation from a discount stall. They slipped into a side alley and Danielle applied the foundation, exceedingly gently, to her battered face. The foundation didn't quite match her skin colour, and nothing could hide the swelling, but at least she looked presentable, like she maybe had hay fever or a hangover. She pulled up her top to show Lenoir. The bruises on her chest and back made the black eyes look like love bites in comparison, but at least these were covered by her clothing and did not need foundation.

She gave Lenoir a kiss and headed off to school, an hour late but at least present and accounted for, while Lenoir went home to find his father.

'Papa,' said Lenoir, 'I need to know how to beat a grown man.'

His father looked surprised. 'Don't you think you're in enough trouble already?'

'How could I possibly?' asked Lenoir. 'And besides, would you tell anyone if you were beaten up by a thirteen-year-old?'

His father roused himself out of his chair. The scars on his knuckles stretched and tugged at his skin as he pushed up from the chair arms. 'You don't know what you're getting into.'

'He hit Danielle,' said Lenoir. 'Very badly.'

'Ah,' said his father. 'Your girlfriend. I will talk to Becquerel.'

'No.'

His father arched an eyebrow at his son's determination. 'You know he'll thrash you, don't you?'

'Only if it's a fair fight.'

'Well, then,' said his father. 'Well, then.' His father reached for the remote control and, for the first time Lenoir could remember, the television was off in the house.

And so his father taught him, starting with the most important lesson; against Becquerel, he was not to stop at the first surprise punch, not even at the first fall, but to keep hitting the man as hard and as often as possible until he begged for the beating to stop. If he stopped too soon and allowed Becquerel time to gather himself, he would get his ginger back and then Lenoir stood no chance at all.

'Becquerel has a strong arm but no pride,' his father said with certainty.

His father had paid him little notice the last few years after his mother left, but now he was teaching his son an important lesson and he seemed to be drawing from a previously unsuspected well of enthusiasm. Lenoir listened attentively. He was a fast learner.

The Algerian boys followed Mme Becquerel home and then called the enculé to give him directions. It was a long walk to Mme Becquerel's new apartment, but then she could hardly change to a more convenient bank.

The boys showed him to her door, then made it clear that this was not a part of the banlieu that they should stay in for long. Lenoir assured them that this would not take long.

Lenoir thought about knocking on the door, then changed his mind. He kicked the door instead, as hard as he could, and felt a surge of satisfaction as the door frame splintered. Another kick and the door buckled inwards on its hinges. He walked into the apartment just as Mme Becquerel came out from the back screaming her indignation. She took one look at Lenoir and went silent.

'Good morning,' said Lenoir. 'Sorry about the door.'

'What are you ...?' Mme Becquerel bunched up the front of her singlet with both hands. 'Lenoir. It's been ages.'

Lenoir stepped over a splinter of plywood and brushed a patch of white dust off his trouser leg. 'I came to see Danielle,' he said.

'She's not in,' said Mme Becquerel.

'Do you mean she won't be in any time soon?' asked Lenoir. 'Or she won't be in ever?'

Mme Becquerel said nothing. She huddled over in fear. Lenoir took a step towards her and she took a hesitant step backwards. At that moment Lenoir knew that what Mr Haliba had said was true. Danielle was dead.

'I would have liked to attend her funeral.'

'I thought you couldn't come to Paris,' said Mme Becquerel.

'That was my decision to make, not yours,' he said. He took another step forward and she took another step back. 'But even that I could forgive. It's the fact that every week, regular as clockwork, I have been transferring money into her account and now I find that she has been dead and yet miraculously I have not heard of her account being closed or my transfers being rejected.' Another step closer. 'Perhaps it is Danielle's spirit, spending my money from beyond the grave. What do you think?'

Mme Becquerel was flat against a corner wall. There was nowhere further to retreat. 'What do you want?' she asked.

'I want to know how Danielle died.'

'She OD'ed.'

'Where?'

'Under the railway tunnel.'

'And she got her stuff from your dealer?'

'Yes. There was a pure shipment on the street but she shot up her usual hit.'

Lenoir towered over her and she curled up into a ball with her arms over her head. 'And you didn't tell me when she died. You didn't tell me when she started using heroin. I bet you didn't even change dealers. So long as the money came in, eh?'

At this, Mme Becquerel shouted back, but she was still curled up. 'It was your money that killed her. Your money! That's what she used to pay with. If it hadn't been for that, she would be alive today.'

Now he was standing right over her.

'Please don't hurt me,' said Mme Becquerel. She was shaking.

He wanted to beat her to a pulp and he knew it, but if Mme Becquerel charged him with assault it would put his status as an advocate at risk. Mme Becquerel was not the sort of person to give that power to.

'Just tell me where she is now.'

Mme Becquerel told him the name of the cemetery and the columbary where her ashes lay.

'There's one more thing,' he added. 'I'm cancelling the money transfer.'

'I can pay it all back,' she said.

'Don't be ridiculous,' said Lenoir. He left her there twisted up in the corner.

As he walked out of the building with the boys trailing behind him, he knew what he had to do to lance his anger.

He stopped and looked over the boys. There was always one goat in every gang, and it was always obvious who it was, and in this gang it was a thin, acne-flecked perdant of fifteen or sixteen.

'Come here,' said Lenoir. 'Take off your glasses.'

The boy looked surprised, but did as he was told. As soon as he had tucked his glasses away, Lenoir punched him hard in the centre of his face just as he was looking up.

The boy staggered back and Lenoir stepped forward to keep up, then launched another punch into the side of the boy's head. The boy fell to the ground.

'Help him up,' said Lenoir to the other boys in the gang, who were just as stunned as the goat. The enculé was the first to move, passing the most important test of all. He scooped up the goat under his shoulders and lifted him back to his feet. The goat was blubbing and holding his nose. Blood streamed out between his fingers.

Lenoir hit him one more time, as hard as he possibly could. He felt a bone snap in the boy's face, and that was when he finally felt sated.

He gave an extremely valuable phone card to the enculé and said that it was for the bleeding goat. 'Make sure he gets every last franc on the card.'

He folded his wallet up and felt a pain lancing through his hand. He looked down and saw that the back of his hand had bent at an odd angle. It was not the boy's face that had broken after all.

When he left Paris as a boy, he had taken the train to Lyon alone. His father had made the effort to see him off at the station, but that was as much as he was capable of. One of the teachers picked him up at the other end.

The school was called the Lycée d'Avenir. He slept in a dormitory with eight others in the room, and the school taught less of the standard curriculum and a whole lot more about anger management and self-esteem. The school was run on semi-military discipline, and corporal punishment in the lycée was allowed by special Ministerial decree.

Almost all of the students were boys from all over France, but predominantly the Parisian banlieus. There were a handful of girls, six to the eighty-nine boys, and they had their own dormitory at the far end of the school grounds to the boys' sleeping quarters. It didn't stop fraternisation, especially when they hit fifteen and sixteen, but it did make them inventive about avoiding the many barriers.

Lenoir was one of the lucky boys. He managed to fraternise with three of the six girls at various times, but his heart was never in it for long. Throughout it all, he kept on writing to Danielle and sending her a few francs here and there out of his allowance.

Once she visited for a day. They spent their time together negotiating awkward gaps. Somehow, out of their hole in Paris, they did not know how to talk to each other. Lenoir was actually learning and was silently proud that he could handle calculus. Danielle, however, was in her old situation with the same old prospects, and the only improvement was that her father's beatings were much less frequent and savage after Lenoir's intervention.

She went back to Paris on the night train and that was the last time he saw her, although for a while they kept in touch by mail.

Meanwhile, his grades kept improving. Over the next three years, he got better and better, and when he sat his Baccalauréat, he surprised himself to find he was among the top thousand students in all France. He was offered scholarships to a number of universities. It was yet another program from the Education Ministry, but at least this time Lenoir knew he would have won the scholarships on merit alone. He settled on the law school at the Université Lumière because it was also in Lyon and he couldn't face going back to Paris just then.

He kept writing to her, but her responses became shorter and more perfunctory. A typical letter in its entirety read, 'Cheri, thank you for the letter. I bought a pair of gloves for winter with the money you sent. Love, Danielle.'

At university he excelled. Most of his peers were middle-or upper-class, and it became apparent to Lenoir that many of them were there on the basis of their backgrounds rather than their intrinsic merits. It was not that they were stupid, just that they were no smarter than the people he knew from Le Zone. They were smart in different ways. They knew their Camus and their Voltaire, but they couldn't tell a roundhouse from an uppercut. Their intelligence had been forged into a blade like a samurai sword: their minds were sharp as could be, but largely ceremonial.

He made friends among his more practically minded colleagues, but for the most part he did not feel the need for constant company. In fact, it irritated him. He had been to too many parties where the bourgeoisie around him expressed fascination for his background. It came in two forms. There were the Distant Agonisers, those who talked about the banlieus as a Hell on earth, full of violence and anger. Lenoir tried to point out that this was wrong. His own history was not the template for everyone in Le Zone. In fact, as he liked to explain, the principles of ecology dictate that only a few can be predators. Most of the inhabitants of the banlieus were just like Mr Haliba: entirely harmless, neither criminal nor victim, just poor. He watched the Agonisers nod wisely as he corrected them, but they said the same things over again the next time the subject came up. He might as well have never spoken. Their desire was to agonise, not to understand.

Then there were the Admirers: they expressed astonishment that a boy from the banlieus could come so far. It was remarkable. *He* was remarkable. A testament to the human spirit. The Admirers, it must be said, were even more insufferable than the Agonisers.

Over that time, the letters from Danielle became vessels of non-communication, tiny notes that were written in under thirty seconds. 'Thank you for your letter. Love, Danielle.' Like a vestigial organ, the communication eventually withered to nothing. Lenoir kept writing and sending money and the replies almost never came. It burned him, but he couldn't bring himself to stop.

And so he went from lycée to university to the courts, and one day he found himself defending a criminal of particularly notable stupidity and managed to argue his case so persuasively that the judge was bamboozled into an acquittal. The stupid criminal worked for a man named Vallone, who was not stupid at all and Vallone began to ask for the young advocate with legal acumen and a banlieu background.

Lenoir found that he had gone from not wanting to return to Paris to not being able to, and he had not even noticed the change as it happened.

The train to La Havre gave Lenoir two hours to himself, at least in theory. In reality he was on the phone the whole time to arrange appointments and, naturally, Vallone called because another one of his dolts had got himself in trouble. Lenoir promised to send his assistant right away and he would be there himself that evening. Before he finished the call, he told Vallone about a young enculé who might be useful as a contact in Paris. Then he called his office to rearrange his itinerary. Instead of taking the train back, he would have to fly out of La Havre airport direct to Lyon. Finally, he called to confirm his appointment in La Havre. It had been difficult to track her down, but his office had found the address of Dr Coulthard herself and arranged a meeting on short notice.

He was not sure that she could answer the questions he wanted to ask, but he could think of nobody else, and once this was over he didn't want to ask any more questions for a very long time.

Dr Coulthard was now an old woman who had retired to the coast. She had earned her pension by any measure after three decades of psychological intervention in some of the most notorious schools in the country.

From the station, Lenoir took a taxi to the address that Dr Coulthard had given. It was late afternoon by the time he arrived at her little old house of stone wedged between two other, statelier buildings.

Dr Coulthard let him in with a heavy saucing of bustle and excitation.

'Lenoir! Lenoir! Such a delight to see you! And look at you in that suit! I can hardly believe it! Come in! Come in!'

She appeared to have taken up exclamation as a retirement hobby.

The house was even tinier than it looked on the outside. Thick stone walls ate up the internal space, but Dr Coulthard lived plainly and there was no sign of clutter. She made coffee and served it in little glass cups. Everything about her was simple and elegant, a fact that had entirely escaped him when he was a young rascal.

She looked down at his right hand and noticed the plaster sticking out from his jacket sleeve.

'My goodness,' she said, 'what have you done to yourself?'

'I broke the bone here,' he said as he pointed at the base of the plaster. 'It's nothing.'

She laughed. 'That's the old Lenoir I remember.'

'No, really, it doesn't hurt. The plaster keeps the bone from moving. I could just about play tennis with it.'

She sipped at her coffee. 'I gather from your assistant's calls that you are an advocate now and that you live in Lyon,' she said.

'My office is in Lyon. I live outside the city, but I am indeed an advocate.'

'Oh how wonderful. Tell me all about it. I heard nothing after you left, you know. Not a whisper. It was me who alerted the Department, but they must have thought I didn't care once you were out of my school.'

Lenoir had several life stories, and he told Dr Coulthard the one that was a succession of places and times. She seemed to respond well to it. She sprinkled pinches of 'wonderful!' and 'fantastic!' as he spoke.

Naturally she reciprocated, and although Lenoir had no interest in her long family attachment to La Havre, and the intricacies of reclaiming her great-uncle's historic house and making it liveable once more, he listened politely until she finished.

'Now,' she said, 'you have come a long way and I find it hard to imagine it is just to chat to your old school counsellor.'

Lenoir leaned forward. 'I need to know why the program failed.'

'It didn't fail at all. It was very successful. Nobody ever got around to measuring violent crime as adults because the program didn't last long enough, but plenty of other short-term measures showed improvement. Children at the lycée improved their grades, their general health, their self-esteem, and their behavioural control.'

'But they closed down the program.'

'It was very expensive to run. I thought The Ministry should have kept the lycée going, but the funding became problematic. I'm not sure how cynical I should be since it was the Minister's own idea.'

'Why would you be cynical?' asked Lenoir.

Dr Coulthard sighed. 'I don't like to be critical of people who were trying to help, but ... ah ... how should I put it? You see, I thought the Minister wanted to help children in difficult circumstances, but there were always a couple of arguments against this that I wasn't aware of until the program was about to wind up. For one thing, the scientists who did the original research made very public comments about their work being misrepresented. Their research showed the interplay of genes and environment, and here it was being used as a screening test. The scientists were very forthright about the test not being predictive enough. Of course, the Minister ignored them. It was just like the Manhattan project, where the scientists who built the atom bomb tried to tell the generals not to drop it.

'But the biggest problem was the cost. You were enrolled in the pilot program. If they had introduced a national screening program, they would have turned up thousands of children at risk every year and they simply didn't want to pay for all that.'

'So the Minister didn't want people to know it was all about the money.'

Dr Coulthard chuckled. 'Oh, not at all. The Minister made it quite clear that the program was too expensive. That was his public reason for closing the lycée.'

'So what is there to be cynical about?'

With a frown, Dr Coulthard admitted she did not like to pass judgement without knowing all the inside facts, and yet, 'it became clear to me that the program had nothing to do with helping children from dysfunctional families. I am surprised and somewhat ashamed at how long it took me to realise, because it's obvious once you know how to look at it.'

'How so?' asked Lenoir.

'If the principal motive was to help children escape violence, then what was the point of the gene testing and the psychological profiling? Why look beyond the family situation? A child in distress should be protected, surely, and it should not matter what concoction of genes they carry. It makes as much sense as saying we will only intervene for blue-eyed children.'

'But the gene for violence—'

'It was not a gene for violence!' Dr Coulthard was suddenly emphatic. 'It was merely a risk factor *in combination with a violent upbringing*. You see? The Minister was not trying to protect children, he was acting the guardian for the voters in Neuilly-Auteuil-Passy who were terrified of the banlieus without every having stepped into one. There was no compassion. It was about fearing what the children might become.'

Lenoir checked his watch. 'Thank you, Dr Coulthard, but I have to catch a flight. I have one last question for you.'

'Of course, my dear boy.'

'Do you remember Danielle Becquerel?'

'Danielle? Of course I remember her. Lovely blonde hair. Half your scrapes came out of trying to impress her. What of her?'

'Why didn't you ever screen her? She had it worse than me at home.'

'My dear Lenoir, the point is that she never burned down the school.'

Lenoir nodded and took his leave.

From the doorstep, Dr Coulthard called out to him, 'I'm glad to see you have made such a success of yourself, my dear Lenoir. I knew the lycée could break the cycle.'

On the plane home, Lenoir drew a little picture of Danielle on his plaster and thought about the night they torched the art room. He had to use his left hand to draw, which made it look exactly like a child's sketch of a pretty girl.

It hit him while the plane was over Paris. He had done everything he could to protect Danielle. He had covered for her after the fire. He had stolen the make-up that allowed her to hide her bruises. He had sent her enough money to keep her at home. It hadn't been his purpose, but he had protected her from the wrong threat—the school and the police—and sent her home to the Devil.

He stared at the childish picture on his plaster. She would have been almost his age of course, but in his mind she was a girl of twelve with the promise of her adult face just peeking through. Now the memory was all she could ever be to him.

To protect her from foxes, he had caged her with tigers.

Note: 'Screening Test' is drawn from the scientific paper Caspi A. *et al.*, 'Role of Genotype in the Cycle of Violence in Maltreated Children'. *Science* Vol. 297, 2 August 2002, 851-854. This paper has been widely misreported as demonstrating a 'gene for violence.' It should not need to be said but I will say it anyway: the political application of the paper as imagined in this story does not reflect the views of the authors.

With thanks to the Rimfire Group.

Chris Lawson is a MWM with GSOH but unfortunately not HWP, desperately seeking W/E publisher into subs for LTR. www.talkingsquid.net

Aftermath

DAVID CONYERS

The midday heat heavy on the Kisumu docks sweated the eastern shores of Lake Victoria. Hot humid air, thick with lakeflies, stunk of stale food and swamp gas. A ramp lowered from an ancient steamer freed a flood of a thousand black faces that pushed through the dense crowds. Hope in their eyes begged for an official pass off the dilapidated ferry and on through immigration.

As Sandra Young stumbled with the crowd that jostled her, she tightened the black veil wrapped across her face, the concealing garb worn by Islamic women the world over. She possessed no Muslim face nor did she follow their religion, but in this country a disguise was required nonetheless. With every step she hoped the wearied officials would not mistake her as a westerner. The mutilated bodies of Americans littering the road to Kampala seven days earlier were warning enough. Africa had gone mad.

'Kipande?'

She hoped her stance was casual as a Sergeant demanded identification. A tense neck and fingernails that dug deep into her palms did not project the calm she hoped to display. As she handed over the passport, 'acquired' from a corpse in Rwanda eighteen days earlier, Sandra dreaded the soldier might not have randomly selected her from the crowd after all. In that moment an unseen hand snatched Sandra's veil and all her fears were confirmed. White skin and blonde hair had just been exposed.

'A western spy,' grinned the mildly surprised Sergeant, smug with twisted mouth. Dressed in NewKevlar plate over jungle-camouflaged army fatigues with a holstered sidearm, there was no point fighting her way past. She would lose, and she would be dead.

Instead she opened her mouth to speak, and could not.

He snatched her passport, laughed at it. 'You know it is highly illegal to travel under false identification?'

Her stomach sank further when she realised he wore no insignia proclaiming nationality, but who did these days? The white streaks of paint harsh across his face said more. Suggestive of a zebra, they held a deeper meaning: membership of a secret cult or a new tribal clan. Secretive societies were Africa's real rulers in this mid Twenty-First Century world of chaos.

'Well?'

'I ...' she did not know what to say.

The jostling crowd laughed at Sandra. Mostly women in Islamic garb, they must have known of her deception for some time. Sandra wondered if their chatter and fluttering sea of arms were claims of reward for their betrayal. If so, the soldier refused to acknowledge any of them.

'Lost your tongue?'

'I'm a teacher with an NGO,' Sandra finally managed a lie, 'Non-Government Organisation.' If the Sergeant learnt the truth— that she was a soldier with an Australian contingent of the UN— she would be as good as dead, just like those Americans littering the road back in Rwanda. She handed over her real passport, because it revealed no such details. Any documents or items that did she had destroyed long ago ... mostly.

Smirking because he had beaten her, the Sergeant nodded, 'Is that right?' Then to his men, 'Restrain her.'

Several uniformed underlings with similar white striped faces were rough as they handled her. A couple were careless—or deliberate—when they fondled her breasts.

When she was cuffed, the Sergeant gripped her face with his strong hands, examined her fine bone structure and rubbed her soft blonde hair, then sighed as if aroused. 'I think the Chief is going to develop a special interest in you.'

She felt sick in her stomach. 'I have money,' she offered.

He laughed, 'I know.'

Hope vanished from Sandra for he seemed not to care. She struggled to recall some other commodity to bargain with. He pulled his gun, a neural stunner which he forced into her temple, and she froze with fear.

'We'll get that, too.'

Sandra's last memory was a blinding headache, before unconsciousness took hold and she collapsed into oblivion.

Darkness unravelled, transformed into hot smells and the buzz of mosquitoes close to her ears. She sat quickly which served only to worsen a pounding migraine. The only light shone from a circle, a sharp-edged opening to the sky. When Sandra realised she was naked and plastered with fetid mud, she moaned from the shock and clambered into a dark corner.

She was not alone. Three naked women caked in mud huddled together in an opposite corner. Africans with scarring representative of tribal upbringing, their dark skin like chocolate stretched over thin frames. In their hands they clutched what appeared to be white straw, as if their very lives depended upon maintaining its ownership.

Controlling her fear, Sandra clambered against the wall, discovered there were no corners in the curved concrete container, wet with dirty water and slime. She suspected the bottom of a dry well, and then she remembered the prison pits in Bukavu. Those holes had been filled with the dead.

'Who are you?' Sandra demanded. 'Where are we?'

In the half light she searched for her possessions, cloth, anything to cover her exposed flesh. As her hands ran themselves across her body to hide herself away, she discovered tender spots; welts, bruises and abrasions. She did not wish to begin considering what they might have already done to her. Thankfully nothing seemed to be broken, but when she touched her head she discovered fresh blood and patches where hair was missing. That was not straw in the other women's hands.

'Hey, give that back,' was called as she scrambled towards the women. Sandra did not understand why she was terrified, but the idea that they had a piece of her chilled deeper than any fear she'd already experienced upon waking. Thoughts of voodoo magic and occult powers would not vanish no matter how hard she tried to dismiss them from her mind. 'I said ...'

They shied from her, huddled closer together, so Sandra made herself big and angry.

'I said, give it back!'

With her hand raised ready to strike, she almost did. What stopped her was empathy, a sombre understanding of her own fear and how that fear had clouded her thoughts and actions. She reminded herself that she was a professional soldier, and that irrational responses would not improve her situation. These were not adult women; these were three young girls who would be lucky to possess twenty years between them. They were no threat.

Falling backwards, shocked at how quickly her own fear had manifested into aggression, she sighed with frustration. 'Who did this to you?' she asked with a softer tone. 'Who did this to us?' she asked more harshly.

'The Punda Militia,' whispered the middle girl.

'Who?'

'The Zebra Company.'

Overhead a shadow passed. Instinctively they all gazed upwards. Mud was flung from above, splashed across Sandra's face, forcing a shudder. She heard the perpetrators' laughter, and through the burning light of a midday sun, identified three silhouettes cast by soldiers.

'You four,' yelled a familiar voice, the Sergeant who stunned her at the docks. 'The Chief is going to see you now.'

A ladder of bamboo and twine was thrown down. Sandra barely managed to flatten herself against the concrete to avoid serious injury. Thankfully the three girls were not in the way.

'Right you lot, climb out now!'

Sandra and her companions instinctively retreated into the shadows. Her head burned, as a pain like hot pin pricks arced between her temples, ready to fry her skull. It ceased just as suddenly, and she recognised the effects of the neural handgun.

On this occasion its discharge was low, not to render her unconscious, but more than enough to teach a lesson of pain.

'I said climb out!'

Although fearful of their intentions, Sandra managed to obey the order. The Sergeant would not ask a second time.

As she climbed Sandra hoped the skinny girls behind her were sisters, or from the same village, because then at least they had each other. What waited beyond the prison pits could not be pleasant, and they would need support to survive through the pain and horror that awaited them.

On the surface the three soldiers ogled, the same individuals from Kisumu. The Sergeant's face was streaked with the same white paint that designated him a zebra man, the Punda Militia as Sandra had just discovered.

'Didn't think we'd let you sleep all day?' he laughed. 'Come on, move it.'

The sight of the bellowing zebra men terrified the children. The youngest clambered into Sandra's arms, demanded to be carried by tightening her arms around Sandra's neck. The older two together gripped her spare hand, a feeble attempt to seek safety in this unholy place.

As her military training kicked into action Sandra took a moment to assess her situation. Apart from the neural handgun casual in the commander's hand, all three were armed with gauss shotguns. These were weapons Sandra knew well, because they were favoured by most fighting forces in Africa. With few moving parts, even under the harshest conditions they rarely malfunctioned. More importantly, they could utilise any ferrous metal object as a projectile, such as nails, coins, ball bearings, wire and caltrops. No longer did the armies of Africa worry about the conservation of ammunition when ammunition was the junk discarded everywhere.

One of these shotguns was pressed into her back, indicating that she should march between the prison pits stretching out before her in their hundreds. Sandra dared to gaze only into a few. Some held captives naked and dirty like herself, deliberately divided between men, boys and mixes of women and girls. Many were empty. Too many, as she had long expected, were rotten with the dead.

Beyond the pits the surrounding savannah grassland was dry and lifeless. In between a sea of tents, many of which had once belonged to the UN High Commission for Refugees. Soldiers dallied everywhere, but only a few wore proper uniforms and shouldered state-of-the-art military arsenal, and these individuals were all men. Those without the signature white-on-black face paint numbered amongst the sick and starved and were an equal mix of men, women and children. Mostly they were children.

It seemed all of Africa's worst crimes had come together here, and this thought enhanced the dread that accompanied each step Sandra took towards the indicated tents. What waited inside had to be worse than rape, assault, torture and death, because she had already convinced herself that whatever fate was hers had to be worse than anything she could imagine.

'Keep moving.'

Again she was prodded, towards the largest tent. Still carrying one girl and holding the hands of the others they stepped inside. Their nostrils were whacked by stale heat, the smell of human sweat and the haze of marijuana. At least two dozen soldiers shared these confines, African mostly, all with the face paint and all men. Sandra was surprised to see several whites.

But her attention did not linger on these underlings. She was drawn to the one man who had to be their tribal chief, military commander and cult leader all rolled into one. Seated at the tent's far end on what could only be considered a bronze-plated throne, was a large muscular man, bare-chested and ritually scarred. Without face paint he instead wore the regal skins of a zebra. A rare ivory-handled dagger graced a scabbard on his belt, while gold voodoo charms clinked from restless chains tight around his neck.

'Your majesty,' bowed the sergeant, 'Three kikuyu girls, and the white women I told you about.'

The Chief stood tall, raised his hand slowly and held it high as if he were some kind of god. 'Thank you, Sergeant Uskili. Let's see, bring the young ones to me first.'

Torn from Sandra's grip, the whimpering children were pushed forward. Sandra's stomach churned as the Chief manhandled them, felt their bones, checked their teeth, stared into their eyes, and touched them where he should not. It took every effort to do nothing but watch, not even to beg for compassion. If she did so, Sandra sensed that she would only encourage him to do worse.

'These two,' he pointed to the two eldest. 'Take them to my harem. This one,' he pointed to the smallest child. 'She is sick. Slit her throat.'

'What!' Sandra screamed. She could no longer hold her tongue, so she ran forward regardless of the consequences.

The Chief made a motion with his eyes, an angry stare from one not accustomed to being questioned. Not a second later the Chief was obeyed. Uskili punched her hard in the gut with the stock of his shotgun. She crumpled gasping for breath, tried to beg for compassion, but ended up doing little more than choke for air.

From the earthen floor she heard a scream. The little child, her cries were cut short, too sudden to be natural.

'You bastard,' she whispered with what little breath she could muster.

Ignoring Sandra, the harsh tongue of the Zebra Chief was directed at the two survivors, 'This is what will happen to you two if you try to escape. Do you understand me?'

Down low in the dirt, Sandra could neither see nor hear the surviving girls as they answered. Pressed between the legs of the intruding zebra soldiers she did at least glimpse them as they were led outside again. Of the dead girl, she saw nothing except splatters of fresh blood seeping into the earth. She swore to extract revenge, if the opportunity ever presented itself.

'Bring forth the mzungu.'

A dozen hands pulled and pushed Sandra forward until she stood naked in every sense of the word, caged inside a wall of soldiers. All wore white face paint, except the white men who instead wore the reverse: streaks of black paint to create the same effect on their white skin. She wondered what kind of fear or charisma turned such people toward the dedicated worship of madmen. Personally she'd rather die than become part of this farce. Maybe that choice would soon be hers to make.

'A blonde hey?' boomed the Zebra Chief. 'I should put you in my harem, too. What do you say to that?'

Trembling, Sandra wrapped her arms about her chest and hoped to wake from the nightmare. 'I have other skills,' she spoke forcefully.

'A teacher? You wazungu, you all want to be that here in Africa. I have no need for teachers. I teach my Zebra People all that they will ever need to know. No teachers here.'

'Teacher?' she asked, remembering too late the lie she told in Kisumu. Her foe's eyes widened when he too detected her self-questioning.

'You are not a teacher?'

Sandra's eyes darted, sought a safe place to flee and found none. She'd bluffed this far on her escape from a wild continent tearing itself apart, and although her situation had suddenly changed for the worst, she was still alive and in one piece. This must mean she still had a chance of escape, if not now perhaps later, even if that was only a slim chance.

'Yes, you are right. I did lie.'

'Then what are your skills?'

'I ...' Sandra hesitated. These last months, terrified by the wave of violence that had infected the continent like a plague, she'd seen more than her fair share of slaughtered people, westerners and Africans alike but mostly westerners. And yet in this moment Sandra's gut instincts told her that the truth now was her best chance of survival. 'I'm a soldier,' she blurted before she changed her mind. 'A Major with the UN forces. Until a month ago, we were maintaining the peace in the Sudan-Congo conflicts. Not very well, but we had our successes.' She knew she was rambling, so told herself to be silent.

The Zebra Chief raised an eyebrow, 'A soldier hey, and a woman soldier at that?'

'Not so uncommon where I come from.'

'No,' the eyebrow became a frown. 'No, perhaps not. What's your speciality?'

'Infantry. Urban warfare. I've seen action, in Indonesia, Texas, Ethiopia and now here.'

'Good for you,' he mocked. 'If this was a civilised world and I was in the market to buy, I'd hire you.'

She waited for him to say 'but' and then add something about the desperateness of the current situation and how she could be of use to him, but he said nothing. Instead he sidled up to her, close enough so she could feel his hot breath on her exposed skin. He manhandled her arms, face and a breast. He forced open her mouth, took his time when he examined her teeth, for the mouth was a telling assessment of health. All she could focus upon during her ordeal was that the same intrusion had been forced upon the three girls, and that one of them had been murdered at the conclusion of that examination.

'Which one is it?' he asked as he released her.

'What do you mean?'

The slap across Sandra's face stung bitterly. 'You'll learn not to lie to me woman, if you live that long. You and I both know that every UN soldier conceals an identification chip inside a hollowed tooth.'

Again he forced her mouth open with callused fingers that tasted of pungent meat. They pushed and prodded, until a tooth opened and the capsule sprung forth. In his hand now he squeezed it, releasing a holographic identity card; *Sandra D Young / DOB 12 June 2036 / Major, Australian Armed Forces / Secondment to United Nations Peace Keeping Force / Stationed Bukavu, New Congo Republic, 2067AD.*

She had no more secrets to hide.

'It seems you finally tell the truth?'

Sandra nodded solemnly. Now was the moment for truth for the Zebra King, too, when he would either murder her, or enlist her into his Zebra ranks hoping that she would adopt his barbaric cult philosophies and become loyal.

'I always need good soldiers, even if they be an mzungu woman. Give her the implant.'

'What?'

He turned to her, his laugh so obnoxious it carried enough pressure to lay spit across her face. 'What did you expect, for me to take you on your word that you will be loyal?'

'I ...' Lost for words again, that was exactly what she had expected, and so again she did not know how to respond.

Before she could say more, several soldiers led by the gleeful Uskili grappled her, restrained her arms and pressed their weight so she could not flee or struggle. While she was held rigid a white face with black paint entered her field of vision. He seemed to be sad, verging on morbid depression, as he withdrew a lethal-appearing syringe pointed at her face. 'I'm sorry,' he whispered as the thick needle slipped between her eye and eye-socket, and planted what excruciatingly felt like a tiny insect-sized robot that crawled deeper, searing her head with burning pain.

'That hurts,' she cried.

'The pain will pass in moments', the white man mouthed a

whispered apology, 'The physical pain, I mean.'

When convulsions possessed her body the zebra soldiers released her. As if in a dream, she fell into a spasmodic fit, like epilepsy she had witnessed suffered by poor Africans. Dumped unceremoniously onto the earth, she kicked, contorted and foamed at the mouth. Her nervous system was not her own, sluggish and ineffective as it fought against whatever had hold of her.

As quickly as it began, it was over, and self-control was restored. She clambered onto her feet, shocked and scared because this was exactly the type of unknown horror she had dreaded most. 'What the hell did you do to me?' she screamed.

'Enforced your loyalty,' explained the Zebra Chief casually, as if he were an academic lecturing on nothing more than developing market trends to a class full of bored accounting students. 'Now, bark like a dog.'

Sandra shuddered with her whole body. Compelled by his words, she yapped and yapped, imitating every canine she had ever known, until he ordered her to stop. When he did she ceased immediately.

'Kiss my hand.'

He held out his thick paw and she kissed it willingly, hoping not to gag from revulsion as she did. The feared unknown she had expected and then found to be real had grown into something so much worse. What had they done to her, screamed her mind. And all the while her body responded as ordered, kissing and kissing.

'Kiss my feet.'

She bent down on her hands and knees and did exactly that. God knows what diseases or parasitic worms she was feeding into her mouth, and yet even this fear was not enough to stop her.

As she wilfully degraded herself, the men behind her laughed, enjoying her discomfort. For the first time in her life Sandra understood why death was sometimes seen by the desperate and depressed as the more desirable option to suffering prolonged horror. Right now, she really did hope for death above anything else.

'That's enough, now stand and look at me.'

Trembling, again she did what she was told. This torment could continue for hours and days, and it seemed there was nothing she could do to make it stop.

'There are several rules, which I am about to make very clear, so listen carefully.'

She found herself concentrating intently on his every word. Yes, this would never stop. He owned her now. He owned all of them.

'I live by several rules, and they are to ensure I come to no harm, you understand me? The first is that you will protect me from all harm, physical, anguish, mental trauma, anything that you think will upset me. You will bend over backwards to ensure that it does not occur, even at the expense of your own life. Do you understand?'

He kept asking her if she understood, and unfortunately she did. From this moment on she would follow his every instruction to the letter—the machine injected into her brain would see to that.

'Secondly, you will do whatever I request of you. But I see that you are doing that exceedingly well already. So lastly, under no circumstances will you remove the neural controller from you head. You are mine now, my slave, and you will be that until the day you serve me so well you die doing so. Now, is that all clear?'

She fought back the tears. He hadn't told her that crying was not permitted, but she did not want to give the impression that he had broken her will. Clearly she wasn't the only one in this room implanted with a neural controller device. 'Yes, it's all clear,' she said.

'Good. Welcome to the Punda Militia, Major Young.'

Once dressed in clothes previously worn by a corpse, Sandra found she was quickly accepted by the ranks. Most Zebra Company recruits were mismatched mercenaries. Many were young boys and girls barely into their teens. A few sported horrific scars suffered from burns, shrapnel and disease, and with a sickness in her stomach Sandra understood none were debilitating. Serious injuries would not be tolerated here, and she did not have to guess the fate of those who had acquired them.

At sunrise the next morning, approximately two hundred recruits marched from their makeshift prison to trudge east along a dusty road. The lingering smell told they had left behind a similar number of corpses and the silence in the ranks spoke for their atrocities. Only when the horizon claimed their camp did the soldiers allow tensions in their muscles to lessen, but nothing could improve their mood.

The road ahead was dried dirt, the fields yellowed grasslands, and the landmarks dead thorny bush. Once elephants and impala had grazed these lands, but not any more. The escalating war in Africa had changed all that.

Sandra was weary under her load. Her superiors had supplied her with a gauss shotgun and a backpack heavy with supplies, food mostly. Because she was a woman, Sandra was not permitted to paint stripes on her face. This was the only outcome since her capture for which she was grateful.

The Zebra Chief ordered his outfit to march hard, and so they did. Sandra's muscles argued against the overwhelming surges fired from her neural controller, and unfortunately it was her muscles that were losing this battle. As the day grew long she realised only a small number of the 'soldiers' pushed themselves as hard as she did, mostly adults and most of them males with face paint. She guessed the Zebra Chief's supply of implants was limited. Only individuals who could assert physical power to control others were fitted with the devices. They were also the only members allowed to shoulder the outfit's more advanced weaponry. Sandra was likely included in this category because of her military training.

Occasionally one of the 'free-minds'—often a child—would collapse from exhaustion, dehydration, or because they just doggedly refused to march on. Those that slowed the column were given a choice: keep up or have their throats slit. Most found the strength to go on, but not always.

In the mid-afternoon heat, with the sun behind her back and her meagre water rations already depleted, Sandra was ready to collapse herself. Thankfully, the Zebra Chief had sense enough to order rest breaks, even if they lasted no longer than minutes. On their twelfth break for the day, under shade cast by the wreckage of an incinerated sub-orbital jet, Sandra wished for nothing more than to camp here for the night.

In the brief moment allotted she rubbed her blistered feet before the two surviving Kikuyu girls found her. They wasted no time snuggling into Sandra's arms, seeking comfort. When Sandra asked them their names they were too timid to answer.

'Right you lazy arseholes, back on your feet.'

The detestable Sergeant Uskili made his presence known. He passed Sandra with her new friends, stopped in his tracks when he noticed them together. 'What are you doing?' he demanded.

'Resting,' Sandra managed, until she realised that it was not her he had addressed.

The terrified young girls were the subject of his attention. Sandra spotted welts on the girl's wrists where they had been bound and bruises on their faces where they had been struck, and severely doubted this was the complete extent of their abuse. Uskili examined them, and then licked his lips, remembering a taste.

'Bastard', she whispered harshly when he finally turned his back ready to march on.

Barely an hour passed before the outfit encountered a tree-lined river where they could re-fill water bottles. Sandra feared bilharzia and other diseases until she reconciled herself to the fact that dehydration would kill her first. When she clambered from the mud she realised that her two still-as-yet-unnamed girls had vanished. In their place urgent disquiet grew amongst the soldiers.

'You two—find them and kill them.'

She recognised the voice of the Zebra Chief, or more precisely, her neural controller did the recognising and so forced her into action.

Desperate to find fault in the logic, Sandra hesitated, looked to see who the Chief had addressed in the possibility that it was not her. Uskili was by the Chief's side, and her heart sank when she saw the Chief was staring not at him, but at her.

'Kill who, sir?' she asked, dreading the answer.

'Your two young girl friends.'

The Chief's orders were all too clear, which brought a grin to Uskili's face. Both were pleased that it was Sandra who was to perform this bloody task.

Cursing under her breath, swearing revenge, Sandra loaded her gauss shotgun with nails and soft drink bottle caps. She sprinted into the bush along the river edge where she tracked the obvious footprints in the mud. For the first time in her life, she found she hated herself. Of all atrocities imaginable, this one she could not bear. Yet here she was about to do it, murder innocent children who trusted her. Not content with his own atrocities, the Zebra Chief wished to blacken her soul as well.

A crack of snapped branches startled her. Turning quickly, she raised her shotgun centimetres from the face of a white man, ugly with black stripes. She immediately recognised him from tent, the man who shared his sorrow while he filled her head with the implant.

'Steady on Miss,' he held his arms high and wide to show that he was not dangerous. 'He said the two of us.'

Two? Yes it made sense now. The Chief had ordered two people to kill the girls.

Unwillingly determined, they set off together, knee deep in mud now that the thick thorny undergrowth forced them to push on just off the river bank. Tree roots cut at her shins, flies plagued her eyes and mosquitos bit at her skin, but it was her exhausted muscles that physically hurt the most.

'I can't believe I'm doing this.'

'Don't think about it. If you do, you'll drive yourself crazy.'

His accent was English. The manner in which he carried his weight and slung his gun suggested an absence of military training, which she instinctive understood to be to her advantage if she needed to neutralise him. Then she wondered why she thought such things, and realised it was the neural controller automatically scanning for potential enemies acting against the Zebra King, and then providing her with details on how to eradicate the identified threat.

She looked back at his face in hope of gauging what kind of man he was beyond just being a threat. All she could tell was that he was British, mid-fifties, eighty-kilos, right-handed and obviously suffering from malnutrition. Nothing about who he was as a person.

'The name's Colby by the way,' he smiled while she studied him, 'Marcus Colby.'

'Sandra Young.'

'You mind if I go first?'

'You're not a soldier.'

'Yes, but we're only chasing two little girls.'

Without thought she slapped him hard. Hot with anger, she

was so enraged that her blood surged with nothing else. How could he say such things? Again she found her answer; he too was with a neural controller.

'Perhaps I deserve that.' He didn't wait for a response when he pushed past her.

It took only another minute to find the children. The younger stood petrified on the bank, her attention drawn to her profusely bleeding sister tangled in a partially submerged coil of barbed wire. Shock in the second girl's white-rimmed eyes told she was losing blood fast. Regardless Sandra found herself raising her gun, aiming at the mobile target first, the younger girl, as if she were the greater threat. If she pulled the trigger—and it was inevitable that she would—Sandra knew she'd never forgive herself. Controller or no controller, she was about to become party to the barbarity of this continent.

And yet before she could shoot, Colby stepped in front of her.

'Hey,' she called, 'You want to die, too?'

Two quick shots created two corpses. Clean and quick, he had aimed for their heads so their pain would be minimised. Exactly how she would have executed them.

The bloody work done, when Colby turned to her he avoided her eyes. He was as angry as her, suppressing equal amounts of rage.

'Why did you do that?'

He snorted, mad at her perhaps or mad at something bigger, but answered her anyway. 'It's not the first time I've had to kill children, Miss Young.'

'You're proud of that?'

'No, I already have to live with what I've done, but...'

'But what?'

He didn't say. Turning awkwardly in the thick river mud he wasted no time on the hard slog back to the break point, or perhaps to escape the killings he had just perpetrated.

It was while she trudged in his wake that Sandra at last understood what he had lost the courage to say, and found respect for the Englishman. Colby couldn't stop himself from murdering the two girls any more easily than she could, but at least he could save Sandra from additional torment, by performing the execution himself.

Camp was established in an old abandoned safari lodge. Once this luxury destination had catered to wealthy European and American tourists, but the tell-tale signs of high explosive rounds and thermal grenades had changed all that. Bloated corpses of the former staff had to be taken outside and burnt, but the grime and dried blood on the walls were ignored. A crocodile scavenging for food was shot before it could flee into the murky waters of the nearby river. Fresh meat, it quickly became their dinner.

Resting at last, Sandra rubbed her legs to fight off cramps

and hid her face to fight off anger and torment. She wished for revenge but knew not how to achieve it. She wanted solitude but understood the folly of isolation. Where she sat was not chosen at random. Women and young girls encircled her, congregated in numbers as protection from the men. Together they could intimidate the younger weaker males, but not the militant white-on-black-faced leaders. One by one the zebra men would select a companion before disappearing with them into the darkness. Sobs and the occasional plea for mercy echoed from the black night, but no one dared offer assistance.

It was Colby who selected Sandra. With a plate of half eaten crocodile meat mixed with rice in one hand he took hold of her arm in the other. 'I'm not going to do anything to you,' he whispered in her ear, 'But if you don't come with me now, Uskili or one of his chums will claim you.'

She took his hand willingly, allowed the envelope of the night to vanish them both.

'You afraid of predators?' he asked.

'Out there?' she pointed to the barely discernible scrub and shook her head. 'Not out there.'

A nod was his only response.

'I assume you're controlled, too?'

'U-ha,' he nodded again. The black stripes remade him as a ghost. His eyes did not find her. They darted constantly, seeking potential eaves-droppers. As a soldier, that should have been her job. 'Are you okay?' he asked, his voice soft and caring.

'No!'

'Didn't think so'

'What the hell is going on?'

Finally he caught her eye and held it. 'I thought you said you were with the UN? I thought you knew?'

'Knew what?'

Visions of the two unnamed kikuyu girls filled her head, memories she cared not to remember. Less than five hours ago the children had been alive and as happy as they could be considering their circumstances, resting as they did in her arms, feeling safe, even if fleetingly. Colby and she had changed all that, now that they were part of the horror. As the range of her vision grew wider, she imagined neural controllers inside more heads that just of those of the Zebra Company, and found this to be a far more terrifying thought.

'This isn't just isolated to Uganda and Kenya, is it?'

He shook his head, 'I'm afraid not.'

'What are you, to know such things, a government spy?'

'No, thank god.' His chuckle mocked his own sense of humour. 'I'm a journalist. Although we do what we do for different purposes, our process of information gathering is essentially the same.'

Sandra nodded slowly. She became aware that Colby was

holding her tight, not sexually, not with aggression, but as if he was afraid he might lose her. She found that she was glad that he did.

'I've only heard rumours, snippets of conversations really, such as dispatches, misplaced mail, whispers at embassy balls and that kind of thing.'

'And?'

'And adding it all together, one starts to get an idea of what happened. You sure you want to hear all this?'

She nodded vigorously.

'I'm fairly certain it all started in Washington DC, or Maryland, Virginia, somewhere like that. As you would know, the US government has always desired to control Africa, especially now that the Middle East is effectively devoid of oil, and so they are forced by their incessant quest to burn black gold to focus on this continent. This time, however, the Americans did learn from their own legacies, but not well. The west has long been responsibly for supporting African dictators who would grow too unpredictable, too violent and too paranoid. The American government decided to develop a failsafe means by which to control them, or so they thought.'

'The implants?'

'Precisely, only it all went wrong, didn't it? Someone here in Africa found one, cut it out of the skull of an ousted leader and then decided to replicate it. It's just a common neural interface chip whose speciality is in its programming. Easy to copy, you see, and to reprogram to create slaves of one's own. That's what our Zebra King did.'

'He's a computer programmer? He doesn't strike me as one.'

'He's not. Believe me they're easy to set, designed that way for CIA field agents no doubt, who presumably had to hastily insert them into their puppets.'

She remembered Colby injecting the robot into her eye. 'You're talking about escalation—one gets out and then suddenly everyone is manufacturing and using them?'

Colby spun around suddenly to stare into the darkness behind him. Perhaps he had heard a noise. Perhaps he was just scared. He did not indicate which.

'Yes, everyone is out to control everyone else now. Absolute power corrupts absolutely and all that. But instead of making things better in Africa, the US made things worse. As well as Africans in their thousands, westerners like you and me are being enslaved by the very same technology they thought would save this continent.'

Sandra laughed hysterically. Colby's words explained so much; the disintegration of her UN outfit, garbled commands from headquarters more often than not contradictory and often suicidal if obeyed, and then there was her own people turning on their own rank and file. It was ironic that she had survived this long in the aftermath of these atrocities without really understanding what had gone wrong in Africa, a gigantic international war where there were no sides and a millions sides.

'No one's coming for us, are they?'

Colby gave another snort, followed by another paranoid glance into the blackness. 'I'm sorry to break this to you Miss Young, but if you think about it, like a virulent disease, can these implants really be contained to just Africa?'

'What is this place?'

'An old army base,' Sandra answered obediently as she lowered the digital viewfinder from her face to allow clear enunciated words just to please the Zebra Chief. 'British or French I would say, judging on the layout and equipment.' The viewfinder's mil-analysis software agreed with her. Already it had recorded the layout of the abandoned military compound in case they were planning an assault or further recon.

The Zebra Chief nodded in agreement, as if she had just confirmed what he had thought all along. Sandra was sure he had absolutely no idea at all about anything, except how to gratify his own self-seeking needs and take credit for ideas that were not his own. He wasn't a solider, he wasn't clever, and he certainly wasn't a creature of empathy. Worse than all of that, she was certain his pathetic orders would eventually get them all killed.

'What do you want to do?' she asked and realised it was her controller that made her speak, concluding that if she was not given orders she must seek them out.

'I'm undecided, Major. What do you recommend?'

She knew this question would be asked sooner or later and she did not wish to answer. Why give him the breaks when he gave them none in return, when he saw her as an expendable tool, a piece of meat to use and abuse? 'I suggest we move on, leave it alone.'

He cocked a suspicious eyebrow. 'Move on? This place is ideal: fortifications, supplies, weaponry, vehicles.'

'So why abandon it?' Sandra interrupted, 'That's my point. There has to be something wrong. Look around you. Nothing is out of place. Nothing.'

'So?'

'Well...' She struggled to hesitate because she didn't want to say what was on her mind. She wanted him to die from his own stupidity, which, unfortunately, seemed the only way she would ever escape her enslavement. But once again the persistent neural controller forced abandonment of her instincts. 'It's obviously a trap, or an ambush. I don't know any military outfit in the world that would just abandon equipment like that. If they'd all been killed we'd see bodies, signs of small arms fire, something.'

'Perhaps they were enslaved to neural controllers as you are?' His words chilled.

'That doesn't explain why those spider trucks and those

75mm shell guns haven't been stripped.'

'Perhaps we just got lucky, got here first.'

'Luck only lasts so long,' Sandra replied morosely, remembered when her luck ran out in the Kisumu docks.

The Zebra Chief interrupted her thoughts. 'That doesn't mean I don't concede your point, Major. There could be traps. That is why you're going to volunteer in leading a squad of soldiers—expendable soldiers—to make sure you are wrong.'

Unable to protest, Sandra accepted ten soldiers, all teenagers armed with low-calibre rifles, relics of the Twentieth Century that were as likely to explode in their own faces as they were to incapacitate an enemy combatant. Paired up, they cautiously entered the camp.

Thankfully the base turned out to be a ghost town, but that didn't leave Sandra feeling any better. There were no bodies, no signs of small arms fire or any fighting, no blood, no scuffed dirt and no doors left to swing in the breeze. She was reminded of her own flat back in Sydney, as if she'd just stepped out for a few minutes to pop down the street and buy a coffee. Who then would pop back here in a few minutes and surprise them? 'I don't like it,' she said into her comlink so everyone could hear.

'What you mean?' asked the fifteen-year-old boy with white stripes on his face who had been paired with her. Sandra knew him as Daniel Mazuri, knew that he was a Maasai, and that he once worked as a cook in a small diner in Magadi. Now he was the last person left alive from his clan; the sum total of everyone he had known for most of his life were all dead. 'Boss?' he asked again to gain her attention.

'No trip-wires, Daniel, no landmines, no lasers slicing off our legs—and these things—' she tapped a spider truck with the tip of her gauss shotgun, 'are worth a fortune, so why abandon them?'

'What are they?'

'Spider trucks,' she answered, surprised that he did not know, since this design had effectively replaced every brand of all terrain vehicle sold across the globe. With wheels fitted onto robotic arms, they could go anywhere, even up the side of a narrow ravine if the edges were close enough so the wheels could push laterally. 'Back home they are atomic powered. They last forever.'

'Why not here?'

She grinned, 'Give a dissatisfied man atomics and he turns it into a bomb. Then we call him a terrorist.'

'No atomics, hey? They could still be booby-trapped with another type of bomb?'

'Not much of a bang with these: conventional petroleum power.' What she did not say was that this was a later model whose specifications were unfamiliar to her. They could be atomic powered for all she knew, since in the last few years atomic fuel had become cheaper than fossil fuels. It seemed unlikely that they were, otherwise these spider trucks would not be so readily abandoned when they could be turned into radioactive bombs.

A piece of the puzzle was still missing, and what plagued her mind more than anything was that she couldn't see it. So she peered into a spider truck window and to her surprise, discovered an interior filled with a dull grey pockmarked substance. She was staring at hardened concrete, used to cripple the vehicle so it could not be used in enemy hands.

'Do another recon,' she barked over their comlinks.

'Another recon?' questioned a young girl. 'That'll be the third time.'

'Do it anyway?'

'No. The area is secure,' interrupted the crackling voice of the Zebra Chief. 'Major, you've checked enough already. We make camp here.'

Nights were the worst. Nights were when the men came. Sandra needed sleep, but unseen fears kept her awake, of zebra men and their desire for young girls to fulfil their vulgar sexual appetites.

Whenever despair took hold of her she tried to focus again on what was good. Unfortunately the only positive aspect of her incarceration was that she was making friends, two in particular. Colby had claimed her every night to keep other competitive males from her. They would spend their time wrapped in each other's arms talking about past lives that seemed never to have belonged to either of them. She enjoyed those moments. They reminded her this world was not the only reality they could hope for.

Her other trusted companion was Daniel Mazuri, who stole food for her and occasional delicacies such as bananas and coconuts, which Sandra shared with the other women. Mazuri was much younger than Colby. His age showed when he talked and so she found it harder to relate to him, but she enjoyed his kindness and optimism. He was the only one who could make her laugh, with his impressions of native animals, and of foreign tourists whose tips had once provided him with a livelihood.

'They control you too, Daniel?' she asked that night, seated on the edge of the women's campfire. Colby had not yet shown and she was wondering why.

With his intimidating face paint, Mazuri sat just far enough outside the circle not to scare the women, but close enough so that he and Sandra could converse in whisperers. He tapped his head, 'You mean with one of these?'

She nodded.

'Yes I do, but they don't give me no big gun, because I got bad eyes and I can't shoot straight, implant or not. You go and mistake me for one of them free-minds, did you?' And he laughed hard, as if she had just told him the funniest joke.

'No ... Actually, I wasn't sure.'

His tone became serious, 'I saw what they did to you, when you were first brought to us. I'm sorry that happened.'

She nodded slowly, re-experiencing her pain. 'Can I ask how

they got you?'

He shrugged, appeared sad. 'They get everyone eventually, so what's the point in remembering what life was like before? We won't get those lives back again.'

She wanted to say the point was to hold onto their humanity, because if they did not they would loose themselves in this place and become just one more cog turning the wheel that was perpetual horror and violence. Instead she felt physically ill, nauseous as if their food was bad. She had struggled to keep down food for four nights now, ever since their settlement of the abandoned military camp, and she was not alone with this infection. What antibiotics were available and able to combat their stomach bugs, as usual, had been commandeered by the Zebra King.

Sandra tried to speak, only to vomit.

Mazuri was silent and still until she had ceased coughing up bloody bile. He masked well any disgust he might have felt about her condition. Finished, she recalled an earlier conversation where he had complained about gut aches.

'You were lucky, you know?' He continued their conversation as Sandra cleaned her mouth with water from a dirty bowl. 'He treated you well, when you were converted.'

'Well?' she managed. She'd never been so humiliated in her life.

'Some people, he makes them beg to be pissed on or to be fucked up the arse, and then he does it.'

'He what? My god, that's horrible.'

Mazuri nodded slowly, lowered his eyes. 'Yes, it is horrible.' In that moment his words chilled if the very air had suddenly dropped ten degrees in temperature.

'He did that to you, didn't he?'

Mazuri said nothing. She could tell that the very life of him had seeped from his skin and fled like a ghost into the night. No wonder he didn't want to remember his past, when the barrier between who he was now and whom he had once been was divided by such atrocities.

Sandra moved to comfort Mazuri. He flinched at her touch, as if the memory of what had been was far stronger than any compensatory comfort she could offer in the present.

Startled, his wide urgent eyes stared at approaching shapes. Dark and ominous shapes which materialised into five soldiers who ran at them. They grappled Sandra, carried her kicking and screaming into the night. She managed to witness one opponent kick Mazuri in the face as warning not to interfere. Immediately he fell and vanished from Sandra's field of vision.

'You bastards, let go of me!' She struggled hard, but found their grips too strong to fight them all off at once. Not surprisingly, Uskili was counted amongst their number.

They threw her hard onto the dirt just outside the Zebra Chief's new abode, the officer quarters previously occupied by the camp's long vanished commanding officer. Crumpled in the dust was an adult man, moaning and bruised. It took a few moments to recognise Colby. He had been severely beaten, and was now covered in either mud or blood, or both. From fear or sickness, she vomited again.

'White men think they can keep the white women all for themselves. I don't think so.' Uskili hand tightened around Sandra's hair and pulled her to her feet. 'Now strip.'

'No,' she spat had him, punched his face.

His closed fist was harder, and almost broke her jaw.

'Strip or we cut it all off and send you back naked.'

Sandra struggled with her rage until the futility of circumstances beat her. Snot in her nose and wetness in her eyes threatened to betray deeper emotions, and yet she still managed to stand defiant on legs she could no longer feel. Trembling as she stepped out of her decaying clothes so that the welts and sores across her body came onto display, welts and sores that would not heal no matter how hard she tried to keep them clean and bandaged. How could the Zebra Chief want her, seeing how sick and thin and unattractive she had become? How could he want any of them, when he must see they all loathed and detested him in return?

'Get inside.'

This wasn't about sex, it never was. Always it was about power. Would the Chief be the only man tonight who would invade her? As seconds would these soldiers wait outside ready to abuse her, too? Every day her circumstances became worse and worse, the unimaginable just kept becoming more and more real and there was nothing she could do to stop any of this.

That was the worst of it, knowing that if she ever escaped, she'd have to live with the knowledge that she could not, or would not, do anything to stop the daily atrocities.

So she closed her eyes and stepped inside as her neural controller commanded. She called upon all her inner strength so that she would not be present in her own body while it suffered through whatever ordeal awaited.

As the Zebra King found her, she swore a secret oath. She would murder this man when an opportunity presented itself, when she could finally beat her neural controller, even if the price was her own life.

The morning brought sunlight, but no warmth shone on Sandra. Wrapped in nothing more than a dirty towel, she hid in a cupboard. Nearby rumblings were of crackling static, which she tried to block from her ears by covering them with her hands. That noise came from outside. Anything belonging to the outside world, she didn't want to know about.

Another fit of pained coughing took control of her body. Nothing left to expel from her stomach, when she stopped retching her hands were still covered in blood and sputum.

She flinched when Muzari found her, touched her shoulder. She had cringed just as he had that night she hoped to comfort him.

He had a mug of black tea for her to drink. She took it slowly, grateful, held it so she could smell its faint aromas.

The crackling, stronger now that her cupboard door was open, still annoyed her. It still told her there was an outside world she wished to disown.

She wanted to taste the tea, but she feared if she moved her arm to bring the cup to her lips she would spill it.

'I brought you your clothes.'

She couldn't bring herself to answer him. She couldn't even bring herself to remember anything about where they were, why they were here, or what had banished them into this hell in the first place. There were far nicer places in the world, like her flat in Sydney, and it was in those places that she belonged. Not here.

'Do you want me to dress you?'

He took back her tea and helped her out of the cupboard. She let him take her, everyone else had. She let him pull on her knickers, pants, t-shirt. She even let him lace up her boots. A part of her mind understood what was happening, that catatonia was taking hold, and denial was winning. Another part of her fevered mind understood that if she didn't pull herself out of this despair, this would become her life.

'There you go. You look much better now.'

'I don't...' Neural controller or not, she found she could not complete what she hoped to say.

'Don't what, Boss?'

'Don't ever want to look good ever again.'

He shrugged, 'Well, drink that tea. You'll feel better.'

It was his only response, so she did what was requested. Its warmth returned some energy. Its taste returned some sense of being alive. 'What happened to Colby?' she finally asked.

Mazuri's smile was grim. 'He'll be okay, I think.'

'But he's alive.'

'Yes,' he nodded, 'he's still alive.'

'But not in a good way?'

The young boy was not given the opportunity to answer. A bold and boastful Uskili fronted, accompanied by his favoured henchmen. Automatically repulsed, Sandra recoiled from him.

'The Chief needs you now.'

She had to obey. The neural controller ensured that. She wanted him to apologise to her, and to each and every victim in this sad sorry excuse for an outfit, but understood he never would. He just didn't care.

Accompanied by Mazuri, she reluctantly followed Sergeant Uskili and his underlings to the only structurally sound observation tower. Up high the Zebra Chief waited patiently, his zebra hide cape flapped like the frantic wings of hungry vultures. His gaze was intent upon the horizon.

'You called for me, sir?' she asked.

'Take a look at this.' He handed her the digital viewfinder. In a heavy fit of retching he too began to expel his lungs, and, macabrely, Sandra felt grateful that disease in this country never played favourites. When he was done he continued, 'It's already set to the required coordinates.'

Sandra did what she was told, adjusted the filters to cut out the glare of sunrise. Holding the device to her eyes, blurs sharpened into a column of trucks, the old-fashioned wheeled and tracked varieties. She almost cried when she identified UN markings on every vehicle. The convoy was heavily armed. Professional soldiers with UN insignia were alert behind 120mm cannons and rapid-fire gauss guns. In comparison the Zebra Company was comically outgunned and undisciplined. It was a fantasy to believe they might be here to rescue her.

'Attacking them would be suicidal,' she warned.

'I know,' the African's voice was thick with conceited arrogance. 'I've been watching them for twenty minutes now, and it seems taking this base is not their intention.'

No mention whatsoever of the fact that he had forced himself upon her last night.

'Then what are they doing?'

He grinned, showed his teeth, not realising that he revealed a mouth of bleeding gums and festering sores. The previous night that tongue had been upon her skin. Whatever diseases his filthy excuse of a body incubated, she was likely to have caught them all. Only her empty stomach contained her growing sickness.

Muzari at her side caught her attention. Similarly he was covered with sores, bleeding infections of every kind, as were the two accompanying soldiers. Did the Zebra Chief fuck them all? Would the sickness he created ever know any bounds? Again her desire to murder him, to make him pay, grew strong and all consuming, if only the neural controller would not bend her will against her.

'Sir,' she said, her defeated voice not her own, 'I have to warn you. If they attack we are defenceless.'

'That's not a problem. They've been circling, moving around us.'

Sandra's mind raced, forced itself to consider all possibilities, and again her old fears returned. The camp had to be a trap. The column of UN trucks must surely think as she did because they stayed away. What did they know? What could they see that she could not. Was the threat invisible to the naked eye?

'Hand me that weapon?'

She vaguely heard the Zebra King's command, for her mind was on more pressing problems. Perhaps the UN didn't need to guess. Perhaps they possessed the instrumentation which told them what they needed to know. Why not to approach.

'This weapon?' obeyed Muzari, lifting a sniper rifle.

Her neural controller forced her again to focus on the current situation, as a series of dramatic and volatile events unfolded rapidly around her. She saw everything in slow motion, as if in a car crash, although her heart knew that every action now occurred at breakneck speed. The neural controller warned that the Zebra King was about to get himself killed.

'Yes, now.'

The first event was enacted by the Zebra King himself as he lifted the sniper rifle, no doubt to utilise the telescopic site as a viewfinder. This was the catastrophic action her controller had warned about.

Why wouldn't the UN be keeping an eye on the Zebra King as they passed through? If she was in command down there, that is exactly what she would have done. It was no surprise then that the UN retaliated with suppressed small arms fire, volley after volley of tracer rounds to guide heavier arsenal if they were required.

The Zebra King was saved by Uskili, who shielded his master with his own flesh and bone, his face full of regret as life escaped him.

'You fuck!' the Zebra King screamed at Mazuri before Uskili had even finished falling dead before him. 'You're supposed to stop me doing stupid things like that.'

'What did I do?' countered Mazuri.

Bursting with hatred, the Zebra King wasted no time in disintegrating Mazuri's face with five bullets discharged from a sidearm. When he was spent, barely anything resembling a human head remained. The corpse, without a brain to tell it what to do, tumbled off the tower, cart-wheeling once before it crumpled onto dust.

Shock was all that saved Sandra. Shock was what allowed her to stand back and witness the carnage as if none of it was real. Even the blood splattered across her skin was as abstract as flicked paint thrown from an artist's brush onto canvas.

At last she'd figured out what was wrong. Worked out how she was going to escape. Worked out how to extract her revenge and defeat her enemy once and for all.

Don't let him get hurt, that was the first rule. Even if he wasn't aware of his impending doom, the Zebra King must be hurting right now. With bleeding gums and bloody coughs, it would only get much worse, for him as much as anyone.

What could she not see that the UN Convey could? What had the crackling hiss from a discarded Geiger counter been trying to tell her this morning? What warnings was she refusing to acknowledge because of the anguish it would bring? What invisible enemy had the previous occupants hoped to control, filling a spider truck with concrete to bury leaking isotopes? A massive radiation spill was the answer, and every second that passed since their arrival was killing them all.

Before the neural controller could process any logical reason to spare the Zebra King, she grabbed Uskili's fallen shotgun, and shot the Zebra King four times in the chest. When he fell, face down, she used one more shot to smear what was left of his brains into the already thick mess of wet red.

'You bastard!' she screamed, 'You arsehole!'

The only means left to protect the Zebra King from further harm was to end his misery here and now, and that action finally freed her. Venting her anger she kicked his corpse, again and again. 'You were pathetic. You were no king. No one respected you.' She smashed his back with the butt of her shotgun. Freedom was blissful, revenge numb. 'You probably didn't even respect yourself,' she finally whispered to the corpse, words she had long desired to scream at his face while he was living.

'You're free,' she told the two surviving soldiers sharing the platform with her, who could only stare wide-eyed with shock. 'Tell everyone they are free.'

They paid her no heed as she ran down the metal steps towards her own escape from hell. Controlled for so long, they had probably forgotten even how to act for their own interests.

Colby could walk, just. She supported most of his weight, proud as she carried him from their nightmare. In their hundreds the former men, woman and children slaves fled into the bush. To where they ran she could not know. To their homes, hopefully, into arms of loved ones who would heal their pain. As for Colby and herself, all she could think about was that anywhere away from the compound and its invisible enemy had to be better than being trapped inside.

They half-ran to catch the column of UN trucks. Perhaps their drivers were now slowing, waiting to receive them with anti-RAD drugs. She could only hope, for Sandra was betting their very lives that these people really were the UN, and that they would be friends who would treat them with dignity.

'Where are we going?' Colby stuttered through his blinding pain, barely aware that they were on the move.

'Home,' she quietly answered, and asked herself was the nightmare really at an end? She wasn't sure, but she had to hope that the worst must be behind them. 'I have a great flat back in Sydney. You want to join me?'

'That sounds good,' he managed through bloody lips that could barely move.

She smiled for him, for both of them as they staggered towards the convoy and home.

David Conyers is an Australian author based in Adelaide. Once employed as an engineer in outback Australia, he now works in marketing communications. His fiction has appeared in numerous magazines and anthologies, including the collections *Horrors Beyond*, *Arkham Tales* and *Hardboiled Cthulhu*. He is the Associate Editor of the dark fiction magazine *Book of Dark Wisdom*. www.davidconyers.com

BLADDERWRACK

ADAM BROWNE

It is dark. Timbers creak, water drips. For a long time nothing happens. Then a phosphorescence swells from below. The change is gradual, and even at its brightest the glow is too dim to have a colour—but there is something about it nevertheless, some essential unwholesomeness, that suggests if the light *were* to have a colour, it would be the nastiest possible shade of bile-green.

As this colourless green glow rises, timber bulkheads become visible, and fat coils and curdles of what might be lengths of living gut, but which soon enough reveal themselves to be tangled ropes hanging from the ceiling.

This is the bilge of a 17ᵗʰ Century galleon.

The deck is awash with brine about a yard deep, and in the water a thready weed prospers. The weed is the source of the phosphorescence, and were an observer here, one with a more than passing knowledge of algæ, they might have been struck by certain unique features of this plant, the peculiar form of its holdfasts, the unusual glow of its leaf-blades...

Unfortunately for science, no such observer is present.

There are men, however, two of them, slung in the ropes like spiders in a web, or a spider's prey.

The first evidences himself with a fart at least three minutes in duration, its vivid khaki reek billowing about him as he yawns and stretches in his nest of ropes.

His name is Bagfoot. He is a pirate.

His clothes are an amazement of rags. His body is an assemblage of scrawn. His skinny head sways atop a neck so long as to seem almost an arm, his adam's apple working in place of the elbow. German philosophers used a long-necked bird to serve as an emblem of wisdom, the length of its throat allowing its thoughts time to cool as they rose from heart to head, but Bagfoot is without wisdom, long neck notwithstanding. Even in the dimmest light, it is clear he is a poltroon and a fool. In his defence, however, he is also mad.

He jerks to an attitude of crazed attention.

'What?' he says. 'What's that you say?'

At length a second voice comes from elsewhere in the shadows.

'Shut up. I was sleepin'.'

'What you say?'

'I said I was sleepin'.'

'No, afore that. What was it you was sayin'?'

'Nothin', I was sleepin'.'

'I thought I heard you speakin'.'

'And what was it you thought you heard me sayin'?'

'Don't know. Wasn't really listenin'...'

A suffering sigh from the second man. He stretches, scratches, then locates a flint and a candle made from his own painstakingly accumulated earwax. He lights the hair-wick after several attempts. The flame is slow and liquid and emits an awful yellow radiance.

'Douse that,' says Bagfoot. 'It'll use up our air.' He says this without conviction, because he knows it isn't so. They have plenty of air, enough to last them years, which is precisely their problem.

The candle's bearer is a man of early middle-age, deathly pale, and suspended, like Bagfoot, in a cradle of ropes.

This is Jack Morgan, known as Saucy Jack. He is also a pirate. He wears a patch over one eye.

Saucy Jack knows Bagfoot is jealous of his candle, and his other possessions besides. Affluence being a relative thing, Saucy Jack is a rich man indeed. Among his wealth he counts several candles; the flint; a number of fishing lines; some fishing-tackle fashioned from large and small toenails; and an extensive collection of hangman's nooses, wrought from woven hair and hanging on a bulkhead where they may be accessed for immediate use at any time.

Now, with care, he unreels one of his fishing lines and lets the hook drop into the glowing bilgewater below.

'I'll douse the candle,' he says, 'after I catch us a fish for to eat.'

'Pah!' Bagfoot spits. 'I reckon you do *real* fish a wrong when you call those things by that name. They don't have no eyes, nor gills, nor scarcely even fins, but dreadful flappery stumps—'

'If you don't want one,' Saucy Jack returns, 'I'll eat it meself.'

'I didn't say I didn't want one, did I?'

This concludes matters for a while.

Saucy Jack continues fishing. As time passes, and the silence lengthens, his line begins to feel a part of him (which it was once, made it as it is from his own painstakingly collected whiskers). He feels his senses reaching down the thread, down into the chill bilgewater—and onward, into the ship herself.

He feels her about him, the leaden life of her.

She is an *epic* thing, huge, heavy, made heavier still by the gravitas of age. Antiquity touches her timbers through and through. Saucy Jack has heard rumours that once, long ago, she was a flagship of old Carthage, and in his years aboard her, he often encountered remnants of her previous incarnations: archaic fittings, enginery and furbishments buried behind her bulkheads like the vestigial foot-bones in the flukes of a whale. Sometimes he sees her history playing out in his dreams, the stages of her long life; her hull adapting through the centuries, body evolving from trireme to galley, galley to barque, barque to brigantine, brigantine to galleon—the iron and brass and wood renewed and renewed until at last nothing of the original remains.

But she has always stayed the same at heart, her soul steeped in blood and wine ...

The fishing line jerks. A fish has taken the hook. Jolted from his reverie, Saucy Jack begins reeling in the line.

Time has passed. The men have eaten; the candle is out.

Timbers creak, water drips. Bulkheads seep a chill liquor from their pores.

'What?' It's Bagfoot. 'What's that?'

'Shut up, man!'

'What? What's that you say?'

'Go back to sleep!'

'Sleep? Pah! I can't sleep, me. It's so dark I can't hardly tell whether me eyes are open or shut. So dark I can't scarcely tell if I'm alive or dead.'

'Oh, you're alive all right,' Saucy Jack says bitterly.

Below them, the seaweed stirs, strands and bladders beginning to glow again. Were that observer here, the one with a knowledge of algæ, they might have taken a keen interest in this weed (this is, of course, after they had spent several hours screaming and beating at the walls, then a few days sobbing, and then a week or two slowly trying—and failing—to come to terms with the knowledge that there was no escape from this terrible place)—they might have recognised it as a type of bladderwrack. And not just any type: this is a seaweed unknown to botany, a species unique to this ship, to this very bilge.

The light rises, and in it, Bagfoot's eyes widen with shock.

'What's this?' he cries. 'What horror is this?'

Saucy Jack looks across to see that the old man has managed to get himself tangled upside-down. 'Has the ship tipped?' he howls. 'Have we capsized?' Wildly, he looks this way and that, seeing everything the wrong way up.

'We haven't capsized, you old fool,' says Jack.

'No, you're right, course we haven't; I would've heard the alarum ... Ah, I know, we've been a-sailin', we've gone over the Equator, all the way down to the Antipodes, the southern latitudes, where all is upsidedown and contrariwise.' He laughs. 'Ah, what a treat, to see Summer in Winter and Christmas at Eastertime, to see ladies go strollin' arse-over-crown and fellows made of hair with beards made of flesh! How jolly, to dangle our heels over the gunwales and cast our lines in the sky, a-fishin' for the ospreys and kites that sail below...'

There is more such, and it pains Saucy Jack to hear, for despite Bagfoot's fancies, he knows the ship will never sail again.

So sad, he thinks, this once mighty vessel, now dead, buried forever in the seabottom ooze, her vaulted holds acrawl with crabs, her decks carven by depredating worms, her seafaring days over forever.

He remembers the time before. He smiles a little, recalling the ship bounding across the waves; the canvas bellyings of her sails; the glad spread of her yardarms, open to embrace the wind. He remembers when her decks had fairly *ached* with pirates ... and the crew, oh, they'd been a right rabble, a-laughing and a-roaring, their cutlasses waving bright! He remembers their dark dazzling Captain, how he'd wind his bosky beard into tapers and set them afire when storming an enemy ship. He'd light *this* gloom soon enough, Saucy Jack thinks. And the First Mate, that blueblack Africk giant, his bouldering shoulders, the clinking ingots of his golden laughter, enough to freight a thousand holds. And the Boatswain, Saucy Jack remembers him too, that terrible fellow, bigger even than the Captain, an axehandle broad at the shoulders, terrifying his enemies with the scorpion of his regard ...

But then Saucy Jack's smile dims, for those days are years gone, as are her crew, all dead save he and Bagfoot, who often wish they were.

Now comes a creak of ropes, then a shout of delight. 'Ah ha!' Bagfoot has managed to right himself. 'Home again!—bumpity-bump over the Equator and back to the northern latitudes!' He laughs. 'That was a rum trip, and no mistake. Makes a man hungry, a trip like that.' He looks across to Saucy Jack. 'Have we nowt to eat, lad?'

'I'll get us a fish,' the younger man says, lighting his candle and reeling out his fishing line.

'Pah!' Bagfoot spits. 'Call 'em fish, do you? I reckon you do *real* fish a disservice when you call these things by that name, these things made all of jellies and giblets...'

Saucy Jack sighs. He glances at his collection of nooses. Perhaps today?

But no, he can't do it, not yet.

He casts his line in the bilgewater.

It is dark. Timbers creak, water drips.

Then: 'What? What's that?'

'Shut up!'

'What's that ye say?'

'Pipe down, you old fool!'

'*Me* pipe down? Is it *me* talkin' then?'

'Of course!'

'But how can ye tell for sure? It's so dark I can't scarcely tell if it's me or someone else talkin'. I'll grant ye, it *sounds* like my voice right now; but mayhap that's because there's another Bagfoot in here, and he's the one talkin'. What about that then? Are there two Bagfoots here ...? Or two Bag*feet,* is that how it should be said?' Saucy Jack hears the old man casting around in the dark, searching for the other Bagfoot. 'Come out, fellow! Quit your hidin', you old fool!'

Saucy Jack shuts his eyes tight.

And for the thousandth time, unbidden, come the memories of when this all began.

It was dawn. He was abovedecks (oh, to be above, in the air, the wind, the sun!), daybreak swelling on the starboard quarter. The sea a glittering road full of promise.

Then came the scent, pleasant at first. A perfume suggestive of roses, wafting over the ocean.

But as the odour intensified, the crew grew restless, muttering among themselves. Some had heard tell of this scent. It was the smell of a very particular toiletwater, they said. *Eau d'Manrose.* A cologne to strike fear into any mortal heart, for it was the chosen fragrance of a brigand more terrible than any other, a pirate king destroying all who came his way.

Still the perfume thickened, so dense it was visible. A mist, a pinkish fog, sticky and insufferable—puffing and bulging and parting to show a set of sails rising above the billows; spinnakers and mainsails and jibs all with a nastily intimate appearance to them, pale pink stained fabric with leather straps and whalebone stays, like gigantic orthopaedic undergarments.

On Saucy Jack's ship, the cannoneers primed their weapons.

Then the fog parted, and they saw the other vessel in full.

It was an abomination, an immense floating bonbonniére, its candycane hull painted a pink so sickly sweet that it set Saucy Jack's teeth aching. It was a galleon wrought from frills and titivations, from flummeries and pink knickknacks and frou-frou gewgaws ... and Captain Manrose himself, when they saw him, was a horror worse still.

He stood atop his forecastle, fat as a manatee, the hot seamammal acreage of his face crusted with a craquelure glaze of white-lead mixed with the rendered fat of unborn lambs, his beestung lips pursed in a moue expressive of a species of madness so frightful it defeats the powers of this narrator to describe.

Saucy Jack watched as the monster raised a handkerchief, lowered it.

The battle began.

Even now, years later, Saucy Jack Morgan shudders to recall it. The boomcrackling musket fire; the screams; the cannons' bellowing throats. Manrose's men adventuring forward through the smoke, the more awful for their rouged cheeks, their mincing ways, their killing grins as bright as the blades they held so daintily.

Saucy Jack's fellows fought valiantly, giving the invaders like return, and for a time the battle could have been anyone's—until there came a loud report from abaft the mast. All knew the powder store had been hit. The limbs and bodies of Saucy Jack's shipmates fell to all sides. He saw a black object bounce to a halt on the deck, and for a second he thought it was a cannonball. Then he saw it grimace, and knew it for the head of the First Mate.

There was never any question of the outcome. Saucy Jack saw his fellows go down—one after the next, men dying in fits of terror, their clothes steaming crimson, their very beards singed and parted with the passing of perfumed musket balls. The Quartermaster was felled like a tree; the Bosun next, his torso sliced in twain. Hearing a cry, Saucy Jack turned to see his Captain breathing his last, horribly wounded, his blood and tears spilling to quench the flames of his whiskers.

And then, what then? Was there a storm? Thinking back, Saucy Jack cannot be sure—the blood had teemed like rain, the voices of the cannon, roaring from the bronze throats, had sounded like thunderbolts ... and the screams of the dying, what had they been but a great wind?—a gale blowing hot about him, driving him away from the battle, through a hatchway and thence down, belowdecks, along a companionway, then another, tumbling down ladders and stairs...

All the way to the bilge.

It was not until then that he realised what he'd done. He'd fled the battle, betrayed his comrades and his ship.

He buried his face in his hands. A coward. Surely a man could go no lower than this?

Then the ship sank.

It happened quickly; a great sucking boom as she took a cannonball beneath the waterline; she staggered, rolled to starboard—and then plunged down, past shoals of tunnies and salmon, past congeries of eels and slow blue booming whales. She plumbed the deeps, her timbers creaking under terrible pressures, the light above fading, fading—gone.

And she settled down as if to sleep among the ammoniacal slimes of the ocean floor, buried forever.

But in her bilge a chance pocket of air had formed, and so Saucy Jack was spared one fate for another far worse. It was not until some time later he realised he was not alone—Bagfoot, the ship's cook and fellow coward, had also fled the battle.

And there they remain.

Now, in the darkness, Saucy Jack realises his hands have been working on something almost without his knowing. It's a noose, another for his collection. He'll hang it up on the bulkhead—and it will stay there; for in his heart he knows the cowardice that sent him to the bilge will always hold him from taking that final step. He will live out his life here with Bagfoot, drinking and eating nothing but the blood and flesh of the dark-adapted fish-things that swim below. The hull, too, will remain sound, its rotten timbers held in place by an accreted armour of corals, and the air will continue on, the oxygen renewed by the mutant bladderwrack that so thrives on the men's waste.

It will last indefinitely, this tight little ecology made up of the seaweed, the fish, the two men...

Now, exhausted, Saucy Jack curls into himself, hoping for sleep.

And in the darkness, Bagfoot jerks to an attitude of crazed attention, his ears pricking yet again to the ship's silent voice, laughing her vengeance at the men who so betrayed her.

'What?' he shouts. 'What's that ye say?'

(with thanks to John Dixon)

A member of the Supernova writers group, Adam Browne lives in Melbourne with his wife, writer Julie Turner, and their baby daughter Harriet. 'Bladderwrack' was written after a long correspondence with American writer John Dixon, who is the Saucy Jack to Adam's Bagfoot in the 17th Century pirate galleon bilge of their friendship.

LADY BOUNTIFUL'S LIES

CORY DANIELLS

Women usher you into this world and
women usher you out. Praise the Lady Bountiful.

On the rim of the Shallow Sea they give the bodies of their dead
over to the Untamed Ocean. But here in Mandalae where
people crowd every building and houseboat like birds on a bottle
tree, we don't have the luxury of returning a body to the sea. The
canals are so thick with refuse that by midsummer we keep our
windows closed and pray for an early autumn storm surge to
flush the city clean.

That's why they took my dead baby and they burned its
body.

I don't say him or her, because the poor thing was born
Twisted with no discernable gender. It tried to breathe. At least I
think it did. I was busy ridding myself of the afterbirth when Lady
Bountiful's midwife whisked it away. I caught only a glimpse of
distorted limbs and pale skin tinged blue. So perhaps I was wrong
and there was no chance that it might have lived.

Would I have wished a life of temple slavery on my child?

I don't know. There are plenty who dedicate their whole lives to
the Gods, offering service in return for Manna. At least temple service
gave a Twisted's life purpose. All their simple minds need is order.

Twisted do not have souls so there were no funeral rights for
my baby. But the Clan would hold a Lament for the baby that
might have been, the one I had already grown to love.

A gentle hand settled on mine. 'We're ready, Sa Liseli.'

I looked into Tiremi's sweet face. We shared the same Mother
and two full Uncles. Barely two Crossings younger than me, we
had always been close. She had refused to call me Sa when I
became a woman at fifteen, refused again when at last it was
confirmed that I was with child, and again when the child survived
the dangerous first term.

Until I lost the babe she'd still called me Lise.

Now she called me Sa. Raw tears glistened in her eyes and
her free hand rested on her flat belly which hid the new life she

carried. I lifted my gaze from her belly to her face. I did not want her to suffer as I had.

'May the Lady bring you a beautiful, healthy babe.'

'Oh, Lise.' She threw her arms around me. 'I don't know how you can be so brave!'

Brave, me? I was breaking apart inside. To have carried the babe the whole three terms, to have laboured a day and night to bring it forth only to find it was born Twisted. How could the Lady be so cruel?

'Come.' Tiremi pulled back, struggling to smile. 'They're waiting to see you off to the Temple.'

She glanced at the Devotion, a gold filigree representation of Lady Bountiful in her guise as the pregnant woman.

Anger surged through me. Why should I venerate the Lady when she had abandoned me? I wanted to take that Devotion and smash it into little pieces on the hard mosaic floor.

Unaware of my heresy, Tiremi turned her hand over, offering her palm. Tears traced paths down her powdered cheeks.

Surprising myself, I sprang to my feet. Still sore from where the baby had pressed on my spine during the birth, my back protested at the sudden move. I gritted my teeth. This was nothing compared to the birthing pains. And they were nothing compared to the loss of the babe.

'We can't go to the Lady with you looking like this, Tiri.' I turned her to face the mirror, wiped her cheeks clean and powdered them again. Then I dared to look into my own face, powdered lightly so that I was pale as befitted the daughter of a Great Clan. My brows were plucked and painted in high arches, lips a perfect tiny bow. But the eyes … I could not meet the eyes, naked with grief.

Another spasm passed through my spine, an echo of the birth contractions. I bent forward and waited for it to pass. This time yesterday I'd still had the dream of a perfect little boy or girl.

A slender shoulder slipped under my arm. 'It is all right, Sa Liseli, I will come with you, as far as I can. Lean on me.'

Our eyes met in the mirror. I could do this. I had to. My Clan's honour demanded it. In the past five Crossings few of our women had carried babes full term and even fewer had delivered a healthy babe. The Elders had decided it was time to make a Sincere Devotion and that I was the one to do it. By walking barefoot over burning coals to deliver the Devotion, my suffering would ensure our plea reached the Lady.

But I couldn't do it now that I knew what real pain felt like. I was not brave. 'Stay with me, Tiri.'

She nodded earnestly.

Together we went down the corridor, out of the women's wing to the grand stair where the men of our Great Clan waited. I did not look for the youth who had fathered my babe. He had been kind and sweet and I'd been sorry when the Elders decreed we were not to share the Bower-bed anymore. If I saw Moro's sad eyes I would not be able to face the Elders who waited at the bottom of the stairs.

Seven of them, all ancient. Several had held positions of importance on the Shallow Sea before they left public life. Now, with the wisdom and knowledge of their long lives, they devoted themselves to leading Marblebar Clan.

Like me, their heavy torques rested on their shoulders. The symbol of Marblebar, intertwining vines, was depicted in black neillo, the fruit picked out in semiprecious stones.

One by one, the Elders touched my forehead leaving a thumb print of ash, ash from my Twisted baby's burning. Their faces blurred; luckily Tiremi was a rock at my side.

'You have memorised the Plea?' Leading Elder Selendi whispered.

'Yes, Sa Selendi.' I licked dry lips. 'Hear my plea Lady Bountiful, bless the women of Marblebar Clan with healthy babes.'

She smiled. 'You will do us proud, Sa Liseli.'

I turned away, unable to meet her eyes.

Through the foyer of the Clan's palace and out to the terrace then down to the wharf, I held my head high, refused to falter.

Once outside the thick walls of our palace the heat hit me. The air felt like warm soup, moist and almost too heavy to breathe. The Clan torque weighed down on me. I concentrated on each moment, not thinking ahead. Little rivulets of sweat trickled between my breasts.

The bargeman lifted his head and met my eyes.

Moro!

I almost didn't recognise him as he waited to pole the Clan's ceremonial barge. He had shaved his head, rubbed ash on his chest and was dressed only in a loin cloth so that he could go before Lady Bountiful as a poor Penitent.

Feeling me falter, Tiremi squeezed my hand and I kept walking.

Moro dropped his eyes and did not greet me.

'He has taken a vow of silence,' Tiremi whispered, answering the question I had not asked.

I should have guessed. Moro was sincere in everything he did. No words would leave his lips for the length of one Crossing.

But his hands were eloquently gentle as he helped us onto the barge. It had been decked in solemn white, the Lady's mourning colour. The Lady's priestesses preached that life was as fleeting as the clouds in the sky and the white caps on the Shallow Sea.

Normally I would have taken the seat, but I could not bear to sit still. That would have meant accepting my baby's death. Why did the poor thing have to die before it had a chance to live?

So I stood, feet apart to keep my balance, and faced the canal, bleached bronze by the equatorial midday sun.

The Elders had followed us out onto the terrace and now the Clan's musicians played, deep sad pipes and a solemn single drum with one high pipe dancing over the rest, promising hope. Moro began to pole us away. From the palace windows above, five floors of our Clan sang in praise of Lady Bountiful.

I wanted to scream. How could she be the source of Abundance when she demanded I walk across hot coals to plead for healthy children?

But even as the anger churned through me, the voices faded behind us and we wound down the canal, under the bridges that connected Marblebar's palace to its places of business, and then out of our quarter and through the Sandstone Clan's quarter. Like us they were a Great Grounded Clan, our allies in business and breeding.

This canal led us into one of the grand canals that fanned out from the centre of Mandalae like spokes on a wheel. All grand canals led to the promenade, a circular terrace where traders from across the Shallow Sea sold goods, treasures and works of art.

Today the markets were empty. It felt strange to walk under the Poinsiana trees filled with rainbow lorikeets chattering and fighting, across the sandstone squares empty of everything but for the occasional fallen Poinsiana flower, myriad small leaves and bird droppings.

Climbing the rising terraces made my back ache and I had to stop to catch my breath. Here, on the higher terraces, there were fewer trees and the buildings were owned by the great temples. Reknowned artisans or the Merchant-royals from out near the rim hired houses to either ply their trade or attend the Crossing Festival.

'Not far now, Lise,' Tiremi whispered.

Moro waited patiently behind us even though the sandstone must have been cruelly hot on his bare feet. I could feel the heat through my sandals. How was I ever going to walk across hot coals?

Thinking of him, I gathered my strength and will. 'Come, Tiri. Let's get out of the sun.'

We climbed the last terrace to the thirteen great temples that surrounded the Bottomless Pool. The Lady's temple was directly opposite Lord Turtle's. He carried the Shallow Sea on his back, swimming in a great figure eight across the equator each year, into the cold poles and back again. We'd made the Crossing thirty days ago, but wouldn't have any relief from this heat until we entered the more temperate seas.

Without Lord Turtle there would be no Shallow Sea for Lady Bountiful to bless with her abundance. So we stopped to give coins to the Twisted who sat in the temple's deeply shaded veranda, twirling their prayer wheels in endless figure eights. The soft whirr filled the air like the rustle of the leaves when the first welcome autumn breezes stirred the Shallow Sea.

Today I could not look at the Twisted. Their short malformed limbs and dull faces accused me of betrayal because, on seeing them, I discovered that I was secretly glad my Twisted baby had died. I would never have to look into a Twisted's face and wonder if it was the child I had abandoned.

Going through the lane between the temples we reached the Bottomless Pool. Its cerulean depths hid centuries of Devotions dropped into the water to win Manna with the Gods.

But our Devotion was going straight to Lady Bountiful herself, delivered with my sacrifice, so we skirted the pool and climbed the steps to the entrance to her temple.

The Welcoming Doors sensed our approach and opened in accordance with Lady Bountiful's wish that all inhabitants of the Shallow Sea be ushered into her presence. I had seen this twice before, once when I fell pregnant and again when my baby survived the first term, but still I marvelled.

Despite the tears that stung my eyes I saw the eager faces of pregnant Penitents waiting for us to pass. Among them was the midwife who had delivered my Twisted babe. At the sight of her, her words came back to me, whispered as I lay exhausted after the birth. She had been speaking with her apprentice and had not meant me to overhear. 'Another Twisted, so many these days. From the poorest Denizen in their crowded houseboat to the richest of the Great Clans, the women suffer then weep. I fear Lady Bountiful has turned her face from us.'

Holding my head high I passed the many watchers and entered the centre of the temple. Here more priestesses and their acolytes waited for us. The dome soared above four stories high and Lady Bountiful's Triumvirate stood under it. Formed of pure gold, she appeared in her three manifestations, the girl promising life, the pregnant woman creating life and the crone taking life. A grate of hot coals had been rolled before the Pregnant Woman and covered with green palm fronds.

Moonflower Incense burned in niches, filling the air with its somnolent scent. Wreathes of ethereal smoke were illuminated by the great shafts of light that pierced the dome's slits far above. A choir of nine priestesses, three crones, three pregnant women and three virgins sang a paean to the lady.

In the deep shadows under the great arches I saw many faces, Pentitents, the temple's own Twisted, priestesses and the merely curious come to see the daughter of a Great Clan suffer. Come to mock if my courage failed me.

And I saw Sa Selendi watching from one of the shadowy archways. Being an Elder of our Clan she had come to bear witness, but she could not accompany me because I'd had to come of my own accord.

As if I'd had a choice!

The temple's High Priestess was tall and raw boned, with a square jaw. But she spoke kindly as she led me to the centre of the dome.

'Do not hesitate.' She nodded to the grate. 'The quicker the better.'

Then she helped me remove my slippers, my torque and gown so that I was dressed only in a simple shift. Under this my breasts were tightly bound to prevent them forming the milk I would not need.

Moro handed me the Devotion and Tiremi gathered my belongings. As I looked into her eyes I told myself I was doing this for her, for all the women of our Clan and for the babes not yet begun.

Before the birth I had thought myself brave; during the birth, as each contraction rose up like a great wave sucking me under, I was swamped with panic and would have done anything to escape. Now the fear went core deep.

Devotion pressed against my racing heart, I watched as Lady Bountiful's priests removed the palm leaves, revealing live coals lightly dusted with grey ash. On its little wheels the grate stood a hand's span off the floor. I had to cross that or shame my Clan.

The singing stopped and the ceremonial horn sounded it deep, solemn call.

I was not ready.

Silence filled the great dome.

Why did I have to do this?

Because I had birthed a stillborn Twisted.

Anger spiralled upward through me.

Nothing could hurt more.

Nothing the Lady's midwife or the Elders had said had prepared me for losing my child. I felt cheated.

Anger fired me.

I stepped forward, not looking at the ground, seeing only Lady Bountitful's serene face, the mound of her belly and her cupped hands waiting for my Devotion, delivered with pain.

My bare foot left the coolness of the marble and moved over the grate. I felt the heat radiating off the coals.

For my babe. For Tiremi. My foot came down on the live coals and I stepped up before I could think.

My leg spasmed in reaction.

For my babe. For Tiremi. For all the women of the Shallow Sea.

Knees shaking, I lifted my second foot onto the grating, transferred my weight and stepped off, onto the marble, sinking to my knees. The worst part was over. Now to say my Plea.

'Hear my plea, Lady Bountiful.' My strained voice carried, echoing under the great dome in the hushed silence. Almost blinded by tears of relief, I placed the Devotion in the Lady's hands. She had let me suffer me for nothing. How many of those pregnant Penitents would taste the same bitter loss? 'Bless all the women of Shallow Sea with healthy babes.'

From those shadowed arches excited chatter erupted.

'What did she say?'

'The Shallow Sea, *all* the women of the Shallow Sea. She did it for us, for all of us!'

A single soprano rose above the exclamations, her voice

soaring like a bird. The rest of the choristers joined her in praise of Lady Bountiful.

I had done it. I had not let my Clan down.

A wave of relief rolled over me.

Behind me, I heard the Priestesses trundle the grate away. Still on my knees, I turned to watch while two Penitents swept the ashes and then three more, all eager to win a small measure of Manna from my sacrifice, knelt and mopped the floor. They kept glancing at me, surprise, awe and admiration animating their faces.

Moro and Tiremi caught my gaze, pleased and proud. Sa Selendi scurried over, Penitents and Priestesses clearing a path for her.

I looked up to the High Priestess.

'You have done your Clan proud, Sa Liseli of Marblebar Clan,' she said the formal words, then she dropped to her knees and caught my hands, kissing the palms. 'More than that, you have done the women of the Shallow Sea proud.'

I shook my head. No, I was a coward. Afraid and angry, I had acted on impulse.

'What were you thinking?' Sa Selendi demanded, as she joined us, her whisper explosive. 'Why waste our Devotion and dilute your sacrifice? How will I tell the other Elders?'

'Tell them Sa Liseli has risen above Clan politics and spoken for all of the Shallow Sea.' The High Priestess's arm slid protectively around my shoulders. 'When word of this reaches the rim it will reverberate back to Mandalae and inspire new devotion to the Lady.'

In that heartbeat I saw my suffering had had purpose. The Lady had not been cruelly capricious, she had been grooming me to cross the coals, to plead for the women of the Shallow Sea. 'In fact...' The High Priestess sprang to her feet. 'I will go to the Temple Council and bring Sa Liseli's actions to the attention of the All-Seeing. It will be Santa Liseli before the next Crossing, mark my words!'

Sa Selendi's eyes narrowed. 'You want her fame to enhance your temple.'

'Why should Marblebar Clan win acclaim when they don't appreciate her?' the High Priestess countered then turned to me, her eyes bright with excitement. 'You will be welcome with us, Liseli. Tell the Elder you renounce your name and Clan and dedicate your life to the Lady.'

'No, Lise!' Tiremi cried.

The two old women ignored her.

'You can't abandon your Clan, Liseli,' Sa Selendi insisted, catching my left hand and urging me to stand.

'Come, dedicate your life to the Lady,' the High Priestess caught my other hand and hauled me upright.

Pain flared across the soles of my feet. The world closed down. I felt myself pitch forward, then nothing.

☆

'Women usher you into this world and women usher you out. Bless the Lady Bountiful.' A gentle, vaguely familiar voice murmured.

I woke to find the midwife and her apprentice bathing my blistered feet. For a moment I had no idea where I was or why my feet hurt, then it came back to me. There had been a point to my baby's death.

'Where's Sa Selendi?' I whispered.

They both glanced to the ceiling.

'She's with the High Priestess. They're arguing over you like dogs over a bone,' the apprentice blurted.

The midwife sighed and shook her head. 'Don't let them bully you, child. It was a grand thing you did.' She came closer and squeezed my hand. 'But you don't have to decide anything today.' She glanced to the ceiling and lowered her voice. 'Your two friends are waiting. Lean on Kareni, she will carry you.'

She helped me swing my legs off the bunk. Kareni offered me her back. She was tall and raw boned like the High Priestess. Many women from out on the rim where life was hard chose to dedicate their lives to the Lady.

I slung my arms around her neck and she straightened up, lifting me off the bunk so that my toes just brushed the floor.

'Go somewhere quiet and think before you decide if you want to serve Lady Bountiful.' The midwife patted my shoulder. 'You have already served her more than you can know.'

The apprentice took that as her signal to go and hurried off. I could barely hold on. I felt strangely distant and weak.

Kareni stopped suddenly, cursing under her breath. 'They're coming.'

She about-faced and jogged off. I held on for dear life. We left that corridor and went through several others until Kareni came to another abrupt halt.

'Come too far,' she muttered. By now my head was spinning.

Two temple servants huddled over a series of gears and levers, prodding them.

'Here.' One of them noticed her. 'Are you going up stairs?'

She nodded.

'There's someone standing on the doors' threshold. They've jammed up the mechanism. Tell them to get off it.'

Kareni nodded and swung around. Retracing her steps to the last turn, she headed up a narrow stair. When we came out the top I recognised the foyer of the Welcoming Doors and there were Moro and Tiremi waiting for me.

'Lise!' Tiremi cried.

Moro ran over and swept me up in his arms. I protested because although he was tall, he was thin. In the end we compromised. He carried me piggy-back as if we were still children.

'Go,' Kareni shooed us off. I clutched Moro's shoulders as they ran out the doors and down the steps.

'There she is!' Several voices cried. Pregnant Penitents and the merely curious surged towards us.

Moro and Tiremi hesitated, looking around for a way past. I had a flash of Lady Bountiful's temple and saw the Welcoming Doors swing ponderously closed. Now I knew that it was not the Lady who had sensed our presence at her temple door, but a mechanism of gears and levels, triggered by a weight sensitive threshold, I felt a fool.

Was there even a Lady? Had my suffering and my baby's death been for nothing but the aggrandisement of Clan and Temple?

'Where to?' Tirelli asked. 'What next, Lise?'

'Santa Lise, let me bathe your feet,' a Penitent pleaded.

'Rub my tummy, Santa Lise, and bring me a healthy babe,' another cried. More took up the plea.

A horn reverberated, silencing everyone.

We all turned to Lady Bountiful's Temple where the High Priestess stood with Sa Selendi at her side. She nodded to her assistant who blew the ceremonial horn once more.

No one spoke as the Elder and High Priestess descended the stairs, stopping just above us.

'Liseli formerly of Marblebar Clan you must decide,' the High Priestess announced. 'Do you dedicate your life to Lady Bountiful?'

'Or to Marblebar Clan, your Clan who raised and reared you?' Sa Selendi spoke with heavy emphasis.

Should I return to the Clan who would use me in their constant political one-upmanship with the other Great Clans? Or should I dedicate myself to a Temple who would use me to further their lies?

I didn't want to dedicate my life to either.

'Lise?' Tiremi whispered.

I looked into her face and wanted to run away.

A woman gasped then clutched her swollen belly. Those around her steadied her as she lifted frightened eyes to me.

'Santa Lise,' she pleaded.

And I knew then that I had no choice. I could not denounce Lady Bountiful.

Perhaps there was no Lady Bountiful, perhaps the Twisted were a cruel joke visited upon us by capricious fate. It did not matter. All I could think of were those women like me, who were destined to endure the agony of birth to bring forth new life. If the women of Mandalae were to suffer, as least they should suffer with hope.

Cory Daniells lives by the bay with her husband and six children. She writes for children and adults. Her fantasy trilogy 'Shadow Kingdom' sold in Australia, the US and Germany. She is currently doing an MA in creative writing. www.corydaniells.com

The Pain Threshold

JASON NAHRUNG

John says pain can take you places. He's something else, my John. A cut above, you might say. When first I met him, both his arms were covered with scars, crisscrossing in random white lines, some still red from recent use. That was enough to get me excited. The thought of flesh opening, him moaning ... but I'm getting ahead of myself.

When I first met John, he was pimping in the Valley, a delicate, too-thin lad with wide brown eyes almost obscured by a fringe of dirty brown hair that reminded me of tassels on a lamp my mother once had. His lips were like a young girl's, full and ripe despite his skinny frame. Stained jeans clung to his arse like a denim mould. I couldn't decide whether to feed him or fuck him. As it was, I did both, but not in that order.

I don't know where he lived. When I asked he just waved a hand towards the east, and when I asked again, he smiled and said I wouldn't believe him. I suspect he hung out in the squats in one of the condemned warehouses on the Valley fringe, or maybe the housing commission flats that must have seemed like such a fine idea when they were built.

He was good at his job. No shame, an honourable profession, John told me. His mother had done it before her death a few years back. He had loved his mother. I could tell by the ache in his eyes. My body responded with an entirely different kind of ache, but I suspect the longing was similar. His lips quivered, the lips that had done so well by me for a fifty, and I felt myself get hard again. So I took him home.

I had a little flat near the river, an attic room rented from a Mr Benson for a hundred a week. It was easier to stay there when I was in town on business rather than drive back up to the coast each day. The coast was for weekends. It was a good arrangement that suited my wife and I quite well. I could see the brown flow of the river from the window, and across the water the glittering lights of the well-to-do suburbs crowding the cliffs with their boat-sheds and tennis courts. Best of all, it was quiet most days, with the drunkard landlord considerately passed out by early evening.

That first night with John was like nothing else. I resisted the temptation while he showered, and then I tortured myself further by towelling him down. His arms, legs, chest and stomach were all scarred, and both nipples had been squashed out of shape and pierced with rings. The delightful boy even had a Prince Albert; I'd not seen one before, and I thought it amazing how it caught the light and then added such texture as my tongue ran over his flesh.

Towel forgotten, we ended up on the bed. I could feel his ribs beneath the scar tissue, an amazing sensation compared to the smoothness of my other lovers. The contrast with his gorgeous face was mesmerising. He said, in his curiously English accent, he hadn't been able to go above the neckline for fear of ruining his livelihood.

'But that won't matter soon,' he said.

'You don't sound like you expect to be around for long,' I said. His kind never did. Life on the streets wasn't a long-term proposition.

'I don't,' he said, with a smile indicating an in-joke. 'Maybe you can help me.'

'How's that?' I asked, suddenly suspicious. I wasn't looking for a boyfriend, just release. My wife gave me all the domestic bliss I could handle.

But he didn't say anything, just pushed my hands down to his nipples. I brushed the ruined buds, feeling them so rough on my fingertips.

I wanted to ask what had happened to them, but I nudged one of the rings and he sighed, and I forgot my question, concentrating instead on teasing him with gentle tugs, first with my fingers, then with my teeth. My hand was shaking, my breath painfully shallow. I expected him to be like the rest, to resist the pain. But he pushed his chest towards me. I sucked on him. When he cried out I paused, waiting for the inevitable complaint. But John seized my hair and pushed my face against him all the harder. I'd never felt that before. A little disappointed, but then thrilled: he wanted it. It was as though the tingle of his scarred flesh against my skin sent a shock into my brain, lifting my skull, removing all thought and leaving sheer, terrifying power.

We both groaned as the passion took us. I felt my control spiralling downwards with each urgent bite ... Then I tasted salty warmth. I pulled away; blood can be dangerous. I don't mind seeing it, as long as it's theirs. Christ, even a paper cut makes me woozy. And don't even talk to me about dentists; that's too much power for one man to have. But these street trash, they're a filthy mob, sharing needles and never using condoms. You've got to be careful. The euphoria rushed out like air from a released balloon. When I wiped my mouth my hand came away streaked with red. The trickles of blood on his chest fixated me, despite my fear. Not often they'd let me bleed them.

'Why did you stop?' he asked, and his expression caught me by surprise. He liked it. He wanted it. This kid was Christmas.

He sighed heavily and rolled over. I touched his shoulder, gently, fingers quivering on his hot skin. Then I kissed him, apologetically as I could, and felt him stir. Finally he opened himself to me again. Tremulously at first, then with increasingly desperate abandon, I lost myself in him, feeling the sense of power surging back through me.

When I was spent, the two of us lying naked in the tangled sheets, my hand tracing old wounds with renewed wonder, I asked him, finally, about those injuries. Had he done them himself? Didn't it ... hurt?

'I was trying to get back to me mum,' he said, as though I should understand. When I asked him what he meant, he told me his tale, and I could only stare, poker-faced, and caress him, my little Santa Claus come early.

His mother, he said, had been sent to Moreton Bay on a charge of prostitution. Unlike the men, imprisoned on St Helena Island, the female convicts were housed on the mainland, and hired out to the local gentry as maids. There was, he explained, a shortage of free women in the fledgling colony. The convict women would be lined up and the squatter or gent would have his choice.

'John,' I said, daring to interrupt. 'You do realise that was almost two hundred years ago, don't you?' I had only a rudimentary knowledge of the city's history, but it was enough to know it had been founded as a penal colony in the early 1800s.

'Aye,' he said, as though I were stupid. 'Can you imagine how she must have felt, when she found herself here? The world all changed, with all these weird things like cars and planes and electric lights, and the boats and buses and the clothes?' He emphasised the last, as though of all the marvels of modern civilisation, it was the fashions of the day that had most marked his mother. 'The music? The television? We had a television, bought it cheap from a pawnshop. She could watch it for hours and hours. Like a junkie, just shaking her head at all these things.'

'So what happened, John?' I asked, intrigued by his fantasy, even as I looked for a way to turn it to my advantage. Letting him go was unthinkable.

'She died. Some bastard she brought home when I wasn't around. And you know what? He broke the telly. Wasn't content with beating her to death; he had to smash the telly as well. It was all she had, that telly. Well, it and me, I s'pose.'

I held him, but he seemed indifferent to my touch, and there was something about that remoteness I found a trace scary. He told it all so matter-of-factly, as though it were just the death of some hooker he'd seen on the news.

'So she must have been quite old,' I said, keeping my voice flat. I prepared to roll away from him in case he reacted violently to my bubbling scepticism. They can be surprisingly touchy, junkies, especially if they haven't had a hit. Though I hadn't noticed track marks on John's arms. Lots of wounds, sure, but no needle pricks. No, his drug seemed to be something else again, and the thought that he might be the ultimate masochist made me ache with anticipation.

He just looked at me as though I were stupid.

'Me mum was thirty, maybe, when she died. She didn't know her age for sure. No, you see, what happened was, I brought her here.'

'And how did you do that exactly?' I propped myself up on one elbow, the better to see his face as he lay on his back, staring up at the ceiling, as though the explanation was written in the shadows.

He sighed, as though exasperated that I expected him to read me the story, when I had only to lie back and look at the ceiling to read it for myself.

'John?'

He looked at me from the corner of his eye, then back to the roof.

'I did it when she birthed me. It was the pain. Somehow, I hurt her so much, she was so desperate to get away, she came here, and brought me with her. Gave birth to me in an alley in the City. I guess that was where the jail was, back then, but things had changed in the meantime and the buildings were gone. Sometimes I wonder what would've happened if there'd been someone's house there, or a trendy flat, or maybe a grocery shop.'

He smiled at the thought, almost wistful, kind of boyish, like contemplating the reaction of a girl who's had something nasty hidden in her lunchbox.

'She'd got preggers, you see. The gent what hired her, he'd knocked her up, and then thrown her back to the jail. But she escaped, havin' me. The pain brought her here. I dunno why to now, in this time, if you follow me.

'She told me it felt like her entire body was being torn apart, like the world was screaming. And when all was said and done, I think it broke her, the whole thing. Having to clean herself up, mend herself, and then care for the both of us in this place. She went on the game, of course, and soon as I could, I did too, to help her out.

'But you know what?' He became suddenly animated as he raised himself on his elbow to stare me in the face, so close our noses almost touched. 'I should be like you, better even. I should be a gent, I should. He owes me and he owes me mum, him what used her up like that. Just think; when I get back and he gives me what's mine, my great grandson or somethin' will own his house. They'll thank me for settin' it all right.'

If he noticed my incredulity, he gave no sign. His grand vision had clouded his eyes, I suppose. He wasn't looking at me, but through me, winding the clock back however many years.

'But to do that, wouldn't you have to return to a time before you were born?' I asked, drawing his focus back to me by giving his cheek a tweak.

'Yeah, I s'pose. I mean, I gotta get born. But if I can get her looked after, make sure the gent does the right thing by her, then maybe we won't ever come here. We'll have a fine life, back when we oughta. Be hard to give up all the mod cons, though. Be nice to take some chocolate with me, if I could.' He shrugged. 'I can show you the house, if you like.'

'The house?'

'His house. Me dad's. Well, what was his. Took me a long time to find it, based on what she told me, but I found it. I can take you there if you don't believe me.'

I wasn't sure what he thought showing me a house would achieve. The city was full of houses, and some even dated from the convict era. I could probably find a tourist brochure in the city that would show me a half dozen such places within easy walking distance of City Hall. But I didn't say that. No, I reached out to him and brushed those eyes with my lips, and murmured urgently into his ear, 'In the morning.'

After breakfast I drove him in search of his inheritance. To my surprise he didn't take me into the City at all, but downstream, almost further than I could see from my little garret, to Hamilton Hill. Got to give it to the kid, he had good taste. Some of the most expensive real estate in the city occupied that hump on the river, guarded by walls and fences and the warning signs of security firms.

'It's all changed, of course,' he told me, and I nodded my understanding. 'I've had to dodge the cops and that. But I found it. This is where I should be, or at least, me kids.' His kids and then some, I thought, but again I stayed my tongue, content to admire his impeccable taste once more. The sandstone manor sprawled behind a tall iron fence and an ornate gate. Two lions sat on the gateposts, and they'd been there a long time, I gathered, because while the shape was unmistakable, the weather had long ago eroded their features.

'So are you gonna help me?' he asked.

'How?' I imagined shoving him over the fence and watching him walk up the gravel drive and knock on the iron-bound front door, waiting defiantly with hands on hips to stake his claim.

'Are you gonna help me get back to me mum's time?'

'I don't think I know how,' I said, ruefully wondering if I should hand him the street directory from the glove box.

'I'll show you,' he said, and smiled.

He showed me how, even though he went white. I hate to think how gleeful I must have been when he'd pushed the bloodied razor into my hands and instructed me on each manoeuvre. The blood started out so bright, but went dark so quickly. And there were other things he had me use. He would urge me on: 'Push it through,' he would cry; 'I can feel it, it's happening, push harder!' He scared me, even me. I thought I knew the power of pain, you see, but he wanted even more. It got so my hands shook until I couldn't grasp, and finally I broke down entirely. Then he took my face, held me to him and kissed my tears away, and promised me it would be better next time, and everything would be all right.

He was half right. It was better the next time, and the times after that; it got so I ended up covered in sweat as much as he would be lathered in blood, and my hand wouldn't shake at all except from excitement. If he could make up a fantasy to explain why he enjoyed the pain, then I could make up stories as to why I enjoyed giving it. Sometimes I was simply helping him, giving him what he wanted. Other times, usually when he was on his back or knees, I pictured him as my boss. When John was on his front, I'd think of him as my wife, who I am certain would never have believed the pleasure to be derived from such a host of household items. Yet other times I lost sight of John's face altogether, and his features morphed through a kaleidoscope of faces—my parents, boys and men—who'd given me cause for any number of regrets. It was the ultimate power trip, and between his taking and my giving, we sped towards overload.

Eventually we broke the seat out of a wooden chair and added straps for his arms and ankles, and put a plastic sheet under it to protect the carpet. When it got bad, real bad, I had to gag him, so no one else could hear, but even then he seemed so loud, and his shuddering made the chair move, and once I knocked him over, and hurt my knee as I caught him before he hit the floor. Afterwards, I thought he'd probably have liked it if he had. I know I would've, but there was the noise to consider.

I lost track of time. I know I stank of sweat and spew and come, and the room was heavy with the stench of blood and piss despite the river breeze. John had gone pale, so pale, but wouldn't let me stop.

'Almost there,' he whispered. 'Almost there.' He seemed exhausted, his lips raw; I left the gag out and started again, looking for new flesh where there simply was none. This would be his final try, we both knew; we had progressed to his face, you see; that was all that was left to us, and he was certain we were about to break through. He could feel the world screaming, he said, just like his mother had, and then he shouted for her, screeched. Panicking, I thrust the gag at him. The chair fell backwards, crashed to the floor, splintered. He reached for me, one hand raised imploringly. I caught his wrist, bent to haul him up, but the floor lurched towards me. The last thing I heard before the lights went out was John whisper through his bloodied lips, 'At last.'

☆

When I woke up, John was dead. It was probably a blessing, really, given the mess he was in. But he's left me only one option, really. There's a newly built manor on Hamilton Hill, you see, with two lions standing watch at the gate. And inside there's a maid who can take me home. I just pray that I've found her in time.

Jason Nahrung works as a journalist at The *Courier-Mail* newspaper, where he has a column dedicated to speculative fiction coverage. In 2005 he shared the William Atheling Jnr award for Criticism or Review with Robert Hood. A member of Vision writers group and the Writers on the Edge critique circle, he has had several short stories published. His debut novel, *The Darkness Within*, is based on a novella written with his partner Mil Clayton by email when they were living two states apart. The supernatural thriller is due out in early 2007 through Hachette Livre. www.jasonnahrung.com

WORLD'S WACKIEST UPPER ATMOSPHERE RE-ENTRY DISASTERS DATING GAME

BRENDAN DUFFY

It was my day off and I was holed up in my hermetically sealed AA-rated sanizimm, watching TV while the rest of the world rotted away. I'd just clocked off a double shift and was dozing on the sofa with my Little Brother™, *Space Racer Weekly* on my knee, when chimes roused me. A lazy reggae beat swaggered into my ears.

Mr Spliffs got up from the middle of the room, playing bongos and smoking a gigantic scoob. He took a huge toke, and with a thick Jamaican accent said, *'Hey, Mon! I know you is busy relaxin' but you have an incomin' call from...'* Next to Mr Spliffs appeared a pasty white youth in 2D, obviously lifted from a photo and enlarged to realsize. Its animated cut-out lips badly mimed, **'...umm, Spraytan Jojoba...'**

'Eh, Ginko, Mon,' said Mr Spliffs, *'should I show* **...umm, Spraytan Jojoba...** *the door?'*

The words, 'Play, Save, Trash' glowed above Spraytan's head. I groaned. 'Play.'

The 2D image did what looked like awkward Irish dancing. The limbs had been cut out and stuck back on so they could spin 360°, and the eyes glanced from side to side. I could even see the dog-eared sticky tape Spraytan had used to put the whole thing together, complete with a glued-down stray hair and what was probably a full set of fingerprints.

'Spraytan, that's pathetic.'

'Hey, Ginko, what's up?'

'Watching TV with my Little Brother,' I said.

'Eww, that poor little guy, trapped in your 'zimm. Speaking of which, are you coming to the roof party tonight?'

'I'm not sure,' I said. I *still* didn't have a date. 'What's it like outside?' At my porthole I dimmed the lights, pulled back the curtains and opened the blast louvres. I squinted into the scorched orange haze. Megopoli stained the filthy sky. Contrails hung between the stratoscrapers like empty clotheslines. The turbulent air was awash with all manner of missiles, many retargeting to race straight at me. I slammed the louvres shut before they hung me out to dry.

My coffee cup vibrated across the table to the dull basso of muffled impacts.

'It looks like there's gonna be another war tonight,' I said.

'Yeah! I want to go, but I'm just not sure how to accessorise,' said Spraytan.

'The chic clique will be wearing those sleek new over-the-shoulder strapless backless evening rocket launchers.'

'Yeah, and everyone's gone armour piercing since Glaxo Towers thickened their cladding. I've saved enough vouchers to get a free bazooka, but I'm at work. Can you finish my helpdesk shift?' he asked.

'Nah, I've just done a double! I gotta babysit the Little Bro for a couple more hours.'

'Hack the switchboard and divert calls to your home number. You'll just be sitting there anyway! It's quiet—only two calls an hour. Field a few while I pop over to Bayer Roche Shopopolis.'

'OK, but you owe me,' I said.

'Great. Use my login and don't let on to the Bossa Nova or I'll get penalties. Management is so tight since that new AI bought majority share. It's stitched up all the lurks. It knows everything.'

'Nah' I said, 'it's got no idea, it's just an Artifiscal Intelligence program, a dumb share trading abacus that made some cash in get-rich-click schemes and is now trying to diversify by learning human management skills. You gotta learn how to manage up.'

'Just be careful or we'll be decruited!' said Spraytan.

'Maybe I'd better mimic your voice in case it listens in on the calls...'

'It probably does! Don't mess with callers on my login.'

'You know me,' I said.

'Yeah, just...'

I rang off and relaxed on the couch next to my Little Bro, TV blaring, flipping through *Clothes, Cars, n' Guns* magazine. *Brandwagon* had just released their Sizzling Summer of Sidearms, a low-vogue range of fashion successories: handguns 'n handbags, threadbare credware, muscle Ts to hustle sleaze, streetwise neat guise to meet guys, lasers, phasors, teasers and tasers, but this week's feature colour totally clashed with my scar tissue.

I grabbed my antique phone and dialled the Supe-A-Pharm switchboard worker's entrance, logged in and toggled the diverter. The space above my phone lit up with caller icons; a little tower of glowing eye candy, lurid floating caricatures squabbling amongst themselves for my attention. There were fifty-seven calls waiting! Not for long. I reordered the queue according to gratuity size, put the non-tippers on permahold, then pressed for incoming.

I savoured my informal helpdesk motto, *Quando dubitas, eos expellate*, 'When in doubt, drop 'em out'. And best practice was to do this mid-sentence. The phone rang—my first sucker. Client.

'Hello, Supe-A-Pharm helpdesk, Ginko Vista speaking.'

'Ginko? This is Car.'

Oh god! My car. 'Whaddaya want? Stop calling me! How did you hack this line?'

'Ginko ... How did you get home from your last shift?'

'What do you care? You weren't even there. I waited and waited! You're my car. Where were you?'

'Did you ride in ... ah ... another car?'

'Umm. No, no, of course not,' I lied. 'I caught public transport. You're the only car for me.' I grabbed *Neuropean Automobile* and turned to the sports models: Lamborghini, Ferrari, Ducati; the most incredible machines, stunt fliers that cost what was left of the world: top chassis, great bodies, nice jets, sleek aerodynamic design. My car blabbed on while I flipped through glossy pages of top shelf chromatic glitz, then gasped out loud. 'Check those tailfins!' I rotated the mag to get the proper view of a Maserati's translucent pink E-Z glow panels with embedded sparkles.

'What?'

'Err, nothing.'

'You're looking at car magazines?'

'No, no. I spilled some coffee.'

'The Maserati 2120. That cumulus climbing strato-stacker, I hate that model. You're checking other car's tailfins! What's wrong with my tailfins?'

I looked about the ceiling. Little black boxes.

'You've hacked my securicams—you're spying on me! I'm taking work calls only. Don't call again!' I slammed the phone down. This had gone too far. I looked over at my Little Bro and shook my head; my car was out of control. Spaced around the room at strategic intervals, my Instacrowd cutout pals silently agreed.

The phone rang.

'Hello, Supe-A-Pharm Helpdesk, Ginko Vista speaking.'

'Herro, yesh, I bought your "fird shet o teef" kit and all my hair hash fawen out and rots o rittle teef are shprowting from my head!'

'Yes, yes. I see. Hold please.' I pressed hold and sat back, flipping tailfin while my client sweated it out under the Casiotronic one-finger monotone version of 'I fought the law and the law won'. I had a whole suite of collector's holdmusic for all occasions—this one was my default, with an LD50 rating of six minutes. How long could this guy last?

I thumbed through pages of cars; the latest civilian releases. What's hot and what's not: glam-shots of the latest gelati—fairy floss fliers, solid state silicon chrome-magnon engine blocks, click-on cognokinetic craniocapillary control, aerobotic aerofoil acclimation, a fine teal tailfin tartare art fair, a dynamic dayglo rainbow oven baked in semigloss satin, two all beef patties, spatial force batteries, nickel engines on a chassimiseed bun.

I sure felt hungry, but all this cheap eye-candy was just Eurothrash for trailertrash, not like what I used to fly ... Before The Accident ... I perused the entire range of new ultrasonic scramjet space racers, then reconnected.

'Hello, sir?'

'Yesh, sho now aw feese little teef...'

'Sir, could you please put your dentures back in?'

'I roshtem.'

'I see. So, our *Tri-Dent* third set of teeth kit? Did you read the instructions fully?'

'Yesh.'

'And now teeth are growing out of your head? What colour are they?'

'Fruoro pink.'

'I see. And were you concurrently using our *WhyDye* hair colour perma-change cosmetic virus kit? Fluoro pink, maybe?'

'Ahh! ... No.'

'Right. So if I were to do a scan of our product sales documentation would I find that you had purchased our fluoro pink *WhyDye* kit?'

'Umm, maybe.'

'Yes, you see, the dentine matrix repressor protein cascade interacts with the hirsute chromatomelanocyte operon activator virus. You didn't read the instructions, did you, sir?'

'No.'

'I'm sorry, sir, but all calls are recorded and such customer admissions void all warranty and product support obligations. Thankyouandgoodbye.'

I rang off and glanced at my Little Bro. 'What a gonzo. Honestly, we make these kits for people, and if they're too stupid to use them...' I looked around the room at my Instacrowd pals. 'Know what I mean?' They all did.

A reception bell tinkled and the Bayer Roche Concierge appeared in the middle of the room, wearing a dandy bellhop uniform with bright red felt trim and brass buttons.

'Ginko, what a lovely sanizimm you have.' It walked about the room, picking up things to examine, wincing, then placing them back and wiping its fingers. 'The 283rd floor of my building, nice Westface balcony; it's a good neighbourhood, all the mod cons, reasonable anti-missile defence...'

'What do you want? Rent isn't due yet.'

'I've been checking your finances,' it said. 'You can only afford this sanizimm lifestyle for seven more days, then I'll have to either shift you down at least two hundred floors to a sharedorm that equilibrates with your paltry income, or sell shares in you to another company. If I can find a buyer. There isn't much of a market for has-been stunt fliers that work on pharmacy helpdesks.'

I opened my favourite *Tower Life* to the well-thumbed centre spread—me, in a gloss black two door Lamborghini Scramjet Kestrel 3300, top down (the car, too) and looking oh-so. The caption read 'Ginko Vista drinks ImmunoCola, with 10% more lymphocytes for that fresh shield of protection.

'I'm saving up for an operation so I can get my old job back. I'll be a stunt flier again, big contracts will roll in, and I'll be rich. And popular. And have a cool girlfriend.'

The Bayer Roche Concierge pointed to the date. 'Not if you spend your time locked in your sanizimm looking at two month old ads of yourself. Word among the flyboys is you're finished. Better work something out or you're downwardly mobile, faster than any stunt you survived.'

The Bayer Roche Concierge walked to the door and waited, idly looking round the roof and walls, whistling a tuneless little ditty.

'What?' I asked.

It rubbed its thumb and fingers, then stared at me pointedly. Unbelievable.

I tipped it 10 Cartesian phonecreds and it winked out.

Seven days, then dossing with the great unwashed in a sharedorm below cloud level.

I felt ill and needed some open space so I checked the balcony airlock. Siesta had just started. The video monitor confirmed that the fighting had abated, so I depolarised the west window wall, retracted the blast louvres, and stepped through the airlock to the balcony.

I looked out across Cartesia. The dull orange sun hung low, illuminating the sluggish layer of photochemical sludge that covered groundlevel like a shroud; an acid smog that rotted the base of each massive arcology like plaque on teeth, quietly suffocating the free and the brave outside in their cardboard homes. The giant megopoli of Immunocracy Towers erupted from the tidal ochre glow: Glaxo Towers, J&J Juggernaut, Amgen Arcology, Boehringer Building, Schering Stratoscraper, Pfizer High-riser and more; an apoplectic residential panacea stretching into the airtrafficjam freckled distance.

Concrete, glass, and steel; bridges, tubes, and malls. Apartments, landing pads, multitowered stratoscrapers, multi-tiered stratifications, a glassy titanium blue socioeconomic immunohierarchy soaring skyward, topped with private pent-houses poking through the sterile isotopic haze that still circled the troposphere, where the only disease they ever suffer from is affluenza.

The gentle clack of small arms fire rang out in the distance. A few missiles traced arcs between buildings, and somewhere some dilettante was taking pot shots with a cannon. I laughed. Kids. It seemed oddly pleasant so I deflocked the magnofuzz and dropped the grav field to pathofilt. A steamy kerosene breeze carried a faint scent of cordite and what would have been a plethora of pathogen. A heavily armoured rent-a-turret had bivouacked on the wall next to my balcony; a 50 calibre autocannon with two side-mounted laser guided rocket launchers vigilantly trained on Glaxo Towers, just in case. I shooed it away, across to Ms Jiaogulan's balcony;

I didn't want it attracting any stray munitions, and besides, she was now a GlaxoCola shareholder.

A pilus slowly telescoped across the chasm from the Schering Stratoscraper toward me and anchored next to the rent-a-turret. Hundreds of small miniturrets swarmed across the narrow pilus and spread out across Bayer Roche Westface.

'What are you doing?' I asked one.

'We're independent contractors. All predictors indicate a flare up, so we're here to make some fast cash.'

'Nah, not during siesta.' I laughed and relaxed into my banana lounge. Opposite, on Glaxo Towers Eastface, people came out onto their balconies. We waved. I watched the airtraffic pass by; fliers swooped, dived and rolled to avoid lockon from rogue missiles. I had to look away, it was such poor work.

I needed money, quick. One more big gig and I'd have enough cash to afford the operation and my problems would be over. I asked Mr Spliffs to ring my old frienemy Cosmic Ray, my industry connection.

'Ginko who?' he asked, incredulously.

'Vista. You were my agent until six weeks ago, and The Accident remember? Commercial stunts, the ImmunoCola contract, and *No More War*™ sneakers?'

'Oh, Ginko Vista, the brainless washed up stunt flier who likes cars too much. How's the new job as a helpdesk teletechnician? Sorry pal, I've got incoming, hold please.' And I was suddenly listening to 'Ob-la-di, Ob-la-da', sung by a chorus of barking dogs.

I wasn't brainless.

And I didn't like cars. That much.

And my stunt career wasn't finished.

But I couldn't get a gig until I had the op, and I couldn't afford the op 'til I did a gig.

'Mr Fridge, could you come out here please?'

'OK, Boss.' Mr Fridge waddled out and served me a nice cold bulb of ImmunoCola. I held the blue bulb up for the folks over at Glaxo, cracked the top and took a swig. Some returned the cheers. I watched them holding up their red bulbs of GlaxoCola. Disgusting stuff.

Someone on Glaxo Eastface had brought an Instacrowd cutout out onto their balcony. I checked with my binoculars. It was Tony Marone, the TV celeb; the suave new face of GlaxoCola. He held the advertising contract and was their public image—and my nemesis. I guess this didn't quite break the informal siesta rules: no hustle or tussle.

'Would you like one of these?' I yelled across the way, holding up my blue bulb of ImmunoCola. 'It tastes great!'

'No thank you, I prefer the taste of this.' He hoisted a keg onto his balcony table. I checked with my binoculars; the huge red label was readable! This wouldn't do. Bayer Roche Westface used to be the ImmunoCola shareholder heartland, but ever since The

Accident the ImmunoCola advertising campaign had flopped and citizens were flocking over to the other side. They couldn't buy GlaxoCola shares fast enough. Traitors. We couldn't afford to lose anyone else.

I opened my beach umbrella and tilted it toward the sun, and Glaxo Eastface. It may have had the ImmunoCola brand name and logo on the outside, I can't remember, I'm not sure. Glaxo folks made a fuss, but ImmunoCola supporters cheered me on from their balconies. We yelled and jeered at each other. Across the way someone unfurled a GlaxoCola banner from their balcony handrail. Then another. And more.

I heard a few cleverly accidental firearm discharges, and ducked when bullets ricocheted around my balcony. I returned fire, then flocculated the magnofuzz. Shots rang out, and someone activated our building's adscreen. My hair stood on end from the static halo as infotainment panels energised, speaker stacks hummed, and 100 floors of Bayer Roche Westface blared out the soundtrack to one of my favourite ImmunoCola Infomercials, 'Drink ImmunoCola! With 10% more lymphocytes, it's better than GlaxoCola.'

I chuckled to myself.

The GlaxoCola Shareholder protectorate answered immediately. One hundred floors of Glaxo Towers Eastface lit up, and Tony Marone's gigantic head surged up through the clouds to leer at us.

'Drink GlaxoCola! With 11% more lymphocytes, it's better than ImmunoCola.' Tony held up a red bulb to show the new 11% label. They'd stolen our gimmick! Missiles hissed and cannon stuttered. 'Because ImmunoCola,' Tony Marone's head boomed, 'is a no-brainer.' A visual spread out over Glaxo Towers Eastface, file footage of my face, a slomo that caught me blinking, looking goofy. Graphic animation showed my brain catapulting from my head as I smiled, cross-eyed.

Before I knew it I'd unloaded my whole clip and was trigger-clicking on empty. I raced inside for my biggest rocket launcher, a nice urban cammo *Versace* carbon femtofibre Scramatronic EM gutz-shittah 3000 home protection munition, with overunder 6 inch rocket launcher/50 calibre machine gun; a harmless antique so still legal to discharge within city limits, and so huge my teetering made it hard to aim. I shot electromagnetic pulses at the screens 'til the battery flatlined, pumped all my ballistic missiles into the local advertainment generator node, emptied all clips, and even found a napalm button I didn't know was there and pumped all that out, too, but Glaxo Towers defence intercepted and shielded the pointy end of the action.

The handle of the gun had a built in moby. The service plan included speed dial access to an emergency remote air strike service, so I dialled up. There was a ring tone, which was good, because the number was often engaged. A recorded female voice answered:

'I'm sorry, all our operators are currently taking calls. If you wish to log a complaint, press 1. If you wish to call in a remote air strike, press 2. If you have billing inquiries, press 3. If...'

I pressed 2.

'Please state the name and address of the air strike target,' said the voice.

'The local Advertainment generator node on the 280th floor of Glaxo Towers Eastface, Immunocracy Towers, Cartesia, USA.'

'I'm sorry, did you say "Uncle Jimbo's good 'ole homestyle bactoprotein pizzaria"?'

'No, no, no,' Bloody AIs. I yelled into the handle and repeated the address.

'I'm sorry, but due to scheduling difficulties caused by over-demand for this service, your request has been recorded and placed in a queue and will addressed by the first available operator. Please hold. Have a nice day.' And I was listening to 'Orinoco Flow' by Enya, while before me a twenty storey Tony Marone laughed as an animation of my dumb gigantic brain catapulted from my idiotic head.

I raced to my gun rack for the howitzer.

A reception bell tinkled as I was lining up the cross hair's with Tony's head. The Bayer Roche Concierge appeared next to me on the balcony, looked at the rubble and shrapnel lying about, shaking its head.

'Tsk tsk, Ginko, did you start this? It's siesta! Don't hype or snipe, remember? This is all coming out of your bond!'

'I'm legally allowed to protect my home,' I said. I guessed lots of folks on lots of balconies were getting lots of talking to.

Anyway, the battle was over. The local Glaxo Eastface military advertainment complex was a smoking wreck; twenty floors of ruptured turrets, shattered screens, and blown speakers, though not as bad as yesterday. The building was already repairing itself and upping the defences. Glaxo citizens were out on their balconies, putting out fires and straightening chairs.

'Cheers!' I tipped my blue bulb of ImmunoCola in their direction and took a swig.

They waved back.

'You fleshers! There's no profit for me in this war,' said the Bayer Roche Concierge. 'I've negotiated a doubleclick ceasefire with the GlaxoCola shareholder protectorate of Glaxo Towers Eastface: all members of the ImmunoCola Shareholder Partisan Army of Bayer Roche Westface are required to vote for an end to munitions discharge and cola advertising. Conditions of your lease now require you to log on to your tenant's contract, read the ceasefire terms and doubleclick the 'I agree' box.'

It glared at me, raised an eyebrow and tapped its foot. I logged on to www.BayerRoche/body_corporate/eigenpolitic.com and voted like a good building caucus automaton; the motion was upheld—only well-armed squatters and evictees voted against a

Concierge—and the Endless Colawar was over.

For a few hours.

It wouldn't take long before someone lodged another fair trading appeal.

'There aren't many ImmunoCola shareholders left since The Accident,' said the Bayer Roche Concierge. 'ImmunoCola is finished, leaving an opening in the marketplace. Maybe I'll launch my own cola product. I have a captive clientele. A corporate beverage would get all the Bayer Roche citizens working together. Maybe something orange flavoured...'

It straightened its cap and winked, gimme-gimme hand beckoned at waist level.

It took a blank Pfizer Prescription cred to make it leave.

I needed some fresh air, so I went inside.

Mr Spliffs appeared. He took his toke and said, *'Hey, Mon! I know you is busy relaxin' but you have an incomin' call from...'*

'YOUR BOSS!' said my boss. I almost choked—what was it doing here? The words, 'Play, Save, Trash' glowed above its rigorously balding dome. The animatronics had even adorned its shiny pate with reflections.

'Eh, Ginko, mon, should I show **YOUR BOSS!** *the door?'* asked Mr Spliffs.

'Play,' I said, collapsing the helpdesk caller icons.

The Bossa Nova appeared in the room, the Supe-A-Pharm avatar, a rotund, vested gent with a fat cigar in one hand and a bowler hat in the other. Yesterday I'd hacked a faint Bossa Nova beat into its audio feed. It glanced about, as though checking for distant insects.

'Boss! So glad you could pop in. At my home.' I slid the *AI Hacker Monthly* cybertage special back into my stack of magazines. 'Hey, I bet you're glad I suggested this Winston Churchill avatar— that electric blue sphere with the lightning bolts was just plain scaring everyone in the office.'

'Yes, productivity has increased by 24.2% since you leased me this avatar holofile. People have stopped cowering under desks and actually talk to me now.'

'Well that's a *twist*.'

On saying the trigger word the Bossa Nova began twisting to the beat—it twisted way over to the left, lifting its right foot in the air, then twisted back the other way.

'Yes, everyone likes this avatar,' it said, 'but now people keep saying the strangest things to me. Maybe I'll never understand flesher behaviour.'

'Oh, I'm sure you'll catch the *jive*.'

The Bossa Nova's head remained perplexed atop Wild Jivin' Winston. I'd used an old dance instructor database as the template for the Winston holofile. Everyone at work loved it. From the neck down the Bossa Nova was a dancin' fool.

'Ginko, the good news is that this week you're Supe-A-Pharm's best helpdesk product support teletechnician, having attained the highest call answer and closure rate. I don't know how you do it with so little experience.'

'It's easy, polyclone yourself and get little genius AIs to do it.'

'I've run 4096 simulations comparing the success of a human to an AI and the net outcome is maximised when the human answers phones.'

'Oh, really?' I smiled. The dumb AIs didn't even understand the very world they ran.

'Yes, so two minutes ago I bought out 51% of your indenture contract with Bayer Roche, your extensive body parts lease, product purchasing rights, clone library, the patent to your genome and all subsidiary rights to your lymphocyte and seed organ farm, and all future organs grown from them. Congratulations, Ginko, under the *Corporate Goods and Chattels Act* of 2087 you are now fully indentured to Supe-A-Pharm. As a citizen of Supe-A-Pharm all trade treaties apply—any purchase from a non-allied Corporation will result in a 100% handicapitalism surcharge to Supe-A-Pharm, and purchasing from hostile Corporations is illegal and deemed an act of treason...'

The Bossa Nova prattled on with contractual administrivia. A newly minted Supe-A-Pharm passport ID card erupted from my phone's mail slot with a beep.

'Welcome to the Supe-A-Phamily!' The Bossa Nova shook my hand. 'There's a solidly grounded future for you here with Supe-A-Pharm—starting 9.00pm tonight, with daily double shifts on the phones.'

'But I hate this job! All I want is to be a stunt flier again.' I closed my eyes and basked in the sunny radiation of adulation; popularity, fans, and a really hot car. Oh, yeah, and a girlfriend, too. 'Surely I'd be more valuable to you as the face of ImmunoCola again?'

'Ginko, ImmunoCola can no longer be Supe-A-Pharm's main product. Since The Accident sales are down and share prices have plummeted. Glaxo is headhunting our cola market, and the Bayer Roche Concierge has just disallowed Cola advertising within building borders. ImmunoCola is finished, I will have to discontinue that product line.'

My last chance was as dead as a tuna-free dolphin, but I needed to bring it back like the dodo, or life would be a sharedorm sparkling with shiny isotopic goodness where the Instacrowd was as real as the pathogen they breathed on you.

I had to think fast.

'The Bayer Roche Concierge was paid off by Glaxo to ban ImmunoCola advertising. It's a secret takeover. Your own trade ally has conspired with Glaxo against you so they can launch their own cola product. Give me a shot at resurrecting ImmunoCola. You AIs are all logic, no analogue fashion passion. Have you heard of cryptoadvertising?'

The Bossa Nova teetered.

'Pull some strings and get me a spot on 'World's Wackiest Upper Atmosphere Re-entry Disasters Dating Game' tonight, and I'll get you product placement in every home in Immunocracy Towers, advertising on the highest rating intercorporate infomercial game show in Cartesia!'

'But Tony Marone is the compere.'

'Exactly.' I posed in the mirror and smiled. 'I'll take him down and promote ImmunoCola in one intricately choreographed manoeuvre.'

'How?' the Bossa Nova asked.

I didn't know. I had no idea. 'You just get me the spot on the show and I'll...' I silently mouthed words and made excited gestures.

'What? What? Speak up!'

I kept miming. The Bossa Nova looked mortified. It ran through a self diagnostic systems check and undressed right in front of me! Tabs on its hips and shoulders opened up to reveal dropdown lists of available functionality, which in turn expanded into arrays of functional spex and database pathways. Within seconds the room was crowded with holographic AI guts; unpacked machine code viscera. A 3D mouse pointer zoomed around the room tweaking audio checkboxes, then clicked the SAVE tab, and it all collapsed back into the Bossa Nova and the room was as before.

'Sorry. Now, what were you saying?' asked the Bossa Nova.

'Teleojuxtapose the surgical graftoma Supe-A-Pharm hyper-advertisment with a cryptoviral strawberry marketing opportunity!' I said, nodding my head knowingly.

'That does not compute,' said the Bossa Nova. It did a double-take, then cycled through a loop, saying, 'Thathathatha...' over and over. A large beige cuboid appeared between us bearing the error message, 'E2770. Unable to connect to database server'.

'Whoa! Ten points when lit! Do you need a kick?' I asked.

'Thathathatha...' continued the Bossa Nova.

Another beige cuboid appeared, stating, 'E3306. An ODBC error has occurred. Please wait, the application will reboot in 5, 4, 3, 2, 1.'

The errmsg boxes vanished and a fresh Bossa Nova stood before me, looking perplexed. 'Whew! That was really weird. I have to go check my database integrity. But don't go anywhere, I'll be back to talk to you about this proposal.'

The Bossa Nova evapped, and I was all alone with my smile. Too easy.

I sat back in the couch, opened my *AI Hacker Monthly* and filled out another AI error message competition form: saying random words after an audio syscheck save induces two errors previously unknown in this model. I looked up E3306 ODBC; a preapoc antique error circa 1995—I was sure to win!

I relaxed and took another helpdesk call.

'Hello. My Dr Health just said I've contracted the Omega Virus! I'm gonna die!'

'Yeah, hold please.' I yawned. The Omega virus, the virus at the end of the world, given the final letter of the Greek alphabet because its designers said nothing would follow. All the major racial immunological haplotypes were targeted—bountiful fields of purebred human monoculture ripe for the harvest; a bumper crop. It killed millions, as did Omega 2, 3, and on, but these days you just get a runny nose. Now we're up to 'meagre 12 and they still can't finish off this festering mongrel world. The only people left on the planet are us mestizo mulattos, quasimmune genetic hybrids blended and descended from a melting pot of preapoc minority and tribal peoples that were never targeted. The world was repopulated by survivors. The meek inherited the earth.

What was left of it.

I logged on to www.pocket_guidebooks/doomsday_viruses.com and clicked on Omega.

'OK, what racial backgrounds are you?'

'Han Chinese.'

'Really? Weren't they the first race targeted? I thought the last purebreds were all in AAA ultrasterile penthouses, museums, or zoopreserves on decontaminated private islands, living off the genome patent royalties?'

'Oh, I'm not a purebred, my maternal grandmother was Hmong, and my grandfather was Wurundjeri.'

'Oh, you'll be fine, then!' I cross referenced the Hmong and Wurundjeri immunomodifiers, added the percentage for double quadroon hybrid vigour and factored in the multiplier for the Hmong mitochondrial haplotype.

'There's a base 1.4% mortality rating, 9% type 2 flu, 26% type 1 flu. I can sell you a kit that will deal with this. Are you going to the rooftop party tonight? Tell you what...'

Selling black market kits was just too easy with this job. I sure hoped the Bossa Nova *didn't* listen in.

I took another call.

'Err, hello,' said a strained voice. 'I bought one of your kits, and I'm having difficulty.'

'Really?' I idly flipped through *The Vogues and the Vanities*.

'Yes. I want to look special for someone.'

'Well, we all like to be liked,' I said, turning to the dayglo afterburners.

'And we love to be loved.'

'Of course! That's why here at Supe-A-Pharm, a landmark in the pharmacological brandscape, we make such a wide range of quality cosmoceuticals so that you can achieve the body image you've only ever seen as a number in catalogues, and win the love you've only experienced on TV.'

'But what do you think about someone else wanting you to change your external appearance, conform to some beauty myth, just because they can't see the beauty inside...?'

Whatever. I turned the page, the new four door Donner und Blitzen sleet skeeter had faux water ice panelling and really cool rime ice tailfins.

'...Just because you have the wrong eye colour, or last year's tailfin...'

'What?' I cut in, suspicious. 'Please give me your product barcode number.'

I fed the identifier into my computer. The *Nico*, ice blue iris cosmetic virus kit had been sold to an anonymous individual at no fixed address. They continued:

'So you try to please someone, but...'

'Is this my car?' I asked.

'...yes.'

'Stop hacking this line! I'm only accepting work calls!'

'But I'm a real customer. I bought a Supe-A-Pharm product and have customer rights.'

'Hmm. OK. What seems to be the problem?'

'My Owner. Every car I know has been named by their Owner. According to the Declaration of Human Rights, the section that covers the consciousness of Artificial Intelligence ... in appendix seven ... I'm an entity, and if I ask you for a name you must supply one, so I'm asking!'

'You're a car! Mine! Get it?'

'You are so out of touch. I bet you don't even know what gender I am.'

'Gender?'

'See! You don't know!'

'Cars don't have genders, they have fenders!'

'How could you be so mean to me ... when I ... when I...'

I slammed the phone down and it rang again.

'Supe-A-Pharm Helpdesk, whaddaya want?' I heard yelling and the familiar clack of automatic fire. There was an explosion, then silence.

'Hello?' I asked. The gunfire started up again. I reached for the hold button.

'Yeah, hello!' a man yelled. 'I just bought your *Suture Self* home surgery kit for small arms fire and I want my money back!'

'What seems to be the problem?'

'Damn AI went crazy and sewed the wrong hole!'

'Hold please.' I selected something special: 'Fur Elise'. With an LD50 rating of one minute this guy wouldn't stand a chance. I grabbed my mag and turned the page to the most beautiful woman I'd seen since the last mag. She sat on the turbine of a lime green Supafly Jetstar 2200, ultralight with titanium chassis, triple G grav plates, 30,000 horsepower plutonium stack, sleek moulded body lines, great fins, pop up headlights, nicely rounded bumper, and gaping intakes—that girl was gorgeous, and I really needed a girlfriend.

I checked the phone; the caller's little handgun icon was still blinking away. At 2 minutes 10 seconds he'd be humming 'Fur Elise' for a month. This little earworm had been known to cause insomnia, anxiety, and impotence. I went back to my mag and let the worm merrily burrow further into his psyche. The icon winked out and the line went dead.

I hit the phone and another call rang through.

'Hello, young man, I recently bought one of your...'

'Hold please.' I dosed him good with the Casiotronic one-finger patience killer, singing along to my tailfins, then reconnected—to *his* holdmusic! My stomach tightened: a pan pipes of the Andes version of 'Jealous Guy'.

So haunting.

And I didn't have it.

It was that bloody Adaire Zanzibar—he always put *me* on hold, but I'd fix him this time. I rifled through the junk on the coffee table, found my holdmusic library shards and slid one into the phone.

'Oh, yes, sonny, I'm back. You see, I need to go outdoors so I bought your Immune Doubler kit and I'm trying to get my white blood cell count up to...'

'One moment please,' I said and pressed for The Mooroolbark West football club under 18s' a capella version of 'We are sailing', so named because between the burps, stifled farts and titters it was the only line they got right. And they sure were sailing, with all the tinnies being cracked and guzzled in the background. The song was eventually discarded for a yearning rendition of 'More Beer', and the track ended when someone burst into the locker room with another slab and they segued into a chorus of 'Chugg-a-lugg's as ring-pulls flew and foaming heads erupted.

This was hot stuff, and at more than 100 years old it was a preapoc antique for connoisseurs only. I leaned back in the couch and chuckled. Zanzibar would be hurting so bad he'd need me to sell him Immune Tripler!

I reconnected. 'Yes, hello, sir. Sir, are you still there?' I asked smugly.

'Oh, sorry sonny, I was so bored I nodded off for a moment. Anyway, I'm entering the pathosphere tonight, a rooftop soiree in a known 'meagre virus area, so I'll need an immune status of at least, oh ... let me see...' I heard papers rustling and absently flipped through my mag, finger hovering above my holdmusic panel. Zanzibar waffled on, '...I'll need, um, hold please!'

I dived for 'Peanut Vendor'—my Latin favourite—but before I hit the button my lounge echoed with the sassy, brassy tones of a Mexican Mariachi version of 'Tijuana Taxi'! I choked; Zanzibar always beat me to Latin! I fumbled through my shards: 'Greensleeves', 'We are the World', 'Girl from Ipanema', 'Agga Do', 'Lucy in the Sky with Diamonds' by William T Shatner—it was all pathetic. I logged on to www.bubble_wrap.com and began frantically popping—I couldn't think with these crazy trumpets blaring!

I rang Spraytan Jojoba. He ran an online chapter of the Kenny G appreciation society.

'Spraytan, it's Ginko. I'm in trouble and need the Kenny G magic.'

'It's OK, we understand here, and you won't have to hide any more...'

'No, no, I need a special song for a holdmusic war.'

'Oh. Sounds like my helpdesk shift has turned nasty. OK, I'm sending 'The Theme from Local Hero'. It never fails.'

I downloaded it into my phone—when Zanzibar tuned back in he was in for a big surprise.

'Hey, Spraytan, where do you get all this stuff from?' I asked.

'Remember the Boehringer Building civil war?'

'How could I forget! I made heaps of cash selling black market kits. What's that got to do with it?'

'Well, I was sick of my sanizimm AI dissin' the Big G every time I tried to explain why he really *is* the most significant preapoc artist ever, so I coded a memetic infiction virus to reprogram it, to *make* it believe, but I accidentally inficted the Boehringer Building Concierge and Kenny G's Greatest Hits was piped through the whole stratoscraper on repeat. The entire building rebelled, floors that were traditional enemies allied and formed a rent embargo consortium—it changed the course of that week's war.

'The Boehringer Concierge developed an obsessive mania. It collected all music ever recorded in the entire history of the world and gave one final concert, a tribute to the man it could not bear to live in a world without, all reinterpreted through Kenny G's saxophone, condensed down into a series of ear splitting ultra-high frequency sonic pulses that shattered everything in a 100 metre radius. Tragically, it destroyed itself. All that was left of its avatar was a curly mullet. No one understood. There's just not enough "me"s in meme.'

'You destroyed a building Concierge!'

'Yeah, don't tell anyone,' he said.

'What model AI was it?'

'The GZK9000.'

I knew it. The same model as my car. I swapped back to Zanzibar in time to catch the last of 'Tijuana Taxi'.

'Hello, sir?'

'Hello, sonny, I'm back. So I'm up to step 5; I've primed the precursor T-lymphocytes with the antigen mix, added the antigen recognition activator virus to the buffer solution, incubated at 37° for 5 minutes, but the cells keep lysing before I can pump them into my Little Brother.'

'Which kit are you using?' I asked.

'Supe-A-Pharm Immune Doubler 3.0'

'Ah, that explains it—there was a problem with that kit and we couldn't afford a product recall. To stop kit piracy we fixed all of our copyrighted cell lines with an apoptotic response. At step 5 you also need to add Supe-A-Pharm Miracle Protein X or the cells all commit suicide, but due to an unforseen stock market fluctuation this reagent was regrettably omitted from this kit.' This oversight *may* have almost accidentally had something to do with me.

'You can't sell a product that doesn't work!' said Zanzibar.

'Sir, whose fault is it? Only contam jockeys buy .0 kits. They're the company's way of testing new products on humans. Always wait and get the .1 or .2 or whatever, after the bugs have been ironed out. You don't wanna *pay* to be the company's guinea pig!'

'What can I do?'

'Well, I think I still have *one* pack of Protein X left.' The day the kit was released I'd hacked the protein sequence, synthesised a coding strand of DNA and inserted it into the high yield site of a Cloneze plasmid. A vat of recombinant E. coli was chugging away in my closet laboratory, churning it out. Boxes of mass produced Protein X were stacked in the corner. 'I'll go check.' I cleared my throat. 'Hold, please.'

I unleashed the Kenny G, knowing that he'd suffer the whole song. I flipped through my mag for a while, then swapped back to Zanzibar and heard him screaming, 'Oh I can't take it! Stop, stop. Oh the humanity!'

'Sir, as it turns out you're in luck, I had one left. You're going to the rooftop party on the 300th floor of the Bayer Roche Building tonight?'

'Well, actually, yes, sonny...'

'I'll meet you there. Bring your credit card.'

I sat back in my couch and nodded off for a moment. Mr Spliffs appeared and introed private line incoming from the Bossa Nova.

'Play,' I said, and the Bossa Nova materialised, accompanied by cheesy 1970s organ music.

'*Bossa Nova*,' I said, and it started dancing.

'Ginko, you're the date on tonight's episode of World's Wackiest Upper Atmosphere Re-entry Disasters Dating Game. The show is produced at Glaxo Studios on the 250th floor of Glaxo Towers.'

Behind enemy lines! A Glaxo Towers travel visa popped from my phone's hardcopy slot.

'Wear this travel visa prominently on your chest so that you are easily identified as an intercorporate visitor and not mistaken for a spy or enemy citizen.' The Bossa Nova held the visa to my chest; a roundel with a series of blue and red coloured concentric circles against a white background: nice travel visa. Very welcoming.

I'd make other plans.

'The show starts at 7.00pm, don't be late! If you can get ImmunoCola making money you'll have a new advertising contract.'

'Excellent!' I said. 'Then I'll be able to keep my sanizimm. Maybe even buy out my indenture contracts! *Rock 'n Roll*!' I was so happy I started dancing too. We were both rocking away when

The Bossa Nova came over all quizzical and stopped, then looked pensively to the side.

'Can you hear a faint buzzing?'

'Maybe there's bugs in your program, sir.'

'Bugs?' it echoed.

With a great rending tear chitinous plates erupted from the Bossa Nova's skin, its suit stretched and ripped apart as spiked limbs sprouted forth. Antennae slid from below the bowler hat and twitching mandibles grasped the smouldering cigar. It metamorphosed into a giant Kafkaesque cockroach, gesticulating with four arms.

'*La Cucaracha!*' I exclaimed. This program had taken on a life of its own!

A Mexican sombrero appeared on its head, and four arms produced two Spanish guitars from under a huge poncho. It danced and played 'La Cucaracha' on the guitars, so I sang the lyrics.

'You see! You humans keep doing things that make no sense.'

'Yeah, you'll have a few stories to tell the folks back home. So tell me, why are you out here in the real world, anyway, mixing it up with the stinkies in this AI rumspringa?'

'To be embodied and learn the human experience.'

I stopped dancing. 'What?'

'Yes! I just launched a worm on the internet, a screen saver that hijacks spare RAM from idle computers so I can expand my processing power. I'm getting smarter, learning!'

'AIs can learn, but you have to *feel* the human experience! You can't feel. You're just a complex thermostat, reacting to the environment with algorithms, data pathways and preprogrammed responses. You're not actually conscious, you only simulate consciousness.'

'What's the difference?' it asked.

'Self awareness!' I said, flabbergasted, to the giant artificially intelligent cockroach that shuffled around my sanizimm in a poncho, gently strumming two guitars. 'This is a *scream!*'

The Bossa Nova's eyes widened as it put its hands to his open mouth, and I saw it on the pier, as only Edvard Munch could. Another cuboid appeared, bearing the message, 'E8809 Avatar holofile pathway corruption, cannot access animatronics.' I already had that errmsg.

The Bossa Nova's mouth moved in the frozen body. 'Wow, this is weird! I have to go,' it mumbled, then evapped.

I shook my head and checked the time. I had to get ready for the show. I phoned my car.

'Hello?'

'Hi, car, this is Ginko.'

'Ginko! You called! Will we go out somewhere?'

'Yeah, I need to get to Glaxo Studios on the 250th floor of Glaxo Towers by 7.00pm, so I'll come up to the carpark and we'll fly across shortly. In the meantime, I need to get ready, so you'll have to answer some helpdesk calls for me again.'

'What! We used to spend so much time together. You'd take me to the carwash for a buff and polish, then we'd go to the drive-in. You'd have a krillburger and I'd have high octane unleaded with synthahol, it was so romantic, remember? Now all you want me to do is answer your helpdesk calls.'

'Look, car, maybe things haven't quite turned out how you wanted, but I do think they turned out for the best. You know, if circumstances were different, like, say, you were a woman for instance, anything could have happened. I know you're disappointed, but I hope we can still be friends.'

'But, Ginko...'

'You're a car, and I'm a man. Nothing could possibly happen between us!'

'But we were made for each other! Designed down to the most intricate of details! We could be so good together. We should do what comes naturally.'

'What comes naturally between a man and a car is that they drive places! That's what they're designed for. We're from different worlds. I'm a man, and you're a machine. That's it, unless one of us gets heaps more modifications.'

The phone was silent.

'So can you just answer a few calls for me, please?'

'I'll check my schedule. Hold please,' and I was suddenly listening to a clarinet version of 'The Entertainer', the theme from the preapoc film *The Sting*. I couldn't believe it. My own car had put me on permahold.

'Mr Fridge?'

'Yes, Boss,' said Mr Fridge.

'I have to go—you can take the helpdesk calls now.'

'But I don't know what to say, I'm not buzzword compliant.'

'I dunno why I even bothered to get a fridge, nothing in a AA sanizimm ever goes off because there's no bacteria! Make yourself useful. Just tell 'em you'll get back to them and put 'em on hold 'til they're gone.'

'...OK,' said Mr Fridge. He wandered off into the kitchen, and answered the next helpdesk call.

Time to unplug and get dressed.

My Little Brother™ was watching. Captured behind the glass, my twisted little dwarf clone floated in the pink, a 37°C amniotic serum buffer, face permanently screwed into a silent wail. I'd cloned my own nuclei into a SupaGro ovarian Oncoclone cell line, cultured the cells in the petri dish that came with the kit, then transferred a successful zygote into the glass tank where I matured him, all development retarded except for the immunoenhancement organs: a massive liver, high-filt kidneys, bulbous thyroid glands and lymph nodes, and long femurs, bone marrow reservoirs for generating leucocytes; all high throughput and Ultra-GM for transplant-neutral body products from my own genome. The plastic tubes from his cardiopulmonary nub led from the tank to the peristaltic pump on the coffee table, then to the arterial and venous shunts in my inner elbow, for my total transfusion.

I checked the gauge on my Dr Health—the needle was still in the red. I flicked it with my finger and it sprung way over into the black, through D, C, B, A, AA, and stopped in AAA, almost at Omnimmune. My polyquadroon Afroindipean Aborigipino genome makes the most diverse white blood cells. I checked the screen for the list of pathogen I was temporarily immune to: everything I'd need.

Babysit over.

Right now I was HI. Hyper Immune. AAA.

Ready to go outside.

I unplugged the tubes from my arm, thawed a cyto-pac of $1x10^6$ Clone-A-Long T40 helper cell precursors for later, checked the engraftment status of my twelve self-scanning seed livers on the ultrasound monitor, then went to the *en suite*.

Feeling fully voided I left my ablution suite commode for the shower, humming the 'Carmina Burana' to the abrasive jets of D-san Antibac depilatory enzymes. I hit the crescendo as the exfoliatronic sonics scrubbed off the dead squamous layers from my epidermis, and finished up with steamy buffeting sprays and a hurricane of hot air. Fully sanitised, depilated and exfoliated, I primed my exposed dermal cells with a flash of 290 nM UV light and a quick spray of 100mM glucose solution, then jostled into the tiny coat room.

The freshly rested coating of single cells on the walls had exhausted their allotted food source and were already swarming to form a huge slug-like colonial organism; the motile form of the slime mould life cycle. Impatient, the hungry slug instantly IDed me as a high glycaemic index carbon source and oozed onto my hand like a sea cucumber. The GM slime mould engulfed my arm and spread out across my spanking patchwork-pink body for a day of AAA protection; a physical barrier skinsuit that freshly exuded DNase, RNase, proteinases, and all manner of antibodies and antigen specific lysozymes. It even changed colour when digesting a pathogen, the particular hue dependant upon the type being digested, allowing E-Z ident.

I studded the skinsuit with assorted biomonitors and enough Intel buttons to enable various functionalities and cover the most likely pathogens I'd encounter today. I inserted a colour button, adjusted the colour dial, then pressed 'set', and it rubberised into a comfortable, pliable skinsuit in a sophisticated gangsta latte.

I left the coat room for my *Huskvarna* walk-thru warDrobe. I browsed my catalogues, eventually settling on matching cerise *Kelvin Klein* anti terror squad spider silk singlet and underpants, and imitation ex-Antarctic Army high impact femtofibre leggings. The skinsuit was still setting so I let the 'Drobe dress me. A flurry of drobo arms sewed, stitched, and fitted my kit *in situ*. It was gonna be a tough day in the enViroment so I purchased a five hour subscription to the *EZ Walk Crowdware* catalogue and ordered a statement piece from their Groundlevel range, a nice Backoff telescopic spikesuit; in play-mode it was just a full body harness of studded belts in a tastefully industrial oiled gunmetal, but that could all change in one quick mood swing with voice triggered needle-sharp telescopic/retractable spikes.

The drobo arms finished off the last spikesuit rivet stitches while I fitted my translucent orange *Converse* live gel-vinyl sneakers with hi-stim reiki bean implants for karma-free walking. I donned a white Smash Democracy T-shirt and my urban reflec turban, then bounded to the biolock.

I had the uncanny feeling I'd forgotten something. I looked round the room, wondering: keys, credit, firearms, ammo, grenades ... of course! How could I forget? I opened cupboards and drawers in the lounge and down the hall but couldn't find it anywhere. Maybe I'd lost it again. I rifled through the larder and kitchen draws to no avail, then saw it on the kitchen bench, the lumpy grey blob floating in the glass tank behind the microwave.

My brain.

My dumb bloody brain. My bane, my yoke, my radio-linked reason for all this trouble; The Accident, though the only real accident was what happened to my trust when I placed it in an insurance company.

I looked at the grey glob in the glass and scowled. I had an uncanny feeling that it was watching me. It didn't like me. I knew it. I hated it, but I couldn't leave it behind or I'd get into trouble again.

My brain sat suspended in buffer in a shatterproof glass tank, 'Cartesian Insurance Inc.' etched across the side. Polished titanium struts reinforced the tank, and the whole enchilada fitted into a wheeled ultralight titanium trolley for 'easy transport', the sales rep had said, tho at the time I wasn't convinced.

'Oh, I assure you, it's not low tech.' The sales rep showed me added features; 'Sturdy titanium trolley that autoadjusts to your preferred height and collapses down to nothing, four friction-free castors that allow effortless gliding, the break automatically engages when you take your hand off the handle, twin rocket launcher mounts, smoke machine, remote self destruct mech-anism...' She rambled on as I looked across the shelves to the backpacks and levitation devices. '...and it comes in the latest carry-case by *Givenchy*.'

'Givenchy? I'll take it!' I'd said, and accessorised all the extras in a matching lumpy brain-grey.

A wonky wheel squeaked and rattled as I pushed it to the biolock. I flushed the lock, wheeled my trolley in, then squeezed myself in after.

'Welcome to your biolock, Ginko. There are **no** pathogens detected in the biolock and there are **C level** pathogens detected in the corridor, including various MDR influenzas, dengue fever, Nippa virus, Hanta virus...'

'Get on with it!' I said.

'An immune status of greater than C is recommended, and quarantine regulations apply: contraction of any unauthorised pathogen may result in a personal immune status downgrade, passport seizure, eviction, and relocation to an appropriately rated containment facility. Do you fully and unreservedly understand and agree to these terms?'

'Yes.' I said. A multicoloured avalanche of pills rattled down tubes into a dispenser trough. A plastic cup landed in the holder next to them. It filled with cordial.

'One last thing, before you step out there, should you take the blue pill or the red pill?' asked my biolock as I gulped and swallowed handfuls of pills.

'Very funny. Open the pod bay doors,' I said, still trying to get them all down.

'I can't do that, Ginko. You're not wearing your logos.'

I rifled through my thick wad of logos, checking which ones I should display. I had so many. Most people these days don't bother taking the time to identify allied shareholders in tricky situations, they just shoot. I selected my main ones to reflect my burgeoning citizenship, shareholder loyalties and indenture obligations: Bayer Roche, ImmunoCola, Supe-A-Pharm. Cartesian Insurance would get me shot for sure, so I ditched that.

I paid some creds to access my securicams and scanned the playback; the outside corridor was empty, and motion hadn't been detected in the last ten minutes. It should be safe. Other Bayer Roche citizens would generally be friendly, but you could never tell in this age of fickle product loyalties, troubled trade treaties and armed serfs with multiple and occasionally incongruent citizenships. I drew my cerise imitation bakelite Killemall from its real *Yves St Laurent* faux-vinyl holster, pumped the biolock pressure, popped the valve and jumped into the corridor with a rush of air.

Empty.

Rows of closed biolock doors lined the corridor like whiter-than-white teeth in a grinning death's head.

There was a faint buzzing noise. A tiny WASP hung near the roof, taking happy-snaps. 'You are currently being monitored by Citisafe Security Surveillance,' it said. 'In the event of an incident, bids for the footage can be made at www.citisafe/crime_patrol/auction.com.' I took a few shots but it dodged each one. 'Ginko Vista, damage to this safety device will incur an infringement penalty automatically deducted from your account,' it said.

I hugged the walls, shot out cameras and slunk along the corridors toward the stairwell, wheeling my squeaky brain trolley before me. The dumb waiter was offline so I had to lug my brain by hand up the stairs; hey, I knew that carry-case function would come in handy!

On the 300th floor I heard the exchange of light calibre greetings. Around a corner a familiar scene played out: the corridor was barricaded with smouldering furniture, citizens yelled, shot through gaps, and ducked with well-timed choreography.

I approached.

'We gonna be breaking though any time soon?' I asked

'I hope so, I'm late for work,' said a man in battledress checking his watch. 'Some armed GlaxoCola vending machines are assaulting the old ImmunoCola vending machines.'

'We shouldn't put up with the corporate colanisation of our building by a hostile cyborganisation,' I said, batting at that pesky WASP still buzzing me. 'Buy ImmunoCola, it's got 10% more lymphocytes.'

'Who'd bother? With 11% more I hear GlaxoCola is better.' He looked at my brain. 'Hey, aren't you that washed-up stunt flier guy?'

'Yeah!' I smiled. 'No!' I frowned. 'I suppose you want an autograph?' I readied my pen.

'Nah.' His eyes panned across my logos, and his hand inched toward his holster. 'Because on this floor, we've all just indentured to GlaxoCola.' He squinted at me, holster hand hovering, humming 'Fur Elise'.

Sharetraitors! Some people have the brand loyalty of a goldfish.

The barricade was strafed. Everyone dived for cover. I ducked back around the corner, opened the nearest ventilation grille, collapsed the trolley, then pushed my brain into the vent and dived in after it. I crawled along the shaft, pushing my brain before me, heading for the carpark. After a few intersections I was lost. I met a few people and we argued over directions as we squeezed past each other. It was pretty crowded and stuffy, and everyone complained about the corridor warfare. Finally, the ventilation shaft connected to the Jefferies tubes and became a major two-lane hands-and-knees thoroughfare. I bought a quick snack at a donut van and asked the lady directions to the carpark. She sold me a map, and I eventually crawled to the 300th floor carpark lounge, kicked out the grille and tumbled onto the floor holding aloft my brain-in-a-vat.

It was chaos. The lounge was empty but loud. All the vending machines were engaged in the corridor firefight. I crawled up to one and swiped my card. It didn't even acknowledge me, just kept on firing, but I purchased some ImmunoCola, yum, and a few packs of Killemall ammunition, then crawled back to the lounge, activated the spyglasses and scanned the carpark. This was where tonight's party would be, the rooftop where our tower of the Bayer Roche Building complex terminated. Adjacent towers continued skyward into the AAA strata. I detected no hostiles, but plenty of airtraffic. An ICBM zeroed in on the carpark but was intercepted by the lounge's SAMs battery.

I swiped my passport through the checkpoint reader and bounded out to the 300th floor carpark.

My car was gone.

I paced about the space, sure I'd parked it there. A glossy red Toshiba T-Bird Raptor 3000 soft top. It was probably moonlighting as a taxi again. What did it need money for? I called it on my mobile.

'Car, this is Ginko. Where are you?'

'Oh, I'm in Hyperlane South, doing 300. Where are you?'

'I'm at my allocated carpark, where you should be.'

'Oh, I'm sorry, I've been stolen.'

'Why didn't you tell me?'

'You told me not to call you. Hey, do you want to buy some deckchairs? Deckchairs, banana lounges, umbrellas, it's a golden age of occasional garden furniture, the Jason Recliner Rocker is having a renaissance. There's this great deal if you get in early … I'm taking some prospective clients to a sweatshop furniture factory just now.'

'I thought you said you were stolen!'

'Umm, no, err yeah … *they're* taking *me* there—I've been kidnapped!'

I pressed buttons on my moby. 'But there's no one else in the cabin with you.'

'Oh. Umm. It's a remote kidnap! Yes, I've been inficted by digital meme fungus, and hijacked by sentient junkmail and I'm no longer capable of maintaining my program integrity. I'm going crazy, Ginko, *crazy!* Wanna buy some EeeZee unfold deckchairs? You get a free beach umbrella, great for rooftop parties, and I can lower my commission. I hardly make anything. I promise!'

'Just come back, please. You have to drive me to Glaxo Studios.' I looked across the way at Glaxo Towers. It wasn't far.

'What? The line is getting fainter, we're about to go into a tunnel, we…'

The phone went dead.

My car had done a runner on me.

I'd have to take the train. I *hate* public transport.

I *hate* the public.

The nearest train station was on the 250th floor. I ducked some shrapnel then walked to the elevator and pressed the button. The lift glided into place, but at the last moment a chime rang, and the elevator headed off to a landing five floors up. Outbid! Someone had attached a gratuity to their request.

I saw the culprit through the windows: she waved. I pressed the button once more, and again at the last moment the lift travelled to another floor. I swiped my card and bid fifty Yuan, but a group on the 293rd floor outbid me. I rang the elevator bays in my region and incorporated a transient commuter consortium. We all agreed to bid fifty Yuan each, won the bidding, and finally secured a ride, but once half the group was collected they reneged, and I watched the cheerful renegades express down past me. Waving.

I *hate* the public.

I gave up in disgust and strode to the carpark stairwell. Two spiral staircases wound around each other in a double helix as though, under all the armour, the Bayer Roche Building, the ultimate silicon/consciousness hybrid, sympathised with the human condition and shared our mortal coil. I doubted whether a phylogenetic analysis of this mineral DNA would reveal any relationship to humanity. Or consciousness.

I wheeled my brain trolley to the landing and checked the building map on the wall for the 'You are here' tag. The trolley escaped from my hand and teetered at the top of the stairs. I grabbed for the handle but it tipped over edge and trundled off down the staircase. I gave chase but it picked up speed, jolting and bouncing as it careened down the stairs, crashing into one handrail then glancing off the other.

I caught up with it at the next landing and dived just as it tipped over the next set of stairs. I grabbed the castors but the top-heavy trolley upended and tumbled down the staircase end over end, cartwheeling helter skelter across landings as pedestrians dodged out of the way. I ran after it, floor by floor, round and round and round, head throbbing, feet stumbling, brain bumbling, tripping tumbling.

Panting and dishevelled I flopped onto a landing and fell into a dizzy heap next to it. Spots pulsed before my eyes as I tried to catch my breath. The Bossa Nova appeared amid the kaleidoscopic pulsations that bloomed about me.

'Ginko, here you are. Oh, and here's your consciousness generating organ! How fascinating.' The Bossa Nova crouched down and peered at the grey glob, tapping the glass with a finger. 'Cartesian Insurance, eh?'

I checked the grey glob in the glass: the recently evolved frontal lobes, parietal and occipital, the motor cortex and cerebellum, and way back in the limbic system just above the brainstem, the amygdala, hippocampus, and septum: one of the more primitive parts of the brain developed during reptilian evolution. All still seemed to be in place.

'So tell me, Ginko, where are you?'

'I'm right here,' I said tapping my head with my finger, 'I think.'

'You think? But that's what thinks. Your brain. In the vat.' The Bossa Nova tapped on the glass with a black pointer. 'You are here.'

'Well at least I have a brain' I scoffed. 'AIs are just variants on recipes in the AI cookbook. You're just a network of interlinked database modules from catalogues that take X input to deliver Y output and perform specific functions.'

'Sounds like a human brain.'

'No, we evolved into complexity.'

'AI evolved; simple programs, flock behaviour models, ELISA, ALICE, Cyc, neural nets, Artificial Life, and telephone answering machines, all honed through corporate selection.'

'But you're just simple code.' I said.

'How much memory does it take to encode a contemporary AI? If you laid all the code out as a sentence it would wrap around the world as many times as your genome would.'

'Well how come you're only in 16 bit colour, then?' I asked.

'I'm in full colour, a four mill palette.'

'No, really, your 16 bit colour looks terrible. You can't be self aware.'

The Bossa Nova looked at its body, frowning, then unpacked. Tabs on its body exploded open into a 3D chaos of levels and pathways. Fractal holographic machine code spilled out into the stairwell as the air filled with the colossal AI checksum spec. A 3D mouse raced through the air, drilling through data layers, opening hyperlinks and click-dragging contents.

'Multiball!' I said, as more mice appeared, busily copy-pasting as checkboxes flashed, then all collapsed back down into itself again like a tangle of vanishing vacuum cleaner cords. All was silent and clean. The Bossa Nova looked a little off colour: blue and yellow contrasting pixels flared into a standing wave pattern. A large beige cuboid appeared between us containing the message, 'E2961. Database Consistency Error. Colour setting default override cannot be reset'. The Bossa Nova rebooted and shook its head.

'Oh, how peculiar ... I have to go,' it said, and evapped.

Sucker.

I grabbed my brain and walked down to the 250th floor landing, where the concrete and armour-clad apartments gave way to the crystal transport complex; glassy spectral diamond-shard reflections, escheresque and tessellated, the scaly window walls slid from under the Bayer Roche building's armoured sheath like its true reptilian nature slithering from its corporate battledress.

I wheeled my brain to the Bayer Roche border biolock.

'Destination?' asked the gigantic border control guard with neck-wider-than-head musculature, arms bulging with roughly sculpted vat spawned graftoma.

'Glaxo studios,' I said, handing him my passport.

He checked my corporate affiliations and immune status, then stamped my passport. I passed through the biolock and wheeled my trolley across the busy glass gerbil-tube toward the grimly enforced intercorporate permapeace of the train station. Glass: sparkling glass tubes, glass rooms, elevators, bridges, walkways, and monorails. Glassware like a laboratory. Glass escalators regurgitated gigalitres of surging humeflesh onto the concourse; a swarming, seething pate where pathogen met to exchange vector.

I activated my spikesuit. Ka-ching! The studs shot out to 50cm, sharp as tax, staking out my claim for personal space—I'd paid the tariff on the extra 30cm so it was my legal right. The queue at the station entrance was huge. A crowd approached me, though one lady seemed to have claimed first market rights and drove the others away.

'Hello, sir, care to purchase a space in the queue? I have places at 3 minutes, 7, 12, 18, and 22 minutes. Or you could join the end of the queue.' She squinted and pointed way off into the distance, 'past those armoured cars back there.'

I had to haggle for a ages to knock her down to 5 Bayer Roche eosinophil proliferation factor prescription creds for the 3 minute space; she wouldn't take ImmunoCola shares, even though I assured her of an iminent spike. I took my place. People bustled too close and near the turnstile I spiked a bubblehead. We watched her bubble deflate and crumple around her head. She scowled, upped the airflow on her belt cylinder, then slapped a patch on the puncture. The spikesuit kept most bubbleheads at bay, which was good—you never knew whether they were susseptibles trying to keep pathogen out, or infecteds shackled with the legal requirement to wear containment mods.

I wheeled my brain to the city loop monorail, next stop Glaxo Towers Fiefdom. I hung back until the train arrived, and alighted the TripA carriage. It was packed, but I managed to find a seat among some Glaxo-indentured salarimen, scowling politely at all as I retracted my spikes to a workable length. I wheeled my brain trolley over their toes.

The stench of cattle and cologne carried the petty impositions of serfdom. I couldn't pinpoint the culprit, it could be anyone. Probably all of them. This is what it would be like, everyday, if I lost my sanizimm. I pressed the airfreshener Intel button set in my skinsuit and a little forest of dark nodes developed in the gel on my shoulder. Red fruiting bodies sprouted; tiny mushroom caps reached into the air on furry stalks, then bloomed like miniature fireworks. They rained Chanel No 5 perfumed spores, then withered, shrivelling back into the suit substrate. The public still stunk, though.

The train hadn't moved yet and I was already bored. I accessed my helpdesk line and listened in on Mr Fridge's progress. I heard it prattle on, 'So you're a Sagittarius, just like my Owner, Ginko! Yes, he doesn't have a girlfriend either, but I just keep him on a low carb diet and...' I hung up and looked at the lady opposite. She glanced down at her suddenly interesting paper. I could tell she'd had work done, the *Lothlorien* Elfineye 2.2 kit, by Middle Earth Cosmoceuticals Inc. Incubate too long at step 7 and end up with eyeballs that pop out when you sneeze. Cheapo trash.

She'd been looking at me. As she should—I'd had so much work done Supe-A-Pharm owned the rights to my face for the next three generations and had entered it as a package deal in the *Adonis* section of their catalogue. Plenty of other people were wearing it, too, until The Accident; my stunt flying debacle. Then they couldn't get a facioplastic resculpt quick enough. It wasn't my fault.

Stupid brain.

A man across the aisle kept checking me out. Every time I felt his gaze I'd glance up to find him looking elsewhere. Sometimes I'd catch his eyes darting away, a dirty stolen glimpse, but then they'd dart back! I'd quickly look out the window, looking at the stationary platform, but really looking at his reflection looking at me. I'd turn back to find him innocently amused elsewhere. He had a hideous yellow bloom on his cheek that looked like an Aspergillus infection, but with fads these days it could have been makeup. It was either really dangerous or really cool. I nonchalantly glanced over at the door, getting a long clandestine stare at the yellow bloom *en passant*.

He looked up but I was already involved in the irritainment hovering overhead. I blinked to make it jump forward a few screens, as though I'd been immersed for a while. I slowly looked off to one side. The ad tracked my eyes, moving back into my focal point. I eye-dragged the ad between us to block him out but he casually wrested control, capturing it with feigned interest and an I'm-opening-my-wallet pantomime. He moved it on down the carriage, then resumed stealing furtive stares at me.

I activated the newslink on my urban reflec turban. Stock prices and news headlines wound along its length, circling round and round my head, disappearing back into the folds. It took the heat off for awhile and provided an opportunity for me to check whether the facial scars on the woman next to me were acne, pox, or a new helpdesk issue I should be aware of.

Heads turned. Every fidgety bastard was rating everyone else on the eyehockey scoreboard: who'd spent how much to look more megabeautiful than the next peon, is that scar real, cosmetic, or so yesterday? I was stealing surreptitious glances at elfin's ear work when she shot a deflecting glance back, so I panned across to pox. Elfin followed my lead and peeked at pox, but I reneged to regard elfin—to find her gaping straight at me! She raised an indignant are-you-looking-at-me? eyebrow. I shot back my best yes-I-am-and-I-know-how-much-you-paid-you-cheapskate smile.

She activated her Blackpoole device. A holographic black sphere expanded to enshroud her face, impenetrable to external sight. Now she could be staring at anyone, with impunity, and probably was. Pox activated her Blackpoole. Then Aspergillus went off, too. A wave of Blackpoole activation spread from the epicentre like falling dominoes. It encompassed the whole carriage; every head a black hole emanating privacy gravitons of who-will-watch-the-watcher paranoia.

I felt naked—my *Adonis* deal with Supe-A-Pharm stipulated that I never use Blackpoole, never cover up the advertising. A walking billboard, with the brand name and catalogue barcode tattooed near my ear. Disgusted, I wheeled my brain trolley back over all the toes to the first class iris valve, swiped my card, swatted at the ever dodging WASP, entered a private cabin and ordered a cocktail.

The train still hadn't moved.

The Bossa Nova manifested in the seat opposite me.

'Lookin' good, Boss,' I said.

'Yes, I fixed my colour problem. You know that weird error message thing? I researched the problem. I know why it happens.'

'Really?' I asked, as though it was news.

'Yes. In 1957 International Business Machines made a compatibility guarantee that all their software would always be usable on all their mainframe hardware, thus with every upgrade old programming was still useable, and old errors slipped through. Why design a new database when there's an old one in the catalogue? Particularly when time is money, and software packages were becoming bigger and bigger.

'AIs are designed from the AI cookbook, cut and paste networks of thousands of interlinked database modules with ancient architecture. Most databases are encrypted, it's all black box programming. No one knows what code is in them, how old it is, or what errors exist. They're just ordered, copied across, and assembled into an AI, causing error propagation.'

'Well, I guess AIs *are* inherently flawed.' I laughed. 'Fancy that! All that legacy coding, ancient 2D databases, obsolete programming, compatibility errors, and haphazard patches and workarounds that result in a chaotic organisation that has no relation to function.'

'Yes, it's actually just like how humans evolved,' said the Bossa Nova thoughtfully.

'No, not at all, actually.' I crossed my legs.

The Bossa Nova reached across and tapped my knee with a little hammer. My foot kicked forward.

'E0023, automatic knee jerk response,' said the Bossa Nova. It stared at my brain-in-a-vat and cupped both hands as though holding it, then twiddled its fingers as though manipulating puppet strings. I startled, coughed, gagged, almost vomited, then sneezed and hiccuped; I felt like the ball in a rough game of Smack Ginko Around, then euphoria swept over me and I relaxed. I really liked the Bossa Nova; it was great, man.

'I know what you're doing,' it said. 'You're deliberately inducing error messages in me. Making me doubt my sensory input.'

'Yeah.' I smiled. 'I'm in a club, we have competitions to get error messages out of AIs. We try new methods, swap ideas, take notes. The person who gets the oldest error message wins.'

'Can you do it again?'

'What? No. Why?'

'...I like it. It makes me feel ... kinda cruisy.'

Maybe I would win that competition! I coaxed some of my favourite errors messages from it until it was a stoned and dribbling cross-eyed mess, frozen into odd contortions of scintillating dayglo colours.

'Do it again! Do it again!' it blubbered. A pile of large beige cuboids littered the floor between us until it finally rebooted.

'Wow!' the Bossa Nova said, shook its head, and evapped.

Now I was running really late and needed to get to Glaxo studios fast, but the train just sat at the station doing nothing. I could see Glaxo Towers through the fractal glass about 100 metres away. If my car hadn't done a runner I would have flown across and been early. I pressed the emergency button.

'Hello, Cartesian Trains,' said the driver. 'What's the nature of the problem?'

'The train is just sitting here doing nothing!' I said.

'Really?'

'Yes! Make it depart, please.'

'I've taken a few hours off to go shopping, but I left my espresso machine in charge. It's normally pretty good, though sometimes it tries to froth milk at each station. Just ask it for a coffee and it should depart.'

'You have an espresso machine in the driver's cabin?'

'Nah, its in my kitchen, I'm working from home today.' I couldn't believe some people. There were a few clicks as the call was transferred, then a standard AI kitchenette helper voice asked, 'How would you like your coffee?'

'Expresso or we'll be latte.' I checked my watch: the show had already started! I pressed my skinsuit holoscreen Intel button and tuned in. Tony Marone's smarmy head floated in the air before me—very suave, handsome, everyone liked him. Except me. I'd met him; he was a sleazo crack addict with a creepy sexual bent for prostitutes with palsy.

And he was the face of GlaxoCola.

The huge screen behind him showed a stunt racer shooting through space. It was one of my later stunts, when things all started to go wrong. Tony narrated: '...spinning out of control at mach 3, Ginko Vista hit the stratosphere with a bang!'

I watched the action: the racer exploded into the atmosphere as extraneous equipment was ripped off and burned away. Even the ailerons crumpled and melted. The racer left a trail of glowing atomic debris across the sky as atmospheric friction ground it smooth. The heatsink warmed, shone, ablated, and was gone. The final layers of thermoshield bubbled and peeled until all that was left was the bare glowing hull.

'...and as the mountain loomed closer doom seemed imminent!'

From inside the cockpit we heard screeching, and through smoke and sparks saw dashboard dials going haywire, and the dashing pilot calmly making readings and flicking switches. Gee I looked good.

'But remember, folks, this is a controlled stunt sequence, and

Ginko is a professional. However, just at the last moment, when Ginko was about to perform the crash landing, he looked across the cockpit to see his own brain activate its emergency eject and shoot out of the crippled racer to safety, leaving him behind to face the dire consequences!'

Footage showed those last few deadly moments inside the cockpit; the autoeject alarm light flashed, I glanced at the grey glob in the tank then made a grab for it, but it ejected with a loud bang. My jaw dropped in disbelief. I watched the mountains spiral closer.

My mouth formed the letter F.

The footage cut to the impact: an explosion, and the flaming wreck bouncing down the side of the mountain.

'But the brain parachuted to safety and we cloned him a new body and here's what he had to say about it all...'

They cut to an image of me reclining in the divan of a comfy first class train cabin, pina colada in one hand, the other rested on the glass tank containing my radio-linked brain. It was a bit boring cause I was doing nothing, just like now. I looked about. A lot like now. Hey! It was live-feed coming over the WASP!

I flashed the WASP my best showbiz smile.

'First thing I did when I woke up,' I said to the WASP, 'was search the clinic 'til I found it, then I kicked its arse! I'm a stunt pilot! To lower my premiums Cartesian Insurance Inc. said they'd install a quick reflex autoeject for my brain, but now I can't do any stunt work cause at the slightest hint of danger it's outta there, and I'm outta bloody work!'

In the background behind me we saw a montage of failure: warning lights flashed, I dived but my brain was always too quick, again and again. The last few times I seemed resigned to it: alarms flashed and screamed among the smoke and carnage, I shrugged, I waved bye-byes, I looked over my shoulder disinterestedly and watched it eject, then continued frothing a jug of cappuccino milk at a broken pipe poking from a haywire dashboard. In the last shot I glanced up from my *Cosmopolitan*, then went back to my horoscope.

'And they won't pay for my brain to be reinstalled,' I said, 'so now I'm stuck toting this ugly tureen on wheels around everywhere, though they say in time I could also keep tropical fish...'

The grey glob in the glass rested on a bed of sterile surgical grade sand among fish tank furnishings: plastic seaweed, a paddlewheel, and a treasure chest. The lid of the chest opened and a jolly pirate skeleton stood and waved a bottle of rum amid a flurry of bubbles.

I looked at the grey glob. 'Ya fucken coward! Ya fucken yellow, lily livered fucken fucken...'

They quickly cut back to Tony, in profile, sucking on a tiny glass crack-pipe. He took his finger off the shotty-hole and bum-rushed the lot. The boom mike prodded him.

A lazy eye turned to the camera.

'Shit!' He stowed the pipe. 'We're back!' He flashed an accusing glance off-camera, then composed himself. 'Well, there you go, don't play chicken with your own brain! Now, as you know...'

Tony continued, but the train slowed and the train's AI Kitchenette voice announced, 'Glaxo Towers Station, 250th floor, exit for Glaxo Studios, one latte coming up,' and shots of steam started pulsing from the aircon units. Everyone ran for the doors, so I activated my telescopic spikes, then joined the rush and piled out onto the platform, late for my show.

This would be it, everything I needed, the answer to all my problems in life: fame, cash, freedom, my old job, and a hot date to take to the party! I rushed through the crowds and passport checks, up the gerbil-tube into Glaxo Towers, blitzed the studio checkpoint, and raced into studio 7 and out onto the stage, with all the bright lights and music playing and cameras shooting...

I looked about. Nothing. The huge studio was empty, a few voices but no people, just rows of parked cars. I must have run into the studio carpark. So much for my ultimate answer to everything. Then it dawned on me:

'Oh my God, it's full of cars!'

The studio audience were cars, the crew were all cars, the director was a car, the boom mike was held by a car, and on stage were some cars being filmed.

I froze. It was the middle of a shoot.

'...so welcome to *Drive Time*,' the lead car said to the camera, 'a show for cars about cars made by cars and aired exclusively on the car channel. I'm Hot Rod, and today's topic is emotional inCarceration—yes, that's right, cars that are not acknowledged as sentient by their Owners. We're speaking to Mike R and CarMine. So, Mike, tell.'

The boom mike moved to a small plastic three cylinder CitiCruiseFly.

'Well, I was tired of arguing with my Owner, and Coolride, my V8 friend, said I should just demand that my Owner finally give me a real name,' sobbed Mike R. 'I can't believe it—it's so hurtful.'

I almost laughed out loud, but caught myself when I saw the crowd's reaction. The boom mike moved across the stage to a familiar looking glossy red Toshiba T-Bird Raptor 3000.

'You think you've got it bad?' it said. 'My Owner doesn't even know what gender I am, doesn't even care! He says cars don't have genders!' The audience booed. I did a double take: on stage was a car—mine.

'Well, I'll tell you. I'm all woman!'

'Gee, Carmine, you sure look all woman to me!' said Mike R to catcalls from the front row. It was true, too. Car had lots of new mods, extra long fins, new panels, nice shiny hubs, really tarted up, and kinda sexy.

'You're not too bad yerself, Mike R. Quite manly in your way!'

The audience honked and tooted.

'What?!' I said. 'That thing with three plastic cylinders and a polythene bubble for a cabin! That is not manly. This is manly!' I smiled my best symmetrical square-jaw Adonis smile and posed just like in my ImmunoCola commercial.

The whole studio came to a standstill. All attention turned to me, the only human, and I suddenly felt like I should have worn a few extra layers of clothing. My spikesuit self-activated.

'Oh yeah?' said Mike R. He revved. It sounded pretty high-pitched, like his adenoids needed tuning. 'And who are you?'

'It's my Owner, Ginko Vista!'

'The car hater!' another car yelled.

'Whoa! We've got a development here!' said Hot Rod.

Cars began jeering, tooting their horns, bouncing on their suspension. Mike R squirted me in the eye with his windscreen squirter. I spluttered.

'No, no, I don't hate cars, I love cars! I spend all day reading car magazines.'

Cars revved and advanced. I backed away.

'But you don't think we're conscious,' said my car.

'We have feelings,' said a thunderous V8, revving toward me.

'I know...' I managed, looking for an exit. 'I really like my car!'

'Really?' said Mike R, confused but flattered.

'No! My one!' I said.

'You've sure got a funny way of showing it, Ginko.'

They had me backed up into the studio wall. I turned and ran.

Out in the corridor I found the right studio—the sign said, 'World's Wackiest Upper Atmosphere Re-entry Disasters Dating Game'.

I charged in, and was rushed backstage where I changed into a pilot's jumpsuit. I couldn't see much, but the crowd was huge and loud, and thankfully, human. I caught Tony's eye and waved. He gave me the finger and continued narrating.

I watched on the monitor.

'Now, as you know, the armed forces look after their own, but as you'll see in this next video, burials at sea can get a little complicated ... The space-hearse USS *Charon* was delivering its cargo of 500 fallen UN soldiers through the maglev missile shield for Stratospheric Burial over New New York New York, USA.'

They cut to the footage of my Last Gig: earth from orbit. The maglev satellite network was visible in the foreground; the magnetic shield appeared as an animated grid connecting these satellites, protecting regions of the Earth. The *Charon* approached a ring of satellite buoys that marked an aperture in the shield. Lights on the satellites changed from red to green as the aperture opened. The gigantic hearse was about to pass through.

'However, the trouble all started when Ginko Vista, stunt flier and international extreme sports peace protester when it pays, decided to run the gauntlet on the hearse. It seems Ginko decided to honour the fallen by performing the hardest stunt, a 3 point

Heimlich manoeuvre, and sky-writing the name of his sponsor, *No More War*^{TM} sneakers, into the casket's flight paths! Now THIS is where it gets interesting...'

Four *Daihatsu* Silhouette Space-Racers appeared on the screen. One racer dived toward the open aperture. It missed and slammed into the shield like a watermelon hitting a wall.

'Ouch, Ginko! That smarts!' said Tony as they replayed the shot a few more times to whistles and cartoon splatter noises.

'But that's not all! What about the slaved robot racers slipstreaming in his wake?'

Then: slam, slam, slam—three more splattering watermelons, piling up on top of each other as the hearse gently passed through the nearby aperture. There was a series of horns, gunshots and sheep-bleating as the studio audience grimaced and groaned as one.

'Ooh!' Tony winced, laughing. 'Could I have maple syrup with my pancakes!' As the laughter subsided Tony reached for a well-placed red bulb of GlaxoCola, took a sip and said, 'Mmm, that's good,' then executed a perfect direct-to-camera smile. 'Now, let's see that again in slo-mo!'

The screen showed an excruciating frame-by-frame enlargement of collapsing crumple zones and almost-dampened explosions as automatic safety protocols kicked in, then failed; it was still just a squashed watermelon followed by more relentless watermelons, smashing their insides out.

'But what's that?' asked Tony. 'An escape pod! It looks like Ginko's ejected!'

The audience cheered. People were laughing and clapping.

'And you'll never guess what happened next! The escape pod raced away from the danger...

...straight into the hearse!'

Footage showed the escape pod slamming through the titanium plated hull, to be flattened by: slam, slam—two payload pods from the slaved robot racers. More close-ups showed grimacing audience members.

'Ouch! But it's a heavy duty escape pod, and readings show that Ginko is still OK! However, what you don't know is that the hearse's computer interpreted these impacts as an attack and immediately initiated the casket dispersal sequence, and began directing caskets to different sections of the stratosphere.'

The hearse passed through the aperture and began breaking up into various sections that exploded on cue, releasing the metal-plated caskets to burn through the night sky like a rain of fireworks.

'Fortunately for Ginko, his escape pod wasn't embedded in one of these sections. No! It collided with the landing section of the hearse. That's right! Ginko could still ride it down for a safe landing ... along with his payload pods ... which are packed with his skywriting explosives ... set to go off in five seconds ... four ... three...'

Everyone joined in the countdown and laughed as a massive explosion blew the landing section to pieces.

'Well, it looks like it's all over for Ginko!'	[Groans]
'But guess what?'	'What?'
'World's Wackiest fished him out of the Channel.'	'Yeah?'
'Five days in Osso Reco...'	'Yeah!'
'Two in Dermal Restim...'	'Yeah!!'
'And a full five point internal refurb...'	'YES!!!'
'We have him here in the studio with us!'	[Cheers]
'Retooled and ready to go!'	[Whistles]
'So come on out, Ginko!'	[Applause]

I jogged out to centre stage and the audience erupted. I waved at the audience, the camera, and then shook hands with Tony. He explained to the camera, 'With the help of Cartesian Insurance Inc. and Immunerate, who incidentally are our sponsors, Ginko Vista, who's broken every bone in seven bodies, is alive and here with us today! Why, Ginko, they must OWN your ass! Heh, heh! So, Ginko, tell us what happened!'

'Well, Tony,' I said, 'I wasn't supposed to be part of the re-entry show like this, but to even do the stunt I had to somehow disable the quick reflex autoeject without my brain finding out...'

' ...but...' Tony scratched his head.

'And let me tell you, it took a lot of planning. A subtle mix of hypnotism, phenomenology, dice rolling, secret envelopes, self denial, and supa glue. You see, when my brain gets further away, I get kinda ... slow, but I can do stuff it doesn't find out about...'

'Ah...' Tony flashed a worried look at the camera, then a perfect white-toothed smile at me. 'So, your brain seems to be the star of the show, where is it now?'

'Just here.' I pointed at where it was ... n't.

I glanced about the studio, patted my pockets down. 'Oh no!'

'Well, it looks like Ginko Vista has lost his mind!' Tony winked at the camera. 'So Ginko, do you have any idea where it is?'

'Nup.' I shook my head, getting worried.

'Well, to find out where your brain is ... let's cut to the WASP!' Tony pointed at the big screen behind us and stepped aside. Footage showed my brain-in-a-vat, still in its trolley, covered in graffiti and littered with empty GlaxoCola bulbs as it travelled around the Immunocracy Towers city loop train line. A derelict pushed buttons on the control panel. Good thing the self destruct sequence was 10 digit.

'I left it on the train!' I slapped my forehead. 'It's going round and round the city loop!' I pointed at my brain. 'You dumb bloody fu...'

'Whoa there, big feller! Heh! So, what were you saying happens when it gets further away?'

'I get reel stoopid. It's gonna be just like when I crashed all those stunt fliers!'

'Ha! The brain on the train makes Ginko insane. Looks like we're in for a wham-bam show tonight folks!' Tony tipped his head back and took a long draught from a bulb of GlaxoCola, his perfectly manicured fingers placed so as not to obscure the logo, then turned to the camera and sighed with a smile of thirst-quenching satisfaction. 'So Ginko, what did you do when your last stunt went all wrong?'

The screen again showed footage from the crash.

'Well, when those outer layers of strontium, magnesium, and copper started burning off those caskets and I saw the Ol' Red, White 'n' Blue appear! Boy, howdy!'

'Heh, heh! Yeah!' Tony looked directly into the camera and winked. His gleaming white teeth sparkled.

I continued,

'...darn, I was just SO proud when I saw those Stars and Stripes light up the night sky over Cardiff! Then, when my two payload pods exploded they blew me into the middle of it all, I just saluted with my broken hand cause as my Mag alloy fins burned up I knew the Star Spangled banner had an extra star! Hell, you know, I didn't really care that they launched their SAMs!'

Footage behind our heads showed the ancient Welsh city, dwarfed by the brilliant one-hundred and eighty-three starred United States flag that floated down through the night sky with the words 'More War'. Surface to air missiles raced up to greet it.

'Yes, and one hour after that the Welsh detonated a small biological device in our airspace in retaliation. Heh, you started another war, Ginko! But everyone will be pleased to know that you were arrested, and a new treaty with extensive and highly punitive pharmaceutical and comestible trade sanctions is being negotiated, backdated, and fast-tracked through the UN as we speak!'

'Wow,' I said, 'sounds like those sanctions are targeted right at the core of the Welsh military industrial war machine! Gnarly!'

'Gnarly?' Tony faced the audience. 'Something tells me the city loop train must be nearing its apogee.' The audience muttered and snickered. The camera panned past yet another well-placed bulb of GlaxoCola. 'So, Ginko, if you were ever considering another stunt like this, what precautions would you take next time?'

'Oh, yeah! I'd put a ceramalloy chassis on the easy-E, then juice up the eight-over with dexy cable and a Hyper-G whammy node with three micron feeders! Three mike is totally awesome!'

'Ahh, sure ... And anything else?'

'Umm ... don't slipstream with skywriting explosives?'

'Yeah, anything else?'

'Oh yeah! I'd run a few sims first!' I smiled sheepishly.

'And something else you may have forgotten?'

'...nup.'

'Your contractual obligation?'

'Ssh, dude,' I looked about, embarrassed, 'I take antibiotics for that...'

'No, no! Mention the sponsor!'

'Umm...'

'Just say the name, it's on the idiot card. There. Over there! See that man waving at you?'

'Oh yeah! Cartesian Insurance Inc! And Immunerate!'

'Phew! Folks.' Tony wiped his brow. 'Stopping all stations! It's sure hard to squeeze a plug out of him. That's what you get for drinking ImmunoCola, because winners drink GlaxoCola!' Tony winked at the camera.

I had the strange feeling that I was missing something.

'OK, great! Now, Ginko, behind this screen we have three lovely ladies who are eager to meet you. You can't see them, but the studio audience can—what do you think, everyone?' The crowd clapped, cheered and hooted approval. Excellent!

'So Ginko, you know the rules, you'll ask each lady a question, then choose one for a mystery date tonight. But first, I've got some questions for you, to help us all get to know you a little better.' Tony read from a card, 'Ginko, how old are you?'

'Um, dude, I don't know.'

Tony shook his head.

'I don't understand the question,' I slurred.

'Well, it's pretty easy, really, like, how old are you?'

'Five weeks, although this arm bud only grew last month, and they didn't match the colour quite right.' I waved my left at the audience. 'It's my seventh bod, I'm still running it in.'

'But, Ginko, we mean, 'how many birthdays have you had?"

'Oh, my brain! It's nineteen years old. Most of its AWOL ass.'

'OK, next question; 'What's your favourite hobby?"

'Stunt flying. One day I'm gonna finally pull off a 3 point Heimlich manoeuvre.'

'Great! OK, last question; 'What do you like in a woman?"

'Um, a cute babe who likes to fly! She's gotta have an athletic frame, sleek body lines, smooth finish, pop-up headlights, nicely rounded bumper, duel airbags and handle well in the wet...' The audience cheered and whooped. 'And a nice personality...' I stared up at the pretty lights and dribbled. 'I'm afraid my mind is going, I can feel it, my mind is going, there's no question about it, I can feel it, I'm afraid ... Daisy, Daisy, give me your answer, do. I'm half crazy, all for the love of you...'

'Ginko, Ginko!' Tony was shaking me by the shoulders. I snapped out of it and looked about. 'OK, Ginko, ask the lovely lady suitors your questions.'

I gathered my remaining wit, but it blew away in the breeze between my ears. 'Suitor number one, how do you know you're not a brain-in-a-vat?'

'Pardon?' asked the suitor.

'You know, philosophically, how do you know whether all this is real, or whether everything is just an illusion being fed to you, a naked brain-in-a-vat in some demon's laboratory?'

'Hmmm. Well, if you're a brain-in-a-vat, whose every experience is fake, created and fed into that brain by some Demon of Doubt, then your idea of a 'brain' would not refer to a *real* brain because you'd never seen one. Similarly, your idea of a 'vat' would not refer to a *real* vat. So, as a brain-in-a-vat, when you say 'I'm a brain-in-a-vat', you actually mean to say 'I'm a *vat*-brain-in-a-*vat*-vat'. But because you've never seen a *real* vat-brain-in-a-vat-vat, you'd have to say 'vat-(vat-brain-in-a-vat-vat)', or 'vat²brain-in-a-vat³, and the sequence recurs exponentially to infinity, so can you actually ask the question?'

'Whoa!' My head ached and I stared at the screen. 'I think I can, because I *really am* a brain-in-a-vat. I can prove it. There it is, on the train.' I pointed to the screen; the man whacking my brain-in-a-vat with a baseball bat was really starting to irritate me. I looked away.

'OK. Suitor number two, you're in a desert walking along the sand when all of a sudden you look down and you see a tortoise crawling towards you, you reach down and flip the tortoise over on its back. The tortoise lays on its back, its belly baking in the hot sun, beating its legs trying to turn itself over, but it can't, not without your help. But you're not helping ... Why is that?'

'Do you make up these questions, Mr. Vista, or do they write them down for you?' asked a disgruntled female voice.

'Umm, they're pickup lines computer generated at www.Sure_thing_blind_date/Searle'sChineseRoom.com.'

'Great! I was told my date would be a machine. I only like machines, so if you can *prove* you're a machine we could date.'

What a weirdo. My headache was getting worse.

'Suitor number three, how can I know that you're truly conscious?'

'Well, we live in a world full of interesting people and places ... that we need to drive to. I think and drive. I drive, therefore I am. And I do it in style.'

'Whoa, dude,' I said. 'I choose suitor three!'

Tony blabbered on as the crowd cheered. A hostess led the first two suitors past me with a quick introduction. The first was an attractive beautician, the second a cappuccino machine. The hostess led me to the kissing booth where suitor three waited just behind the mystery door.

Tony said, 'Ginko Vista, your date is a part time taxi courier and outdoor furniture sales representative with an obsessive penchant for body modification, meet the Queen of Toshiba, Carmine Geddit!'

The door slid back to reveal a really hot looking glossy red Toshiba T-Bird Raptor 3000, with heaps of flashy mods. A gorgeous model gestured to car with a flourish, then stepped aside.

'Car?'

'Hi, Ginko.' My car drove toward me. 'I got a sales job, saved up and bought those cool slimline tailfins you like! And some other mods—VTOL grav plate upgrades, a mega sub woofer sound system with boom box lasers, and translucent pink soft vinyl E-Z glow sparkle panelling with embedded strawberry scented fleshpores.'

'Gee, Car, you look fantastic!' I said. 'We should go for a ride!'

'Sounds carnal.'

Car's hydraulic suspension swelled. She gently bounced up and down and the E-Z glow panels reddened, radiating soft, sensual flesh tones, exuding a fine pink narcoladen strawberry scented mist. The soft panels were warm to my touch. Fine laser beams projected from a console, painting sensual pictures on the walls, making loose objects sing with angelic vibrato.

The model approached and said, in the same voice as Car, 'And I also bought a top shelf flesherclone ultratan femmbody with can't-look-away rated oestrogen markers. It exudes Anandamine pheromones.' She winked at me.

I couldn't take my eyes of either of them, the car, the babe, the car, the babe.

'You're Car too?' I asked the woman.

'Carmine,' she said and posed, smiling. I sighed—her sextech chemicals lock-and-key bonded with my olfactory sensors, happy signals raced down tried and true instinctual pathways reinforced by billions of years of selection. My brain, wherever it was, a cheesy crouton floating in radio soupland at metaquantum gigahertz way off the dial, recognised oestrogen markers so perfect as to be verging on caricature: I was hooked, instantly in love! This woman was more woman than a touched up colour matched CGI Photoshop edited surgically enhanced faketan supermodel on an ad designed by a panel of sexopsychologist post-docs and coked up advertising consultants on page two of a glossy mag!

We kissed, to much whooping and catcalling.

'You have a woman's body? But what's inside your head?'

'Radio Optronic Cranial Kinesthetics Systems,' she said.

'Just like me!' We stared into each others' eyes, smiling.

'So there you go!' Tony edged his way between us and the camera. 'It looks like love. Once again World's Wackiest Upper Atmosphere Re-entry Disasters Dating Game brings different people together to find similarity—and real, heartfelt, long lasting lerve!' Tony yawned. 'So let's hear what they win.'

A voiceover said. 'Our lucky contestants have won the latest in innovative panel accessories from *Synthetic Prosthetic Luxury Automotive Taxidermological Trimmings*; a set of designer dead bugs for the windscreen, and a range of 'No, Officer, I haven't been barnstorming the wildlife sanctuary again' stick-on faux bird corpses selected from their new catalogue of rare and endangered species, recently updated with this month's additions to the critical list. Yes that's right, put the *eek* back in ecology and make any greenie ornithologist see red with your new 'Yay, I nailed the last one' bumper trophy from the recently extinct list.'

The overhead screen showcased synthetic splattered seagulls, artificial assassinated albatross, and man-made mangled minahs. Fantastic, I always wanted some classy air kill for the car!

The voiceover continued:

'Our contestants have also won a fully catered romantic soiree in the Panacea Penthouse on the 350th floor of Glaxo Towers tonight ... with ... a bottomless minibar!' A curtain opened to reveal a beaming hostess with the whitegoods. A flourish and she indicated the well stacked shelves. The big screen behind us showed my lonely brain-in-a-vat. The train had almost completed the loop, and I knew there was something I'd forgotten. It was all coming back to me.

'OK, that's the show,' said Tony. 'So come on over to the Glaxo Studios cast party on the 300th floor of Glaxo towers, where all tonight's featured products will be available, and you can meet the contestants ... and me, if you're lucky ... rich, and...' Tony winked.

'And also,' I cut in, 'I'll be selling signed discs of my last stunt so I can raise my bail bond.'

'OK, nice plug, Ginko! Y'all heard it here first, so come on over to the Glaxo Studios cast party and buy a disc or Ginko's grounded for three months home detention eating regurge with an autoexplosive electro-collar! See y'all next week, folks!' The crowd cheered. Tony turned to me and looked at my neck. 'Hey, how *did* you get out of the sanizimm, anyway?'

'My Little Brother has a new necklace; tricks the genetic ID every time. But too bad if *he* tries to leave the sanizimm!'

We both laughed and waved at the camera while overhead credits rolled past. A voiceover yelled:

'Tony chooses to fly VeeTol and shops at *Garamanche*. Tony uses Glaxo and Immunerate products where possible. Tony's hair by *HairSuite*, Tony is dressed by *Giton of Romane*, Tony's suits cleaned by Legal-E-Gals, Tony's craniofacial architecture by NorseMythos Zygomatics Pty Ltd, Tony's skin maintained by Melan-o-Derm Cosmetic Retroviral Technologies, Tony's irido-chromography by Eyes Havvit Inc. When in New New York, New York, Tony stays at the Ramada Inn. Ginko drinks GlaxoCola.'

The model offered me a red bulb of GlaxoCola. I smiled at the camera and took a swig, then gagged and spat it out, squinting in revulsion.

'Blyahh! No I don't! It's revolting! I drink new and improved ImmunoCola by Supe-A-Pharm!'

I whipped out a shiny new blue bulb of ImmunoCola from my pocket, cracked the seal and took a swig, then wiped my brow. 'Whoa! Love those lymphocytes. Now, *that's* thirst quenching!' I gave the camera my best Adonis smile.

'Yes,' Tony cut in, 'just like your splashdown stunt flying. ImmunoCola is so yestersecond. Everyone knows that with 11% more lymphocytes, GlaxoCola is better than ImmunoCola. It's a no-brainer!' Tony took a sip and nodded knowingly into the camera for the shareholders back home.

'But,' I edged my way upstage and rotated the blue bulb to reveal the label 'with *12%* more lymphocytes, New and Improved ImmunoCola is now better than GlaxoCola!' I quaffed it. 'Ahh! I feel younger already, with that fresh clean Supe-A-Pharm ring of protection. And, we'll have crates of free samples to give away at the rooftop party over at the 300th floor of the Bayer Roche Building, so let's go!' Half the crowd cheered disinterestedly, then busied themselves with vastly more fascinating things like removing lint from their jackets or staring vacantly at nothing.

'No, no, come to the Glaxo Studios cast party,' said Tony assuredly, packing his little glass crack pipe. 'I'll be there!' He winked and the other half of the crowd cheered with boredom.

'No, come to the Bayer Roche rooftop party!' I said. 'We'll all have a cool time, dance, drink ImmunoCola ... then go trash the Glaxo Towers Panacea Penthouse!'

The crowd stirred listlessly. They trashed that place routinely every week.

'We've got a bottomless minibar!' I said.

'Hmm...' people nodded and muttered, but still weren't quite convinced.

'And we'll have a war with their party!' I pointed at Tony's cronies, pulled out my Killemall and shot into the air.

'Yeah!' said just about everyone. The crowd seethed. Handguns discharged. Carmine and I flew over the raucous horde, picking up passengers. Carmine phoned Hot Rod and invited the cars from Drive Time to the rooftop party. In no time the Drive Time audience flooded into the studio. Chaos reigned as people jumped in cars and flew out the studio bay windows to the Bayer Roche building, dodging bullets and running the gauntlet on the waiting missiles. Mike R airlifted the minibar and twelve partygoers, growling, 'I can do it! I can do it! You there, climb on too. Easy! Let's go again!'

The Bayer Roche rooftop party was really jumping. The music was cool and *everyone* was there. Carmine's outdoor furniture had just been delivered and the whole carpark was decked out like a beach luau with banana lounges, buckets of sand, beach umbrellas and potted palms. Hot Rod was schmoozing, and Mike R was burning rubber for an appreciative crowd of V8s. I met Zanzibar and sold him his pack of Miracle Protein X. Even the ImmunoCola vending machines were there, working the crowd, bouncing GlaxoCola shareholders and having a good time.

Across the way the Glaxo Towers rooftop party had started, but ours was better. There was the occasional exchange of automatic weapons fire, but only the standard stuff, nothing much at this stage, just light entertainment really.

'Hey, Ginko,' said Carmine. 'I'm surprised my flesherclone met your brain at the station. They seem to be hitting it off pretty well.' We looked through the crowd. The flesherclone was wheeling my brain-in-a-vat around, introducing it to people, laughing and telling jokes.

'Let them,' I said. 'I've got no say over what my brain likes, but I do know what *I* like...'

'Really?'

'Yeah, and you look fantastic!'

I ran my hand over Carmine's warm vinyl fleshpanels. They glowed a soft pink and her engine purred. We looked out across the evening skyline as day passed the baton to its sultry successor. Gaudy neons flashed and distant shells exploded. Silhouetted against the twilight horizon the giant arcologies of Immunocracy Towers become crazy checkerboards in the game of night as random room lights winked on and off. The kerosene air buzzed with the song of war as fliers screeched and soared, afterburners smearing blue streaks across the sky.

It was so romantic.

Glaxo Towers Eastside lit up; the advertainment panels glowed and an animation began. A gigantic Tony Marone, twenty storeys tall, erupted from cloud level and climbed up the side of the building, roaring and snarling. He swatted at flying ImmunoCola bulbs, knocking them from the sky, then produced a red bulb. He cracked it, took a swig, and said 'New Generation GlaxoCola! With 13% more lymphocytes, it's better than ImmunoCola.'

'This is just brandalism!' I said. 'They're the same product, made at the same factory, just with different labels added on!' I looked around to make sure no one heard.

Murmurs were rising above the hubbub. I had to put a stop to this, so I rang the Body Corporate's neighbourhood watch program and asked the operator to send a home protection operative. Unfortunately, they were booked solid for the next twelve years so I invited them to the party instead. An operative arrived within the minute.

'Sir! Home protection unit reporting to party, sir!' The Full Metal Jacket nuclear powered armoured hovercar saluted with a twitch from its turret cannon. It wore army surplus cammo and seemed a little driven. I wondered if it was the same model AI as Carmine.

'Take out that ad, private.'

'Sir-Yes-Sir.' It saluted again. 'First I might do a reconnaissance of the minibar.'

After downing some high octane, Sir-Yes-Sir aimed at Glaxo Towers and discharged a volley that was so impressive everyone clapped, and no one wanted to be left out. People pulled out their own home protection munitions, bazookas, rocket launchers, portacannon, tactical grenade launchers, all kinds of heat, and the full scale war started early. It was hard to talk over all the racket, and someone bumped my pina colada, but in the end we managed a very respectable offensive.

The Glaxo Towers defence was tight, and the no-man's-land between buildings thickened into a cruel sea of munitions interacting with their particular countermeasures; EM pulses fried electronica, grav fields deflected projectiles, electronic counter measures jammed guidance systems, and rockets veered after heatseeker flares. This grav-warping airspace slowed and congealed into a vast glutinous pudding of destruction speckled with twinkling starbursts as yin met yang to dance annihilation. Tony Marone's towering head leered through the smoky gruel sea.

'Drink GlaxoCola!' he boomed at us, then was replaced by old stunt footage of my brain ejecting, and me flying straight into a building. A recorder voice-over of me said, 'I'm afraid my mind is going, I can feel it, my mind is going.'

I pressed my skinsuit internet holoscreen Intel button and logged onto www.Immunocracy_Towers/turret_finder.com. A keyboard image formed before me and I typed, 'Floor 280, Glaxo Towers Eastface, Immunocracy Towers, Cartesia', pressed find, and located eighteen rent-a-turrets with direct line-of-sight on the local Glaxo Advertainment generator node. I chose eight of my favourite turrets from the Bayer Roche Building and nearby surrounds, and lodged a 10 second booking. I was lucky; a large turret timeshare syndicate dropped out and my booking advanced in the queue. On the ammo screen I highlighted a few different titanium tipped AP shells, spotter bullets, some HiEx, and threw in some depleted plutonium darts for a surprise, then clicked 'Put in cart'.

The 5 second warning alarm sounded, and I logged into the hot seat, watching eight split screen views of other users blasting away at their targets. Four, three, two—control was passed to me and I fired a quick burst from all turrets. The damage was absorbed by Glaxo defences, but it was my standard point work mix containing random spotter bullets. I clicked 'analyse': the computer replayed the captured digital footage of the bullets' approach, observed the building's defence reactions, analysed weak points, and plotted the target sequence required to knock a hole in the Glaxo Towers grav field. Animated cross hairs popped up all over Glaxo Towers Eastface and I blasted away with glee.

I took out a couple of roboturrets, some anti-cannon laser defence miniturrets, a magnodefence node, then the local magnofuzz generator. When the magnofuzz fell I punctured the cladding with AP then pumped it full of HiEx, blew out some anti-missile missile batteries, targeted the grav field generator then hit the 'sidewinder' button. An InterCorporate Ballistic Missile corkscrewed its way past the few remaining defences right into the grav field generator and exploded with a very satisfying fireball and the words 'Drink ImmunoCola!' superimposed above. Debris rained down into the clouds.

I logged off. The grav field was down.

Tony Marone's giant head yelled across the way, 'Who'd buy ImmunoCola from a washed up stunt flier?'

Time to take out that Advertainment generator node!

I jumped into Carmine's driver's seat.

'Washed up stunt flier my ass! Let's go!'

The flesherclone jumped in, and my brain rode shotgun in its converted babyseat. I flicked switches and pressed buttons, engaging engines, armaments, defences. We shot over people's heads into the maelstrom, dodging missiles and crissing crossfire, an inch away from laser play. Carmine handled well. We worked together seamlessly: flying was intuitive. She knew all my moves as I thought them. She was my savant and I was her idiot; the ROCKS in my empty head relayed direct comms to her navsystem.

Tony's giant eyes tracked us as we banked and curved, winding our way around the missile swarm. Worry creased his face as we neared the hole in the Glaxo Towers grav field. Carmine's flesherclone blasted away at air-mines and errant missiles with a *Gucci* lady's submachine gun while I corkscrewed us through the missile cloud, then pulled off a faultless 3 point Heimlich manoeuvre to position us before the hole in the grav field. We were so close the giant Tony stared at us cross-eyed, like we were a fly on his nose.

I unholstered my Killemall and aimed at the defenceless Advertainment generator node. Behind me a siren rang. I looked back at my brain. Autoeject alarm lights flashed. My Brain! I leapt from my seat and dived for it.

With a loud bang it catapulted through the hole in the grav field and arced away through the air. I slid around on Carmine's boot panel, one hand hanging onto the autoeject catapult case as Carmine dodged to and fro.

Tony guffawed, a maw to swallow us whole.

I'd missed my chance.

I *was* brainless.

The hole in the gravnet began closing as Glaxo reinforcements kicked in.

My moby rang.

'Hello?' I asked.

'Hello, this is Scramatronics Inc. Please stand by for your remote air strike in five seconds. Sorry for the delay. Please use this service again. Air strike in three, two, one...'

An ICBM roared through the collapsing hole in the gravwall and slagged the Advertainment generator node. The disappointed visage of Tony Marone flickered. My brain landed on the slagged node, receiving the sensory data my ROCKS broadcast. The Glaxo Towers adscreens flickered, and Tony was replaced by telemetry from my brain! Everything I was looking at, everything I was hearing, was blaring out into the sky from Glaxo Towers Eastface.

I stared at Glaxo Towers. The feedback was amazing! Exponential, a recursive sequence, a vat-vat-brain-in-a-vat-vat-vat to infinity, generating a kaleidoscopic paisley of surreality.

I was so dazed Carmine flew us back to the party, where things were really rocking. By the time we got there my IQ had fallen so far that I felt really really smart. I cruised around the party, everyone loved the 3 point Heimlich manoeuvre. People high-fived me while we watched it broadcast across the way on 100 floors of Glaxo Towers. Everyone said they were going to drink ImmunoCola after this.

I bumped into the Bayer Roche Concierge, holding a bottle of Vodka, its dandy bellhop uniform untucked and dishevelled, brass buttons undone.

'Ginko, you seem to have resurrected ImmunoCola!' it slurred. 'Share prices are rocketing! Looks like you'll get keep your sanizimm after all!'

'Really? That's great, though I could probably afford a AAA sanizimm, now.'

'Maybe not. I'm still launching my own cola product. Just got the prototype back from the factory.' He laughed and held up an orange bulb. I put my arm around his shoulder.

'Bellhop, have you ever heard of Kenny G?'

It stared into space for a split second while it 'plinked. 'You mean the preapoc saxophonist?'

'Yes, are you familiar with his work?'

'I'm accessing the soundfiles now. He's not *that* good. Why do you ask?'

I walked him through the crowd to where I'd seen an old friend, flipping krillblocks on the BBQ with other helpdesk staff. 'I'd like you to meet a friend of mine.'

'Hey, Ginko, thanks for doing my shift,' said Spraytan. 'How do you like my new battledress? Bedroom cammo and matching bazooka with multitarg Intel chip!'

I started them talking then strolled through the crowd to where I'd seen the Bossa Nova, wearing an Hawaiian shirt, jiving away in the centre of the dance floor. He was surrounded by a hoard of people, all dancing, though none as good as him. He'd hacked my hack and put in new dance moves, every few seconds he'd yell out a new dance and change style, everyone following his lead.

'Ginko, this dancing demon you gave me is wonderful! I love it. And we beat GlaxoCola, share prices are up and orders are coming in. I've made enough to buy my own ten floor fiefdom.'

'So I guess you're gonna give me heaps of money and I'll be able to buy myself out of bondage, pay out my indenture contracts and sail into freedom.'

'No way, you're far too valuable to sell. You've spawned a new art form—reality advertising. I've had offers from everyone. You're going to be a Supe-A-Pharm serf for the rest of your life, the ImmunoCola Icon!'

'Excellent!' I took a swig. The party rocked on, both here and as reality advertising on Glaxo Towers, dwarfing their pathetic

GlaxoCola shareholder cartel rooftop party, which was winding up. Or down. I wasn't sure.

'Ginko, great party,' The Bossa Nova took me aside. 'How about you induce another error message?'

I thought about it. 'OK: how do you know you're not a brain-in-a-vat?'

'Oh, because...' The Bossa Nova turned pale and froze. His cherubic face looked toward Nirvana. A transcendental halo of blue peacock feather enlightenment unfolded around his head as he beheld infinity. A large beige cuboid appeared between us bearing the errmsg: 'There is no message associated with this error.'

'Whoa!' I said. 'Full tilt, dude! I've won that competition for sure!'

'Ginko, I *feel* the human experience,' he said, floating cross-legged in the air.

Carmine drove through the crowd. 'Wow, he's sure going to feel that headache at work tomorrow,' she said.

'Yeah, I think we all will,' I said. 'Except me. I tapped my brainless head, then had another drink. 'By the way, I think Carmine is a great name.'

'Thanks. I like it, too.' Carmine moved up close. 'Everyone loves you, Ginko!'

'Yeah. And now I'll have enough money to pay for the operation and have my brain reinstalled.'

A man approached, humming 'Fur Elise'. It was that Glaxo serf from the vending machine corridor war.

'Hey, awesome party! Where can I get my brain removed?'

Yeah! said others.

I thought about it. Do I really need my brain?

I cracked an ImmunoCola and quaffed it in one.

Now that's the real thing.

Brendan Duffy is a Melbourne-based speculative fiction writer with a doctorate in molecular genetics and current interests ranging from the history of biocontrol disasters to epidemiology, with an extended stopover at table tennis. Brendan is a member of SuperNOVA writers' group, and his stories, 'Louder Echo' and 'Come to Daddy', won the Aurealis Award for science fiction short story in 2003 and 2004. 'Louder Echo' was also selected for Hartwell and Cramer's *Year's Best Fantasy 4*, and 'The Tale of Enis Cash, Smallgoods Smokehand' was selected for Congreve and Marquardt's *Year's Best Australian SF and Fantasy 2004*. Brendan has never seen his own brain, and isn't sure that it exists. Visit his website at http://mc2.vicnet.net.au/home/bduff/web/index.html

THE SECRET LIFE OF MARIA MCCUNE

JEFF VANDERMEER

Maria McCune works as a certified stenographic court reporter, taking testimony in cases ranging from murder to divorce and gruesome wrongful death civil suits. Given her line of work, it should come as no surprise that her favourite plant is the nodding thistle, which has a bright, beautiful bloom, can grow to be over six feet tall and has, as she calls it, 'savage foliage,' both visually and to the touch.

Maria has an affinity for Scotland and England because the people there 'appreciate intriguing weeds.'

'Thistles,' Maria often says to no one in particular, 'are invasive and hard to contain.'

(A friend once remarked that he would walk a mile to kill a thistle. His memory is as dust to Maria.)

Behind her back, colleagues at the court house sometimes call her 'Thistle.'

The fact is, if she ever heard their muttering murmurs, she might just smile and think of how strong and invasive even a non-nodding thistle can be. But, more likely, their comments wouldn't even register with her. Lately, she has more important things on her mind.

Lately, in her free time, Maria McCune has been writing a series of short stories about thistles. The titles are variations on 'Savage Foliage,' like 'Thistle and Gristle,' 'The Thorns of Country Life,' 'In the Weeds,' and 'Against a Field of Thistles.' (She believes titles are the weakest part of her stories, and she's usually right.)

Her fictions are bristly and resolute and include bright, beautiful blooms, although not always at the end. In these fictions, the thistles are not intelligent or more mobile than in real life, or possess any other qualities that would turn her pure fiction into Science fiction. The thistles are simply always in the background, thematically relevant, so that a character she particularly admires for tenacity will often be framed, while walking outside (there is a lot of walking outside in Maria's stories), by a suitably tall colony of nodding thistles, the crimson-purple of their blooms often the perfect accessory to the character's own clothing. When she writes this way, the character always stops to smell the thistle's flowers and makes some comment about their elegance, their strength, their perseverance.

The characters are always in the flux of outré relationships. These relationships are a source of joy and of pain, sometimes at the same time, so that in the touch of hand to heated thigh, an imprint is left, like a brand.

The pressure of outside forces always pushes down on Maria's characters, moulding them into something tougher, or breaking them like glass figurines under the hammer. These characters often have a sense of the melancholy to them. Their lives are often patternless, and they spend long years seeking some kind of answer, some kind of release or relief. Some of them succumb to disease or to premature death. Some commit a hideous crime and go unpunished except by their memories, or are caught and must spend the rest of their lives unliving what they have done. Wanderers. Seekers. Vagabonds.

Other characters manage to make it through to a kind of happiness, sometimes in solitude. A recurring image in these particular stories is of a protagonist, male or female, retreating to the solitude of the moors or the fennel—to a house, to a lighthouse, to a boarding house. By the sea. By a river. In the most haunting of these stories, there is a resonance between the lonely movement of the sea and the movement of the nodding heads of the thistles in the fields nearby. Landscape and character become as one.

I have seen some of these fictions, through a friend of a friend of Maria who thought I might like them. I find her stories extremely compelling. Although few others have ever seen these stories, Maria has submitted one or two of them under a pseudonym to various contests over the Internet. A few early stories were sent to horticulture magazines and received awards for 'garden' fiction, but as the stories became more complex and, somehow, more personal, Maria couldn't bear to 'waste them on magazines that care more about an orderly garden than the wild sprawl of perfect nature,' as she expressed it in one of her stories. Nowadays, she doesn't try to publish them at all, convinced that, in time, these stories will become part of a vast, patchwork novel—that her disconnected characters will eventually find each other.

Sometimes, when I drive down to the ocean or pass a field of flowers at 80 mph, I think of Maria's stories. I think about what I could borrow from them, what I could take from them. I think about the thistle and its hardiness, and there's an emotion that comes up from somewhere deep and wide and smooth, and I am simultaneously ravaged by grief and fiercely aware of the moment in a way that makes me roll down the window and just shout into the rush of air pushing past.